DEFIANCE

Dean Crawford

Copyright © 2015 Fictum Ltd
All rights reserved.

ISBN: 1512040916
ISBN-13: 978-1512040913

The right of Dean Crawford to be identified as author of this Work has been asserted by him in accordance with sections 77 and 78 of the Copyright, Designs and Patents Act 1988.
All rights reserved.

Also by Dean Crawford:

The Warner & Lopez Series
The Nemesis Origin
The Fusion Cage

The Ethan Warner Series
Covenant, Immortal,
Apocalypse,
The Chimera Secret,
The Eternity Project

Atlantia Series
Survivor, Retaliator,
Aggressor, Endeavour,
Defiance

Independent novels
Eden, Revolution,
Holo Sapiens, Soul Seekers

Want to receive notification of new releases? Just sign up to Dean Crawford's newsletter via: www.deancrawfordbooks.com

We should have known better.

We know that there are few survivors, few of our kind still clinging to life.

They say that when the end came some embraced it willingly, shrugged off their lives like old skins and allowed the Legion to infiltrate their minds and their bodies and become one with the machine. Most, however, did not. Most fought, and died, trying only to remain who they were.

The Legion, the instrument of the Word, our governing law, took life across all of the colonies. Worlds fell; Ethera, Caneeron, Titas; the mining settlements and the outlying systems and the uncharted clouds of asteroids and meteors beyond consumed by the monstrous and insatiable thirst for knowledge and power that is the currency of the Word. The greatest creation and achievement of our human race turned vengeful deity, the destroyer of worlds.

We now know that there are several forces at work within the Legion, an immeasurable swarm of mechanical devices ranging in size from as big as insects to as small as biological cells. There are the Infectors, the smallest and most dangerous, for it is their mission to infiltrate the optical nerves, the brain stem and the spinal cord of human beings, turning them into mere instruments dancing to the macabre hymn of the Word's destructive passion. Then there are the Swarms, the clouds of tiny but voracious feeders who break down all and any materials into the raw ingredients for more of their kind: metals, plastics, even human tissue, consumed en masse and regurgitated into further countless devices, all of which evolve with startling rapidity as though time were running for them at breakneck speed. Finally, there are the Hunters: bigger than the rest and with only a single purpose – to find and to kill intelligent biological life wherever it is found in the cosmos.

We are the last of our kind, and despite the horrors that we witnessed when we fled the only star system we could call home, we now know that we must return. There is nowhere else to run to, nowhere else to hide, for if we do not make our stand now then we condemn our children or their children after them to face what we could not. We must fight back and step by step, system by system, we must take from the Word that which was ours and liberate ourselves from the living hell that we have created and endured.

The Atlantia, a former fleet frigate turned prison ship, is the last home we have. Our crew is comprised of terrified civilians, dangerous former convicts and a small but fiercely patriotic force of soldiers and fighter pilots for whom there is no further purpose in life other than to fight for every last inch of space between here and home.

Our lives may become the last that will ever be lived, and thus we tell our story in the hope that one day others will read of it and remember our names.

Captain Idris Sansin

Atlantia

DEFIANCE

Dean Crawford

I

'I don't like this.'

Captain Idris Sansin stood upon the bridge of the Atlantia and stared out into the absolute blackness of the viewing screen, as though if he looked hard enough he could see beyond time itself and prepare them for whatever unknown fate awaited beyond the veil of darkness. He didn't take his eyes off the screen as he spoke.

'Stand by for sub–luminal deceleration,' Idris ordered, 'on my mark.'

The circular bridge deck was silent but for the hum of super computers and the soft hiss of air conditioning. Idris saw his reflection in the viewing screen, glowing in the dim light from the control panels as though a ghost were standing outside the massive frigate and looking in on him, an accusing expression on its features.

At super–luminal velocity, Atlantia was travelling at several times the speed of light and all light information was thus stripped from the cosmos around it. Although safely ensconced within a bubble of neutral mass through which no attack or intercept could penetrate, the Atlantia was also blind, deaf and mute. Somewhere alongside her, her sister ship Arcadia travelled at an equal velocity, likewise entombed within a void of absolute blackness.

'I said I don't like this.'

'I heard you,' Idris uttered in reply.

He did not look at the rotund face of Councillor Gredan, the bloated bureaucrat gripping the command platform's guard rail and staring out into the blackness just as the captain did. But where Idris was emboldened by preparedness, Gredan was beholden to fear.

'There could be anything out there,' he said, his voice a whisper.

'That's why we're coming in hot,' Idris murmured in response, one eye casting across a bank of screens where images of Raython fighters waiting on the forward catapults and Marines preparing to repel boarders met his gaze. 'This is the way it's always been done.'

Governor Gredan did not reply, his skin sheened with sweat, the bridge hot despite the air con' systems recirculating the air through the ship. Behind Idris on the command platform were arrayed a series of command posts handling communications, weapons systems, the Commander of the Air Group's station, helm and navigation, each manned by officers who had served under Idris ever since the terrible apocalypse that had consumed their home world of Ethera. Each of them watched the screen with equal earnest as Lael, the communications officer, began counting down on a ship-wide broadcast channel, her metallically tinted hair sparkling like chrome in the dim light of her station. Her voice echoed through the huge frigate's decks.

'*Seven, six...*'

Gredan turned to the captain. 'Lazarus led us here, but how can we trust that…, thing? It's a machine, it's The Word. This could be a trap.'

'This could be our salvation,' Idris growled back as he glanced at the navigation screen, its normally detailed data now presented in blood-red graphics to signify that they were projecting calculations rather than absolute positions. Atlantia's precise location in super-luminal travel could only be estimated from the point and trajectory of its initial leap.

'It's an unexplored world on the fringes of the Icari Line,' Gredan snapped. 'We don't know what we're getting in to.'

'We know what we'll be dealing with if we don't find supplies soon,' Idris shot back. 'Drought, starvation and disease. The fleet has not been replenished in almost four months. It's your call, Councillor. Tell the people that we won't try. See how they react.'

Gredan's features folded upon themselves in silent fury but he said nothing as Lael's voice echoed through the frigate.

'*Four, three…,*'

Idirs grabbed the command platform's rail a little tighter and hoped against hope that Lazarus, the digital ghost of a man trapped inside a machine and the creator of the most horrific technological terror mankind had ever created, was right.

'*…two, one, sub-luminal engines engaged!*'

The bridge deck of the frigate seemed to surge as the light was momentarily polarised around the captain, a snap-shot of tense faces and flickering screens as Atlantia's sensors suddenly received information from the surrounding cosmos once more.

Idris's brain rushed to re-calibrate as a flood of information plunged from dozens of screens all around him and a frenzy of calls rang out from the command crew.

'Sub-luminal attack velocity, all systems operational and at maximum power!'

'Sheilds engaged, all plasma cannons active and charged!'

'Reaper squadron launching off cat's one and two!'

Idris saw a pair of sleek, curved-winged Raython fighters rocket out into the void ahead, their exhausts flaring blue-white against the dense star fields.

'Akryan V in sight captain,' Lael called, 'four planetary diameters, port bow elevation three niner!'

Idris' gaze flicked to the upper left quadrant of the viewing screen and almost immediately he spotted the looming shadow of a planet silhouetting the star fields, almost invisible due to the lack of a parent star. Akyran V was a so–called "orphan" planet, ejected from whatever system had nurtured it millennia before due to gravitational interactions with other planets. Wandering alone in the infinite void it was frozen solid, a gigantic ball of ice. *Pristine ice.*

'Renegade flight launching!' Commander Andaim Ry'ere, the CAG, called from his station, his youthful features pinched with concern. 'Eight fighters now aloft and heading to patrol coordinates.'

Idris nodded. *So far, so good.* Once a perimeter was established, shuttles could be sent down to the surface and begin the process of transporting water to Atlantia and Arcadia and replenishing their parched reservoirs.

Idris turned to another display panel nearby, clear plastic that was arrayed with digital displays including one detailing Arcadia's position alongside Atlantia. He could already see that Arcadia was breaking away to take up a defensive position out to starboard, separating the two vessels to prevent them from being attacked all at once.

Alongside the panel was another that displayed radar returns from Atlantia's powerful sensors. Although set to *passive*, to prevent any emitted signals from betraying their position, Idris could see no returns out in the endless void that gave him cause for concern. The largest return came from Akryan itself, the image of the world slightly hazy on the radar screens due to dense clouds of debris orbiting it.

'Residue from whatever impact event broke the planet from its parent star's orbit,' Andaim guessed as he noted the captain's gaze. 'If there's enough ice in there it might mean we can collect what we need from orbit instead of having to take the risk of landing.'

'Agreed,' Idris replied as he turned to the CAG. 'Prepare the shuttles but hold them until the defensive perimeter is secure. Where is Reaper Flight?'

'Out bound at zero point eight planetary diameters,' the CAG replied. 'They'll be on station within a few minutes.'

'Divert two of them toward the orbiting field, have them check it out. Our radar won't penetrate debris of that density. Let's make sure there's nothing lurking out there that shouldn't be.'

Andaim turned and began conveying the captain's orders as on another screen an image of Arcadia's captain appeared. Mikhain, a dark haired, powerfully built man with equally dark eyes, raised an eyebrow as he spoke.

'All quiet,' he murmured. 'We never get things this easy.'

'Lazarus said that this would be a safe spot to attempt to recover supplies,' Idris pointed out. 'He says that The Word could not have spread this far out yet from the core systems.'

'He's a computerized faÃ§ade of a man who died decades ago and who destroyed entire worlds,' Mikhain scowled. 'I wouldn't trust that short–circuit as far as I could throw him. I'm not willing to move in until the scout ships have reported clear.'

'Agreed,' Idris replied. 'Reaper Flight is almost there. We'll let them finish their sweep and then head in. Maintain position on the starboard flank and keep everything charged. I want out of here in five minutes or less if something goes wrong.'

'Roger that.'

Mikhain's image vanished as Idris turned to screens displaying the tactical dispersal of two squadrons of sleek Raython fighters toward their assigned Combat Air Patrols far out at the limits of Atlantia's sensor range.

'I hope you're right about this,' Governor Gredan said from somewhere behind the captain.

'So am I,' Idris murmured softly.

*

'Battle flight, go now!'

Evelyn glanced out of her Raython's cockpit to see Teera Milan's oil–streaked fighter break crisply from close formation flight and rocket away until she was a bright speck among the countless stars.

Ahead through her canopy Evelyn could see the looming shadow of Akyran V, a featureless blackness where the dense star fields vanished as though a black hole were swallowing them one by one. The faint starlight was not enough to illuminate the planet in the manner that a parent star would, and thus the bitterly cold and lonely world seemed all the more sinister for its impenetrable darkness.

Evelyn looked down instead at her instruments and saw there the planet more clearly, along with its orbiting belt of icy debris. The debris was indistinct, the Raython's radar not powerful enough to provide a high resolution return.

'We're not getting much in the way of signals,' she reported to Teera as she scrutinized the image before her on her cockpit screen. 'You seeing anything?'

'Nothing but icy junk,' Teera replied.

'Looks like we're going to have to do this the old fashioned way,' Evelyn said as she eased back on her throttles.

The Raython slowed as it closed in on the dangerous belts of tumbling rock, and in the dim glow of the starlight Evelyn thought that she spotted reflections flickering in the blackness, starlight caught on the surface of icy boulders spinning through the vacuum of space.

'Here we go,' she said, and flipped a switch on her instrument panel.

A pair of vivid beams of light burst into life from her Raython as she activated her landing lights, the beams illuminating a misty field of icy debris. Some chunks of rock were the size of her fist, others twice as large as her Raython, others still almost as big as Atlantia herself. They tumbled and drifted in a silent, chaotic dance high above the surface of the planet, itself now so close that Evelyn felt as though she were staring into a black hole for real.

'Damn,' she muttered. 'It's too dense. Nothing's getting in there and surviving.'

Evelyn glanced out to her left and called for Renegade Squadron's lead CAP aircraft.

'Segei, you see anything out there?'

*

Segei Voont squinted into the icy wastes outside his Raython's cockpit and shook his head as he replied.

'There's nothing here, Evie,' he said. 'No signals from the field, no way through it though either. The shuttles could use scoops, but it'll be risky.'

'You think we could maybe use grapples and haul one of the bigger ones out of the field?' Evelyn suggested.

'It'd be safer boss,' Segei agreed as he scanned his instruments. 'There's a big one just ahead of me, looks like mostly ice rather than dust. Enough water there for one of the frigates for months.'

'Roger that,' Evelyn replied. *'We're on our way. Stand by.'*

Segei peered ahead through the gloomy dust and ice at the large rock floating in silence before him. He edged his throttles forward and his Raython crept into the veil of debris, the sound of smaller pieces of rock and ice rattling against the fighter's fuselage as it eased between the tumbling clouds.

The larger rock was over a thousand cubits long and five hundred deep according to Segei's instruments, and likely partially hollow as its mass did not match its predicted volume. It glowed a strange, misty white in the harsh glare of the Raython's landing lights as his fighter edged closer.

'Segei, hold position,' Evelyn called across to him. *'There's too much debris.'*

Segei saw something flicker briefly on his radar screen. 'I've got something, a weak signal.'

'Hold position,' Evelyn repeated.

Segei saw the signal flicker again, a minute heat source, as though perhaps a candle flame was gusting in the wind that he knew could not exist in the brutal vacuum of space. A sense of dread enveloped him as he retarded the throttles and engaged reverse thrust.

'There's something in here!' he shouted.

The tiny heat signal flared suddenly on Segei's screen and his gaze flashed to the view outside his cockpit as from the massive icy rock a blast of ice crystals were ejected into space and a huge, pulsating black tentacle of oily liquid rushed out toward his fighter.

'Renegade Four, there's something here, it's coming for me!'

Segie slammed his throttles to maximum power and his Raython lurched into reverse. Sergie saw the vast, swarming black tentacle writhe toward his cockpit, its surface undulating like a sea of oil, billions of countless waves. And then he realized what he was looking at.

'The Legion!'

Segei's head slammed into his headrest as the Raython plowed backward into a tumbling chunk of rock and spun over, out of control. Segei rocked the throttles and tried to right the fighter, and as it spun back over so the blackened swarm of Hunters smashed into his cockpit screen.

Segei screamed and fired his plasma cannons at the massive cloud of tiny machines, each no larger than his thumb, but already his canopy was disintegrating as it was instantly fogged by a million tiny pincers scratching at the glass. His Raython's engines failed as the Hunter poured inside and tore through power cables and fuel cells, and Segei reached for his service pistol to take his own life before the Hunters broke through.

The canopy failed and Segei screamed one last time, his cry snatched away as the atmosphere was ripped from the cockpit and the Hunters poured inside in their thousands. Segie felt a moment of unimaginable pain as they tore into his body, his flesh ripped apart and his limbs and neck severed within seconds as the Hunters literally tore his fighter to shreds.

***

II

'Segei!'

Evelyn shouted his name at the top of her voice as her Raython streaked toward Segei's fighter, the Raython lost in a dense cloud of misty white ice and something else that writhed and coiled around it.

Evelyn's blood ran cold as she saw the roiling mass of the Legion's Hunters consuming the Raython, sparks of energy flickering among them as they fed.

'The Word is here!' she cried out. 'The Legion's here!'

Evelyn activated her plasma cannons and opened fire, knowing that Segei was already nothing more than a memory. Blue–white pulses of fearsome plasma energy thundered from her Raython's cannons to smash into the Hunters' feeding frenzy and a brilliant explosion dazzled Evelyn as the stricken Raython's engines exploded. The blast blossomed out in a terrific fireball that sent debris radiating away from it and out toward Evelyn's Raython, and as she broke away she felt her guts plunge within her as from behind the expanding debris cloud she saw a vessel lumbering toward her.

In the fading light of the explosion she caught a glimpse of a cylindrical hull, a functional rather than aesthetic design, festooned with countless grappling arms and plasma cannons, but the craft was clearly not designed for war. A mining ship, she realized, that had most likely become infected while going about its business near the edge of the Icari Line collecting minerals for sale on Ethera and the core worlds.

'All fighters, break off!' Evelyn heard the tension in Captain Idris Sanin's tone as he roared the command across all frequencies. *'Return immediately for departure!'*

Evelyn hauled her Raython around in a tight turn and accelerated away from the debris field, knowing that she could outrun the mining vessel, and then looked out to her left for Teera's fighter.

'Reaper Two, report in!'

'I'm under attack!'

Evelyn's eyes widened as she saw another craft emerging from the debris field in pursuit of Teera's Raython, this one some kind of luxury yacht that looked oddly out of place amid the fighters and the darkened wastes of the lonely planet's orbit. Faster than the mining craft, it was keeping pace with Teera's fighter.

'It's an ambush!' Idris snapped over the communications channel. *'All craft prepare to depart!'*

Evelyn saw Teera's fighter being intercepted by the yacht, the pursuing vessel sleek and white like a paper dart but speckled with a black sheen where the Hunters infecting the craft were using the material of its hull to replicate.

Ahead, Evelyn could see both Atlantia and Arcadia moving toward them, but both frigates were out of firing range.

'Teera, break right, now!' Evelyn ordered.

'I can't, they'll cut me off!'

'I'm in–bound, do it!'

Evelyn broke hard left and advanced her throttles to maximum power as she rocketed toward Teera's Raython, using her instruments to guide her. She spotted the yacht rushing across her bow, and then moments later Teera's Raython curving toward her at maximum velocity as she tried to cross the yacht's bow and make a run for Arcadia.

'That's it,' Evelyn said as her thumb hovered over the trigger on her control column. 'Now, break left!'

Evelyn's Raython broke away from Evelyn's fighter and the yacht turned to track it, presenting its hull broadside to Evelyn's guns as it crossed her nose from left to right, its engines clearly visible.

Evelyn lined the yacht's engines up in her sights and opened fire. A brilliant stream of plasma pulses rocketed out from her Raython and smashed in bright blue and white blasts against the yacht's hull and engine bays. The yacht broke off its pursuit to defend against her attack, but then its starboard flank rippled with bright explosions as plasma lines were ruptured by Evelyn's gunfire and the yacht began to veer to port and trail clouds of debris and unburned fuel.

'Your tail's clear!' Evelyn yelled. 'Let's get out of here!'

Evelyn had barely gotten the call out when another was broadcast from Arcadia.

'New contacts, bearing zero three eight, elevation minus two four!'

Evelyn craned her head over her right shoulder and saw a flotilla of vessels emerging from the depths of the debris field, all manner of craft illuminated by the savage flares of light from plasma cannons as Renegade Flight's Raythons opened up on them.

A rain of plasma fire crashed through the emerging flotilla, but Evelyn could see that the Raythons were heavily outnumbered already and that the

Legion was emerging from the attacking vessels in writhing coils, the Hunters on the outside revolving around and then plunging back inside the coil to prevent themselves from being exposed to the frigid vacuum of space for too long.

From the flotilla erupted a barrage of plasma fire in return, and Evelyn saw one of the Raythons hit as it turned to flee the attack.

'Renegade Five, I'm hit! I'm hit! Get me out of here before they…'

The cry abruptly mutated into a grotesque scream of agony as the wounded fighter smashed into one of the Hunter tentacles. It rocketed out of the other side, consumed by the tiny machines and broke up in mid-flight. Evelyn saw the fragments of the fighter continue on into space as they were torn apart by the frenzied cloud of machines, the pilot's remains trapped among the torn metal plating of his Raython.

'All fighters retreat immediately!' Idris ordered once more.

Atlantia and Arcadia were turning already, crossing each other's flight path with Atlantia higher than her sister ship as they reversed course while presenting the aft landing bays to the fleeing Raythons. An invitation for a tactical landing, Evelyn saw Renegade Flight break off from the flotilla of vessels and make a run for it as a hail of plasma fire rocketed in pursuit.

'Renegade Flight, retreating under fire!'

Evelyn turned toward the fleeing Raythons. 'Reaper Flight, covering fire!'

Reaper Flight's eight Raythons rocketed toward the fleeing fighters, and Evelyn gasped as she saw the sheer number of craft emerging from the debris field.

'I'm hit!'

Evelyn saw a Raython veer to one side as a lucky shot struck its aft starboard quarter and one of its engines exploded. A trail of sparkling energy spluttered from the wounded fighter as it turned violently, its pilot struggling to maintain control under the asymmetric thrust from its remaining engine.

Behind it, half a dozen infected craft broke off from the main group on an intercept course.

'Renegade Four, hold position, we're on our way.'

Evelyn accelerated toward the stricken Raython, Teera on her wing and four more Raythons pursuing her as she saw the mining craft swarm toward the Raython. Evelyn aimed for the gap between them and then lined her weapons up on the leading infected craft.

'All fighters, line astern, hit them one at a time!'

Evelyn opened fire on the lead craft, a wedge–shaped vessel of a type she did not recognise. Her plasma blasts smashed through the hull's armour plating and its cockpit erupted into flames as clouds of vaporised Hunters spilled away from it as though the craft were a comet trailing fire across a blackened sky.

She pulled up in time to see Teera's Raython open up on the same craft, and it exploded into a brilliant fireball as the shockwave hit Evelyn's Raython and shuddered through it.

'That got 'em!' Teera yelled jubilantly as she pulled up and away from the blast.

Evelyn pulled up high, her Raython wheeling around for a second pass as she saw the remaining craft of Reaper Flight hammering the freighters below them. Immense clouds of Hunters burst like fireworks as they were melted and spat out from the blasts like embers from a raging fire, the spacecraft they occupied pitching and yawing out of control as their bridges and cockpits were blasted into oblivion.

'Renegade Four clear, landing now!'

'That's it,' Teera yelled. *'Let's get out of here!'*

'Reaper Flight, disengage and land immediately!'

The Raythons broke off their attack and swept past Evelyn's fighter as she cast one last glance across the advancing flotilla of vessels. They had been concealed behind or within the larger asteroids and rocks, with the infecting Hunters likely hibernating around the crafts' fusion cores to maintain their heat and emerging only when unwary travellers were detected closing in on their position. With so many humans likely fleeing the core systems into deep space and on the lookout for resources, Evelyn realized that the Legion had evolved its tactics once again, no longer actively hunting humans in individual ships but bedding down in wait to ambush them *en masse*. Yet despite the change in tactics she could not fathom how the Legion had managed to reach out so far into deep space.

'Reaper One, retreat immediately!'

Evelyn blinked herself out of her reverie and shoved her throttles wide open as she accelerated away from the flotilla of captured and infected vessels, maintaining maximum velocity for as long as she dared, Atlantia and Arcadia looming before her until it seemed a collision was inevitable. She could see the last of Reaper Flight landing already, disappearing into the frigate's stern.

She hauled back on her control column and flipped the Raython over, her blazing engines now directing their enormous thrust in the opposite direction as she simultaneously lowered the fighter's magnetic undercarriage. Before her cockpit she saw the pursuing infected vessels closing in on her fighter and suddenly the Hunters reached out for her, writhing and twisting tentacles of machinery stretching out toward her Raython's bow. A sudden dreadful realization poisoned her thoughts.

I'm not going to make it.

The Raython's velocity slowed dramatically toward tactical landing speed, allowing the flotilla to catch up with her. She saw the billions of Hunters that made up the writhing arm reaching out to her from the mining craft, glistening like black scales in the white glow from her landing lights. She looked down at her velocity indicator: *five more seconds.*

A sharp crack hit her canopy and she flinched as she saw a Hunter land there, its metallic pincers scraping at the glass. Another joined it, and then another. Evelyn's hand went to the service pistol at her waist as cold dread swilled through her belly.

A blinding flare of light smashed past the Raython's nose, and in the glare Evelyn saw the Hunters on her canopy melted as they were seared by terrific heat. The flare of light vanished as it crashed into the nose of the pursuing mining craft and smashed the entire vessel's bow clean off. A brilliant explosion of countless millions of Hunters blazed before Evelyn and then were shouldered aside with brazen courage as she saw Arcadia's massive bow plunge past her Raython with scant cubits to spare.

Evelyn gaped in amazement as she watched the huge frigate lumber by, saw distant flashes over the hull from its massive plasma cannons as they opened up in tremendous broadsides upon the flotilla advancing upon Atlantia's stern. Captain Mikhain's voice rang out over the intercom.

'What are you waiting for, a red carpet?! Get aboard, now!'

Evelyn grabbed the control column once more as she flipped her Raython over and saw Atlantia's landing bays wide open, a warm and inviting orange light glowing within as she lined up for an arrested landing. The Raython soared in beneath the frigate's enormous hull and then plunged into the landing bay. The magnetic clamps on her undercarriage were dragged to a halt by the deck's opposing magnetic field and the fighter decelerated violently, Evelyn hauled forward in her harness as the Raython was brought to a dramatic halt.

'Reaper Flight recovered, close the doors!'

Atlantia's massive landing bay doors lumbered downward, and Evelyn craned her head around her seat to see Arcadia disappearing from view and the flotilla of infected craft looming toward her in the bay, many of them aflame and with a field of carnage behind them from Arcadia's massive broadsides. Hunters writhed in glowing hot tentacles as they tried to reach out for the frigate, to infect it with as many machines as possible.

The massive doors thundered down and then the light in the bay became polarised as the frigate's mass–drive engaged and Atlantia was hurled into super–luminal velocity.

***

III

'It was a damned shambles!'

Captain Idris Sansin stood before the Board of Governors with his hands behind his back and his chin held a little higher than usual.

The Governor's Chamber was a converted homestead within Atlantia's sanctuary, a forested valley that emulated their home world of Ethera and was contained within a revolving cylinder inside Atlantia's hull. Arcadia contained a similar sanctuary, built after the end of the frigates' military service and designed to provide a hospitable living quarters for the correctional officers deployed to serve as prison warders. Both frigates had been prison ships prior to the appalling catastrophe that had befallen mankind.

'It was an ambush,' Idris replied. 'All things considered our extraction and escape could hardly have gone better, despite the sad loss of two of our pilots.'

Governor Gredan was flanked by Governors Ayek and Vaughn, a prim woman and a young man respectively. On the ends of the table sat Governor Ishira Morle, a former ship captain herself and thus Idris's only real ally on the board, while at the opposite end sat Governor Meyanna Sansin, his wife and, alarmingly, often his greatest foe.

'How?' Governor Vaughn asked with a tight smile. 'How could this be an ambush? We're on the edge of the Icari Line, far from Ethera. How could the Legion have penetrated this far out into deep space and lain in wait for us?'

'The Word was in control of our people long before we knew it,' Idris replied. 'And we now know that our own government sent Special Operations teams beyond the Icari Line to find out what lay there, after our last encounter with the Morla'syn. It is entirely possible that The Word could have despatched small groups of Hunters or Infectors out with them, to begin its conquering not just of Ethera but of the known cosmos. We must assume from this point onward that The Word is not just intent on destroying what's left of the human race, but of expanding its reach indefinitely.'

Idris knew that The Word, a creation of quantum physics, was in effect a computer. It had evolved out of a major milestone in human engineering, *The Field*: a digital record of all information that had been accessible to all humans. The growth of human knowledge had accelerated wildly in the years following the creation of The Field, reaching all corners of the colonies through the sharing of information, and technology had likewise grown and expanded at a phenomenal rate. This massive database of information had been fused with quantum computing to create *The Word*, a depository of knowledge designed to be able to make decisions based on pure logic and an understanding of myriad complexities that were beyond the human capacity to assimilate and form cohesive responses. Tasked with finding solutions to the most complex problems in history, ranging from space exploration to crime to medicine, The Word eventually became the founder of laws, the arbitrator of justice and the icon of mankind's prolific creativity.

The one thing that nobody could have predicted was that The Word, through its sheer volume of thought and understanding, would have concluded that mankind, its very creator, was a greater threat to itself than any other species and thus must be either controlled or eradicated. Thus had been born the Legion, and mankind silently infected with nanobots capable of controlling the brain stem long before anybody realized what was about to happen.

'Then we must re–think our strategy, don't you agree, captain?' Governor Ayek snapped primly. 'Our path of traversing the cosmos from supply source to supply source without a common goal in mind has run its course entirely, don't you think?'

Idris ground his teeth in his jaw and clenched his hands behind his back as he formulated his reply.

'It has served us well up to this point,' he replied.

'Indeed,' Governor Vaughn agreed, 'right up to the point where we were ambushed by the Legion on Akryan V having been sent there by Lazarus, the very man who created The Word! Has it not crossed your mind that whatever is left of the man inside that machine might have led us there on purpose, captain?'

'I doubt that very much.'

'You *doubt* it?' Governor Gredan chimed in. 'But you do not deny it, either?'

'These are hardly ordinary matters we're talking about here,' Governor Morle said finally, coming to the captain's aid before even his wife, Idris noted. 'Lazarus is an unknown quantity, but he got our people off Endeavour and helped us win in battle against a much more heavily armoured Morla'syn battleship. There has to be some credit in there for his intentions.'

'There is,' Governor Sansin replied finally, hiding from her husband behind a veil of her long dark hair that had fallen across one side of her face. 'But that credit can only carry us so far. The Word is known to be a cunning and duplicitous foe, and Lazarus's assistance in battle against the Morla'syn could easily have been a sleight of hand to win our trust.'

Idris snorted and shook his head. 'Even if that were true there is no way for Lazarus to communicate with the Legion, especially not in super–luminal cruise, which I should add we've been in for at least forty per cent of the time we've been running from…'

Idris cut himself off, appalled at his choice of words. Governor Gredan did not miss the slip up.

'Running,' he echoed as he folded his thick fingers beneath his bloated chin. 'That's what we've been doing for the vast majority of the time since the apocalypse, captain. When is it that you're going to admit that we're unable to face this challenge alone, that we cannot take the fight to the Legion and to The Word on Ethera? With every passing month we find ourselves further from our homes, further from any hope of enlisting help in fighting the scourge that decimated our home world. Sooner or later, captain, we're going to be too far away to ever hope to return and fight your promised battle against The Word.'

Idris allowed a cold little smile to form on one corner of his lips. 'Strange, Governor, but I seem to recall it being you who demanded that we flee the Legion rather than face open battle, and you who almost fainted on the bridge deck during the last engagement.'

Gredan's florid features paled a little. 'I am not conditioned to the command demands of a warship, captain.'

'How true.'

'We need make no apology for the fact that we are not people of war, captain,' Meyanna said. 'We are, however, of the people, the very thing that placed us on this governing board – the common vote. We speak for the last two thousand human beings known to be alive in the cosmos, and you're not listening. How much longer do you plan to ignore the wishes of the people you purport to protect?'

'For as long as it protects them,' Idris growled back.

'It isn't protecting them!' Governor Vaughn snapped. 'They were almost overwhelmed less than two hours ago! And right now your command is actively interfering with the on–going trial of a Veng'en murderer, is collaborating with a computerized reincarnation of the man who created The Word, while leading a military contingent that is fifty per cent comprised of convicted felons! You're also insisting that we should not attempt to enlist the help of the Galactic Council in eradicating The Word on the battlefield, based on the opinion of the one machine aboard this ship that we have considerable reasons not to trust!'

A deep silence followed the councillor's outburst, and Idris could almost feel the watching eyes of the audience of civilians behind him as he attempted to gather his thoughts.

'Kordaz is under protective custody because without it he would probably be murdered by our own crew,' Idris replied. 'As a Veng'en he is seen as an enemy, but I have seen what he is capable of and of what he has achieved in the name of our cause, and I will not allow him to be harmed ahead of a proper trial. Lazarus is our only hope of understanding The Word and perhaps finding a weakness within it, and we have it on his authority that the Galactic Council created the Icari Line to keep human beings *in*, not protect us from what was *beyond*. They cannot be seen either as allies or as a means to fight a war.'

'So says Lazarus,' Governor Ayek uttered. 'And as for that woman *thing* you brought back from Endeavour – do you intend to put her in command soon, captain?'

Idris felt his blood boil and he was about to reply when Meyanna cut across him.

'Her name is Emma,' she growled at Ayek, 'and she is as human as you or I.'

Idris raised an eyebrow in surprise at his wife's sudden defensive stance. The ship's chief physician, she had not taken kindly to Ayek's tone.

'Says who?' Ayek retorted. 'Emma and that other one, the former convict…'

'Evelyn,' Meyanna replied, 'her sister.'

'Sister,' Governor Vaughn almost chuckled. 'They're a hundred years apart and yet genetically identical. They're clones, not sisters. Can we agree that nobody here really knows what the hell is going on with those two?' Vaughn looked at Idris. 'And if you can consider the Galactic Council as a potential enemy based on the opinion of Lazarus, then is it not a logical progression based on the same evidence that we can consider both Emma and Evelyn potential foes based on their apparent origin with The Word?'

'You could,' Idris replied, 'if you were idiot enough. Both of them have risked their lives on more than one occasion to protect us.'

'And there we go again,' Gredan snapped with a click of his podgy fingers. 'Somebody throws themselves in the line of fire for you and suddenly their opinion matters more than ours, regardless of their questionable motives or history.'

'Their opinion is irrelevant,' Idris said. 'Their acts are unquestionable.'

'We can't all be heroes in the line of fire, captain,' Vaughn pointed out. 'If we were we'd all have died long ago. There are two thousand humans known to be left alive, and yet you're defending a Veng'en killer and a genetically cloned woman who may or not be something created by The Word. You understand our concern, do you not?'

Idris sighed. 'I can only continue on the course that is safest for us, and the Galactic Council is not a safe haven for humanity. We have no representative there and we know for sure that they don't trust us. If we travel there, the chances are they'll blast us from existence on sight.'

'But they may not,' Gredan countered, 'whereas the Legion certainly will. Captain, this is no longer a decision that can be placed in the hands of Atlantia's command crew and certainly not Lazarus. We put it to the people that the decision to avoid, or approach, the Galactic Council for assistance in our war should be put to a referendum. Our survival is a universal concern, not just something for military officers to determine.' Before Idris could open his mouth to protest, Gredan addressed the gathered civilian onlookers seated behind him. 'All those in favour?'

Idris did not turn to look as he heard a shuffling from the hundred or so civilians chosen to witness the governor's meeting on behalf of Atlantia and Arcadia' passengers. He watched as Meyanna counted the hands behind him, and then glanced across at Gredan.

'Eighty five in favour,' she said. 'The decision will be put to a referendum of the ships' company.'

Idris managed to somehow prevent himself from cursing out loud, and instead turned on his heel without another word and marched from the homestead into the cool air outside.

The sanctuary's forested hills basked under a broad sky, a mock sun blazing brilliantly as it descended toward the horizon. The sanctuary's rotational velocity perfectly replicated Ethera's gravity, avoiding the need for the magnetic gravi–suits and boots worn by crews in the rest of the ship. Filled with negatively charged particles of iron that pulled them down toward the positively charged cylinders beneath the deck plating, the gravi–suits prevented muscle loss and preserved bone–density that long periods of zero–gravity would otherwise degrade.

Idris could see the rolling ocean in the distance, the sense of depth remarkable although entirely an illusion created by the ship's powerful computers. In actual fact, although the sanctuary seemed to go on forever, it was only a thousand cubits long by some three hundred wide. But the air was cool and the sunshine felt warm on his face, and Idris closed his eyes and tried to relax and let the tension bleed from his pores in the wake of his grilling before the council.

'They're only thinking of the people.'

Meyanna's voice reached out to him but he did not turn as he replied. 'And you?'

'Don't be like that. The people voted me as their governor. You supported their choice to vote!'

Idris sighed as he looked out over the rolling ocean sparkling in the setting sun like a sheet of rippling copper, aware of his wife's elegant features bathed in the coppery light beside him but unable to bring himself to look at her. 'We have enough enemies out there, Meyanna. I don't want to be dealing with them aboard ship too.'

'Then stop viewing us as enemies. The people are as trapped aboard Atlantia and Arcadia as we are. If you choose to go into battle they are forced to come with us. Don't they have a right to say whether the stakes are high enough to risk their lives, as you and the Marines and the pilots risk theirs?'

Idris knew that his wife was right, and he turned to look at her. Meyanna had always appeared more youthful than he but now, with the sunlight caressing her skin and her long dark hair, she looked decades younger. But her mind was as sharp as his, and he knew better than to underestimate her instinctive feeling for the mood of the governors.

'Maybe you're right,' he said finally. 'Maybe that's what's holding us back?'

'What do you mean?'

Meyanna moved to slip one arm through his, and they turned together to look out over the stunning vista of a world that no longer existed.

'Governor Vaughn was right,' he said. 'We're running away, every thought of offensive action tempered by the fear that failure will cost all of our lives. If we want to strike back, we need the civilians sent somewhere safe.'

Meyanna raised an eyebrow. 'You mean a haven of some kind?'

'They need a home, so that we can fight on their behalf without fear for their safety. We can't keep running like this, or before we know it we'll have run out of places to hide.' Idris looked down at Meyanna as a fresh resolve began surging through his veins. 'It's time,' he said softly. 'No more running.'

Meyanna searched his eyes and he saw the concern etched into hers.

'What are you going to do?'

***

IV

'How they did they get so far out?'

Evelyn reached up and hung her flight suit on a hook beside the entrance to the tiny cabin she shared with Teera Milan, ready to grab again at a moment's notice if the Reapers were scrambled once more.

'I don't know,' Evelyn replied. 'We're right out on the Icari Line. The Legion shouldn't have gotten this far and yet, there it was.'

'Most of those ships were mining vessels,' Teera said. 'Andaim said the techs had identified them in debrief – the Legion must have had control of them long before Ethera fell.'

Evelyn nodded. The Word's Legion, the innumerable army of tiny machines that had overwhelmed mankind, had been dispersed among the populace initially through the use of dangerous street drugs, most notably Devlamine, the *Devil's Drink*. Tiny *Infectors* contaminating the drug entered the human body and gradually colonised the spinal column and then the brain stem, multiplying using the human body's own resources until they took control of the victim. Alive but unable to control their own bodies, the victims then passed on the Infectors to others, spreading the mechanical contagion like a virus.

Nobody knew when the Legion first began dispersing among humankind, but what was now certain was that it all began long before The Word issued its command to annihilate human beings wherever they were to be found. By that time, more than eighty per cent of mankind had already been infected, tiny machines coursing unnoticed through their bloodstream or hiding away in their brain stem, waiting to strike.

'Mining companies used to spend years on a single voyage, hunting out minerals in the asteroid belts,' Evelyn said thoughtfully. 'Those ships might have been infected decades ago and lain in wait ever since. It could even have been part of The Word's long–term plan, to organise a series of ambushes on distant worlds to capture any fleeing humans. Who knows?'

'Lazarus knows,' Teera replied. 'Maybe we should have him wired up to something, get him to talk, y'know?'

Evelyn couldn't help the smile that crept from her lips as she zipped up her uniform jacket and looked at Teera. 'We're not a dictatorship, remember? Lazarus may be a machine, but it's pretty clear that there's a human being in there, no matter how odd it seems.'

'And what about...?'

Teera cut herself off, but Evelyn smiled again. 'You mean: what about Emma?'

Teera shrugged. 'I don't get how she can be your sister when she's supposedly a hundred or more years old.'

'Believe me, I don't either,' Evelyn replied. 'But she's a human being too, and treating her any differently isn't going to make things easier.'

'But, she can *hear* The Word, can't she? That's what everybody's saying, that the Marines with her aboard Endeavour said that she talked to the machine.'

Evelyn nodded. When the fabled, long–missing exploratory vessel Endeavour had been found by Atlantia, adrift beyond the Icari Line, they had found aboard her Lazarus. The great inventor, realizing the horror that he had created in The Word as he neared the end of his days, committed suicide after uploading his consciousness into a computer and sent himself to Endeavour, already far beyond the Core Systems and beyond the reach of The Word. Lazarus had then taken control of Endeavour and silenced her communications suite to prevent The Word from pursuing him, thus starting the mysterious legend of what happened to the enormous vessel.

'Emma is special somehow,' Evelyn replied. 'And we all have our immunity to the Infectors because I too have some connection to The Word. You don't see me as any less human, do you?'

Teera shrugged. 'That all depends on your damned mood in the mornings.'

Evelyn grabbed a pillow and tossed it at Teera, who ducked and feigned drawing her pistol. A buzzer sounded in the cabin and Evelyn hit a switch on the wall. The cabin door hissed aside and Commander Andaim peered inside.

'Captain's orders,' he said, briefly glancing at the pillow now hovering in mid–air in the cabin and at Teera's hand on the butt of her pistol, 'we're to assemble below decks.'

'Below decks? Any idea what it's about?' Evelyn asked.

'No, but Emma's been called in too along with most of the senior personnel.'

'So it's a fashionable party,' Teera quipped.

'Ten minutes, Deck H, aft quadrant,' Andaim said, and then turned and marched away.

'Soul of the party,' Teera observed as Evelyn closed the cabin door. 'He still got the hots for you?'

'Give it up,' Evelyn smiled to herself.

'Come on, you know he likes you,' Teera nudged her friend. 'How come you two haven't got it together and…'

'I said enough,' Evelyn snapped, and then softened her voice. 'I think Emma's appearance has made him nervous. Can't blame him, really.'

'Most people were nervous around you anyway, so it figures,' Teera replied as she hid behind the pillow still hanging in the air.

'Something's up with the command crew and I want to know what,' Evelyn said as she checked her uniform in the steel mirror bolted to one wall of the cabin. 'C'mon, let's move.'

Evelyn led the way out of the cabin and aft toward the deck elevators. Since the fleet had doubled in size with the addition of Arcadia, when Salim Phaeon's pirate fleet had been defeated on Chiron IV, Atlantia's decks had become less packed with officers and civilians. Evelyn and Teera made quick progress through the ship on the shuttle system toward the stern, just aft of the sanctuary's gigantic revolving cylinder.

Deck H was a storage deck and held most of the ship's supplies along with the plasma armoury, itself further for'ard and with a specially armoured containment system that ensured any un–commanded detonation would expel plasma out of specialized vents in the hull rather than allow it to expand into the ship.

Evelyn and Teera walked along an access corridor between storage depots, the corridor passing through bulkheads that ran the length of Atlantia's keel. Their boots echoed down the immensely long passage and Evelyn noticed something as they moved.

'The crew's been dismissed,' she said as she realized that none of the storage personnel were at their stations.

On a vessel like Atlantia, with a compliment of a thousand souls, there were always supplies being moved by man and machines alike. But now, the depots were silent.

'They cleared the deck,' Teera agreed. 'Must be something big going down. Got any ideas?'

Evelyn shook her head as she saw two Marines standing guard outside one of the storage depots. She slowed as the soldiers moved to meet them, checking their identity badges before waving them inside the depot.

The depot was roughly fifty cubits on all sides, used to store dry goods and foods for the crew and compliment. It was a measure of how short of supplies the fleet had become that this particular depot was virtually empty. Evelyn's boots echoed as much as they had in the access corridor as she walked toward a small group of officers gathered in a loose circle in the centre of the depot.

Captain Sansin stood with the commander of the Marines, General Bra'hiv, and the CAG, Andaim Ry'ere. Alongside them were Arcadia's captain, Mikhain, who had evidently travelled across from his ship via shuttle, and Lael, Atlantia's communications officer and a woman whom Evelyn recognised as becoming something of a surrogate first officer for Captain Sansin. Her metallically-tinted hair, a fashion during the last days of Ethera, twinkled like chrome in the low light. Finally, standing to one side, Evelyn saw Emma waiting patiently with her hands clasped before her.

'Lieutenants,' Captain Sansin greeted them.

Both Evelyn and Teera saluted. 'Where's the fire?' Teera asked.

'Where isn't there one?' the captain replied, and then looked at the officers before him. 'Now we're all here I'd like to point out that this meeting is between us and us alone. It is not to be shared or discussed with anybody else aboard. *Anybody*, is that clear?'

A murmur of *yessirs* fluttered across the group. Idris slid his hands into his pockets in an uncharacteristically casual manner. 'We got ambushed this morning on a planet far from the home worlds. The Legion is spreading, or has already spread, far beyond our expectations and will continue to do so. Given that we have encountered the Legion this far out, and assuming that The Word attempted to extend its reach in all directions, the infection that destroyed Ethera might now cover a sphere some one hundred lights years across, with the core systems at its centre.'

Evelyn heard a soft breath of distress from the gathered officers as they considered the extent to which The Word and its Legion might have infected and colonized other worlds.

'We cannot allow this to continue,' Idris went on. 'Already, the Legion's advance represents a battle-front that is far too vast to contain or effectively combat. If we stem the tide in one area, it will simply continue to expand in another. We are but two vessels and a very small tactical force, and we have to face the fact that we are doing ourselves no good by running any further. Wherever we flee, the Legion will eventually reach and we will be forced to fight anyway.'

Andaim frowned. 'I thought that we were fighting.'

'We are,' Mikhain said, 'but we're only winning battles. We're losing the war.'

Idris nodded. 'We cannot do this on our own. Today, the Board of Governors voted to put our future to a referendum, to let the civilians decide by democratic vote whether we should continue on our own or attempt to approach the Galactic Council for assistance.'

'The Council wants us dead,' General Bra'hiv growled. 'The Morla'syn told us that much, that the Icari Line was conceived to keep us away from them.'

'Nobody is saying that it will be easy,' Idris admitted, 'but right now, facing what we're facing, the only way for us to win this war is to recruit allies.'

'We don't have any allies,' Mikhain pointed out. 'Besides, we tried it with Taron Forge and his pirate buddies, and look how that turned out.'

'Pirates and the Galactic Fleet aren't quite the same thing,' Evelyn said, speaking out for the first time. 'The combined worlds could amass a huge armada, maybe enough to overwhelm The Word.'

'Maybe,' Andaim cautioned, 'but certainly enough to blast us into history.'

'Lazarus said that the council will destroy us,' Teera added.

'Lazarus also said that Akyram V would be a safe place to look for supplies,' Bra'hiv countered.

Evelyn, and everybody else, looked at Emma. Even now Evelyn felt unusual whenever she looked at her sister, her every feature and expression like looking in a mirror. Emma was wearing civilian clothes, probably to help the rest of the group tell them apart, because they were otherwise utterly alike down to the finest detail. Both had short–cropped light brown hair, the same elfin features, the same green eyes and curious smile that could be both friendly and lethally dangerous by turns.

'Despite his fears Lazarus considers it unlikely that the Council is unanimous in its desire to destroy humanity,' Emma said. 'It would serve no purpose and they would still then have to face The Word in open combat without the benefit of what we have learned of its weaknesses.'

'So only *some* species want us dead,' Bra'hiv replied. 'That's good then.'

'If the council itself is divided over the fate of humanity, then how can we trust them when it comes to battle even if they do agree to act with us?' Evelyn asked.

'We don't have much of a choice,' Idris replied. 'I have every expectation that the people will vote to head for Oassia, the Galactic Capital. My wife, as you all know, is their governing representative and she believes that they are more tired, afraid and in need of safe haven than they have ever been. I'm inclined to agree with her, and ask you to support the vote.'

Mikhain raised an eyebrow. 'You're *agreeing* with the governors?'

'I'm agreeing that we cannot fight this war with one hand behind our backs,' Idris insisted. 'Atlantia and Arcadia are warships, not cruise liners. We need to be able to use them as such.'

Evelyn folded her arms as she looked at the captain. 'You want the civilians off our backs.'

Idris sighed, but gave a little shrug. 'If the Galactic Council can be convinced that we're not the enemy, that the Legion is their foe and that we should be allowed to assist in its eradication, then our people will have a safe haven from which to begin again. There are many unpopulated worlds out there awaiting discovery – there is no reason we should not be able to colonize one for the future of our children, and theirs after them.'

'And Ethera?' Lael asked.

Idris's expression became grim. 'We take it back, or we destroy it ourselves.'

Andaim studied his boots for a moment. 'We have a lot of issues to resolve. Both the civilians and the council are baying for Kordaz's blood at trial, they're screaming blue murder about us having Lazarus aboard and they've never been happy about an armed force of former convicts patrolling the ship. All of that's going to count against us with the council too – they may demand some kind of compromise.'

Idris nodded. 'I know, and we may have to bend to their will in order to gain their fleet as allies.'

'We can't give up Lazarus,' Emma said with some force. 'To do so would be as foolhardy as welcoming The Word aboard.'

'Which is exactly what the Galactic Council will think we've done,' Mikhain replied. 'They're not going to see it our way and to be honest I can't blame them. Lazarus, no matter how well–meaning he might be, is a liability in too many ways to count and now he's been wrong twice. We're better off without the machine.'

'We'll likely be dead without it,' Evelyn snapped. 'Lazarus is the key to understanding The Word. Knowing your enemy is the key to winning battles, captain, or have you forgotten that?'

'And a spy in the enemy camp?' Mikhain challenged. 'We still don't know that we can trust him!'

'I'd trust a man over the machine any day,' Andaim admitted.

'Lazarus saved my life,' Emma shot back. 'I wouldn't be here if it weren't for him.'

'You shouldn't be here at all anyway!' Mikhain blurted.

Emma's anger was whipped away by the harsh strike of the captain's words, and Evelyn stepped forward as one hand drifted toward her service pistol of its own accord.

'None of us should be,' she hissed at Mikhain. 'We're here because of each other, and like it or not that's the way it's going to be, understood?'

'Are you threatening me, *lieutenant?*' Mikhain snarled. 'Because last time I looked, threatening a senior officer was punishable by…'

'Enough,' Captain Sansin growled. 'We don't have time for arguments. I need to know that you will all back me up when we reach Galactic Council space. We will be intercepted and likely threatened. We may even be fired upon. We *must not* return fire. We *must* make them aware that we come in peace.'

Evelyn looked at Andaim, who in turn looked at Bra'hiv. All eyes finally settled on Emma.

'I will inform Lazarus of your decision,' she said. 'I doubt that he will do anything but offer as much assistance as he can.'

'Are we all in agreement?' Captain Sansin asked.

'Aye,' Evelyn replied.

A chorus of muted consent that sounded anything but content rippled across the officers.

'Then let's get to it,' Sansin said. 'Plot a course for Oassia, and we'll await the decision of the people.'

'What happens if they vote against it?' Evelyn asked.

'Then we've got another problem,' Sansin replied with a tight smile. 'But right now, they're not my main concern.'

***

V

'I don't know what to think.'

Evelyn walked alongside her sister, Emma's elegant white dress flowing like water in the breeze as they strolled through the sanctuary. It was one of the major benefits of super–luminal travel that all combat operations were ceased, allowing aircrews the rare chance to rest and recuperate before the next cycle of patrols and engagements.

'You need to trust Lazarus,' Emma insisted as they reached the brow of a low hill that overlooked the forested valley. Nestled deep within the woods were the homesteads of Atlantia's civilians and the Governor's Chamber, and beyond were the patchwork fields where the civilians grew crops in an attempt to sustain Atlantia's compliment while away from external sources of food.

'Trust,' Evelyn echoed, 'is a rare commodity these days.'

'All the more reason to foster it wherever and whenever we can.'

Evelyn sat down on the grass and breathed deeply on the fresh air that circulated through the sanctuary. Many of the crew limited their time inside the dream–like sanctuary, unable to bear the grief of knowing that it was an illusion, that the billions of people who had once lived on Ethera were gone, that perhaps even the planet itself was now unrecognisable. Back in the day, so Evelyn had heard, some of the crew went insane down here, unable to leave, unwilling to accept that the world outside existed any longer, that they no longer had a home to return to. Two were found hanged in the forest, poignant suicides that unveiled the torment that Atlantia's crew had suffered.

'The civilians don't trust the officers,' Evelyn pointed out. 'The officers don't trust the civilians, everybody hates Kordaz despite the fact that he's probably the most honourable soul aboard the ship, and nobody at all trusts the Marines of Bravo Company because they're all ex–cons.' Evelyn shook her head. 'I have no idea what they think of you and I.'

Emma smiled as she sat alongside her sister.

'I don't care what they think. I've got you now, and you've got me. That's something I never would have believed possible. Lazarus gave me a second chance at life and I'm not about to waste it.'

Evelyn smiled softly. Emma was something of the image of who Evelyn used to be: before the carnage of the apocalypse, before her arrest and imprisonment for the murder of her husband and child, crimes she had not committed. Back then Evelyn had dressed in similar clothes, had possessed an easy smile devoid of the shadows of grief that now clouded her thoughts. She realized that the person she had been was forever lost now, Evelyn a volatile mixture of feared former convict, fighter pilot and uneasy ally to Lazarus. Evelyn stared out across the sanctuary for a long moment before she spoke, checking around them in case anybody was listening.

'I can hear Lazarus,' she said.

Emma stared at Evelyn for a long moment. 'Since when?'

'Since we left Endeavour. I could hear a whispering all the time, calling me in. Not as loud as you, not as clear, but it was there.'

Emma thought for a long moment. 'Lazarus engineered me to be his failsafe, in case he was overcome by megalomania as The Word was on Ethera. I don't know what he did or how he did it, but since I've awoken from stasis I've been both his spokesperson and the one thing that means he can be trusted by humans. Lazarus can make no command and take no decision without it first passing through me – that's why I hear him. But you, you have had no such engineering performed. How could you possibly be capable of receiving signals from him?'

'I don't know, and we need to find out,' Evelyn insisted. 'Do you know what happened to me, what The Word did to me on Ethera?'

Emma's features darkened and she averted her eyes from Evelyn's as she nodded. 'Captain Sansin informed me of some of what happened.'

'I was a reporter,' Evelyn replied, 'a damned good one. I was chasing up a story on the spread of a dangerous new street drug called Devlamine, and when I got too close to The Word it murdered my son and my husband and had me imprisoned for the crime aboard Atlantia. No trial, no due process. It put a mask on my face that silenced my voice by placing probes in my throat, the same mask that we found you wearing aboard Endeavour while you were in stasis.'

'Lazarus used the mask to keep my airways open when I climbed into the escape capsule aboard Endeavour,' Emma replied. 'The per-fluorocarbon can become gelatinous over long periods of deep cold so it was considered the safest way to survive long periods of suspended animation.'

'You're sure about that?' Evelyn asked.

'I could have refused,' Emma replied. 'Why else would he have asked me to wear it?'

Evelyn stared down the hillside at the forest and watched the breeze move through the trees.

'The mask doesn't only silence the wearer,' she replied. 'Doctor Sansin discovered that it is capable of extracting genetic information. DNA, Emma, the very thing that would be needed to create a clone.'

Emma stared at her sister for a long time.

'But Lazarus had no contact with The Word. That's why he fled to Endeavour.'

Evelyn nodded. 'So he says.'

'You think that somehow my genetic code ended up back on Ethera, and from there…'

'Was used to create me,' Evelyn finished the sentence for her sister. 'I was born immune to the Infectors, Emma. I didn't know that of course, not until I was captured by Tyraeus Forge and he attempted to infect me and failed. Lazarus must have known what he was doing, and somehow managed to manipulate your genetic code to reject the Infectors before sending that code home. He was trying to destroy The Word from within, before the apocalypse could be started.'

Emma shook her head in amazement. 'Have you told anybody about this?'

'Not yet. I wanted to see what you thought before I brought it up. It explains why The Word wanted me out of sight so badly, was willing to risk exposure in murdering my entire family in order to get me under its control. My immunity was all that kept me alive because The Word wanted to study me and figure out how I'd become immune in the first place, and likely to see what Lazarus was up to. It didn't get the chance.'

Emma's face was enraptured with intrigue but Evelyn could see the questions racing through her mind.

'But how did the genetic code Lazarus sent end up inside you?' she asked. 'He must have sent it to *somebody* before you were born.'

'That's what we need to find out,' Evelyn replied. 'If we're heading to the Galactic Council, they're going to want a damned good explanation of who we are and how we're even possible, or they'll assume we're agents of The Word and shoot us on sight. Lazarus needs to explain everything or this is all off for us, you understand what I'm saying?'

'Yes,' Emma nodded.

'You'll back me up?'

Emma reached out and grabbed Evelyn's hand. 'All the way.'

*

'The vote is in.'

Governor Gredan scanned an electro–sheet he held in one hand as data streamed in from a dozen automated polling booths that had been installed around both Atlantia and Arcadia to allow the entire ships' compliment to vote in privacy.

'What's the verdict?'

Governors Vaughn, Ayek and Morle stood near the main table in the Governor's Chamber and waited as Gredan finished scanning the document and looked up.

'It's unanimous,' he replied. 'Almost ninety per cent of the ship's compliment voted in favour of the fleet approaching the Galactic Council and pleading for asylum and assistance in fighting the Legion.'

Vaughn nodded and ran a hand through his thick black hair. 'Pretty much as I expected. Captain Sansin will hit the ceiling when he finds out.'

'I doubt that,' Morle said.

'How so?' Gredan challenged her. 'He's all for fighting this war with Atlantia at the forefront. He doesn't want to hand control or command over to the council.'

'He doesn't want a couple of thousand civilians hindering his battle plans either,' Morle pointed out. 'If there's nobody aboard but those who have elected by choice to wear Colonial uniforms, then he can fight the Legion just as he would have fought any other adversary back in the days of the Veng'en wars.'

Governor Ayek stared vacantly into the middle distance for a long beat and then looked up sharply at Morle.

'If he intends to send the civilians elsewhere then we'll have to go with them, which will mean…'

'That Atlantia will be beyond our scope of influence,' Gredan muttered and tossed the electro–sheet to one side. 'Damn it, the old man's trying to get rid of us. I should have known better.'

'The captain knows what he's doing,' Morle insisted. 'This is a warship. He can't fight effectively with a civilian contingent getting in the way.'

'And he'll have full power in his hands with us gone too,' Vaughn pointed out. 'Sansin's always resented our presence ever since the board was created. The sooner we're out of the way, the sooner he can carry on as he wishes without any democratic checks and balances that a civilian contingent demands.'

Governor Gredan nodded. 'And right now we need them more than ever, because Captain Sansin is the least of our worries.'

Gredan picked up the electro–sheet once more and selected a new file which he activated as he laid the sheet down on the table. The data stream disappeared and was replaced with a recording that every person in the hall could see. In it, Captain Mikhain was seen entering the War Room of

Atlantia, a secondary bridge buried deep inside the hull of all Colonial warships that allowed the command crew to maintain control of the ship in the event of being boarded and losing the ship's main bridge.

In the recording, Mikhain was seen informing the legendary pirate Salim Phaeon of Captain Sansin's plan to send a Veng'en to sabotage his compound on Chiron IV. Kordaz had duly been captured by the pirate and later infected by the Legion during a calamitous escape under fire from the pirate lair.

The Governors remained quiet until the recording came to an end and Gredan looked up at them.

'It was agreed that we would maintain our silence over this matter, and our word given to Arcadia's Executive Officer, Lieutenant Scott, that we would not reveal that it was he who brought us this recording. However, now that we're approaching Galactic Council space and the rule of law once more, I must ask you all to re-consider our position on this matter. Mikhain is the traitor who exposed Sansin's rescue mission on Chiron IV, a course of action that resulted in the deaths of many Colonial soldiers and civilians at the hands of Salim's pirates and later an ambush by the Legion. Such a treasonable act surely cannot go unpunished?'

None of the governors spoke for a long moment, each of them weighing the consequences of speaking out against Mikhain.

'If we reveal what happened before the Galactic Council, it may weaken our position in their eyes,' Morle pointed out. 'If our own house is not in order, what can they expect of us as allies?'

'And we don't know for sure whether or not Sansin knows about all of this,' Ayek agreed. 'If he does not, then he looks weakened before the council. If he does, then he looks corrupt and untrustworthy in command both before the council and the civilians: one rule for officers, another for the rest of us.'

'He knows,' Gredan insisted. 'At the very least he must *suspect*. How could he not?'

'Mikhain's a patriot,' Ishira Morle added, 'and a long service officer. He must have had a reason for this.'

'I agree,' Vaughn said. 'He's a long service officer without a command of his own. My guess is that he wanted Idris's rescue mission to fail so that he could step up and command one of his own. I asked around after Lieutenant Scott brought us this evidence. Mikhain was actively whipping up support among the rank and file aboard Atlantia before the attack on Chiron IV, trying to build a following among the crew. Why else would he do that unless he had designs on the captain's chair?'

Gredan looked at the document one last time and then he made his decision.

'We need to resolve this issue before we reach Oassia,' he said. 'We need our house in order and be able to show a united front. Any weakness, any injustice among our ranks will go down badly with the council.'

Ishira Morle shook her head. 'That's a bad idea. Mikhain is in command of Arcadia and if he realizes what's about to happen there's no telling what he might do. You're risking splitting the fleet that we do have.'

'And how can we trust Mikhain to stand by us if the going gets harder?' Gredan challenged.

'I don't think that anybody has the right to question Mikhain's courage or his patriotism,' Morle snapped back. 'He's come through for us on numerous occasions, and only this morning put Arcadia in harm's way to rescue Evelyn from the Legion's ambush.'

'Evelyn,' Vaughn uttered as though he had tasted something unpleasant in his mouth. 'There's another thorn in our side, along with her sister and that damned machine below decks. All of them, along with Kordaz, threaten any chance we have of garnering the sympathy of the council. We need this to be a ship of upstanding examples of humanity, not Veng'en assassins, convicts and genetically cloned minions of The Word.'

'You don't know what you're talking about,' Morle shot back. 'You haven't seen them fight, for the fleet, for us. Evelyn and Emma both are as human as we are.'

'Or something more,' Gredan mused. 'Vaughn's right, it's all acting against us. We're struggling to cope with these individuals and learn to trust them, and we've shared a ship with them for months, years even. The council may have just days or even hours to make a decision.'

'Then what the hell are you suggesting?' Morle asked. 'That we just get rid of them somehow? Turn them over to the council as enemy combatants?'

Vaughn raised an eyebrow and Ayek appeared almost delighted at the thought, but Gredan shook his head.

'No, we give the decision to somebody whose responsibility it is to control all of these factors,' he said finally. 'We'll give Captain Sansin the chance to do the right thing, and if he doesn't…'

'That's blackmail,' Morle gasped in horror. 'You're risking the cohesion of the entire command structure if this gets out!'

'Who said anything about revealing this to the public?' Gredan asked. 'We inform the captain of everything we know and then observe his response. If it does not fall within the rule of law, then he can be removed from his role as captain for treason.'

Morle shook her head. 'And you do realize that if Mikhain is brought to trial then you're also effectively sinking the trial of Kordaz, who is in the cells right now for the murder of Mikhain's former XO, Djimon?'

'Murder is murder,' Gredan replied, 'and must be tried as such. Furthermore, if Idris Sansin is found to have known about Mikhain's actions at Chiron IV, then he becomes implicated in all of the deaths that occurred at that incident. In effect, the act of Lieutenant Scott becoming a whistle–blower on this entire sorry affair could remove both captains from their positions, which would require new commanders to take over their roles.'

Vaughn, Ayek and Gredan grinned at each other. Morle almost snorted in disbelief.

'We're here to speak for the people, not organise a mutiny.'

'It's not mutiny, it's justice,' Ayek shot back, 'or do you condone supporting murderers and liars as senior officers aboard this ship?'

Ishira Morle ground her teeth in her skull and strode toward the exit. Gredan's voice pursued her.

'Not a word of this beyond the hall, Ishira,' he warned. 'Treason comes in many forms.'

'Yeah,' Ishira snapped over her shoulder. 'So does betrayal.'

**

Dean Crawford

VI

The *Lazarus Chamber*, as it had become known, was a heavily fortified and guarded storage depot deep inside Atlantia's hull, formerly an armoury used when colonial frigates had powered their weapons using plasma–filled projectiles rather than the plasma–gas lines that now fed the turrets directly from the fusion cores.

Evelyn walked toward the chamber entrance with Emma alongside her, the guards making way for them as they passed by. Few members of the crew were allowed access to this most dangerous and feared quarter of the vessel, but under the captain's orders both Evelyn and Emma were allowed to speak to Lazarus at will, provided each and every engagement was monitored by a team of engineers assigned the task of preventing Lazarus from gaining direct access to any of Atlantia's systems without prior permission.

The chamber was cold, the heating disconnected by the engineers, who were fearful that Lazarus might somehow be able to manufacture a single Infector and begin the process of colonizing the ship: the tiny machines of the Legion were known to be slowed by the cold. The fact that Lazarus had no appendages with which to construct physical entities had apparently escaped them, but such was the deeply ingrained fear of The Word and its Legion.

The guards behind them sealed the doors to the bay, leaving them alone with the machine.

The box–like depot was bare but for a single generator bolted to the deck in one corner of the room, which provided manually controlled power to Lazarus's terminal. Devoid of any automation, and ringed with explosive plasma charges that were connected to a detonation unit outside, Lazarus was effectively a prisoner not just within the cabinet–like terminal in which he resided but also aboard Atlantia herself.

The original, aged terminal recovered from Endeavour had been replaced with a more modern and powerful machine, and the flat screen was now a holographic emission unit that projected Lazarus's image upward from a light source alongside the terminal. The projection glowed a vivid electric–blue and shimmered like water, shot through with twinkling points of white light that sparkled like stars.

Like a sick man attached to a computerized lung, Lazarus stood beside his life blood and turned as he sensed their presence. Lazarus's voice rang out in the chamber, digitized and in–human and yet possessed of a desperation, a genuine need for human contact and shared emotion.

'Emma?'

Emma walked forward and stood before the terminal. 'I am here.'

Evelyn joined her sister in time to see Lazarus's eyes open and a vivid expression of relief blossom on his face, then joy, like a grandparent seeing their grandchild for the first time.

'I have missed you so,' Lazarus said, and then looked at Evelyn. 'And you've brought your sister.'

Evelyn felt slightly perturbed by the fondness with which Lazarus regarded them both. Even the biological man had been no blood–relative of theirs, and as such should hardly adore them in the way that he did.

Dr Ceyen Lazarus had been a legend in the development of the quantum computers that gave rise to The Word. A programming genius who had likewise mastered the fields of quantum physics and molecular biology, Dr Lazarus had been instrumental in giving The Word sufficient intelligence and autonomy to be able to govern effectively in place of human beings. Celebrated as the saviour of mankind, in the last days of The Word his name had become an icon for destruction, his memory tarnished by the devastation wrought by his own creation. To *'become Lazarus'* was a slang term that suggested brutality or betrayal of one's fellow human being, hinting at crimes too hideous of which to speak.

'We've got a problem,' Evelyn said without preamble.

Lazarus's smile did not slip. 'I am provided with a limited stream of information from the bridge, and I am aware of the referendum among the crew and the decision to approach the Galactic Council for assistance. It is most regrettable, but a democratic vote cannot be ignored.'

'Regrettable how?' Evelyn challenged. 'The council could help us, could provide a fighting force of hundreds of warships.'

'Evelyn,' Lazarus said as though speaking to a child, 'our race is not highly regarded across the known cosmos. We are viewed as savages, much in the same way as we view the Veng'en. For instance, the Icari Line was never a barrier to the Veng'en because despite their war–like nature their aggression is only directed at humans. They have had a representative upon the Galactic Council for decades. But humans are viewed by the council as dangerous because we're as likely to destroy each other as anybody else. There was much fear of human expansion into the wider cosmos long before our people even learned the art of space travel.'

'Humanity is not that bad,' Emma argued. 'The wars that our ancestors fought on Ethera ended long ago, and we've come a long way. The Word was supposed to end all conflicts, military or otherwise, and it did so. It was the machine that turned against us, not people.'

'Sadly, the council will not see it that way,' Lazarus replied. 'A moratorium on artificial intelligence governing or controlling global affairs was created by the council centuries ago. It was not devised because of a fear of advanced machines waging war on galactic species, but rather out of a consideration for the *rights* of machines should they become sentient. Races were concerned that switching off a sentient machine was in fact a form of murder, which in some ways it would be – I can vouch for that. They called it *digicide*, the killing of a sentient computer.'

'We couldn't have known that,' Evelyn replied. 'If the Icari Line was created to keep human beings in, then we can hardly have been blamed for knowing nothing of laws in the wider cosmos beyond.'

'The council will not take that into consideration,' Lazarus replied. 'Their view has always been that a species must conquer its own flaws and mistakes before being given access to the cosmos. Using a machine to govern, to avoid the responsibility of finding a way to maintain peace among its own people, is not an option. The moment The Word was given political power and governance, humanity's fate was sealed as far as the council was concerned.'

'How do you know all of this?' Evelyn asked. 'You were aboard Endeavour, which we found adrift, and had never been to the council.'

Emma answered for Lazarus, recalling her time aboard Endeavour.

'Lazarus explained to the crew the real reasons for the Icari Line,' she said. 'We used the ship's sensors, the most powerful ever conceived at the time, to listen in on other races populating deep space. We learned a great deal until the Morla'syn found us and attacked.'

Evelyn stepped forward, confronting Lazarus even though she knew that he was as ephemeral as air itself, a projection of light and not matter.

'How did you manage to get the DNA of Emma back into the population on Ethera, and start the process that led to me?'

'In short?' Lazarus asked. 'I didn't. The crew of Endeavour, before leaving on their epic voyage, were subject to intense biological and psychological studies by the Etheran government and space agencies. The Word, naturally, would have had access to that information. After their departure, The Word began using the crew of Endeavour as the template from which to build genetic clones that it intended to use to infiltrate and eventually take over humanity. However, the process did not go as according to plan. The complexities of human nature and the difficulties in controlling human beings conflicted by devotion to their parents as much to The Word meant that The Word was forced to abandon the plan and instead attempt to build nano–tech devices with which to infect the population. In this, it was more successful.'

Evelyn thought for a moment. 'And my immunity?'

Lazarus smiled now as he looked at Evelyn. 'Just because I did not have anything to do with The Word's genetic tinkering of your sister's DNA, doesn't mean I wasn't hard at work aboard Endeavour. The Word's experiments with nanotechnology were in their infancy, and although it learned at a trimetric rate I was able to ensure that the fundamental basis of its nano–Infectors was presented with a biological foe, a naturally occurring immunity that blocked the paths taken by Infectors in order to colonize and control the spinal column and brain stem and instructed human T–cells to attack the foreign objects. I felt certain that if that immunity could spread quickly enough through the populace, then at least some of humanity might survive the apocalypse that I felt certain was coming. It was too little, too late of course, but it was all that I could do in the time available to me. I sent the altered DNA back to Ethera as a sort of virus, and hacked The Word's experiments. You, Evelyn, are descended from the resulting bloodline.'

Evelyn glanced at her sister before she went on.

'The council is going to be against us, against you,' she said. 'They'll insist that we're creations of The Word and likely imprison us. I have no idea what Captain Sansin intends to do about that, but right now he's got no choice but to go with the referendum vote.'

Lazarus nodded. 'And he's not helping my position by limiting my access to information so severely. We are in super–luminal travel, so I cannot detect anything from beyond the ship, but when we joined orbit at Akyron V the ship's sensors would have been able to collect enormous amounts of data. I would very much like access to it.'

'To what end?' Evelyn challenged.

'To give us as much time as possible.'

'Time for what?' Emma asked, consternation in her voice.

*

'All systems at one hundred per cent, captain.'

Idris nodded as he scanned the bridge displays for any sign of weapons malfunctions, shield weaknesses or structural defects.

'Fighter wing readiness?' he asked.

'The Reaper's pilots will be called back to operational status within the hour,' Andaim replied from his station. 'I'll lead the launch flight.'

Idris did not reply, knowing that Andaim would not be kept on the bridge and away from his Raython's cockpit at such a time. Young for the role of CAG, Andaim had been the most experienced officer and fighter pilot aboard Atlantia when the apocalypse had struck and thus the natural choice to lead the frigate's compliment of fighters. His natural vigour reminded Idris of his own youth, when he had flown Phantoms as a young lieutenant in the fleet and...

'Captain!'

Idris turned, alarm pulsing through his nerves as he saw Evelyn rush onto the bridge deck with Emma in hot pursuit.

'What is it?'

'Get us out of super–luminal now, before we enter Galactic space!'

'We're almost there,' Idris protested.

'It's tracking us!' Evelyn snapped. 'The Word, it knows where we're going!'

'That's not possible,' Andaim replied. 'We're at super–luminal cruise – nothing can track us.'

'It's not the cruise,' Emma wailed in horror. 'It's Arcadia. She must have picked up some of the Legion when she covered Evelyn's escape! They're aboard, and Lazarus heard them!'

Idris whirled and pointed at the helm.

'Emergency stop, break us out of super–luminal cruise right now!'

***

VII

Captain Mikhain sat in his personal quarters, located just off Arcadia's bridge, and closed his eyes as he attempted to silence his mind. His thoughts were overwhelmed with a constant stream of command requests, logistical problems, technical malfunctions brought about by Salim Phaeon's inept slave–labor maintenance on the frigate's hull back on Chiron IV and an endless list of other problems all vying for his attention. And above them all a final voice whispered to him a single word over and over again.

Regret.

Mikhain had served the Colonial Fleet his entire adult life, and almost half of that time in the role of Executive Officer of one vessel or another. His career had been stellar, but due to the vagaries of captaincy availability he had never received his own command despite serving two tours as XO of the Colonial super–carrier *Defiance*. After those heady days at the bridge of a capital flagship and in the twilight of his career, he had seen himself posted to the prison service as XO aboard Atlantia.

Mikhain had always craved command, had always dreamed of being in the captain's chair and leading his crew into battle against whichever foe had threatened the safety and sanctity of Colonial space, but now he realized that it had been a fool's errand, a step too far. The command role was one of adjudicator, engineer, pacifist, warmonger, lawyer, judge and accused all in one, and the stress of dealing with a daily litany of crisis and setbacks was crushing Mikhain beneath a burden his sanity had not been designed to bear.

'Idiot,' he muttered at himself under his breath.

Idris Sansin knew what Mikhain had done on Chiron IV, of that he was sure, but then he had chosen not only to say nothing but to promote Mikhain to the captaincy of Arcadia in the wake of the battle above Chiron IV. True, Mikhain had fought ferociously to protect Atlantia, to the extent of almost losing Arcadia in the process to a more powerful Veng'en vessel's attack, but even so… Kordaz would soon be on trial for the murder of Djimon, Arcadia's former XO. Moreover, Djimon had been in the prison cells in order to kill Qayin, the former convict and Marine who had been so heavily involved in the whole damned process. And all of it on Mikhain's say–so.

Both Kordaz and Qayin were aboard Atlantia and beyond his reach, and truthfully Mikhain was tired of the deceptions and the lies. He had twice almost been exposed, the consequences of which would be charges of treason, dereliction of duty and many more besides. Court Martial would follow and then in all likelihood Maroon Protocol, his abandonment on an alien world to fend for himself for what few years remained to him.

For a brief moment he considered the solitude of being marooned somewhere and found some meagre solace in the idea of finally being left alone for more than sixty seconds. As if on cue a quiet but insistent alarm beeped for his attention, a command request from the bridge where Lieutenant Scott, another of Mikhain's problems, was acting as commander in his 'stead.

Mikhain reached up and activated the intercom above his bunk, where a data screen relayed information to him even when he slept.

'What is it?'

He had tried to keep his tone reasonable but even he could hear the gruff irritation in his tone.

'The port fusion core is fluctuating, captain,' Lieutenant Scott informed him, 'and we're having air–conditioning supply issues in the sanctuary as a result. The civilians are getting agitated at the rising temperatures.'

Can we shoot them? Mikhain thought but did not say.

Arcadia's cores were at maximum output while in super–luminal cruise and as such any power fluctuations could drop them and Atlantia, which was gravitationally bound to her sister ship, out of super–luminal cruise.

'Re–route the power from the weapons systems to balance the core's output,' Mikhain advised. 'But be on stand–by to reverse that if we should drop out of cruise.'

'Aye cap'ain,' Scott replied, and the channel shut off.

Mikhain sighed and dragged a hand wearily across his face, reading the data list above him and wondering at how much longer he could maintain this charade of competence in the face of such overwhelming…

The ship lurched unexpectedly as the light in Mikhain's cabin became briefly polarised. The captain cursed as he was rolled out of his bunk by the sudden change in inertia as he heard the distant hum of the mass–drive disengage and a flickering of the display screens in his cabin as sensor information began streaming in from around them once more.

Mikhain almost roared in anger as he stormed out of his cabin and along the corridor outside. The two Marines guarding the bridge deck entrance snapped to attention as he raged past them and burst onto the bridge.

'I ordered you to transfer power from the weapons systems, not drop out of cruise!' he bellowed.

'It was Atlantia!' Lieutenant Scott snapped back as he gestured at the main viewing screen on the bridge. 'She's out of cruise and has gone full tactical, shields up and she's pulling away from us.'

Mikhain's mind reeled as he struggled to understand what was happening, vast reams of data rushing in upon the ship and his brain as he recalibrated himself to the command position and took his seat alongside Scott.

'Where are we?' he asked.

'Three point four astronomical units inside Galactic Space, and four hundred twenty eight units beyond the Icari Line.'

'Scramble Renegade Squadron to set up a perimeter, all power to plasma cannons and shields, and open a damned channel!'

Arcadia's communications officer, Shah, sent a signal request from her station behind Mikhain and the rest of the crew scrambled to bring Arcadia to battle readiness as a low, mournful alarm began wailing through the ship. Moments later an image of Captain Sansin appeared on one of the display screens before him.

'We're coming up to battle readiness,' Mikhain said promptly, 'Renegades will be aloft in minutes and our plasma batteries are charging. What gives?'

Captain Sansin stared back at him with a sombre expression.

'Maintain your shields but belay the Raythons and seal all hatches, bulkheads, stairwells and decks.'

Mikhain felt the hairs on the back of his neck rise up and he got out of his chair. He glanced at the commander of his Raython squadrons, the CAG a young man like Andaim Ry'ere, and nodded once.

'What's happening, Idris?' Mikhain asked.

'You're infected,' Captain Sansin replied. 'Lazarus says he could hear the Legion aboard you before we departed the ambush on Akyran V.'

All motion on Arcadia's bridge ceased and every voice that had been relaying commands to other areas of the ship fell silent. Mikhain felt the weight of their silence and horror upon his shoulders as he struggled for words.

'And he's only telling us this *now*?'

'Lazarus has been under an information embargo as you know,' Idris replied. 'He could not tell whether the signals he detected came from the Legion's ambush vessels in orbit around Akyron V or from Arcadia as we departed. I allowed Lazarus access to the signals data and he confirmed that they came from your ship.' Idris sighed. 'I'm sorry, captain. Some of them must have attached themselves to your hull when you intervened during the escape.'

Mikhain whirled and pointed at the Marines standing guard inside the bridge.

'Seal all bulkheads, including here. Have the sanctuary sealed and all decks. We're on permanent lockdown until we can locate the Legion and eradicate it!'

The Marines whirled to seal the bridge as Mikhain turned to Lieutenant Scott. 'Alert the ship and tell them that we're on lockdown while we traverse Galactic Space in case we're intercepted. Don't mention the Legion – I don't want the civilians panicking down there. Break out the microwave transmitters and deploy them on all decks and at all intersections to limit the Legion's ability to move!'

'Aye, captain!'

Mikhain turned back to Sansin. 'They've been aboard for hours, they could have moved anywhere. Does Lazarus have any idea of how many might have made it aboard?'

'Not yet, but he's working on it,' Idris replied. 'We both know that it won't take many to start colonizing the ship.'

'I know,' Mikhain replied, 'but an attack by Hunters is something we can defend against. It's the Infectors I'm worried about.'

'The crew's been immunized,' Idris pointed out.

'Yeah, and Veng'en's were naturally immune, right up to the point the Legion worked out a way to infect them too. Ask Kordaz. There's no point in risking all, captain. Right now we've no alternative but to set Arcadia's transponder to the *plague ship* code.'

Mikhain saw Idris bite his lip as he considered the implications of broadcasting Arcadia's status.

'If Galactic warships detect that signal they'll take no chances and blow you to hell.'

'And if we don't broadcast and they too become infected..?' Mikhain challenged. 'They'll wipe us *all* out.'

Idris stared at Mikhain for a moment longer and then he whirled and thumped a clenched fist down on his chair. Mikhain could see Atlantia's bridge crew watching him in silence, Evelyn and Emma close by his side.

'Damn it!' Idris cursed and dragged one hand across his forehead. 'We need to locate the source of the infection and wipe it out as soon as possible. As long as we're out of super–luminal we can be detected, and if we're intercepted before the Legion is wiped out…'

'I'm on it,' Mikhain replied as he turned to Arcadia's helmsman. 'Take us out to ten thousand cubits, real slow and steady, and prepare to launch a shuttle under remote control. I want to take a look at the hull and see where the little bastards got in.'

Mikhain thought for a moment and then turned to Lieutenant Scott. 'You said that the port fusion cores were fluctuating?'

'An intermittent power drain,' Scott agreed. 'If they landed on the outer hull somewhere at the stern near the plasma lines, when we broadsided those mining vessels...'

'Then they could have burrowed their way in,' Mikhain finished the sentence for Scott and whirled to the helmsman. 'Shut off all power to that section of the ship, isolate it from all electromagnetic frequencies and set up a double–screen of microwave emitters on that deck and those above, below and adjacent to it.'

'Aye, captain!'

Mikhain turned back to Idris. 'We need a way out of this and fast. It could take days to root them all out.'

'I know,' Idris replied as he looked at Emma. 'I have an idea.'

**

VIII

'No, absolutely not!'

Governor Gredan stood resolute before the board as Captain Sansin stared back at him, Emma and Evelyn standing either side.

'It's the only way. Emma will accompany him aboard Arcadia as additional security for General Bra's Marines.'

Gredan looked as though he was about to burst a blood vessel, his florid cheeks bright red.

'Kordaz is about to be tried for murder! He was, by his own admission, infected by the Legion and Governor Sansin's medical examination confirmed that he had undergone significant mutation. Now you're saying you want to send him aboard Arcadia?'

'Kordaz can sense when the Legion is near,' Evelyn explained, 'just like Lazarus, but unlike Lazarus, Kordaz can hunt them down. He can root them out before the Galactic Fleet locates us. We don't have time to argue this out, governor. We have to remove the infection before it takes hold aboard Arcadia and threatens her entire crew!'

'And risk Kordaz allying himself with the Hunters already aboard Arcadia and taking the ship?' Vaughn asked. 'You're talking about a suicide mission in more ways than one.'

'It is a repugnant idea,' Governor Ayek snorted.

Idris allowed a smile to creep onto his features. 'I wonder if you would find it so *repugnant* were it Atlantia's sanctuary that had become infected?'

'You're talking about once more placing your trust in a dangerous killer,' Gredan persisted. 'Why do you have such a desire to place your faith in such unreliable allies?'

'Desperate times, governor,' Idris replied. 'I'm not placing faith in Kordaz, although despite the General opinion of him I consider the Veng'en to be an honourable soul. I'm using all of the resources at my disposal to get the job done. Kordaz is our best bet at rooting out the infection aboard Arcadia before we're intercepted. We don't have time to debate this at length and our tactical positon is, to say the least, weak. If we're bounced now, we'll likely be overwhelmed with ease.'

The governors watched Idris for a long moment, all of them stricken with genuine concern and apprehension.

'If we agree to this,' Gredan asked cautiously, 'what makes you think that Kordaz will even consider helping out? He's on trial for murder and faces life imprisonment if convicted. What's his motivation going to be?'

Idris took a deep breath but it was Evelyn who replied.

'Amnesty,' she said, 'in return for risking his life to protect ours, not for the first time.'

Gredan's jaw hung open and his eyes widened. 'Amnesty,' he rasped.

'You may see him as a Veng'en assassin,' Idris said, 'but Kordaz has done as much to protect humanity aboard this ship as anybody, and ended up infected for his troubles. He no longer possesses his own eyesight, relying instead on the monstrous deformations that the Legion created for him. You and I both know that the moment the Galactic Council sees him they'll demand he be executed. This is the right thing to do.'

Gredan appeared lost for words. He turned his bulbous head to look at the other governors, who were all staring aghast at the captain. Meyanna's skin had paled considerably and Even Ishira Morle looked disturbed.

'It's a long shot,' she said finally as Idris looked to her for support. 'I'm not opposed to it, but Kordaz isn't exactly *Kordaz* any more, is he? We can't possibly know what will happen if he comes into contact with the Legion again.'

'He killed a senior officer aboard Arcadia,' Governor Vaughn reminded the captain. 'You send him over there and virtually every person aboard will want to see him dead.'

'They'll leave him be rather than risk exposure to the Legion,' Idris replied with a confidence he didn't entirely feel. 'If Kordaz can eradicate the Legion from Arcadia, we will rid ourselves of two major problems: infection, and Kordaz. With the Veng'en free to leave the system, there will be one less reason for the council to refuse us safe haven.'

'And the small matter of where he will go? As far as we know, the Veng'en homeworld of Wraiythe might already have been overrun.'

Idris sighed.

'I can offer Kordaz no answers or solutions, only his freedom. Executive Officer Djimon was himself a murderer and guilty of treasonable acts for which he too would have been tried and convicted. Had Kordaz not been betrayed by Djimon, we wouldn't have been put in this position.'

Gredan's eyes narrowed and he glanced sideways at his fellow board members. 'You have evidence that Djimon was behind the betrayal at Chiron IV?'

'Djimon was the only link between Qayin, Kordaz and what happened with Salim Phaeon. I have no reason to think otherwise, and Qayin himself has suggested that the only person with a reason to turn Kordaz over in betrayal was Djimon.'

'And yet both of them hated each other with a passion, as I recall,' Governor Ayek pointed out. 'Qayin might have simply pointed to Djimon as the guilty party in an act of revenge.'

'Djimon was already dead by that time,' Idris replied. 'A bit late for such things, I'd imagine.'

Gredan hesitated for a long time as Idris watched him weighing something up in his mind. Gredan was a showman who enjoyed his time in the limelight, enjoyed making people wait as he formulated his responses and decisions. Now, he was playing the moment for all it was worth and his enforced prowess irritated Idris.

'We don't have all day to wait on ceremony for your royal damned command,' Idris muttered. 'Make the call or I'll do it for you.'

'This is a civilian matter, not a military one,' Gredan growled back, apparently equally irritated at the intrusion into his thoughts.

'And Djimon was a Marine and the Arcadia's executive officer!' Idris snapped back. 'Any trial related to his death is a military one and as such can be tried by military court martial!'

'And does court martial apply to Captain Mikhain, or are all senior Colonial Officers immune from prosecution?!'

A ripple of hushed whispers chased around the hall and then fell into silence as Idris stared at the governor.

'What?'

Gredan faltered, unsure of himself in the wake of his sudden outburst. He glanced again at the board, and this time Meyanna spoke.

'We have evidence that suggests Executive Officer Djimon was not acting alone when he betrayed us at Chiron IV. In fact, it suggests that he was not even involved in the treachery.'

Idris swallowed thickly as he felt prickly heat tingle on his forehead and around the back of his neck. He resisted the temptation to scratch away the irritating sensation as he replied.

'What evidence?'

'This isn't the time,' Ishira Morle hissed. 'Division among the ranks could be fatal!'

'What's going on?' Idris demanded.

Governor Gredan turned to a member of his staff, who in turn activated a display screen. Before the governors, Idris, Evelyn, Emma and the hundred or so watching civilians, Captain Mikhain was shown colluding with the infamous pirate Salim Phaeon.

Idris stood in silence and felt his skin crawl as he watched Mikhain warn Phaeon of the impending infiltration by Kordaz into the pirate compound, the lair from which they had eventually successfully recovered the frigate Arcadia from the pirates and doubled their strength in a single move.

The display reached the end of its recording and shut off, leaving the hall in absolute silence as Idris's mind raced to find an explanation for something that he had always suspected and yet always hoped was a mistake.

'Could it be a fabrication?' he asked. 'Some sort of technical bluff to divert blame onto a senior officer?'

Governor Gredan might have attempted to laugh and suggest that the captain was clutching at straws to defend his own people, but in the wake of the recording he too seemed subdued and he shook his head.

'As you know, the exchange took place in Atlantia's War Room,' Gredan replied. 'The access pass of Marine Qayin was used, placing the blame on him. We now know that Djimon stole that pass, and things would have been left at that were this recording not passed to the governors by a senior officer, captain.'

Idris felt a hollow pit form deep in his belly as he realized where the leak had come from, Gredan's implied statement placing the blame squarely with the military contingent. The sheer depths of the fractures in his command staff surprised him and he wondered what other secrets they harboured, that they had not felt confident enough to share with him but instead had approached the governors with.

'Captain,' Gredan said, 'it is evident that neither you nor your command staff can be trusted with the even–handed application of the rule of law aboard this ship. Any Court Martial would be seen as hollow and biased by the civilian contingent and, by extension, the Galactic Council.'

Idris, left with nowhere to go and with his eyes fixed upon Meyanna's as he stood rooted to the spot, replied in a monotone voice robbed of its authority.

'What are you suggesting, governor?'

Gredan drew himself up to his full height and lifted his chin as though buoyed upon an ocean of self–importance. Drunk on his own authority, he almost smiled as he replied.

'Captain Mikhain will be tried by a civil court, and he will be subject to the laws and sentences devised by that court with the assistance of the Galactic Council.'

A rush of whispers hustled around the hall once more and Idris swallowed thickly.

'That would be little more than a death sentence,' he replied. 'The Galactic Council will not waste much time in adjudication of a crime committed by a race they would love to see extinguished. They'll condemn

Mikhain without hesitation, without proper counsel if necessary. He'll get Maroon Protocol if he's unlucky, a death sentence if he's more fortunate.'

Gredan nodded. 'No more, or less, than he condemned our people to during the assault and escape from Chiron IV, agreed?'

Idris looked again at Meyanna, and his wife averted her eyes and looked down at the table before her as, he guessed, she too realized the extent of the council's new-found power.

'And Kordaz?' Idris asked.

Gredan looked at the governors behind him for a brief moment, and then back at the captain.

'An exchange,' he replied. 'If Kordaz is truly innocent as you claim, and it is Mikhain whom we seek and who should be punished for the betrayal on Chiron IV, then I see no problem in cutting the Veng'en loose and improving our chances with the Galactic Council when we finally arrive at Oassia. I suggest he is told that his freedom depends on his ability to eradicate the infection from Arcadia, upon which he may go free and return to his homeworld.'

Idris closed his eyes for a long moment.

'Mikhain is currently aboard Arcadia, which is in lockdown.'

'Then time is of the essence, don't you agree captain?' Gredan asked, basking in his victory. 'The sooner Kordaz completes his work, the sooner Mikhain can be apprehended and the sooner we can progress toward Oassia, upon which time the governors will take the lead with the negotiations.'

Idris was so preoccupied with his thoughts of Mikhain's plight that he almost missed the governor's last.

'What?!'

'We will negotiate with the council,' Gredan repeated. 'The military staff will be represented by yourselves of course, but we have every right to be present and to convey the needs and wishes of the civilians. Unless of course that you no longer consider this board, which you agreed to support, representative of the fleet?'

Idris ground his teeth in his skull but said nothing in reply. Gredan glanced once more at the governors and then smiled at Idris.

'You are *dismissed*, I believe is how you phrase it, captain?'

Idris cast one final glare at the board of governors, and then he turned on one heel and marched silently between the ranks of watching civilians and out of the hall.

***

IX

'You've got to be kidding me?'

Lieutenant C'rairn pulled on his battle kit and fastened his webbing into place as General Bra'hiv shook his head, pulling on his own black body armour and weaponry.

'I kid you not. We're using Kordaz as a bloodhound to flush out the Legion aboard Arcadia, and as soon as we're done we're arresting Mikhain and bringing him back aboard Atlantia for some kind of trial.'

'But I thought Kordaz was the killer?'

The general shook his head as he picked up his plasma rifle and checked the magazine.

'I've always had my doubts about Mikhain,' he admitted. 'I've tried to tell the captain but he wasn't buying it. Guess it's a bit late now anyway.'

C'rairn slammed his locker shut and plucked a spare magazine from where it hung in mid–air between them, stashing it away in his pocket.

'This whole damned charade is getting too complex for me,' he said. 'I prefer it on the battlefield – at least you know who your enemy is.'

'Djimon turned out to be a traitor too,' Bra'hiv pointed out, 'and he was a career Marine.'

C'rairn rubbed his temples and turned to lead the way out of the barracks and toward the landing bays, where a shuttle was awaiting them both along with a small platoon of Marines to back them up. Despite the assertion that Kordaz should be responsible for earning his amnesty, nobody expected him to fight the Legion single–handedly. Then again, Bra'hiv thought as he followed C'rairn, nobody likely trusted the Veng'en to do the job anyway. Better to have a dozen Marines on hand to blast him into history before he got the chance to go over to the other side in full and take control of Arcadia from within.

A capsule–based shuttle system that ran the length of both sides of Atlantia's keel in a large loop transported them across the ship to the for'ard launch bays. Bra'hiv stepped out of the capsule with C'rairn and together they strode onto the flight deck.

Rows of Raython fighters were parked either side of the deck, their cockpits open and maintenance crews clambering over them as they continued the endless task of keeping the sleek craft in battle–ready condition. Closer to the bay doors a pair of Reaper Squadron Raythons sat on the catapults, their systems plugged into power cables snaking across the vast deck that kept them ready for scramble. Both of their pilots were close by, sitting in recliners in full flight–gear should the claxon go off and watching the gathering Marines with interest.

Near the port wall of the bay was a single shuttle, wedge–shaped in design with stubby but aerodynamic wings and a low T–tail, around which stood ten Marines in full battle kit. One of them towered above the rest, his bituminous skin glowing with bioluminescent tattoos from his time among the most feared of all Ethera's street gangs: the *Mark of Qayin*.

'Private Qayin,' Bra'hiv greeted the giant man, his vivid gold and blue locks shaved back close to his scalp. 'So good to see you up and about on your feet.'

Qayin scowled at the General but said nothing. Stripped of his sergeant's stripes in the wake of his desertion at Chiron IV, the former convict was now once again nothing more than a foot soldier among Atlantia's ranks. A fearsome fighter, Bra'hiv would not admit it to any soul alive but despite the man's unreliable nature, if a fight was to go off he would rather be with Qayin than without him.

'Time to redeem yourself,' he added, noting that none of the other Marines were mixing with Qayin. 'We'll be joined by your best friend shortly, upon which we'll travel across to Arcadia and take the Legion on. I'm sure you'll be on point the entire time, agreed?'

Qayin, a full half cubit taller than Bra'hiv, stared back without emotion. 'Kordaz?'

'The same,' Bra'hiv replied, enjoying himself. 'You know that he's going free after this, don't you?'

'Veng'en don't interest me.'

'But, I thought he nearly killed you last time you were together?' Bra'hiv murmured innocently.

Qayin grinned, his glowing tattoos flaring with fiery light. 'He killed a Marine officer instead. Best watch your back, general.'

Bra'hiv kept the innocent look on his face but did not reply. A commotion from behind them alerted him to a dozen heavily armed security guards marching onto the flight deck, and almost immediately all other sounds faded into silence.

The twelve guards surrounded a gigantic figure in their midst as they marched, the only noise the sound of their boots on the deck and the rattle of chains as Kordaz's towering, reptilian form strode among them. Taller even than Qayin, the eyes that had once been bright yellow were now a deep, ominous red and surrounded by flexing scales of metal where the Legion had repaired his eyesight. Likewise, his massive chest was a bizarre patchwork of forged metal that flexed like skin and yet was as strong as steel, engineered by tiny Infectors that had swarmed across his body and healed his wounds using the wreckage of the spacecraft hulls around them in the devastation after the battle for Chiron IV.

The security guards came to a halt before Bra'hiv, Kordaz quiet and calm in their midst.

'Here you go,' the chief security officer said as he handed what looked rather like a leash to the General, attached to Kordaz's wrist manacles. 'Can't say I'm sorry to see this one go.'

The security guards backed away from Kordaz to give Bra'hiv some room, and the General walked up to the Veng'en and looked into his fearsome, glowing eyes.

'You up for this, Kordaz?'

The Veng'en's voice, when he replied, was relayed by a universal translator strapped to his throat that detected vibrations in his vocal chords and constructed words from them. It sounded digital and in–human, especially over the warrior's harsh, guttural dialect.

'You make it sound as though I have a choice?'

'Your freedom's riding on this,' Bra'hiv said. 'You think that you can find the Legion aboard Arcadia and help us rid ourselves of the infection?'

Kordaz looked over Bra'hiv's head to where Qayin was standing among the Marines and watching him.

'I can sense the infection already,' the Veng'en growled. 'It is close by and I can hear them.'

Bra'hiv shivered involuntarily and then snapped himself out of his torpor.

'I'll take that as a yes,' he said and then whirled to his men. 'Mount up, let's get this done.'

The Marines turned and Bra'hiv followed them, one hand holding the immense Veng'en warrior's leash as though he were some kind of horrific pet.

*

'The shuttle's away.'

Captain Sansin nodded as Andaim Ry'ere stood alongside him on Atlantia's viewing platform. A circular construction directly above the bridge and mounted atop the frigate's hull, the platform afforded a spectacular panorama of the surrounding cosmos, Arcadia clearly visible ten thousand cubits away, floodlights illuminating her hull in the absence of a nearby star to light the scene. Vast veils of stars soared across the blackness, glowing galaxies like smudges of candlelight peppering the infinite universe.

'This was the only option you had, captain,' Andaim soothed. 'You can't be held responsible for Mikhain's actions. We both know that he has a reckless streak – his career was filled with incidents like this. It's likely why he was never given a command by the admiralty.'

Idris exhaled noisily as though trying to expel his pain.

'He's a good commander and an excellent Executive Officer. He once served two tours as XO of the Colonial flagship Defiance – he doesn't deserve this. He believed that Kordaz would betray us on Chiron IV and would ally himself to Salim Phaeon's pirates if we cut him loose. He was trying to protect us.'

Andaim smiled tightly. 'Are you sure about that?'

'What's that supposed to mean?'

'You know what it means,' Andaim replied. 'You just won't let yourself see it.'

'Enlighten me.'

Andain sighed and watched as the shuttle shrank to a tiny speck as it slowed and turned to land aboard Arcadia, dwarfed by the frigate's massive hull.

'He wanted your command,' Andaim said, 'and you were feeling pretty low at the time and under a lot of pressure. It seemed to me that part of you wanted Mikhain to take Atlantia off your hands, if only for a while.'

Idris turned to look at Andaim. 'Is that so? You're the ship's counsellor now too?'

'I don't mean it like that,' Andaim insisted. 'I get why you wanted to cover for Mikhain, really I do. But a crime is a crime. He could have dealt with the Kordaz issue back on Chiron IV any number of ways but he chose deception.'

'He did what he had to do to protect us all.'

'He ended up nearly finishing us off!' Andaim gasped in exasperation. 'Why won't you see that?'

'He's being hung out to dry by Gredan and his damned board of governors!'

'And if it had been Gredan who had gone behind our backs and colluded with a known pirate and killer?' Andaim challenged. 'Would you have turned a blind eye then? Would you have covered for *him*?'

Idris opened his mouth to reply but his words felt as though they were trapped inside of him, unable to take form. He whirled away from the CAG, unable to formulate an argument as he heard Andaim's voice from behind him.

'Gredan's right. You can't have one set of rules for the command crew and another for everybody else. It's not going to work and it'll weaken us all in the end.'

'This is a military ship,' Idris growled in reply. 'I can't run it any other way. You can't achieve victory in battles with debate and justice – fighting dirty is sometimes the only way to win.'

'And fighting dirty among the civilians, risking their lives for your own gain? There are consequences for that. Without consequences this would still be a prison ship with convicts running riot throughout.'

'You think that I'm not aware of that?!' Idris roared and whirled to face Andaim. 'I can only do the best I can with what we have! We can't be a democracy and a fighting force at the same time! Either we attack and fight with one hundred per cent commitment or we accept the rule of law across all endeavours and then die because of it! I don't give a damn about the governor's laws any longer, and I'm damned if I'm going to sit here and let them hang Mikhain out to dry for taking chances that none of them would have the guts to even think about let alone act upon!'

Idris turned for the stairs that led down to the bridge, and Andaim stepped to one side and blocked his path.

'You can't do that, captain.'

Idris froze in motion and stared at the CAG. 'I can do whatever I damned well like, *Commander*.'

'It's the same kind of treason that got Mikhain into this mess and exactly what Gredan wants you to do.'

'I'm done with the governors. Move out of my way.'

'I can't do that, sir.'

Idris struggled to decide what to do, his head filled with conflicting loyalties. 'You're in danger of being convicted yourself, Andaim, of insubordination! All I have to do is call the guard.'

'All I have to do is call the governors.'

'They're irrelevant now.'

'So we're truly a dictatorship,' Andaim replied, and suddenly stood aside.

As Idris watched the CAG reached up to his shoulders and tore off his rank patches and let them hang in the air between them in the zero gravity.

'That's not going to achieve anything, commander,' Idris snapped.

'Nor is becoming the next tyrant who dismisses any train of thought that differs from his own.'

Idris felt something in his mind and his body let go, and without conscious thought he swung his fist and it cracked across Andaim's jaw and sent the commander staggering across the platform.

Andaim regained his feet even as the sound of running boots hammered up the stairs from the bridge below. Two Marines rushed onto the platform with Meyanna Sansin in hot pursuit.

'What's going on up here?!' she snapped.

Idris stared at Andaim, his knuckles throbbing and dismay flushing through his chest like a crushing weight as he realized what he had done. Meyanna looked at the CAG's rank patches hovering above the stairwell and at Andaim holding his jaw.

'Idris?'

Idris turned away and rubbed his hands across his face, suddenly feeling more tired than he had ever felt before in his life. He was about to say something, *anything*, when an alert claxon shrieked out from the bridge below and Atlantia's lights went out.

Idris whirled as a speaker near the stairwell blared Lael's panicked voice.

'Multiple contacts, bearing eight five one, in–bound mass warps!'

Idris turned instinctively to Atlantia's starboard aft quarter even as he saw Arcadia's lights flicker out also as she went to tactical alert.

From against the dense star fields he saw a deep warping of the light, as though space and time were spiralling in on itself and vanishing down a tiny vacuum into oblivion. A flare of brilliant energy flickered in multiple locations barely fifty thousand cubits away from the two Colonial frigates, and Idris saw several massive vessels lurch into view as they dropped out of super–luminal cruise with astonishing precision.

'It's an ambush!' Andaim snapped.

'Battle stations!' Idris yelled as he made for the stairwell. 'Prepare for tactical assault!'

***

X

'We've got four Morla'syn destroyers, two unknown battle cruisers and two waves of fighters already launching!'

Lael's voice was clear and steady but Idris could hear the fear in her tone as he dashed down onto the bridge with Andaim just behind him.

'All shields at maximum but don't scramble any more Raythons! Let's not let anybody get trigger–happy out there. Who's on patrol?!'

'Reaper and Renegade squadron have four Raythons each at two hundred thousand cubits,' Andaim replied as he took his seat near the command platform. 'You want them brought in?'

Idris thought hard for a moment. 'No,' he replied. 'I don't want to spook the Morla'syn into attacking if I can avoid it.'

'Avoid it?' Meyanna uttered in bewilderment as she stepped down onto the bridge. 'We're heavily outnumbered by vastly superior vessels. We couldn't stop them from blowing us away even if we had a full fleet behind us.'

'We don't know what they want yet,' Idris growled back, irritated at the intrusion. 'Helm, turn our bow toward them, minimize our profile but don't target them.'

'Aye, captain.'

'Is Arcadia in contact?' he asked Lael.

'All signals are being blocked, heavy jamming from the Morla'syn vessels captain,' she replied apologetically. 'There's no way we can get a signal through.'

Idris cursed silently and watched as Morla'syn fighters spread out from their massive capital ships and began taking up offensive positions that surrounded the two frigates. The Morla'syn capital ships were also splitting up, cutting off escape routes and effectively corralling both Atlantia and Arcadia in place.

'We can't win a fight,' Andaim said, 'we need to barter our way out of this.'

Idris shook his head. 'I don't think that we'll be getting out of whatever this is. All we can do is try to preserve our lives and our dignity.' He turned to the Marines guarding the bridge. 'Contact the governors. They wanted to have their damned say? Let's give it to them.'

Andaim's eyes widened as the two Marines hurried away, one of them already speaking into a comm's radio.

'You're serious?' the CAG asked. 'You want to bring them in on this?'

Idris glared at Andaim. 'Isn't that what you all wanted, commander?'

Andaim said nothing but glanced again at the main viewing screen that showed the massive Morla'syn cruisers now in position and surrounding the frigates, two unidentified vessels flanking them.

'Galactic scout ships,' Lael said as Atlantia's scanners swept the two vessels and data spilled onto the screens near the captain. 'They're from the council's fleet.'

Idris sucked in a deep breath and let it spill out, relief flooding his system.

'At least we're not just facing the Morla'syn,' he said finally. 'Have they attempted to establish contact?'

'Nothing yet,' Lael replied. 'Doesn't look good.'

'Send a signal,' Idris said. 'The sooner we get them talking, the sooner they won't be thinking about opening fire.'

Lael complied as Idris stole a furtive glance across at Andaim. The CAG's broad jaw seemed none the worse for wear after their confrontation, but Idris was aware that now he too had overstepped the mark, his actions liable for several forms of disciplinary action under normal admiralty rules. But, as he tried to remind himself, there was no longer an admiralty and there was no effective structure to enforce punishment on officers convicted of criminal activity. Idris realized somewhat belatedly that despite everything, both Gredan and Andaim had been right. Atlantia's hierarchy had become such that there was nothing but a form of executive power holding sway at the top of the chain, and the whole ship was in danger of slipping into a state of tyranny with Idris at its head.

He felt a pall of shame descend across his shoulders as he realized just how close he was to becoming a dictator, a man who used force and even violence to maintain control over those beneath him in rank.

'Damn it,' he cursed under his breath.

A hand rested on his shoulder and he looked up to see Meyanna looking down at him.

'It's not all on you,' she said softly. 'It can't all be on you.'

Idris offered her a weak smile. 'That's the problem, there's nobody else.'

'Captain?'

Idris looked up and saw Lael gesture to the main viewing screen. 'The Morla'syn are opening a link.'

Idris sighed and wearily got to his feet once more, straightened his uniform and prepared to address whoever had surrounded them, on behalf of the last two thousand human beings alive in the cosmos. He took a deep breath and nodded to Lael.

The viewing screen flickered and a face appeared upon it, a long, regally featured, bi–pedal humanoid species known as the Morla'syn who had emerged as something of an implacable foe to Idris and his people.

'General Veer, of the destroyer *Archangel*,' the Morla'syn announced himself imperiously, looking down at Idris with large, slanted eyes shaded a deep blue that perfectly matched his pale skin, as though all of the lifeblood had been drained from his body. Veer's digitally translated voice sounded far more natural than the series of high–intensity sonar clicks that Idris could hear, the Morla'syn's natural form of communication.

'Captain Idris Sansin, CFS Atlantia,' Idris replied. 'We apologize for not announcing our presence in Galactic Space, but our situation is dire and we have come in the hope of gaining the assistance of…'

'Your vessels are on a watch–list of aggressors known to have attacked Morla'syn ships along the Icari Line,' Veer cut across him. 'You recently disabled one such vessel before fleeing.'

Idris nodded.

'We came under attack, as did the vessel we were attempting to protect, a Colonial ship known as Endeavour.'

'The circumstances of the attack are now irrelevant,' Veer snapped. 'You are targeted for destruction with the blessing of the Galactic Council's Chief of Staff.'

Idris took a pace closer to the screen. 'That would be a mistake, General.'

'The only mistake we have ever made is in believing that humankind would remain within the boundaries of the Icari Line, that you would succeed in overcoming your weaknesses and flaws and grow to become a member of the wider Galactic community. Instead, you are warmongers bent on your own destruction and that of the cosmos around you. No race or species has any interest in your affairs any longer, and wishes only to see you relegated to extinction as soon as possible.'

Idris clenched his fists by his side. 'We've already had this conversation with the Morla'syn once before, and it turns out they were twisting the Council's words to suit their own purposes. None of us trust anything that you're saying, and we will not stand down until the council has heard our plea.'

'There will be no plea,' Veer snapped. 'Humanity has no place beyond the Icari Line and will be exterminated wherever it is found.'

'The Icari Line is a prison that no longer has any walls,' Idris shot back. 'And every species is about to be exterminated wherever it is found as soon as the Legion arrives, which it will.'

'The Legion will be likewise annihilated,' Veer retorted confidently.

'You think so?' Idris asked. 'Because we found the Legion in ambush on a world not more than a few light years from here, and it looked alive and well to us!'

General Veer's skin darkened slightly and he peered at Idris. 'You lie. The Word's Legion has spread only as far as Wraiythe, and the Veng'en are fighting back.'

'The Legion has not just been spreading since the apocalypse on Ethera,' Idris replied. 'We recently learned that elements of the Legion have been expanding into the cosmos for decades and are lying in wait for the right moment to strike, just like they did on Ethera. That's their preferred method of attack, General – ambush, in overwhelming numbers, like insects swarming upon prey. If they're out this far, they've likely already infected the Galactic Centre.'

Veer visibly recoiled from the screen and glanced across the bridge of his warship as he communicated with his own people, his translator temporarily shut–off as he exchanged a series of terse clicks and squeals with his crew.

'That is not possible,' Veer snapped. 'No human vessel has entered Galactic Space since the apocalypse on Ethera.'

'Except a single Special Forces unit,' Idris countered, 'the same one that was being pursued by the Morla'syn destroyer that attacked us and we were forced to defend against. No doubt they forgot to mention that it was us who defeated the Special Forces soldiers in battle, not them.'

Veer's narrow, thin lips twisted in anger. 'The human invaders were killed by a Morla'syn crew in revenge for attacks against merchant ships in our sovereign space. The captain of our vessel was commended by the Morla'syn high council for valour.'

Idris let a rueful little smile curl from his lips. 'I bet he was. I bet the Morla'syn high council will wonder how such a small Special Forces gunship could have caused such immense damage to a Morla'syn cruiser too, the kind of damage that might be caused by, say, two Colonial frigates?'

'This is irrelevant!' General Veer raged.

'Not if the humans were infected when they travelled beyond the Icari Line,' Idris shot back. 'That would place modern, highly efficient Infectors in Galactic Space, and specifically, Morla'syn space. We've managed to figure out how to immunise ourselves against infection, one of the few advantages of having to fight the Legion for so long. You're compromised,

General, and in danger of infection yourselves. The last thing you want to be doing is destroying us. It's *you* who needs *our* help.'

General Veer waved Idris dismissively away as he cackled something to his crew off–screen and the link was abruptly shut off. Idris let out a long breath of air and slumped back into his seat.

'That was gutsy,' Andaim said from one side.

Idris turned to him, wearily preparing himself for another criticism, but none came. Idris sensed an olive branch.

'You think they'll buy it?'

'I don't know,' Andaim shrugged, 'but you've sure given them something to think about. Not sure how you're going to square that off with the Legion aboard Arcadia.'

'I hadn't got that far yet,' Idris admitted. 'We need to speak to Mikhain.'

'We're still being jammed,' Lael said. 'They're not going to let us speak to Arcadia and give us time to formulate an attack plan.'

Idris nodded. 'Where are Reaper Squadron now?'

'Ten thousand cubits,' Andaim said, 'in four pairs, combat air patrols.'

'What about the Morla'syn fighters?'

'Holding their ground between us and them,' Andaim said as he checked his displays. 'They're not attacking. Something must be holding them back.'

The main viewing screen flickered into life once more and General Veer's pale image reappeared.

'You will maintain close battle flight and your weapons systems will be deactivated,' he announced.

'Is that so? On whose orders?'

'Mine,' Veer snapped back. 'You do not have the luxury of leverage over your fate, captain. If you wish to address the Galactic Council and make your plea, you will be required to form a mass–sphere with your sister ship in order that we can travel as a fleet to Oassia.'

Captain Sansin concealed his relief as he nodded.

'Very well, General Veer. We will deactivate our weapons as you request, and recover our fighters prior to leaping to super–luminal.'

'Your trajectory will be guided by our systems,' General Veer informed him. 'Be ready to depart in precisely ten Etheran minutes.'

The screen blanked out and returned to an image of Arcadia in the distance, loomed over by a Morla'syn destroyer.

'Do it,' Idris nodded to Andaim, who relayed the order for Reaper Squadron to land immediately.

Meyanna hurried to her husband's side. 'You're threatening them with the possibility that they're already infected, and then bringing the Legion with us aboard Arcadia to Oassia? If they find out that we're carrying those machines with us, and especially Lazarus and Kordaz, they'll blast us to hell in the blink of an eye.'

Idris nodded. 'I know, but it's either that or inform them that Arcadia is a plague ship and let them vaporize her. I'm not willing to do that to a thousand innocent civilians.'

'The Morla'syn might not hesitate so easily,' Meyanna pointed out.

'Then the burden of guilt will be upon them and not us!'

Meyanna flinched from him and he sighed and reached out for her hand, took it in his and held it quietly for a moment. He turned and looked at the image on the main viewing screen of Arcadia.

'We've just got to hope that General Bra'hiv and his men can clean that ship up before we make it to the Galactic Council, or this is going to be a real short trip.'

***

XI

'And you're sure this will work?'

Mikhain stood before Bra'hiv's Marines and the towering, silent form of Kordaz as they assembled inside Arcadia's flight deck.

'He can sniff them out,' Bra'hiv said as he gestured to Kordaz. 'That's more than we can do, so how about it?'

Mikhain nodded, knowing he had no option but to go along with the plan.

'We won't have long. Atlantia's recalled her fighters from CAP and they're landing as we speak. My guess is that they're going to slave our navigation computers to the Morla'syn ships and we'll all be taking a little ride to Oassia. It's only a few hours away, General. Whatever you've got in mind, that's all the time we have to do it.'

General Bra'hiv whirled and waved his Marines past as they marched toward the deck exits heading aft toward the sections of the ship that had been sealed off by the captain. Bra'hiv hesitated alongside Mikhain as the captain grabbed his shoulder.

'How's Idris holding up?'

'What do you mean?'

'He's been under a lot of pressure lately, and he was making an effort to defend Kordaz from the board of governors before the Morla'syn arrived. Now Kordaz is here and free to wander about Arcadia. What happened?'

The general gave a vague shrug and pushed past Mikhain.

'My rank means I don't have to worry about things like that,' he replied. 'That's your job.'

The general hurried after his men, Mikhain watching them go as his mind raced. Governor Gredan and his bureaucrat friends aboard Atlantia had been screaming for Kordaz's blood for weeks now, demanding an open trial before the civilians rather than the court martial behind closed doors favoured by Sansin.

Lieutenant Scott strode to the captain's side, one eye on the huge Veng'en as he disappeared into an adjoining corridor, surrounded by the Marine escort.

'What's he doing here?' Scott asked.

'They're using him to locate the Legion, wherever it's hiding,' Mikhain replied. 'The governors must have him over a barrel or something.'

'Must've been a sweet deal to get him out of the prison cells and over here,' Scott observed.

Mikhain nodded but did not reply as a tanoy burst into life over the noise of maintenance work ongoing in the hangar.

'*All stations, prepare for super–luminal cruise in five, four, three…*'

'That's it, we're heading for Oassia,' Scott said.

'*…one.*'

The light in the landing bays became briefly polarised and the massive frigate surged forwards and then settled down into super–luminal cruise. Mikhain looked at his wrist–display, noted the time, and then pulled Lieutenant Scott to one side.

'Something's going on here and I don't like it,' he confided. 'The Marines aboard Arcadia could have conducted the search, and why send General Bra'hiv and that damned Veng'en over here anyway when we have our own Marines? We could have used microwave scanners and Devlamine traps to burn the Legion wherever we found it.'

Lieutenant Scott frowned. 'Why does it matter? I think it's quite a good idea: Kordaz can hunt them down more quickly than our teams scouring the ship deck by deck, and we only have a few hours.'

Mikhain nodded, his instincts alive with the sense that he was missing something of great importance.

'You're right,' he said. 'You have the bridge, XO.'

Lieutenant Scott nodded and turned, hurrying away toward the exits. Mikhain waited until he was gone and then activated his communicator. Moments later, a voice replied.

'*Yes, captain?*'

'Lieutenant Neville,' Mikhain addressed the senior officer of Arcadia's Marine contingent. 'I need you to deploy a tracking team, quietly.'

'*Understood sir, what's the target?*'

Mikhain eyed the bay exits where Bra'hiv's men had disappeared. 'Bravo Company's Marines, lieutenant. I don't want that Veng'en secretly communicating with the Legion and placing the soldiers around him in jeopardy. Listen in, and report anything you hear back to me directly.'

'*Yes sir!*'

*

'The locked down section of the hull is just ahead.'

The Lance Corporal leading them looked nervous as Bra'hiv checked his rifle one more time and glanced up at Kordaz. 'You sense anything?'

Kordaz did not look back at the General as he replied. 'They're close. I can feel them.'

'This gives me the creeps,' one of the Marines said from behind the General.

'Focus on the job,' Bra'hiv snapped. 'Qayin, on point.'

The big Marine shouldered his way to the front of the platoon as they neared a series of blast doors that had been sealed shut, microwave scanners aligned nearby to create a shield that prevented the Legion's machines from advancing beyond the doors should they chew through them.

It had been discovered by Meyanna Sansin that although the swarms of machines the Legion utilized were virtually indestructible due to their sheer numbers, their internal circuitry was not immune to attack. Microwave energy, of a frequency that matched the Hunter's and Infector's internal circuits, would result in a build–up of heat energy within the devices that fried their innards and rendered them useless. Likewise, the use of Devlamine as a draw to the machines, due to their inherent programming designed to use Devlamine as a means of gaining control of human beings, meant that they could be corralled and then annihilated by firepower en masse, a tactic deployed effectively on Chiron IV.

The Marines slowed noticeably as they approached the doors. Bra'hiv, like his men, had seen what the unstoppable waves of machines could do to any biological species, rushing over them like glistening black oil and tearing them apart in a fearsome frenzy of countless thousands of razor sharp metallic teeth and claws.

General Bra'hiv moved to the doors' security panel and entered a code. The Marines raised their rifles, the plasma magazines humming into life as they aimed at the doors, two of them hefting plasma–powered flamethrowers into position. Satisfied, Bra'hiv hit the access command button and then leaped back as a hiss of escaping air billowed out in a cloud of vapour into the corridor and the blast doors rumbled open.

The Marines tensed up, then the vapour cleared and revealed an empty corridor descending into the bowels of the ship.

'Kordaz, you're up! The rest of you, advance by sections,' Bra'hiv ordered. 'Stay sharp!'

The gigantic Veng'en turned to the Marine closest to him, and with features pinched with reluctance the Marine activated a swipe–card and passed it over Kordaz's manacles. They clicked open and hung in the zero-gravity as Kordaz quietly slipped them off.

For a moment Bra'hiv wondered whether the Veng'en would attempt to run or perhaps plunge into the Marines in a murderous frenzy. But instead, Kordaz turned and strode into the chilly interior of the passage.

'Follow me.'

The Marines looked at Bra'hiv, who nodded, and the soldiers marched in behind the Veng'en. Bra'hiv took one last look at the rest of the ship and then he followed them in and sealed the entrance behind him, the heavy doors rumbling closed with a resounding boom that echoed through the interior.

'There's no other way out of here,' Emma said as Bra'hiv began marching in pursuit of his men.

'That's kind of the idea,' Bra'hiv pointed out in reply. 'And as long as we're in super–luminal the Morla'syn can't scan us or communicate with us. We need this sorted before we reach Oassia or we'll be vaporised.'

'A comforting thought,' Emma replied in a rare display of humor. 'Kordaz, can he be trusted?'

'He's a Veng'en, what do you think?'

'He's infected, he could be turned.'

Bra'hiv looked at her as he marched. 'We could be asking the same of you.'

'I have no desire to see this mission or the eradication of The Word and its Legion fail, General.'

'Kordaz is battle hardened and has shown a loyalty to us that I would never have believed possible,' Bra'hiv countered. 'You, on the other hand, are an unknown quantity and that makes the men nervous.'

'They learned to trust Evelyn.'

'You're not Evelyn.'

Ahead, the Marines shuffled to a halt and took up positions either side of the wide corridor. Kordaz stood in the centre, looking away from them into the darkness ahead, his breath condensing in clouds that caught the low light from the ceiling above them.

'What's up?' Bra'hiv asked as he dropped down onto one knee alongside C'rairn.

'Don't know, he just stopped.'

Bra'hiv looked at Emma, and she reluctantly moved forward to stand alongside the enormous Veng'en warrior.

Emma had something of Evelyn's spirit, but the sheer size and power of Kordaz intimidated her. Her eyes were barely level with his abdomen, and she could hear his breathing hiss through gigantic nostrils high above her, his breath spilling from them as though he were some kind of monstrous bipedal dragon.

'You hear them.'

It wasn't a question: Kordaz's harsh dialect translated digitally into something that she could understand.

'No,' she admitted. 'I can hear nothing, yet.'

Kordaz nodded once, his gaze affixed to something far off in the distance.

'What does Lazarus want?' he asked her.

Emma frowned as she looked up at the Veng'en. 'What do you mean?'

The warrior's head turned and he looked down at her, his eyes glowing a dull, menacing red and the metallic orbits catching the dim light.

'No machine ever cared for man or beast,' he growled at her. 'Lazarus is here for something and it's not to save our skins. What does he want?'

Emma shook her head. 'I don't know. He's done nothing but protect us.'

Kordaz stared her down, and she realized that even the quickest shot among the Marines would not be swift enough to stop the warrior from reaching out with one of his gigantic hands and crushing her skull before he was cut down.

'You fear me,' he said.

Emma swallowed and lifted her chin. 'I do not.'

'Yes, you do,' Kordaz said, 'because the Legion can sense it.'

Emma stiffened and she turned to look down the corridor ahead. 'I cannot see them.'

Kordaz's reply sent a fresh shiver down her spine.

'They use scouts, just like armies would. They are already behind us.'

***

XII

Emma turned to call a warning but Kordaz's hand suddenly landed upon her shoulder.

'Silence.'

The whisper was harsh, strained, and she looked up at Kordaz to see him squinting down the tunnel.

'If we let them know we're aware of their presence, they may attack.'

Emma swallowed again. 'How can you see them?'

'The Legion repaired my eyes,' he replied. 'They did a better job than they should have. I can see their heat signature. About two hundred of them, clinging to the ceiling, twenty cubits ahead.'

Emma peered into the gloom and thought that she saw a subtle movement across the ceiling of the corridor, as though something alive has scuttled across it.

'Then how can they be behind us?' she whispered.

'They're leaving scouts behind to encircle our position,' Kordaz replied. 'One here, one there. Their numbers will build up and once we're deep enough into the interior they'll attack from both in front and behind. No escape.'

Emma scanned the darkened ceilings but could see nothing.

'They're chewing their way into the air conditioning vents, moving out of sight,' Kordaz explained as though he had heard her thoughts. 'They'll come out behind us again when they're passed.'

'We must tell the General!'

'His men will panic,' Kordaz hissed. 'That's what they always do. We must not let the Legion know that the men have seen them.'

'But we've seen them,' Emma protested.

'Yes, and they know that we have,' Kordaz replied and looked down at her once more. 'But we are not *them*, are we Emma?'

Emma shivered again and realized that the Veng'en's massive hand was still upon her shoulder, gentle now. Kordaz lifted it away and turned to the Marines.

'Move on.'

Without waiting for a response, Kordaz began marching away into the darkness. The Marines hurried past and Bra'hiv jogged up alongside Emma.

'What was that all about?'

Emma watched the Veng'en disappear into the darkness.

'He wanted to know if I'd sensed anything yet,' she replied.

'And?'

Emma shook her head. 'I haven't heard a thing, general.'

Bra'hiv watched her for a moment and then he hurried off in pursuit of his men.

Emma looked around her at the corridor and thought she saw something nip out of sight far behind them, a tiny speck like an insect hurrying across the deck. Revulsion writhed down her spine and she hurried away in pursuit of the Marines.

*

Captain Sansin made his way to the heavily armoured storage depot with his wife and the governors following, two Marines acting as escorts as they descended through the ship. Gredan led the governors with a look of self-satisfaction on his face.

'I'm delighted that you agreed to our requests, captain,' he said as they walked, clearly enjoying himself.

'I didn't agree,' Idris replied. 'You demanded.'

'The governors have a right to know about everything you're getting them in to,' Gredan explained conversationally. 'How else can we convey to the populace your intentions, the reasoning behind your faith in Veng'en warriors, genetic clones and Lazarus?'

'Necessity,' Idris shot back. 'It's called *war*, governor.'

'And that same necessity explains our presence now,' Gredan replied without concern. 'We need to know everything if we're to be a part of any negotiations with the Galactic Council.'

Idris nodded to the guards outside the depot and they immediately unsealed the doors and hauled them open. Idris marched inside, the governors following somewhat more cautiously. The room glowed a soft blue, Ceyen Lazarus's holographic form turning its head to meet them as the door slammed shut behind the governors. The two escorting Marines took up positions either side of the doors and waited unobtrusively.

'Lazarus,' Idris announced, 'these are the governors, representatives of the people who have demanded an audience with the Galactic Council alongside me.'

Lazarus listened as the captain introduced the governors in turn, and to the captain's surprise he bowed slightly at the waist in greeting.

'It's my pleasure to make your acquaintance,' he soothed. 'Forgive my appearance, but it's a considerable improvement on my previous incarnation.'

'Or re–incarnation,' Idris suggested. 'We felt that a holographic representation of the doctor's form was something that people would prefer.'

Governor Vaughn peered at Lazarus in fascination. 'So, you're *alive*?'

'Regrettable so,' Lazarus replied. 'I should have died long ago, governor. But my work is not done and I have much for which to attone.'

'Tell them what you told me,' Idris commanded Lazarus, and the image of the old man obeyed without question.

'I am a machine, much the same as The Word, of that there is no doubt,' Lazarus said. 'But my networking is entirely different, a modification I made to ensure that the fate that befell The Word cannot be repeated with me.'

'Fate?' Ishira Morle echoed fiercely. 'The Word suffered no *fate*. Six billion or so humans suffered a fate.'

'Yes,' Lazarus conceded, 'but the proximal cause of that tragic loss was with The Word. It was designed to be autonomous, to make its own decisions, to be able to weigh up actions and consequences, to arbitrate and judge. Those actions, those capabilities, are what make us *human*, for no other Etheran species possessed such qualities. The Word thus became somewhat human, and without a barrier to its expansion it developed what one might call emotions, or a soul, and above all, *fear*. It learned to fear humans in just the same way that the species represented by the Galactic Council has come to fear humans. The Word's fate was to act out of fear of its creators, not out of a homicidal rage but out of self–protection, an act that we humans are most definitely familiar with.'

'No,' Gredan snapped, 'humanity relied upon The Word, came to trust it. If it was so capable, had such understanding, it would have realized that it had nothing to fear from us, that it was in control.'

Lazarus smiled at Gredan. 'That would be true were it not for all the other emotions that come with self–awareness, like paranoia for instance. Rage, desire, the need for power, control and certainty in our world that is a hallmark of the human condition. The Word could not be sure that we would not someday turn against it and so it acted as we would and prepared for war.' Lazarus sighed. 'By the time that war was imminent, The Word's programming had mutated grotesquely enough that self–preservation had transformed into an inextinguishable desire for domination. By then, there was no turning back.'

Governor Morle took a step closer to Lazarus.

'So what makes *you* so different?'

'When I uploaded myself to Endeavour, I introduced a new protocol into my programming that ensured that I could never again make decisions autonomously of human direction.'

'What kind of protocol?' Governor Gredan asked.

'I chose three members of Endeavour's crew and ensured that they were given unique and complete access to my files and systems, and that my own ability to give commands aboard the ship were slaved to their acquiescence. In short, I could not make any decision or give any command without their verification first.'

Governor Gredan peered at Lazarus closely. 'Which members of the crew did you choose?'

'The captain, and two of his senior officers. Only one of those officers remains alive, and she is with you now. Her name is Emma.'

Evelyn stood forward. 'It's all true, Emma told me as much on numerous occasions. Lazarus inserted the protocols to ensure that whatever madness consumed The Word would not afflict him in the same way.'

'So in effect we have control of you, and not the other way round.' Governor Vaughn said.

'Correct,' Lazarus agreed. 'The task at hand now is to convince the Galactic Council that this is the case, that they do not have anything to fear from me being aboard Atlantia. Likewise, they have nothing to fear from either Evelyn or Emma.' Lazarus frowned, his glowing digital features scanning the crowd before him. 'Where is Emma? I cannot sense her presence?'

'She is aboard Arcadia,' Idris admitted. 'She travelled there before the Morla'syn destroyers arrived.'

For the first time since Lazarus had been given's holographic presence, Idris thought he saw a look of dismay across the man's features.

'The Legion is aboard Arcadia,' Lazarus said.

'We have sent Marines to root them out,' Idris promised, 'and the Veng'en warrior Kordaz is with them. As a team, they should have no problem in clearing up the infection before we arrive at Oassia.'

'Emma is not strong enough,' Lazarus insisted. 'If she is exposed to the Legion she may succumb to its temptations.'

'What do you mean, succumb to its temptations?'

Lazarus sighed despite the fact that he had no lungs with which to breathe. The action was uniquely human despite his digital form.

'The Legion is a conglomerate, a unified force, and the greater its numbers the greater its attraction to those who have in any way been a part of what the Legion is. In order that Emma could control what I can do, she too had to become a part of it. It's why she can sense my presence and that of the Legion too.'

Governor Gredan glared at Lazarus. 'So you're saying that she is as much a part of The Word as you are?'

'No,' Lazarus insisted. 'Emma was infected along with the other two crew members by me on purpose with a weakened version of what you now call the Legion. I only used a single Infector, similar designed to that used by The Word, but instead of being an aggressive invader it was designed merely to allow Emma to develop the senses needed to communicate with me. The Infector I placed inside her was designed to disintegrate after a short period of time, which it did effectively, the disintegration powered by Emma's own immune system. I then sent this information back to The Word on Ethera, concealed within other more mundane data which allowed the information to be absorbed into the system. In effect, I was attempting to create humanity–wide resistance and even immunity to the Infectors. That's how the immunity entered the human line and ended up in Evelyn here.' Lazarus sighed again. 'Sadly, the immunity did not spread wide enough and fast enough to prevent the apocalypse.'

The governors fell silent, Evelyn with them as Idris thought long and hard.

'The only advantage we have is the immunity that we now all carry aboard Atlantia and Arcadia,' he said finally. 'That in itself is a bargaining chip with the Galactic Council. An immunity to the Infectors provides a major barrier to The Word's infiltration of differing races. It served the Veng'en well for some time until they succumbed.'

'The Legion learns fast,' Lazarus agreed. 'Any immunity we carry at this time will not prevail forever. Now that we're seeking the council's assistance it's essential that we also commit them to a major offensive against the advance of The Legion. If it appeared at Akyron V then we know that the Legion is expanding at a trimetric rate and will continue to consume worlds as it expands into the cosmos. There will come a point where it will spread so far that we will be unable to stop it no matter how large a fleet we can amass. In short, captain, you were right. Now is the time to fight.'

Idris looked at the governors.

'You understand the predicament we face?' he asked them. 'That there is nowhere else to run. This is not just about finding a safe haven for what's left of humanity. This is about reaching a point where we must stand and fight back or be destroyed. Are you willing and prepared to stand before the

Galactic Council and barter not just for a safe haven but for the amassing of the fleet sufficiently powerful to take us back to Ethera?'

The governors looked at each other, and Idris realized that even Ayek's normally belligerent expression and softened as she realized the sheer magnitude of what they were about to attempt.

'This is it then,' Meyanna said. 'It's the end of the line, one way or the other?'

Idris nodded solemnly.

'When we reach Oassia we either make our stand or we will be destroyed by the Galactic Council and they will have to make the stand for us. Given the choice, I would rather die fighting The Word than any of the other species that populate our galaxy.' He looked at the governors. 'Are you with me, or not?'

Governor Gredan lifted his bulbous chin and stepped forward. 'Aye.'

The other governors cast each other one last glance, and then they all stood forward.

'*Aye.*'

***

XIII

'You see anything yet?'

Lieutenant Neville did not reply as he crouched in the darkness and listened intently. The blackness was unnerving, as was the cold, the power to Arcadia's aft hull re-routed to deny the infecting Hunters power and warmth, slowing them down enough to perhaps give the Marines some warning of any attack.

Neville was backed by three of his most trusted men, but right now he felt anything but safe. None of their portable detectors was reading a definable heat signature from the Hunters supposedly colonizing the damaged areas of the ship, and as such he had no idea of where to begin looking for them. Not that doing so was a part of his mission, which was in fact to watch General Bra'hiv and Bravo Company, a request that made him feel distinctly uncomfortable.

'Nothing,' he whispered back finally. 'There's nothing here.'

'Where are they then?'

Neville shrugged and looked down at the tracker he held in his hand. The screen portrayed the ship in all directions in a quasi three-dimensional display, with their own heat signatures displayed in blue and those of Bravo Company in red. Bra'hiv's Marines were about a hundred cubits ahead of them down the corridor and close to the hull breach, the section itself sealed off to protect the ship's internal atmosphere and shield it from the intense radiation generated outside the hull by the frigate's tremendous velocity.

Mikhain's orders were clear: Kordaz could be a threat to Bra'hiv's Marines and should be vaporized should he in any way seek to threaten their safety. What bothered Lieutenant Neville was that everybody in the entire fleet knew that Kordaz was an unreliable ally and a carrier of the Legion's Infectors. Did Mikhain mistrust somebody else on the General's team, or perhaps even the General himself? If Mikhain was so concerned for everybody's safety, then why would he demand that Neville report only to him in person and not directly to Bra'hiv? Neville's instincts were alive with the sense that something was amiss and that something was about to hit the fan somewhere along the line, and he was damned if he was going to walk blindly into some kind of…

'What's that?'

Neville looked over his shoulder and saw one of his men pointing behind them. Neville squinted into the darkness but saw nothing.

'You're getting jittery,' he said. 'Secure your nerves and keep moving.'

'No sir,' the Marine said in a surprisingly concerned tone. 'I saw something, it's behind us.'

The young soldier's conviction galvanized Neville and he turned around and aimed the heat detector behind them. Almost immediately the hairs on the back of his neck rose up as he cried a strained order.

'Enemy rear!'

A roar of fear went up from the soldiers as the flashlights on their rifles swept behind them and illuminated the corridor, now filled with a murderous black tide of Hunters that tumbled toward them like thousands of black boulders streaming through a canyon.

'Fall back!' Neville roared as he opened fire.

The Marines let loose a blaze of plasma fire that thundered into the charging nanobots in brilliant flares of bright blue light and clouds of glowing red Hunters incinerated in the blasts.

*

Bra'hiv's Marines crept silently down the corridor, the cold biting deep as Emma followed them through the shadows. Kordaz was still at their head, striding with brazen confidence and forcing the Marines to hurry from position to position behind bulkheads as they covered his advance.

Evelyn pulled her coat tighter about her shoulders and found herself looking over her shoulder repeatedly as though demons and ghosts were hovering in the darkness behind her.

'You feel anything yet?'

General Bra'hiv was looking back at her from where he crouched behind a bulkhead, his plasma rifle clutched in his grasp.

'Nothing,' Emma lied as she peered ahead down the passage that led toward the outer hull where the Legion was presumed to have entered Arcadia. 'They must be too spread out for me to detect them.'

The general looked back to where Kordaz was striding forwards. 'He seems to know where he's going.'

'Yeah, but what's he actually doing?' Qayin muttered from further ahead. 'I've seen the Legion chew through half a ship and turn it onto a million Hunters within days. We should have seen something by now.'

Emma struggled with indecision and looked over her shoulder again.

'What is it with you?' the General demanded of her. 'Why do you keep looking behind us?'

'I don't know,' Emma replied. 'It must be the darkness, I feel like we're being watched.'

A low whistle attracted their attention and Emma looked forward to see Kordaz stop once more in the darkness, the Marines taking up position behind him with their rifles pointing ahead. In the silence, Kordaz's voice was deep but clear as he spoke.

'They are here.'

'They are *where*?' the General hissed.

Kordaz turned to face them, and his red eyes glowed in the darkness like a demon's as he extended his giant arms out to either side of him, his clawed hands almost reaching the opposing walls of the corridor.

'Everywhere,' he growled softly. 'Don't make a sound.'

Bra'hiv crept toward Kordaz from his position. 'What the hell difference is that going to make?'

'They're not hunting us,' Kordaz replied.

'What?'

Suddenly a din of rifle fire echoed down the corridor toward them, mingling with the terrified screams of men. Bra'hiv whirled as he saw flashes of light from rifles flickering off the walls in the distance.

'They're behind us!' Emma cried out.

From the silence in the darkness came a sound, like the scuttling of a thousand insects across a tin roof. Emma felt a frigid chill stiffen her limbs as she looked this way and that for the source of the sound but realized she was unable to track it. The Marines began pulling in without orders and formed a defensive circle in the centre of the corridor as they aimed their weapons outward.

'With me!' the General snapped at Emma and grabbed her hand.

Together they ran toward the Marines, the circle opening to let them in and closing behind them as the General squatted down in the centre and aimed his rifle directly at Kordaz.

'What the hell is going on, Kordaz?!'

The Veng'en's voice roared out above the sound of the advancing hordes. 'They're under threat and are attacking!'

'Under threat from *whom*?!'

From the darkness surged a black wave of Hunters, a shimmering mass of metal that poured along the walls and the ceiling and the deck toward them from both sides. Emma gave a yelp of fright and shrunk back against the General's side as she saw the vast swathes of machines thundering along the deck toward them.

'How come you didn't sense all of them?!' Lieutenant C'rairn shouted at Emma.

Emma could not bring herself to reply as she cowered alongside Bra'hiv.

In front of the Hunters were three Marines, all shouting and firing desperately as they retreated before the hordes of machines.

'Activate the scanners!' the General yelled at the top of his lungs as he took aim and fired a round into the depths of the swarming horde. 'Covering fire!'

Four of the Marines pulled out mobile microwave scanners and activated them, sending powerful pulses of energy toward the advancing Hunters. Emma watched in terrified fascination as the invisible beams of energy split through the hordes of machines, the Hunters flowing like debris–filled oil around the patches of energy and sweeping up across the ceiling as they threaten to colonise the passage above their heads.

'We're surrounded!' C'rairn yelled.

'I knew it,' the General snapped. 'Kordaz, call them off!'

The Veng'en did not reply, still standing with his hands stretched out to either side of him. The general took more careful aim at Kordaz's head and bellowed one more time. A sudden scream shrieked out in the darkness and Emma yelped in sympathy as she saw one of the retreating Marines suddenly yanked sideways out his firing position and hauled feet–first down the corridor. In the dim light Emma saw a writhing black tentacle of machines wrapped around the soldier's boots.

'Covering fire!' Bra'hiv bellowed again as he whirled back to protect the soldier.

The company's rifles opened up as one and a salvo of brilliant blue–white plasma blazed down the corridor and illuminated the horrific wave of Hunters spilling into the corridor behind them, one tentacle extending out to the terrified soldier's entrapped legs.

'Get them off me!' the soldier screamed.

The plasma rounds smashed into the tentacle of machines and clouds of vaporized Hunters blasted in all directions in glowing orbs of molten metal. The tentacle was severed half a dozen cubits down its length, and the soldier slumped in horror as the Hunter's still attached to his boot suddenly swarmed upon him.

The soldier writhed and screamed as the machines rushed across his body, his arms batting and smashing at them as they attempted to tear into his body armour and the soft flesh beneath it. Suddenly, the machines stopped moving, completely covering the Marine but neither advancing nor retreating.

General Bra'hiv whirled back to Kordaz and in shock he realized that the Hunters had swarmed past the Marines, sweeping up across the walls of the corridor and the ceiling as they flooded by. Even more of them were coming from the far side of Kordaz, like a deep river of black that had burst its banks and was thundering downstream toward them.

Emma felt a fresh shudder of revulsion as she saw the black waves of machines crash together at the feet of the Veng'en warrior and then rush up him like a billion black ants climbing a gigantic tree. Kordaz remained rooted to the spot as the thunderous wave of Hunters swarmed upon him and utterly concealed the Veng'en within their metallic embrace.

'They'll kill him!' C'rairn shouted and leaped to his feet as he took aim.

'They're not here for his life!' Emma yelled. 'They're here to take back what's theirs!'

The swarm of Hunters had formed a pyramid where Kordaz stood, and that pyramid was undulating and rippling like some kind of gigantic insect nest.

'Let's go, now!' Emma shouted. 'While we still have a chance!'

Bra'hiv turned back to the Marine who had been entombed in the Hunters, and saw the soldier stagger to his feet, his features twisted with horror, revulsion and yet relief that he had somehow been spared.

'Neville?' Bra'hiv uttered in amazement. 'What the hell are you doing down here?'

'Mikhain sent me to cover your backs,' Lieutenant Neville replied. 'Said Kordaz might turn on you.'

The line of Bra'hiv's jaw hardened. 'I don't think it's our safety he's concerned about.'

'What do you mean?'

'I'll tell you later.' General Bra'hiv stared in amazement one last time at the horrific form before him and knew that he could not torch the Hunters without killing Kordaz at the same time. He turned and bellowed at the Marines. 'Tactical retreat! Let's get out of here, blow the hull wall and send them all out into space!'

The Marines re–formed into a defensive semi–circle in front of Bra'hiv and Emma and then began retreating away from the towering pyramid of Hunters. Emma forced her legs to move as she backed away from the horrendous sight of Kordaz utterly buried among the savage machines.

The light from the Marine's weapons sliced through the gloom and gradually the pyramid of machines was lost to the shadows as, incredibly, it rose up into the ceiling.

'Full retreat!' Bra'hiv called. 'They're going for the air conditioning vents!'

The Marine's defensive circle broke and they began hurrying back along the corridor toward the major bulkhead and blast doors.

***

XIV

'Where is Kordaz?!'

Mikhain stood upon the command platform and listened as replies came in from the Marines deep within the ship. The connection was distorted and crackling with static.

'He's been grabbed by the Legion – they've taken off and we can't keep up,' Bra'hiv replied. *'The Legion did the last thing we expected and moved outside of the hull and back in ahead of us. He's on the move and wherever he goes the Legion is following!'*

Mikhain whirled and pointed at his tactical officer. 'Scan the ship immediately, locate any large moving heat source you can and relay the information directly to the main screen.'

The tactical officer obeyed immediately, and Mikhain turned to a schematic of Arcadia appearing on the main screen. Moments later a small red disc of fluctuating light moving forward through the vessel from the starboard hull.

'That's them,' Mikhain said as he observed the moving orb on the display. 'They're moving for'ard.'

'It's heading for the bridge,' the communications officer said, Shah's tone a little more than concerned. 'It's coming here. The Legion wants control of the bridge!'

Mikhain stared at the blob for only a moment longer, and he knew with a deep certainty that it was not the bridge that the Legion necessarily sought. Kordaz was in its midst, and despite his every sense saying that it was impossible it appeared that the Legion was following the commands of Kordaz and not the other way round. Somehow, Kordaz had become The Word, and with all that he knew about what Mikhain had done on Chiron IV, there could be no doubt as to his intentions. Kordaz had nearly killed Qayin during one such act of revenge, and Mikhain had not nearly the strength of the giant former convict.

'It's not the Legion,' he said finally to the crew around him. 'It's Kordaz, and Kordaz wants me.'

'What do you mean he wants you?' Lieutenant Scott echoed.

Mikhain watched the angry red spot moving through the ship's corridors toward the bridge.

'Kordaz blames me for what happened to him on Chiron IV,' Mikhain explained. 'We can't let the Legion or Kordaz onto the bridge – we need a diversion.'

Lieutenant Scott glanced at the schematic and shook his head. 'There's no way we can intercept Kordaz now, we don't have the manpower and Bra'hiv's men are too far behind.'

Mikhain agreed. He turned to face Lt Scott. 'I will be the diversion. Send a ship wide call for the captain to make his way to the aft flight deck, and set battle stations. I want you to make your way to the War Room and seal yourself inside along with two senior officers, in case the bridge becomes compromised in my absence.'

The War Room was a secondary bridge deep within the ship and a place where in the event of the main bridge being compromised during a boarding in battle, Arcadia could still be controlled by its original crew without the boarders knowing of their presence.

Lieutenant Scott shook his head. 'No, that's a bad idea. If the Legion gets into the War Room then they could take the ship from there.'

'The Legion doesn't know about the War Room and likely neither does Kordaz. If they change direction upon the command call going out, then we will know that it's me they seek rather than to control Arcadia.'

'That's a hell of a risk,' Scott pointed out. 'And what if they cut you off before you can reach the flight deck?'

'That's a risk I'm going to have to take,' Mikhain replied. 'The longer we deliberate over it the more chance there is they'll cut me off. Have all crew evacuate the flight deck and lockdown the rest of the ship.'

Scott frowned. 'What are you going to do when you get there?'

Mikhain ground his teeth in his jaw and clenched his fists by his side. 'What I should have done a long time ago. You have the bridge, XO.'

Mikhain whirled on one heel before Scott had a chance to reply and he marched off the bridge as briskly as he could. The Marines guarding the doors parted for him as the doors opened and he strode through, and even as the doors were closing behind him he heard the ship's tannoy burst into life with Shah's voice.

'Captain to the aft flight deck, all sections on lockdown alert, battle stations!'

Mikhain accelerated his pace, hurrying towards one of the small shuttles that would transport him through the ship. He clambered into a pod and sat down as it began to accelerate, and on his wrist–com he saw a data message appear from Lieutenant Scott.

Legion following you. Hurry, and good luck.

Mikhain gripped the safety rail of the pod and watched the lights of the transport tunnel flashing by overhead. A small screen before him on the panel showed his position in the ship, and he could only estimate where the Legion was. Travelling at such a pace, he could see immediately that he would reach the flight deck before they would.

The pod slowed and Mikhain prepared himself to jump out the moment it came to a halt. The pod hissed as its brakes engaged and it slid in alongside the platform, and Mikhain immediately hurled himself out and began running for the flight deck access doors. His boots echoed down the corridor, devoid now of other personnel as the lockdown took force. He felt his heart beating in his chest and was mildly surprised to see images from his past flash before his eyes as though he were entering the last moments of his life. Time seemed to slow down, regrets and hopes and fears and dreams drifting through his mind and his legs running it seemed of their own accord as he raced to the flight deck and slid to a halt beside the access panel.

There were two shuttles inside the bay, either of which he could use. If he could just slip away and out of immediate guns range, then he might be able to set a course for Oassia and jump ship once he reached a spaceport. He knew it was a hell of a long shot but he had no choice – whatever happened now, his time as a Colonial officer was over.

Mikhain entered his personal security code and the door slid open. He hurried inside into the cavernous flight deck, filled with parked Raython's and shuttles, and then he immediately slid to a halt once more as he saw a platoon of Marines awaiting him with their rifles all pointed in his direction. General Bra'hiv was at their head, his cold gaze directed at Mikhain down the barrel of his plasma rifle.

'That's far enough, captain,' Bra'hiv snapped.

Mikhain stared at the General's plasma rifle and instinctively put his hands in the air beside his head.

'What the hell's going on? You said that you were behind the Legion!'

The general stepped forward from his men. 'Must've got confused. You're under arrest, captain.'

'Under arrest for what?'

'On the orders of Captain Idris Sansin and the Board of Governors,' the General explained. 'We know everything about what happened on Chiron IV, about you selling Kordaz out to the pirates.'

Mikhain felt a flush of anxiety tingle down his spine and weaken his legs as he realized the extent of the General's knowledge, and now that of the men who surrounded him. Lieutenant Neville was alongside the General, his own weapon pointed at Mikhain. He briefly considered denying all knowledge of such an event, but the certainty with which the General spoke meant that they must have conclusive evidence of some kind, something which could not be refuted. At such a crucial juncture, Idris would never have condoned his arrest without being absolutely certain of his guilt.

Mikhain knew that the imminent meeting with the Galactic Council was behind the decision to arrest him. Governor Gredan and his do–gooders on the governing body must have decided that they could not risk having somebody like Mikhain in command, which meant that somebody must have approached them with the evidence that condemned him. Mikhain briefly closed his eyes as he realized who must have been behind it.

'I did what I had to do to protect Atlantia,' he said finally, and felt a surprising wave of relief wash over him as he spoke. 'Kordaz was the enemy, we all knew that. Salim Phaeon was also the enemy and yet Captain Sansin at the time was willing to negotiate with pirates. I had no faith in his command, no faith in a Veng'en warrior's desire to stand by humanity and felt sure that once down on the surface Kordaz would ally himself to the pirates and represent a greater threat to us and the pirate's hostages. It was my decision and I stand by it!'

'I'm not here to judge,' the General shot back. 'In fact, I couldn't give a damn. Get down on your knees and keep your hands behind your head.'

'We don't have time,' he replied. 'The Legion is on its way here.'

General Bra'hiv raised an eyebrow. 'The Legion is down in the 'tween decks and Kordaz with them.'

'Kordaz wants me!' Mikhain shot back in exasperation. 'He knows everything that you do and he'll stop at nothing to get his revenge. I came here to draw him away from the rest of the ship.'

Qayin stepped forward from the ranks of Marines, the towering convict's bioluminescent tattoos glowing malevolently. 'You sold me out and then expect us to believe you were coming down here on some kind of heroic one–man mission? We both know why you're here – you were going to get aboard one of these craft and make your escape.'

Mikhain shook his head vigourously. 'No, I'm here to face Kordaz. You can either stay here and risk being consumed by the Legion or you can get the hell out before they arrive.'

General Bra'hiv shook his head. 'No can do, captain. There's no way we're going to let you out of here, either on foot or in one of those spacecraft. You're going to the brig until we have re–established communication with Captain Sansin and the Governors.'

'There is no damn time!' Mikhain roared.

The Marines began shuffling nervously and looking over their shoulders, and suddenly Emma stepped forward and spoke clearly to the General.

'He's right,' she said suddenly. 'I can hear them.'

Bra'hiv glanced over his shoulder at her and then at the captain. 'And just what exactly are you going to do when they get here?'

Captain Mikhain tried to think straight but his own nervousness was clouding his thoughts. In truth he had no idea what he was going to do, but whatever it was he was going to stand up and face Kordaz down. Running away was no longer an option.

'I have absolutely no idea,' Mikhain replied. 'But it's me he wants and you all need to leave. Get into cover, now!'

The general gripped his rifle tighter and Mikhain watched as he struggled with his decision. Mikhain was about to speak again when Emma suddenly pointed to the ceiling of the bay high above them.

'It's too late!'

Mikhain looked over his shoulder and to his horror he saw countless thousands of tiny black machines spreading across the ceiling, flowing like droplets of black oil streaming down a window.

'Set up the microwave scanners!' Bra'hiv yelled.

It was Qayin who responded as he observed the Legion spreading onto the flight deck. 'That's not going to work, they're spreading out too far and wide, will never be able to hit enough of them once to stop them!'

Mikhain felt horror creeping like lice beneath his skin as he realized the Legion had already adapted to the microwave scanners that they had deployed to prevent their spread. They were moving fast, no longer in a thick, dense morass but scattered as widely as possible so that they spent as little time inside the microwave beams as possible and that as few of them were taken down by each beam.

'Set them up anyway,' the General insisted. 'All around us! Seal us in!'

Behind Mikhain the bay door slid open, and he turned to see Kordaz stride onto the flight deck, the corridor behind him filled with the seething black mass of the Legion. The Veng'en's glowing red eyes fixed upon Mikhain's as he stood in the doorway, his huge frame almost filling it.

'Captain,' he growled in his thick, translated dialect. 'I have waited a long time for this moment.'

***

XV

Mikhain took an involuntary step back as Kordaz advanced toward him, and behind him the Legion swarmed in, scaling the walls and spreading out like thick liquid oil across the deck. Mikhain cringed as he heard the scuttling of their metallic legs, like a billion grains of sand falling on a tin roof.

'Scanners on full power!' Bra'hiv yelled, and moments later the microwave scanners were omitting an invisible energy field around the Marines as they shrank back into a defensive circular formation with the General and Emma in the centre. 'Captain, get inside the circle, now!'

Mikhain looked over his shoulder at the Marines as they crouched in their defensive formation, their plasma rifles pointing out into the bay. The temptation to take a few paces back and join them was almost overwhelming, but Mikhain forced his gaze away and stood his ground as Kordaz paced toward him.

The Veng'en's eyes seemed more malevolent than ever, the deep red glow burning with ferocity as though they were filled with magma. Kordaz seemed oblivious to the Legion swarming around them, but Mikhain could not keep his gaze from sweeping left and right as the machines swept through the for'ard section of the bay. He looked back at Kordaz and realized that the Legion was no longer pouring through the bay entrance, their numbers limited to a few tens of thousands.

Kordaz came to a halt two cubits from where Mikhain stood. At such a short distance, the captain for the first time realized just how large and powerful the warrior was. In the past he had only been in close quarters with Kordaz when the Veng'en had been an ally or otherwise in chains and unable to strike. But now he was exposed to the full force of Kordaz's size and power, with nothing between them to protect him.

'You have not fled,' Kordaz growled.

'I have no reason to flee,' Mikhain shot back with an anger he did not entirely feel.

'You're a traitor,' Kordaz went on. 'You know what you have done.'

'I did what I had to do,' Mikhain defended himself. 'I know that you won't be able to stand there and say that you would have done any different had you been in my shoes.'

'You have no idea what I would have done,' Kordaz rumbled back. 'Just as you have no idea what I'm about to do now.'

Mikhain realized belatedly that the Legion had swarmed around them, giving them a reasonable amount of space but colonizing the deck, the walls and the ceiling far above. Completely surrounded, Mikhain had nowhere to run. Defeated and in danger of imminent death, Mikhain dredged what remaining courage he had from somewhere deep within.

'Do what you will,' he snarled. 'But the last thing I would do to sully my reputation is run from a Veng'en.'

Kordaz leaned forward slightly at the waist and his eyes glowed into Mikhain's. 'That will be your last mistake.'

From behind Mikhain, the General's voice rang out. 'That's enough, Kordaz. It's not your call to make. Call off the Legion!'

Kordaz looked past the captain and his eyes narrowed, Mikhain witness to the intensely detailed replication of his physical features as his metallic eyes mimicked the movement of real flesh.

'You're not in command here,' Kordaz growled at the General. 'This is between Mikhain and I.'

'He's already under arrest!' the General shouted back. 'We know what he did and he will pay for it one way or the other. Kordaz, we have to be seen to treat our own people with the same kind of justice that the Galactic Council expects to see or this is all for nothing. If you kill him like you killed Djimon, then they'll see us as nothing more than savages and we will all be blasted to oblivion by the council's warships.'

Kordaz glared down at Mikhain, standing almost a full cubit taller than the captain. 'He's not worthy of your defence! Men like him will bring about your downfall.'

'And men like us will uphold it,' Bra'hiv called back. 'Warriors like us, Kordaz. There is no punishment in death, no matter how prolonged the pain. If you kill him now it will be over, but then so will the rest of us. Let him go, let us deal with this and I'll see to it that he suffers imprisonment for the rest of his life.'

Kordaz's giant hands clenched and un–clenched at his sides, and his reptilian skin flickered with different colours as emotions rushed back and forth like violent tides. Bizarrely, the Legion around them seem to mimic Kordaz's emotions, surging and recoiling like the tides of some horrible black sea.

From behind Mikhain a softer, gentler voice called out.

'Kordaz, my sister once told me that she had never met a human being more humane than you,' Emma said. 'We can both hear the Legion, and we both know that it cannot be defeated by us alone. If Captain Sansin's ploy to gain the assistance of the Galactic Council fails, then everything is over. *Everything.*'

Emma stepped forward from the Marines and to Mikhain's amazement she walked directly through the protective shield of the microwave scanners, exposing herself to attack from the Legion.

'Emma, get back now!' Bra'hiv snapped.

Emma continued to move as though she had not heard the General, and within a few paces she reached Mikhain's side and stood alongside him before the Veng'en warrior. Kordaz looked down at her in silence, seemingly enraptured by her presence.

'This is not you, Kordaz,' Emma said softly. 'You and I both know it.'

The Legion around them suddenly began to scuttle and dance, and then wave surged towards Emma. Kordaz whirled and raised one gigantic arm and the Legion stopped where they were and retreated once more.

'Yes,' Emma said softly, 'they want me dead should I turn you. You control them, Kordaz. As incredible as it seems, the fate of humanity now lies in the hands of a single Veng'en.'

Kordaz stared at them for what felt like an age and then suddenly he struck forward, one giant leg landing alongside Mikhain as one huge arm swept across and smashed into the captain's chest. Mikhain felt as though he'd been hit by a meteor as his breath was smashed from his lungs. He lifted off the deck and flew through the air clean over the surrounding circle of the Legion. Mikhain hit the deck on his back and rolled over, his vision starring in his eyes and his breath rasping in his throat as he struggled to draw air into his battered lungs.

'Emma!' Bra'hiv bellowed. 'Get into cover, now!'

Emma hurled herself clear of Kordaz and scrambled into the Marine's defensive circle as the gigantic Veng'en spread his arms wide and let out a deafening roar, the throaty yet warbling warcry of his people soaring across the flight deck as he spread his arms to either side like a giant reptilian tree.

'He's lost it!' the General yelled. 'Take him down!'

The Marines whirled to aim their weapons at Kordaz and Mikhain scrambled to his feet and shouted with every last ounce of breath in his lungs.

'The bunker! Now!'

General Bra'hiv looked across at Mikhain and suddenly realized what he was getting out. Mikhain pointed to the bunker where launch crews hunkered down in a sealed environment as the flight deck atmosphere was evacuated during launch cycles and the Raythons, Corsairs and shuttles blasted off into space.

The general turned back to Kordaz and aimed his plasma rifle, but Emma hit out at the weapon and knocked it out of alignment.

'No!' She yelled. 'He's not attacking!'

The Legion were rushing upon the Marines but swerving around them, flowing like a black metallic river around the microwave shield as they rushed upon Kordaz.

'Marines, retreat to the bunker now!' Bra'hiv ordered.

Mikhain dashed away toward the bunker and jumped down the steps as he heard a blaze of plasma fire behind him, the Marines opening fire on the surrounding ring of the Legion and blazing a trail through them. Emma and the General both carried microwave scanners before them, the Legion falling back from the invisible beams as though parted by an invisible hand. Behind them, standing tall in the centre of the bay and with his arms still extended to either side, Kordaz stood as the Legion rushed upon him once more.

Mikhain dashed into the bunker and immediately sealed the flight deck entrance doors, preventing the Legion from escaping the bay. He looked up and saw the Marines and Emma dashing toward him, and behind them half of the Legion following them in a black wave.

His hand hovered over the bunker closing mechanism. Mikhain reached out for the buttons, his finger a hair's breadth away, and then he clenched his fist and pulled it back. Moments later, Emma and the General burst into the bunker with the Marines rushing in behind them.

'Seal it shut!' Bra'hiv shouted.

Mikhain sealed the doors of the bunker closed just as a cloud of Hunters hit the surface of the bunker outside, and his view through the windows was obscured by the metallic black bodies as they swarmed upon the thick glass.

'What about Kordaz?' Qayin snapped.

'He's given us a chance to escape!' Emma said. 'That's why he hit Mikhain toward the bunker! This is it!'

Mikhain looked out onto the flight deck and saw Kordaz once again consumed by a towering pillar of Hunters, only his arms extending out from either side as he stood rooted to the spot.

'They're holding him to ransom,' Emma whispered as she realized what the Legion was doing. 'We surrender, or he dies.'

The Marines and Mikhain all looked at the General, his gaze affixed to the horrific sight of Kordaz pinned within the towering pillar of machines intent on tearing him to shreds. In the moment of silence they all heard Arcadia's tannoy suddenly burst into to life.

'*Subluminal cruise in five, four, three—*'

General Bra'hiv stared at the machines for one moment longer and then he slammed a clenched fist down onto the control panel before him.

'Open the bay doors, launch protocol!'

The light in the bunker became suddenly polarised as Arcadia was dragged out of super luminal flight. Mikhain slammed one hand down on the emergency launch button that controlled both the magnetic launch catapults and the massive launch bay doors. In an instant there was a roar from one side of the bay as the enormous doors suddenly lifted and the air in the entire flight deck turned misty and opaque as the vapour within it was frozen.

In a raging torrent of whirling vapour the atmosphere within the launch bay was hauled out into the chill vacuum of space and the hundreds of Hunters scratching against the glass of the bunker were sucked out along with it.

Mikhain peered through the glass and saw the pillar of Hunters around Kordaz hauled out in one glistening black mass, the Vengen's body trapped within them as it tumbled out into the void. Mikhain watched it go, unable to take his gaze away from the Veng'en's terrible fate. A hand flashed past in front of him and slammed down on the emergency close button, and the bay doors rumbled shut almost as fast as they had opened.

From vents high in the ceiling of the bay fresh, warm air billowed in trembling clouds into the bay and the brilliant red lights warning of the vacuum outside switched to green as the atmosphere was reintroduced and the temperature once again stabilised outside.

General Bra'hiv stared at the now closed bay doors for a long moment before he finally turned and with one hand grabbed Mikhain's collar from behind and pushed him against the console.

'Captain Mikhain, you are hereby being placed under arrest on the orders of Captain Idris Sansin and the Board of Governors, for charges of treason and accessory to murder.'

Mikhain did not resist the General as he placed the manacles around his wrists behind his back, unable to tear his eyes away from the now closed bay doors.

***

XVI

'Subluminal speed in five, four, three, two…'

Captain Idris Sansin gripped the guard rail around the command platform as he listened to Lael counting down, and then suddenly the light in the bridge was polarised as Atlantia was dragged from super luminal cruise. The screens around the bridge flickered briefly and then suddenly data began streaming in. Idris glanced immediately at a screen showing Arcadia in close formation alongside Atlantia as the Morla'syn fleet rocketed out of super luminal cruise alongside them.

'Signals and communications not possible,' Lael reported immediately. 'They're still jamming us.'

'Position?' Idris asked the helmsman.

The helmsman glanced at his instruments and his eyes widened. 'We are approximately ten planetary diameters from Oassia.'

Idris turned as the main viewing screen flickered into life and before him he saw the broad open expanses of a water world. Like a perfect blue marble suspended in the black velvet of deep space, and illuminated by the warm orange glow of an ancient red dwarf star, Oassia was everything that one would expect the galactic capital to be. Only ten per cent of the world was covered in land, the rest of it a gigantic ocean with graceful polar caps and reefs and ribbons of cloud.

'They bought us directly into the system,' Andaim said with some surprise.

'Signal the Morla'syn immediately,' Idris ordered.

Lael sent the signal and the bridge descended into silence as they awaited a reply.

Idris could see the Morla'syn destroyers moving into position, tactically dominating the two frigates as their smaller sister ships formed an outer ring, one at each point of a triangle that surrounded the entire formation.

'Our signal has been blocked,' Lael reported. 'I suspect they are talking to the Galactic Council before we are able to.'

Idris nodded as he looked at the image of the destroyers surrounding them. 'Getting their version of the story in first, no doubt,' he said.

'We are tactically out of position and pretty much defenceless against any form of attack now,' Andaim reported as he scanned his displays. 'There's absolutely no chance of them allowing us to launch fighter screens.'

Even as Idris watched, the destroyers launched waves of fighters that spread out into a defensive screen of their own, the Morla'syn preferring automated drones to manned fighter spacecraft. Idris watched the world of Oassia as he sought to understand why the Morla'syn had brought them so close to the galactic centre's capital world, when their greatest fear surely was exposure to infection?

'We're too far away from Oassia to infect it directly,' he thought out loud. 'But close enough to be blasted into oblivion.'

'Maybe they are willing to talk after all?' Lael suggested.

As if in response the Morla'syn destroyers and the sister ships began breaking away from the two frigates, increasing their distance as the fighter screens also spread apart.

'We're being isolated,' Idris guessed, looking at how close Arcadia had been positioned alongside Atlantia. 'As long as we're in close formation we could be taken down from any angle and both ships hit at the same time.'

Andaim stood from his chair and joined the captain at the command rail. 'What's the plan?'

Idris shook his head as he attempted to fathom what was going to happen next.

'I want all Raythons on full scramble alert,' he replied finally. 'All Marines ready to propel borders. If this thing goes down badly, I'm not going out without fight.'

Idris thought he saw a brief smile cross Andaim's face as the CAG turned and began relying orders to the launch crews and fighter pilots assembled on the flight deck far below them. The captain returned his attention to the screens and moments later one of them flickered into life.

'Incoming signal,' Lael warned the captain, and Idris straightened his uniform just in time before the image of the Morla'syn commander, Veer, appeared once more on the screen.

'General Veer,' Idris greeted the captain. 'I see we have arrived. What happens next?'

'A mission from the Galactic Council is already on its way. You will be held here. You will be allowed to launch four Raython fighters as escorts for the incoming council mission. All other weapon systems will be powered down. Any deviation from these orders will be considered an act of aggression and will be met with lethal force. Do you understand?'

Idris nodded. 'I understand. Thank you for bringing us this far and allowing us the chance to state our case.'

Idris's gratitude was genuine, but at the same time he couldn't help needling the Morla'syn captain just a little with his tone.

'Your fate will be decided by the Council in just a few short hours,' the Morla'syn captain replied, and then added in an identical tone: 'Good luck.'

The screen flickered to blackness and Idris felt the eyes of the bridge crew upon him.

'What makes me think he was less than sincere?' Andaim asked from his command chair.

'I don't care about the sincerity of a race like the Morla'syn,' Idris replied as he turned and marched back to his own seat. 'All I care about is that the council hears our case. We have too many innocent lives aboard and nowhere else to go – anything other than asylum for them would be genocide and the council must know it. All we can hope is the Morla'syn have not painted us in a bad light.'

Governor Gredan stared at the captain. 'We severely damaged one of their vessels and left it adrift in deep space,' he pointed out. 'I don't suppose they're going to sing our praises.'

'I don't suppose they'll elaborate on *why* we damaged their ship so heavily either,' Idris countered. 'The Morla'syn are as guilty as anybody else in that engagement, and right now that's our only leverage over them. Let's wait for the council to get here before we make any further judgements on how this is going to play out.'

Idris turned to Andaim. 'Launch the Raythons, weapons cold, and have them intercept the council mission as soon as it appears on their scopes.'

Andaim relayed the command, and moments later on the main viewing screen Idris saw four Raythons rocketing away from Atlantia, their ion engines in full afterburner.

'Who have we got out there?'

Andaim glanced at the roster. 'Aryon and Miller, plus Teera and Evelyn.'

'Good,' Idris replied. 'We might need Evelyn's cool head if this goes bad.'

'New contacts, visual sensors, multiple craft inbound from Oassia!' Lael called.

Idris saw the four Raythons splitting into two pairs, tiny specks against the vastness of space as they swept out to the left and right. He could remember from his own combat training in the Phantoms to know that the two pairs of fighters were spreading out in order to sweep back in and move alongside incoming craft. His old eyes could see nothing against the bright flare of Oassia's pearly blue disc, so he simply stood and waited with his hands behind his back until finally he began to see a number of small specks moving against the planet's backdrop, gradually growing larger.

'*Atlantia this is Reaper One, diplomatic mission inbound, weapons cold.*'

Lael's reply was as calm and cool as Evelyn's.

'Reaper One cleared to approach, maintain weapons cold.'

'Weapons cold, Reaper one.'

Andaim peered at Idris. 'They're coming aboard?'

Idris was about to reply when Lael spoke once more. 'They're drones,' she said as she scanned her instruments. 'Passive sensors show no lifeforms aboard. They're not coming here – they want us to go there.'

'I'll be damned,' Idris said as he realized what the council intended. 'They're going to try to split our command structure, keep us weak and as far away from the frigates as they possibly can.'

'Divide and conquer,' Andaim agreed. 'If they fracture our command structure and keep blocking our signals, there's no way we can coordinate either defence or attack. We're sitting ducks here.'

As Idris watched the half a dozen ships flying towards the frigates from the planet below split into two, each formation approaching Arcadia and Atlantia respectively.

Idris gripped the command rail more tightly. 'Mikhain will be brought down on the other formation. It's quite likely they will interview us separately in an attempt to prevent us from working together. I didn't anticipate this.'

'If Mikhain is under arrest,' Andaim asked, 'then general Bra'hiv won't be able to release him. He'll be under the impression Mikhain will run if he gets the chance.'

Idris took a deep breath and stood up as he straightened his uniform once more and turned to Andaim.

'You have the bridge, commander,' he ordered. 'If there's a need for close combat with the Raythons I have no doubt you will make for your own cockpit, in which case Lael will take the bridge.'

Idris saw Lael grasp, her eyes wide although she did not look up from her displays. She had never commanded a vessel before her in a life, much less a gigantic frigate like Atlantia in a potentially life–threatening situation like the one they faced now, yet Idris had no choice but to leave her in command should Andaim be needed with his squadron.

'We'll take the lead once we get down to the planet,' Governor Gredan reminded the captain.

'Yes,' Idris replied, 'once the initial negotiations with the council have been conducted.'

'That wasn't part of our agreement!'

'That's correct,' the captain replied briskly. 'But the council is not asking for you, they're asking for myself and Captain Mikhain to speak.'

'A man who has murdered and is guilty of treason?!' Gredan protested.

'Accused of both,' Idris corrected the governor.

Governor Ayek raised her voice. 'Perhaps the captain is right, Gredan. We could be arrested on the surface if this doesn't work out, even imprisoned.'

Idris smiled at the prim little woman.

'You insisted on your right to be heard and claim to speak for the people: now's your chance to speak for their lives. You repeatedly insisted to have your say in the command and control of this fleet, and now I'm giving you that chance. You will accompany me to the surface and we'll state our case together to the Galactic Council. If we fail it may be the end of us, but our place as a unified front is down there on Oassia on behalf of every single soul aboard the ships.' Idris looked at her for a moment to let his words sink in. 'I do take it that you will not back down from this challenge, or shirk your duties in any way, after working so very hard to attain them?'

Governor Ayek stared back at the captain in horror, but she was aware of the bridge crew watching her expectantly.

'Of course, captain,' she uttered finally. 'I merely wish to respect the council's wishes and avoid upsetting them. Our future counts upon it.'

'Agreed,' Idris said as he looked at Gredan. 'Which is why I shall do the talking.'

Idris strode off the command platform and approached Governor Morle.

'Ishira, can I ask you to remain here aboard Atlantia? If things don't go well we may be in need of experienced starship captains to help Andaim and Lael run the ship in battle, as well as maintain at least one spokesperson for the people aboard. You're the only Governor with suitable experience in both fields – can I count on you?'

Ishira nodded without hesitation. 'I'll be here,' she assured him. 'Just make sure you get back aboard in one piece, all of you.'

Idris nodded and with one hand briefly gripped her shoulder in gratitude as he glanced briefly at a display screen to see the council mission's elegant diplomatic vessels cruising in a wide arc around Atlantia as they lined up for landing in the aft bays.

'Our ride awaits,' Idris informed the governors. 'Shall we?'

***

XVII

General Bra'hiv led the way back toward the bridge, Mikhain striding behind him with his hands manacled behind his back and the Marines split into two groups, half in front of their general and half behind the captive captain.

'What the hell are we going to do if Mikhain is imprisoned on Oassia?' Qayin asked the General as they walked. 'Arcadia will have no captain, and Lieutenant Scott is not experienced enough to take the command.'

'Be thankful that's not a problem that you'll have to deal with,' Bra'hiv replied. 'You're just a lowly private now and that's the way it's going to stay.'

Qayin allowed a grin to creep onto his features. 'You say it like you think I care?'

The general did not look at the towering convict as he replied.

'I know damned well that you care. It's all about power with you, and right now you've got none.'

Emma walked up alongside the General. 'This could go down badly. We have no idea what the Morla'syn are doing, or even where we are.'

The bridge doors appeared ahead, two Marine guards still standing either side of them. They looked at the approaching group of Marines and their eyes flew wide as they saw Mikhain manacled between them. Both soldiers however said nothing, parting to allow their general through. The doors opened and Bra'hiv led the way onto the bridge.

Arcadia's bridge was a hive of activity and the General could see from the display screens that they had arrived in the Oassia system, the beautiful blue marble of the planet displayed amid a galaxy of stars and glowing in the distant flare of its red dwarf parent star.

The bridge crew came to a halt at their stations as they observed Mikhain in chains behind the General, and the hustle and whisper of conversation faded away as the General approached Lieutenant Scott. Scott stood from the captain's chair and stared down at Mikhain in disbelief.

'What the hell is going on?'

'Captain Mikhain is under arrest for treason,' Bra'hiv replied without preamble. 'In the absence of any better qualified officers you are now in command of Arcadia.'

Scott stared at Bra'hiv as though he'd gone mad. 'General, I do not have sufficient authority to take command of this frigate without first obtaining the confirmation of Captain Idris Sansin and the Board of…'

'Shut up and take the captaincy,' the General snapped, cutting the lieutenant off in mid–flow. 'I don't have the time for bureaucratic considerations right now. You're in command, start acting like it.'

Scott glanced at Mikhain, who simply nodded in his direction.

'You're in command, XO,' Mikhain said. 'It's the right thing to do.'

'Pity you weren't thinking like that back on Chiron IV,' the General snapped over his shoulder at Mikhain before looking at the communications officer, Shah. 'Do we have any contact with Atlantia or the Morla'syn destroyers?'

'Nothing general,' Shah replied. 'We're under full jamming, all sensors except passive are disabled and all weapon systems are deactivated. Whatever they're planning, it's going to happen soon and there's nothing much we can do about it.'

'There's always something that can be done,' the General growled back. 'Activate the LANTERN system and start signalling them as soon as you can.'

The Lantern system was merely a series of lights that could be used manually to send subtle information back and forth between two vessels that were otherwise unable to communicate. The merchant version was well known, but the military used a different and well–guarded signals alphabet that the Morla'syn may not have encountered before.

'They may be looking for that,' Mikhain pointed out. 'It's why neither Idris nor I attempted to use the system to communicate.'

'Well, things have changed,' the General replied before he looked at the tactical officer. 'Ensign, did you detect any debris on the passive sensors leaving Arcadia when we dropped out of super luminal cruise?'

The tactical officer glanced at his displays and shook his head. 'Nothing, as far as I can tell.'

The general nodded in satisfaction. 'Good, with a bit of luck that means the Morla'syn also did not detect the Hunters ejected from the flight deck. As long as we're sure that Arcadia is clear of infection, both the Legion and Kordaz are now something we don't have to worry about.'

Bra'hiv briefly closed his eyes and hung his head as he realized how quickly he'd dismissed the Veng'en warrior's sacrifice. He spoke up so that every member of the bridge crew could hear him.

'Kordaz, a Veng'en, was probably one of the bravest warriors I've ever met. He was about to be tried for murder but in my opinion he should have been commended for bravery, because he acted with greater humanity throughout his time with us than many of us did ourselves.'

The general could not resist looking directly at Mikhain as he spoke his last, then he spoke to Shah once more.

'Use the lantern system, send a signal to Atlantia that says we are clean and that Captain Mikhain has been apprehended. That's all they need to know for now.'

Shah was about to send the signal when an insistent beeping noise was omitted from the panel and they looked up sharply.

'The Morla'syn are contacting us, they'll be on screen within seconds!'

The general grabbed Mikhain, turned him and pushed him off the command platform as he pointed sharply at Scott.

'You're up, Lieutenant. Make it sound good.'

Scott faced the display screen as the General and the Marines hustled themselves out of sight. Moments later the face of the Morla'syn General, Veer, appeared on the screen and he looked down at Scott.

'Your frigates have been brought out of super luminal cruise and a diplomatic mission is inbound from Oassia. Your captain is to board the mission and will be taken down to the surface along with Captain Idris Sansin of Atlantia. There, you will be able to state your case to the Galactic Council, and your fate will be decided.'

Scott took a moment to digest this new information.

'Our captain is unwell and I am currently in command of Arcadia.'

'Unwell?' Veer echoed suspiciously. 'Captain Mikhain seemed in fine mettle when he assisted in the near destruction of one of our destroyers only weeks ago. What illness has befallen him?'

'Fatigue,' Scott replied on a stroke of inspiration. 'The stress of commanding a frigate and being on the run for almost two years, under constant combat stress with no opportunity for rest and respite can sap the will of even the strongest men. I feel certain that he will recover soon, but for now he will be unable to accompany the mission to the surface.'

Veer turned his head and communicated off screen with some of his crew, his translator momentarily disengaged in order to conceal what he was discussing. Moments later, he returned his gaze to Scott.

'The Galactic Council will not recognise you as a leader and representative of the human race. If Mikhain is unable to join the diplomatic mission, then Captain Sansin will be forced to confront the council alone. The mission is inbound, ensure that it passes through your defences without incident and that your captain be brought aboard.'

The screen went blank and Scott let out a deep breath of air that he felt he had taken an hour before. He turned and looked at Bra'hiv.

'They're not going for it.'

The general cursed under his breath and began pacing up and down the bridge. Mikhain spoke softly from where he stood in his manacles.

'There's too much at stake for me not to go,' he insisted. 'This arrest is the work of the Board of Governors and I can face them at any time at trial. Right now, you and Captain Sansin need me down there on the surface.'

'So you can betray us again?' the General challenged.

'I betrayed a Veng'en and with good reason,' Mikhain shot back. 'At the time it was the right thing to do. Get over it.'

'Kordaz is more deserving of a place here than you,' Qayin growled nearby.

'Says the convicted murderer,' Mikhain replied.

'Silence!' Bra'hiv snapped. He stood for a moment on the bridge and gathered his thoughts. 'Lieutenant C'rairn, released the captain.'

C'rairn moved to the General's side and spoke softly. 'Are you sure about this?'

'Of course I'm not damn sure about it, but what choice do we have? Mikhain's right, there's too much at stake for us to screw this up before they've even got down to the surface.'

'That's right,' C'rairn said. 'But once he gets down there he's got every motive for not wanting to come back, and we can't reveal what he's done for fear of weakening our case before the council.'

The general nodded and then a grim little smile curled from the corner of his lips as he confronted Mikhain.

'When Idris sent Kordaz down to the surface of Chiron IV, you betrayed him because you thought that he would be a threat to our safety. I can assure you, captain, that the moment I even suspect that you have any intention of doing anything other than defending the human race even if it means your own sacrifice, I'll ensure the Galactic Council knows every single thing you've done since you joined this fleet. Your betrayals, your lies, and the lives lost because of them. If it's my last breathing act I will ensure that you spend the rest of your life rotting in a cell and awaiting the arrival of The Word and its Legion.'

Captain Mikhain held the General's gaze and nodded once.

'I wouldn't expect anything less.'

Bra'hiv scowled and turned away, then gestured for the lieutenant to release the captain. C'rairn stepped forward and moments later Mikhain's manacles were released and he stepped forward, rubbing his wrists.

'The missions craft are inbound, one Raython escort each from Atlantia,' Shah reported from her station.'

'Keep our Raythons aboard ship for now,' Mikhain replied, 'and ensure all passive sensors remain operational. If this goes badly we may need some kind of advance warning of...'

'You're no longer the captain!' Bra'hiv snapped.

Mikhain glared at the General, as though he were about to retort, but then he fell silent and stepped back. Bra'hiv looked up at Lieutenant Scott.

'You have the bridge and the command of Arcadia,' he instructed the lieutenant. 'Keep your shields down and your plasma cannons deactivated, but I want every single person on the ship ready for action at a moment's notice.'

Scott nodded, and then he turned and began giving orders to the command crew as the General grabbed Mikhain's arm.

'Remember, your every effort down there, or I will sink you. I'll be watching, one way or the other.'

Bra'hiv shoved Mikhain towards Qayin and the Marines and gestured toward the bridge exits.

'Ensure he gets aboard the diplomatic mission. Don't take your eyes off of him until he's gone, understood?'

Qayin loomed over the former captain and without looking he activated his plasma rifle, the magazine humming into life.

'Don't worry, he's not going anywhere but where we want him to.'

***

XVIII

'Reaper one copy, Atlantia?'

Evelyn heard the call as she banked her Raython over, the sleek fighter descending alongside Atlantia's hull. She watched as a small convoy of diplomatic vessels lifted off and departed Atlantia's launch bay.

'Reaper one, pass message.'

'You're instructed to accompany the diplomatic mission down to the surface, with Reaper Two. Weapons are to remain cold, shields down.'

'Roger that, wilco.'

Evelyn glanced out to her right to see Teera's Raython formating alongside her.

'Looks like we're going for a ride.'

'I don't like this,' Teera replied. *'Sure, I want to still be down there on Oassia and not stuck aboard Atlantia, but I don't trust the way they're doing things. We've got our arms behind our backs and no way of defending ourselves.'*

'They're nervous,' Evelyn soothed with a confidence she did not feel. 'Once we get down there and state our case I'm pretty sure they'll come round to our way of thinking.'

'I'll believe that when I see it,' Teera replied.

Evelyn eased back on her throttles as she allowed her Raython to drift into close formation alongside the sleek diplomatic vessels as they turned toward Oassia, several planetary diameters away. The diplomatic craft were all painted a glossy white, their slender flanks illuminated by external lighting making them easily visible even in deep space. These were not warships and likely only possessed light armaments, and they all carried a blue triangle emblem that signified diplomatic vessels of the Galactic Council. To fire upon such a vessel was considered a galactic crime that was pursued and punished with the absolute conviction of all concerned.

Evelyn had no idea who was aboard the craft, and could only assume that Lieutenant Scott had taken the place of Captain Mikhain aboard Arcadia. As she watched, two of the diplomatic craft moved very slowly together, one rolling inverted and positioning itself beneath the other before closing in.

'They're docking,' Teera observed.

Evelyn could tell that the precision and speed with which the two aircraft docked meant that they were under automatic control, for no pilot could manoeuvre with such accuracy in such a short space of time.

Evelyn glanced at her instruments and a clock in her cockpit estimated their time of arrival at Oassia's atmosphere as just over one Etherean hour.

'We'd best settle in,' she said as she checked her fuel gauges. 'Switch over to autopilot and slave our guidance systems to the lead diplomatic craft. We may as well let them do the navigating once they accelerate to cruise velocity.'

'*Roger that,*' Teera replied.

Evelyn switched over her navigation computer, locking it in to the diplomatic craft, and then stretched her legs out as she folded her hands in her lap and tried to relax. Whatever the Galactic Council had in mind, they were going to have to face it one way or the other.

*

Captain Idris Sansin sat in a luxury leather recliner, a polished glass table before him that contained a variety of fruits, drinks and other refreshments probably laid on for high–level diplomatics rather than the captains of former prison vessels. The other eight recliners around him were vacant, the Board of Governors instructed to occupy another section of the craft for reasons that Idris could not fathom. Despite his suspicion about the way they were being treated he found himself rather enjoying the solitude of the cabin, a rare moment of peace in what felt like a lifetime of war.

The craft's gravity, like that of Atlantia, was created using magnetically charged panels beneath the decks. This worked well for walking about, but Sansin like all experienced space travellers had to take care as he plucked fruit from the bowl and popped it into his mouth. Tiny globules of liquid water drifted up through the air from the bowl and he was careful to mop them up with a napkin as he ate.

The fruits tasted like nothing he could recall, perhaps because they were native to a planet he had never before visited, or perhaps because they had gone so long without adequate fresh food and vegetables that his body craved them more than usual. He was almost relaxed when he felt the pressure change in the cabin as an entrance door hissed open somewhere behind him. Idris turned and saw Mikhain stride into the cabin.

Idris hid his disappointment at the intrusion as he stood from his seat but said nothing as Mikhain walked towards him and gestured to one of the seats opposite.

'Mind if I take one?'

Idris regarded his fellow officer for a long moment before he replied. 'Be my guest.'

Mikhain took a seat and reached out for some of the fruits in the bowl opposite. Idris sat back down and looked out of the craft's viewing ports at the dense starfields and Evelyn's escorting Raython as he waited for Mikhain to say something.

'General Bra'hiv's Marines completed their mission,' Mikhain said finally.

'I wouldn't have expected anything less.'

Mikhain sighed heavily and took a deep breath. 'Why did you do it, Idris?'

'I think that's the question we should all be asking you.'

Mikhain shook his head and rubbed his temples with one hand. 'You know damned well why I did it, why I disagreed with you entrusting such a valuable mission with Kordaz, why I thought the whole crusade was a step too far and could have cost us everything.'

'Every step now is a step too far that could cost us everything,' Idris replied. 'We're stronger together and infinitely weakened by any hint of betrayal or discord.'

'That's how you've always seen it,' Mikhain said. 'It's your way or the highway. Any discord is some kind of betrayal, any disagreement evidence of enmity. Yours is a dictatorship, Idris, and it always has been.'

'That's why it's called the military.'

'Well it's not the military any more.'

'Don't give me the soft-touch approach,' Idris shot back. 'We've been over this before too many times, especially with the Board of Governors. They're aboard, you know?'

'How did Gredan get himself a ride?'

'I had to cut a deal,' Idris replied. 'If Kordaz could be used to hunt down the infection aboard Arcadia…'

'… then Gredan and the governors got me?' Mikhain finished the sentence for Idris.

'And Kordaz walked free,' Idris added.

Mikhain sighed, overwhelmed by the scale of his downfall. 'So you placed a Veng'en murderer's welfare above my own? Charmed, I'm sure.'

'Losing Kordaz and arresting you served the same purpose,' Idris replied.

'So it would seem, but Gredan's only service is to himself. This is about his power, nothing more. He doesn't speak for the people.'

'The governors as a whole do,' Idris replied. 'This ship is automated, but the council's drone insisted we board in separate sections which are isolated from each other. I'm assuming that the Galactic Council wants to keep us separated before meeting us on the surface, which means that they intend already to split us along military and civilian lines.'

'And yet they let our ships dock, and us to talk?'

'I don't pretend to understand everything that they're doing, but they're obviously nervous of us and our intentions. They may suspect that we are infected, or that we're agents of The Word, or that we're as dangerous as any other species that they may have distanced themselves from during their long history. Who the hell knows?'

Mikhain glanced out of the window beside his seat and saw a Raython formating close by.

'They're letting us travel to the planet despite suspicion an infection?' Mikhain asked rhetorically. 'That doesn't make any sense at all.'

'It surprises me,' Idris replied. 'They may intend just to vaporise us, and there's nothing that we can do about it.'

Mikhain shook his head. 'If they were going to do that they would have done it by now. This isn't about destroying us. Whatever they want, they're pretty much going to get. We have no way out of this now.'

'And nor do you,' Idris pointed out. 'By now half of Atlantia will know what you did. You do realize that, don't you?'

Mikhain nodded, staring straight ahead, but he said nothing.

'There have to be consequences. The Board of Governors will not let it pass, and the Galactic Council will certainly want to know everything that's happened aboard our ships. We have to tell them everything in order to gain their trust, and that's what Gredan's angling for, complete transparency.'

'I understand.'

Idris looked at Mikhain for a long beat and then he leaned back in his seat. Ahead, through the viewing port to his left, he could just about see the shoulder of the planet Oassia appearing, looming large before them. The horizon glowed a soft blue against the deeply shadowed surface, the light from the red dwarf star yet to reach that section of the planet, but already he could see the glowing lights of cities far below, and closer still small specks of light moving slowly this way and that as civilian and military vessels moved between the massive orbiting stations and military bases high above the planet's surface.

Mikhain fell silent, and Idris decided to leave him be as he watched with fascination as the diplomatic craft descended toward Oassia. From his vantage point he got his first glimpse of true civilization for the first since leaving Ethera's orbiting prisons so many years before.

The space traffic increased as they closed in on the planet, large mining vessels departing orbit and vanishing in bright flares of light as they leaped into super luminal cruise. Further down, smaller shuttles moved between gigantic orbiting stations shaped like large eggs of steel, rotating on their axes. Although the egg-shaped stations appeared upright, Idris knew that the interiors were on their sides, the rotation providing natural gravity for the countless thousands of species that lived aboard them. Streams of space traffic entered and exited landing bays in a busy but orderly flow, the station catching the light of the star in a deep orange glow.

The entire scene seemed full of peace, as though life were continuing as normal throughout the galaxy, but Idris knew that conflict was only as far away as the nearest of The Word's Legion and that the inhabitants of this world must know it too.

The diplomatic craft descended past the orbiting stations and began automatically changing their attitude as they decelerated. Moments later Idris felt a faint vibration through the craft's hull beneath him as it entered the atmosphere of Oassia, and he looked out to his left to see Evelyn's Raython in the distance, its nose high and bright red flames flaring from its hull as it deflected the enormous energy of orbital re-entry.

The re-entry process lasted only a few minutes, and Idris marvelled at the sight of a bright blue ocean world below, vast ranks and valleys of cloud casting deep shadows over broad oceans as the sun rose over the horizon, the entire scene lit with vivid brushstrokes of copper and gold, vast towering clouds spread like angels wings across the horizon.

He felt the craft slow as ahead he saw an enormous city standing above the ocean waves, immensely strong legs and braces supporting its unimaginable weight and vanishing into the ocean's depths far below. Clouds drifted alongside its flanks, atmospheric turbulence buffeting the wings of the craft as it descended towards a landing pad, one of hundreds encircling the enormous city. Idris could see spires, tower blocks, flying vehicles and even pedestrians as the diplomatic craft slowed to landing speed and lined up with the landing pad ahead. Moments later, the craft shuddered as it touched down perfectly on the pad, Evelyn's Raython settling nearby.

Idris let his eyes drink in the spectacular city, virtually every single building and walkway transparent, the sunlight bathing the entire metropolis in orange light that glinted as though the city were built from burnished gold.

Idris unstrapped and stood up from his seat as beside him Mikhain did likewise, and they stared at each other for a brief moment.

'A unified front,' Idris said, 'no matter what the consequences.'

'Agreed,' Mikhain nodded.

***

XIX

Evelyn unclipped her harnesses and flipped a switch on one of the panels beside her in the Raython's cockpit. The canopy opened and a brisk breeze of wonderfully fresh air gusted around her as she removed her flight helmet and clambered out of the cockpit.

The landing pad was large enough to accommodate both the diplomatic vessels and the Raythons with room to spare, and as Evelyn climbed down from her fighter's cockpit she saw the boarding ramp of the diplomatic craft lower to the sound of escaping pressurised air and a brief cloud of vapour.

From within she saw the Board of Governors stride down onto the landing pad, and then moments later she saw Captains Sansin and Mikhain following them out of the craft. Evelyn managed to cover her surprise at seeing Mikhain and instead approached Idris directly.

'Evelyn, notice anything odd?' Idris asked her.

'You mean apart from us coming down here weapons cold, leaving the frigates at the hands of the Morla'syn, and with no idea what the Galactic Council will do with us? No, nothing out of the ordinary. I only detected a single scan using passive sensors, which identified us as human occupants, that's it. What about you, Teera?'

'Same for me,' Teera said as she approached, her skin not a dissimilar blue to Oassia's vivid sky.

'Never mind the scans,' Councillor Vaughan growled. 'What's *he* doing here?'

Vaughan pointed at Mikhain, who was standing with his hands behind his back observing the governors with guarded interest.

'No alternative,' Idris replied. 'The Galactic Council recognises him as a captain and would accept nobody else in his stead.'

Governor Ayek glanced at the bay exit, which remain sealed.

'Nobody to greet us,' she observed. 'This isn't the reception I was hoping for.'

The whine of ion engines caught Evelyn's attention and she looked over her shoulder to see two of the Galactic Fleet's *Skyhawk* fighters flash by in close formation, low enough and close enough to the landing pad for her to see the pilots looking down at them as they passed by.

'They're checking us out,' she said. 'It shouldn't be too long now.'

As if in answer, the landing pad exit opened with a hiss and a double line of armed troopers jogged out. Morla'syn infantry, their pallid skin stark against dark navy blue combat suits and heavy long–barrelled plasma rifles, jogged in pairs and split up to surround the landing pad. Every one of them was at least eight feet tall, and despite slim physiques they moved with extraordinary grace and speed.

As soon as the troops were in position, their rifles activated, new figures emerged from the bay entrance. Evelyn watched in amazement as the various species walked, crawled and in one case fluttered into view.

She glanced at Idris and saw the same look of amazement on his face despite his efforts to cover it up. It had been many decades since the Icari had brokered *first contact* between humans and other species, an event that had heralded the beginning of mankind's journey into deep space. Many species had been encountered, but it was already becoming obvious that the degree to which humanity had been exposed to them was limited, for Evelyn did not recognise any of the species confronting them now. The last of them, an amorphous blob of gelatinous transparent liquid encased in a thin membrane, travelled out to meet them on a motorised platform. The blob pulsed and glowed with bioluminescent light not dissimilar to Qayin's luminous tattoos, and although Evelyn could see no evidence of true eyes, ears or mouth, there was bizarre intelligence to the way in which the light glowed within its body, as though she recognised emotions there in the same way as she would recognise muscle movements in the face of another human.

At the head of the delegation was the Morla'syn General Veer, flanked by two of his lieutenants. Behind them were two Gaollian dignitaries, quadrupedal creatures with solemn, bulbous blue eyes that belied their ferocious nature. The only other species that Evelyn recognised among the twelve that greeted them was a Veng'en, his reptilian form covered in a thin one–piece jump suit of velvety purple material, the collars laced with a thin line of gold that seemed to represent perhaps a form of royalty from their homeworld, Wraiythe.

Veer halted a few cubits away from Captain Sansin.

'Greetings, captain. I apologise for the cautious nature of your transportation here, but as I'm sure you can appreciate there is much for us to fear.'

'I understand,' Idris replied. 'There is much I wish to tell you and the council and I do not believe we have much time.'

'The council is convening as we speak,' Veer informed him. 'They have agreed to hear your plea, although I feel it is unlikely that they will be willing to put much stock in the presence of two human frigates. Your ships are no match for The Legion, and nothing in comparison to the Galactic Fleet.'

'Which is why we are here,' Idris pointed out in reply. 'We are stronger together.'

If Veer agreed with the captain he showed no signs of doing so. Instead, he turned to one side and gestured for Sansin, Mikhain and the governors to follow him toward the bay entrance.

The captain caught Evelyn's eye with a meaningful gaze and she hurried to catch up as they began walking.

'Keep your eyes open,' he suggested in a whisper. 'There's something I don't like about this.'

'How come they haven't searched our ships?' Evelyn asked in a whisper. 'The Legion could be aboard for all they know.'

'I don't know,' Idris admitted. 'This all seems incredibly hurried, like they wanted out us out of the way as soon as possible.'

'Do you think they know about Lazarus?'

'Not yet, but it's only a matter of time until their deep scans of Atlantia figure out that there's something aboard. What's worse is that with you here and Emma aboard Arcadia, Lazarus has no power at all. At least if we came under attack there's the chance that he might be able to act in our defence.'

'So you're finally coming round to Emma's way of thinking then?'

Idris kept looking ahead as they walked. 'Let's just say Lazarus is beginning to represent the closest thing to an ally we have in a galaxy filled with enemies.'

Evelyn looked about her as they entered the reception bay. The interior was filled with transparent walkways of armoured glass, allowing the pedestrians a vertiginous view of the rolling oceans far below and an equally dizzying perspective of the soaring heights of the city spires that reached high into the cumulus clouds drifting through the blue above.

'Oassia is a city built upon the belief that transparency is the key to noble leadership,' General Veer said from where he walked alongside Idris, his strides slow to keep pace with the smaller humans. 'The city is deliberately designed to hide nothing and promote trust in member species.'

'Would have been nice for us to have been a part of it sooner,' Idris pointed out with a touch of irony in his voice.

'Your representative on the council was vocal in his support for human interaction with the greater cosmos, captain, but the General consensus was that humanity was a danger to other species, not yet mature enough to master and control its impulsive desire for domination, nor its paranoia and mistrust of strangers.'

'You're talking about traits that have evolved over millennia,' Evelyn pointed out, her voice translated into a series of grunts and growls that the Morla'syn could understand. 'They can't be simply erased overnight. It takes time.'

'Indeed,' Veer agreed. 'Time that you had not yet spent overcoming your shortfalls as a species. Too often your kind reaches too far over the cliff of endeavour, and falls to your doom in the pursuit of things that you cannot understand.'

'And the Morla'syn didn't before your species was taken on by the Galactic Council?' Idris challenged.

Veer did not reply except to glance at the captain as though somehow offended.

The transparent walkway crossed the vast city, most of the buildings perhaps a hundred cubits below where Evelyn walked, the rest towering into the sky around them like gigantic steel spears. Streams of craft travelled between the towering spires, their sleek hulls gleaming in the sunlight as they moved this way and that. Across myriad transparent walkways Evelyn could see species of all kinds moving to and fro, and she for the first time realized the sheer extent of the Galactic Council's reach into the galaxy, of the importance of Oassia as a galactic hub and a mixing place for species of types she could barely begin to imagine.

'How big is the known galaxy beyond here?' Evelyn asked Veer. 'How much has been kept from us?'

General Veer looked down at her and for the first time she saw something approaching humour sparkling in the towering Morla'syn eyes.

'Far more than you can know,' he replied, and then the humour faded slowly. 'Which is why it must be protected without compromise. The Galactic Council on Oassia cannot be responsible for allowing the Legion to spread further than it already has. This is our corner of the universe and we must both defend and if necessary destroy it to protect species that we do not even know exist yet. That is the responsibility of all species under the governance of the Icari.'

'And where are these Icari?' Evelyn asked. 'We've heard so much about them over the decades, but I've never known anybody who was ever met an Icari.'

The Icari were known to be tenuous beings, consisting mostly of light information, that had forged an existence in the atmospheres of giant stars. Nobody in all of human endeavour had yet discovered how intelligence could have developed in such a hostile environment, so devoid of the normal processes that had led to the evolution of intelligent species across the rest of the universe. But the Icari, virtually invulnerable to any kind of weapon, had evolved during immensely ancient times, perhaps even since the evolution of the very first stars. Their invulnerability had made them devoid of the need to conquer, for they had spread as simply as had the chemicals of life throughout the universe since time immemorial: the Icari were ubiquitous to the universe, as common as stars and yet rarely seen.

'Direct communication and observation of the Icari is generally considered to be impossible for most species,' Veer explained. 'It is more the case that they communicate on occasion with the Galactic Council with generalised direction, in the sense that they give an impression of where the council's governance should lead the species under its command. The rest they leave to us, and observe from a distance. The Icari do not wish to directly control the evolution of our species, merely to adjudicate and advise. Their wisdom is unquestionable.'

'And do they condone the destruction of the human race?' Idris challenged Veer.

The Morla'syn shook his head. 'On this they have made no comment. As I said, they advise when necessary but do not directly interfere unless it is absolutely required.'

'It's absolutely required by *us*,' Evelyn snapped.

Veer slowed as he approached a large, transparent vessel that was shaped like an elongated teardrop and carried the blue triangular markings of the Galactic Council.

'This vessel will carry us to the Galactic Council chamber,' he informed them. 'No weapons are allowed in the chamber.'

Veer waited expectantly, and with some reluctance Evelyn pulled her plasma pistol from its holster and handed it over to one of the Morla'syn guards.

'I hope they're being as transparent as they claim to be about everything,' she murmured to the captain as she watched her pistol being taken away.

'You and me both.'

***

XX

'What range are they at?'

Andaim Ry'ere sat in the captain's seat on Atlantia's bridge and looked at the tactical displays. Atlantia was portrayed as a green icon in the centre display, Arcadia close alongside and their escorting fleet of Morla'syn destroyers portrayed in red and located further out in a loose ring.

'Fifteen thousand cubits,' Lael reported. 'They're holding station, weapons hot, and the scanning is continuous. I'm detecting multiple frequencies, some of which are in the ultra–high range. Some I can't identify at all.'

Andaim dragged a hand across his chin as he looked at the Morla'syn destroyers and tried to figure out what they were doing. None of them were close enough to fire immediately upon the two frigates, and he could tell that they would have time to raise shields, power the plasma cannons and begin defensive manoeuvring in order to attempt an escape from Oassia. In short, they were not being penned in as before.

'Do we have any records of Oassia possessing large bore surface to orbit plasma cannons?'

Lael shook her head. 'Nothing that I'm aware of, but Colonial records regarding Oassia are scant. No Etheran fleet ever was granted permission to enter the system.'

Andaim scanned the instruments for a moment longer and then he made a decision. 'Divert all available power to long–range passive sensors. I want to know what's out there beyond our patch of space.'

'Stand by,' Lael replied.

Andaim watched the scanners flicker as the range altered and they began detecting signals from further out, fleeting glimmers of other spacecraft and of orbiting stations many times larger than even than the Morla'syn destroyers. Andaim slowly got out of his seat and walked toward the viewing screen, and as he did so he captured a brief glimpse of a shimmering object orbiting on the far side of the planet.

'What was that?'

He pointed at the fleeting return, and it vanished almost as instantly as he had seen it.

'Analysing the data,' Lael reported. 'Stand by.'

Andaim waited and watched the viewing panel but the strange signal did not return.

'There's not much to go on,' Lael replied finally as she scrutinised the display. 'The sensors detected a very large object, almost continental in size, possibly a metallic emission on the spectrometer. It appears to be concealed on the far side of the planet in an orbital position the mirror image of our own.'

Andaim glanced again at the position of the Morla'syn destroyers. 'What's our orbital velocity?'

'We are matching Oassia,' the helmsman reported, ' in geo–stationary orbit.'

'Damn,' Andaim murmured. 'They're hiding something there.'

'It could just be another orbiting station,' Lael suggested. 'Atmospheric disturbances sometimes distort signals, stretching them out and giving them an appearance much larger than they actually are.'

'True, but they don't become the size of continents,' Andaim pointed out. 'The Morla'syn are keeping us here in exactly the opposite position to whatever is on the other side of that planet.'

'What are you thinking?' the helmsman asked.

'I want to know what they're hiding, fast.'

Andaim thought back to the encounter with the Morla'syn in deep space, when they had been forced to abandon the wreck of Endeavour. General Veer had said then that the Galactic Council was amassing a fleet, one of the biggest ever created, in order to fight The Word and its Legion. They had said that they intended to destroy Ethera if it was required, and with it every last trace of humanity.

'Lael, set passive scanners to detect ion traces instead. Direct everything we have at where the anomalous trace appeared.'

'Stand by,' Lael replied.

Almost all modern spacecraft of suitable size possessed antigravity devices that allowed them to travel through atmospheric conditions, and also allowed them to maintain steady orbits without the use of constant fuel. However, no planet's gravitational field was entirely uniform: there were fluctuations, patches of higher and lower gravity, the effects of magnetic energy in planetary fields and even the negligible effects of constant micrometeorite impacts that would affect over time the orbit of any craft no matter how large. To counter these effects, all spacecraft would periodically fire either retro rockets or ion engines in order to maintain a perfect orbit and sustain the required velocity and trajectory.

'I've got it,' Lael reported and then looked up at him. 'You were right. There's a very large area with trace signatures of ion exhaust comparable to the anomalous signature we detected moments ago.'

Andaim grinned, but his triumph of deduction was tempered by an anxiety that he could not conceal from his voice. 'It's a fleet, a big one. And they're not telling us about it.'

'General Veer did mention just such a fleet when we last encountered the Morla'syn,' Lael said. 'Maybe they've got further with it than we thought.'

'Then why the hell aren't they out there and engaging the Legion wherever they find it?' Andaim demanded. 'What are they waiting for?'

Nobody on the bridge crew answered him, and perhaps for the first time Andaim began to feel the true burden of command, the price of obtaining the captaincy of a major frigate in a war situation. There was nobody else to turn to, no Admiralty to ask for help, nobody to take responsibility for what to do next but himself. Unless…

Andaim drew himself up to his full height as he considered the implications of what he was thinking. No doubt the Board of Governors would be appalled that he would even consider it, but right now he could not think of any other way of analysing the situation better, and he was completely unable to take action on his own. The moment the frigates lifted their shields or charged their plasma cannons, the Morla'syn would be on them.

'Lael, you have the bridge.'

'Where are you going?' Lael asked, a touch nervous.

'Down to the pilot's crew room,' he lied. 'I want to brief them quietly on what we discovered.'

Andaim stepped off the command platform before Lael could reply and walked out of the bridge, but instead of turning towards the crew room he turned instead aft and began travelling down through the ship. He boarded a shuttle pod and allowed it to transport him across the vessel and down towards the storage depots. Within two minutes, he was standing outside a heavily guarded depot deep within the bowels of the ship.

The Marine guards standing outside the depot moved aside as he approached, both of them saluting.

'At ease,' Andaim saluted back. 'I need access. The situation is changing rapidly, and without Captain Sansin here I need all the assets I can get on my side.'

The Marines stepped forward without question and tapped in their access codes, and the depot door opened with a hiss. Andaim strode in, blinking as his eyes adjusted to the blue glow of the holographic projection unit within. Dr Ceyen Lazarus turned to face Andaim, a look of some surprise on his face.

'Lieutenant, what brings you down to my humble prison?'

Andaim waited for the depot doors to hiss shut behind him, and then he approached Lazarus.

'How much do you know about where we are?'

Lazarus shrugged. 'I know that we were required to head for the Galactic Council and I can tell that the mass–drive is now disengaged, so I assume we are in orbit around Oassia, but I know nothing more than that.'

Andaim nodded.

'We're at ten planetary diameters, escorted by Morla'syn destroyers and being constantly scanned. Despite the measures we've put in place to prevent your access to Atlantia's systems, which will also help block their scans, it's likely only a matter of time before they discover your presence here.'

'Where is captain Sansin?' Lazarus asked.

'On Oassia, with Captain Mikhain and the Governors. They're preparing to plead our case to the Council Chamber.'

'And if I am discovered..,' Lazarus said.

'Then we could find ourselves accused of infiltrating The Word into the Galactic Council, or similar,' Andaim finished the sentence for Lazarus. 'Whatever trust we may foster within the council will be lost if we are found to be deceiving them.'

Lazarus offered Andaim a kindly smile. 'You wish me to be handed over to the Council?'

'No,' Andaim replied, 'because they're not being entirely honest with us either.'

'How so?'

'We've detected a large fleet in geo–synchronous orbit on the far side of Oassia, the biggest I've ever seen. Analysis of what data we can uncover is still coming in, but at first glance I'd say maybe five hundred large vessels.'

Lazarus's eyes widened as he stared down at Andaim. 'That's a serious force, do you know if they're military?'

'Can't say from this range and we're on passive sensors only under orders from the Council. If we start active scanning it may be seen as an act of war.'

'They don't want you to detect the fleet,' Lazarus said. 'But why bother? You already know that the council has been considering a war–footing against the Legion. There's no reason to hide the fleet.'

'That's what's bothering me,' Andaim said. 'They base their criticisms of the human race on our lack of transparency and supposed tendency to deceive – that'll be demolished if we can prove they're hiding something from us also.'

Lazarus grinned, his hands folded before him as he stood in front of Andaim.

'Your sense of tactics is admirably shrewd, commander,' he said. 'But do you make your play now, or do you hold off until you receive word from Captain Sansin?'

'Idris is down there in the company of Mikhain, who now has every damned reason to try to protect himself at the expense of us. I wouldn't be surprised if he were to inform the Galactic Council of your presence here in return for his own asylum on Oassia.'

'Mikhain's is a soul obsessed with self–preservation,' Lazarus lamented, 'as are those of so many human beings, and understandably so. We wish to live. However, the council will see any such act as one of cowardice and it may serve to strengthen Idris's position.'

'We can't rely on that,' Andaim insisted.

'I agree. What would you have me do?'

'You said that you cannot carry out any act without Emma's acquiescence?'

'That is true – I inserted the requirement into my own program. It cannot be revoked.'

'We're being jammed and cannot send signals to Arcadia, but you and Emma could both hear the Legion's presence despite the jamming.'

Lazarus nodded as he realized what Andaim was driving at.

'You think that if I can communicate with Emma, I can take control of Atlantia and protect us? Perhaps, but the problem will be whether Emma can hear me.'

'I need to know what's hiding on the other side of Oassia,' Andaim insisted. 'If I can give you control of Atlantia's systems would you be able to hear the Legion?'

Lazarus stared at Andaim for a long moment. 'You would trust me with such control?'

'You handled Atlantia well enough against the Morla'syn before,' Andaim pointed out. 'I'm sure you can handle a secure communications channel and avoid detection by the Morla'syn.'

Lazarus nodded.

'Enter the standard frequency into my terminal and open a link to Atlantia's communications terminal, but I cannot promise anything. Emma's sensitivity to the Legion is not as developed as my own.'

***

XXI

The Galactic Council Chamber was a vast amphitheatre that resided within the very heart of the city and was entirely surrounded by transparent walls, floor and ceiling. Evelyn felt her heart lurch in her chest and her legs weaken as her mind struggled to orientate itself to the vertigo–inducing panorama around her.

The chamber contained some five hundred seats arranged around the amphitheatre in stacked galleys, those seats variously designed for the bi–pedal, quadrupedal and non–limbed species who now populated the chamber. Almost full to capacity, Evelyn figured that this appearance by the scant remains of humanity was as important a meeting to the rest of the known cosmos as it was to the humans at the heart of it.

'Looks like we've drawn quite a crowd,' Teera said as they stepped out into the centre of the amphitheatre.

Evelyn almost hesitated as she looked down. Beneath her boots were several inches of perfectly clear glass, and below that a two hundred cubit drop to the vast ocean below. She looked up and almost lost her balance as she saw a huge, clear dome above them, the blue sky above flecked with clouds. Here in the heart of Oassia no towering city spires obscured the view of the heavens above, whether by day or by night.

The walls of the chamber were likewise transparent, and displayed the city around them in all of its technological glory, a reminder of all the many species represented here. No politician, no governor or councillor, could speak or act in this chamber without being both seen and heard by every resident of the planet if they were so inclined to listen in.

General Veer led them to a podium, likewise transparent, in the centre of the amphitheatre, where several discreetly hovering translator *bots* and sensors would amplify their voices and translate them into the countless dialects required for so many differing species to communicate effectively.

The commingled conversations of a thousand races, their homeworlds scattered across countless light years, filled the dome of the amphitheatre and made it seem as though the waves far below were making sufficient noise to be heard by Evelyn as she stood to one side and allowed Idris to take the lead. Mikhain, perhaps chastened by his recent arrest, likewise stood back discreetly as Idris followed Veer up onto the podium.

Evelyn watched them both, and realized with a sudden belated gasp that all of the air traffic outside had ceased motion and that countless pedestrians and wheeled vehicles had stopped. Literally, it seemed that the entire population of Oassia was watching the chamber. The only thing she could not see beyond the chamber itself was evidence of a single human being.

'You really think we're the only ones left now?' Teera whispered to Evelyn, evidently having realized the same absence of humanity. 'I haven't seen a single human being on Oassia since we arrived, apart from us.'

Evelyn shook her head. 'Nor me. I can't believe that nobody else thought to come here. I'm sure we would have done ourselves, if Captain Sansin hadn't believed that we could fight back on our own.'

The buzz and whisper of the countless conversations faded like an errant wind into a deep silence as thousands of eyes, ears, antennae and sonar detecting whiskers were directed down toward the podium.

'Councillors,' General Veer said, his voice carrying across the vast auditorium and echoing around them. 'I give you the last survivors of the human race, led by Captain Idris Sansin of the Atlantia, and Captain Mikhain of the Arcadia, two surviving frigates of the Etheran Colonial Fleet.'

A deep silence followed, and Evelyn briefly wondered whether the captain was supposed to get the proceedings underway. With everything so rushed and with no Etheran ambassador to guide them, she had no idea of the accepted protocol.

Any doubt was dispelled when a bloated, jelly–like species in a tub–sized seat rose up before the podium, bioluminescent algae flickering deep within its torso. The same creature that had accompanied Veer out onto the landing platform when they had arrived, Evelyn could see no eyes to speak of, merely diaphanous black dots either side of a bulge atop its form. Almost as transparent as the amphitheatre itself, the creature pointed one tentacle like appendage at the captain and its translated dialect, a series of deep and tremulous blasts like the sound of horns underwater, echoed around the chamber.

'Captain Sansin, my name is Rh'yll, and I am both a native Oassian and spokesperson for the Galactic Council. Your crew and dependents have been allowed into the Oassia system in order to state your plea for asylum from the terror you call The Word, and its Legion. This welcome has not been granted lightly and there are many here who would like to see what remains of your species eradicated before it can cause any more damage to the galaxy we share. What do you plea on behalf of your people?'

Captain Sansin lifted his chin and spoke clearly.

'That we are granted the same humane rights as any other species represented by the council. That we are granted asylum and a safe haven from which we can launch an offensive against The Word.'

A sudden awful cacophony filled the chamber, and Evelyn winced at the raucous noise as it ebbed and echoed around them. Captain Sansin remained admirably silent and still as what Evelyn could only assume was laughter among the chamber died down.

Rh'yll peered down at Sansin. 'The council finds your notion amusing, captain.'

Idris glanced around him at the surrounding chamber. 'I would like to know what they find so amusing about the genocide of an entire species? Would they laugh if, tonight, ninety per cent of their own people were slaughtered?'

The remaining chortles fell silent as Rh'yll's gelatinous form reared up once more.

'The council is not here to be judged, it is here to *pass* judgement,' he rumbled back.

'The definition of a dictatorship,' Idris replied calmly.

This time the sounds of gasps and clicks of horror fluttered like a live current across the chamber and Evelyn winced again.

'You insult us when you have come here for help?' Rh'yll growled.

'We did not come here for help,' Idris snapped back. 'We came here for asylum, to state our case, to plead for a safe haven for the civilians who travel with us. We came here in search of a safe place for them to stay in order that we could take the fight back to our enemy without fear for their lives.' Idris looked around him at the chamber. 'We came here for the chance to fight back, so that none of you would have to. This is our mess, but we cannot clean it up with one hand tied behind our backs.'

Rh'yll remained motionless for a long moment as he stared at the captain and then looked up at the species populating the countless seats in the surrounding amphitheatre.

'This council has represented our known and shared territories within this galaxy for over two thousand of your Etheran years,' Rh'yll said. 'Worlds have risen and fallen in that time, species joined and later become extinct due to their conflicts and mistakes, their technological errors born of a desire to overreach what they were capable of managing. But never, in all that time, has any endeavour by a single race threatened the entire galaxy, perhaps even the universe, as this Legion that your humanity has created.'

Rh'yll shifted position, his glowing innards flickering at the movement as he pointed at Idris.

'You have, as a species, already lost a great deal. Vessels travelling through or nearby Ethera detected the millions of distress signals coming from the system and warned us of the apocalypse. We know well, all of us, of the terrible slaughter that must have occurred on your homeworld and of the losses that you have all endured. What you ask of us now, captain, in light of all that humanity has already done, is to throw our lot in with the handful of human beings remaining and say that we shall stand alongside you against this tyrannical force that you created, and risk our lives doing so.'

Idris shook his head.

'We did not create The Word,' he argued. 'It was created by people long before we were born, and it was designed to emulate what this very council champions as the ideal governance – devoid of greed, of malice, of the desire for revenge or dominion.'

'A machine is not a species!' General Veer raged. 'A machine cannot be trusted to have any biological creature's best interests at heart, especially not one that has attained self–awareness. Look around you captain, at all of these species with whom humanity shares the cosmos. All of them achieved their status with time and with effort and mutual respect, not by displacing responsibility for their actions onto a computerized dictatorship.'

Evelyn could see Idris grinding his jaw as he formulated a response.

'It's hard to see how my forebearers could have developed mutual respect when we were imprisoned within the Icari Line, denied exposure to the richer cosmos beyond, subjected to scare tactics to prevent us from travelling further.'

'For good reason,' Rh'yll replied calmly, 'as we have now seen.'

'Are you going to help us or not?' Idris snapped.

Rh'yll reared up in his seat once more, and Evelyn saw his gelatinous body shudder as though he had been struck.

'The council feels unanimously that humanity has done quite enough damage, and that the threat that comes from the Legion that you created cannot be dealt with adequately by the few humans left remaining. Your fleet is weak and obsolete, your crews tired and dejected, your supplies low and your enemy growing stronger with every passing moment. This is not an act of punishment, captain, it is an act of mercy. Your vessels will be impounded and your crews, military and civilian, transported to a safe haven as you have requested while the council organises a response to the Legion's threat.'

Evelyn could not help herself.

'You're burying us?!' she gasped, the microphones hovering alongside the podium sensitive enough to detect her exclamation. Two of them suddenly zipped across to her side to better pick up her response.

Rh'yll and several hundred delegates all turned to look at Evelyn.

'We're removing the root cause of the problem,' he responded.

DEFIANCE

'You're also removing the cure,' Idris fought back. 'Evelyn here is one of a very few individuals who is naturally immune to the Legion's Infectors.' A gasp went up from the delegates as Idris went on. 'That immunity has been synthesized and used to vaccinate all of our people against the Legion. We have learned much on our journey. To hide us away now would be to abandon the very knowledge needed to conquer The Word.'

Rh'yll peered suspiciously at Evelyn.

'How does a human being develop a natural immunity to machines?' he murmured. 'Machines are mechanical, not biological, and thus could not be identified by any known killer cells.'

Evelyn thought that Idris would reply on her behalf, but instead the captain stood to one side on the podium and beckoned her to join him. Gingerly, Evelyn stepped up alongside him and spoke to Rh'yll.

'It's a long story but given the circumstances we face, I believe that you should all know the truth.' She looked at the captain for acquiescence, and he nodded once. 'I am effectively the great–granddaughter of a clone, one designed specifically to defend against The Word's Infectors.'

More gasps, this time louder and more alarmed, conversations rippling through the council.

'You are a creation of The Word itself?' Rhy'll rippled in horror.

'No, merely the descendent of one,' Evelyn replied. 'The creator of The Word, on his deathbed, realized what he had done, the danger he had created. He thus created a defence against it, and inserted that defense into the human population in the hope that it would grow and come to prevent any apocalypse. He failed, but the creation lives on in me and in my sister.'

More horrified exclamations and Rh'yll visibly shuddered. 'And you know all of this, *how?*'

Evelyn swallowed. Although she knew of the danger of revealing everything to the council now, honesty seemed by far the best policy. There had been too many lies, too many deceptions that had held humanity back on its quest for freedom from the Legion. Now was the time to come clean and begin a new journey.

'The creator of The Word, Doctor Ceyen Lazarus, lives on as a holographic projection. He uploaded his consciousness before his death in order to combat the spread of The Word.'

An uproar surged from the crowd, and despite the coalesced commotion of hundreds of different dialects, Evelyn could detect the sense of panic poisoning the atmosphere around them. Rhy'll appealed for calm and the delegates fell silent once more.

'You realize, do you not,' Rh'yll said, 'that you just broadcast to every single living intelligent being in the Oassia system that you are willingly collaborating with the Legion?'

'Lazarus is not the Legion, and we believe that he is key to understanding the nature of The Word – know your enemy, as we often say.'

Rh'yll stared down with his tiny black light sensors and then spoke softly.

'Know your enemy indeed,' he replied. 'An idiom we have applied to humanity on every occasion possible.'

'We can fight The Word,' Idris insisted. 'We have the skills and the knowledge to turn the tide of this war if you'd only have some faith in our determination to rid the galaxy of this…'

'Thing that you've created?' Rhy'll cut across him. 'This monstrosity that is consuming entire worlds even as we speak? You believe that you can destroy The Word, eradicate its Legion, and yet you have no knowledge of what it has achieved. You have been running blind, captain, and behind you is the wake of your species' hideous legacy.'

Evelyn gasped as from nowhere appeared a massive, shimmering hologram that filled half of the amphitheatre and allowed every member of the council to see the display. It was a beautiful, glowing series of lines and lights that she recognised instantly as the local area of the galaxy in which they all lived, several tens of thousands of light years' worth of stars, nebulae, black holes and stellar nurseries.

'You want to know what you are facing?' Rhy'll challenged them. 'This, captain, is what you believe that you alone can fight.'

As Evelyn watched, so from one side of the three–dimensional map began to spread a dark, scarlet patch. Evelyn saw Ethera, the Core Systems, Caneeron and other local planetary bodies suddenly consumed by the red glow as though the galaxy were bleeding from some horrific wound.

The red patch spread, not evenly like a blood stain but in jagged red spikes, like the tentacles of some unspeakable beast as it writhed and coiled and reached out to consume and destroy. The cancerous stain swallowed whole worlds and began to fill the amphitheatre around them, the light from the sky streaming in from above stained a dull red that reflected off their faces as though they were once again aboard Atlantia and under battle conditions.

The stain expanded to contain almost a quarter of the galactic plane, the Veng'en homeworld of Wraiythe almost within reach of its tentacles, and now a thin stream like a blood–red knife blade reached out to the small world of Akyron V, on the edge of the Galactic Council's space and where Atlantia had encountered the Legion in orbit.

The amphitheatre fell silent as the gathered species observed the sheer magnitude of the Legion's expansion in the space of the past three Etheran years. Evelyn looked at Captain Sansin and felt dismay settle heavily upon her shoulders as she saw the captain's upright stance slacken and his head hang low as he realized the true scale of what they faced.

Rh'yll looked down at them, his form now resting back in his tub–like seat.

'This is what we all face,' he said solemnly. 'This is the legacy of mankind, captain, and we will tolerate further contamination of the Galactic Plane no more. Your frigates are hopelessly out–classed and would be annihilated should you attempt to face the Legion in open battle. Surrender completely to our forces now and we will attempt to protect your people as best we can. Refuse, and we shall have no option but to destroy your frigates where they are.'

Idris, his shoulders sagging, stood for a moment in deep contemplation, the silence drawing out around him. Then, slowly, he looked up at Rh'yll.

'I'm sorry councillor but I cannot do that,' he said slowly. 'If you take the stance that our refusal to cooperate will result in our destruction, then we have gained nothing by coming here. We seek allies, not enemies; assistance, not ultimatums. If you cannot help us, then we shall go on our way.'

Rh'yll's gelatinous form reared up once more, but before he could reply Governor Gredan strode to the platform and one flabby arm pointed at Idris.

'That's no longer your call to make!' he roared.

***

Dean Crawford

XXII

'It's too damned risky!'

Governor Ishira Morle walked alongside Andaim as he marched down to the storage depot and the Marines guarding the entrance made way for him to pass. The doors hissed open and Andaim walked inside.

'We don't have any other way of getting a good look at that fleet and what they're hiding,' Andaim replied. 'We're sitting here at the mercy of a Council that claims to be absolutely transparent and yet is anything but. If they permit us to ship the civilians down to the surface, I want you to do it.'

'Deception isn't their game,' Ishira insisted.

'And the Icari Line?' Andaim shot back. 'Was that not a deception?'

'They feared what The Word might become,' Ishira pointed out. 'Rightly so, as it turned out. You can hardly blame them.'

It was Lazarus who replied as they moved to stand before him.

'Ishira is right. The council indeed fears The Word and likely enforced the Icari Line barrier due to that fear. They knew what might happen, and in truth I wish they had been more vigorous in sharing their fears with us, with humanity. It might have spared us the losses for which we now grieve so deeply.'

Andaim walked up to Lazarus. 'Have you established contact with Emma?'

'I can sense her,' Lazarus replied, 'but I cannot communicate with her. The Morla'syn are using a complex frequency modulation algorithm that I cannot break, possibly due to quantum programming. I do not believe that I will be able to pass any form of message to Emma from here.'

Andaim turned away from Lazarus. 'Then there is no way to warn the captain unless somebody goes down there.'

'Which would be a suicide mission,' Ishira pointed out. 'Any attempt to get one of our ships around the far side of the planet would be a one way trip ending in a bright flash and families sending flowers. It's just not possible.'

Andaim turned to Lazarus. 'Would you be able to shield a craft from their scanners?'

Lazarus shook his head, and Andaim wondered briefly whether the scientist could actually feel his body or whether the movement was some kind of deeply programmed habit, a remnant of the human being that Lazarus had once been.

'No craft can leave either Atlantia or Arcadia without being detected,' he replied, 'and besides the Morla'syn would never… allow… anything…'

Lazarus's voice trailed off and his gaze became vacant, in as much as a hologram's gaze could, as he stared at the opposite wall. Andaim frowned as Ishira stepped forward.

'What is it?'

Lazarus did not reply but Andaim could hear the processors in his terminal humming with activity, and the scientist's holographic lips were trembling with barely whispered words as he seemed to vocalize the new information streaming in toward him.

Suddenly, his eyes flared wide and he looked directly at Andaim.

'Time has run out,' he said sharply.

'What do you mean?'

Lazarus turned, looking through the walls of the depot as though peering through Atlantia's hull and out toward the distant stars beyond.

'The Legion,' he replied finally, 'it is here.'

Andaim felt a tremor of consternation pulse through his abdomen as he paced closer to the scientist's hologram.

'Where away?'

Lazarus frowned in concentration, his aged brow creasing and his eyes squinted tightly shut as he focused on some unheard data stream.

'It's not coming directly from the Legion,' he whispered as he replied. 'It's being relayed somehow, from farther afield. There's a distress signal going out, very faint, and a reply coming back much stronger. Something here is communicating with the Legion.'

Andaim's eyes widened and then he whirled and dashed from the depot with Ishira in hot pursuit. Andaim hit a button on his wrist–com and yelled into it.

'Bridge, battle stations, shields up! Warn the Morla'syn that the Legion is coming!'

*

Emma stood in silence on Arcadia's bridge, Lieutenant Scott sitting in the captain's chair and looking as though he would rather be anywhere else. Military officers like him were not used to sitting about and doing nothing, especially not after the last three years of being in a constant state of battle–readiness, and now he fidgeted as he scanned the tactical displays for some signal from Captain Sansin.

'It won't be long now,' she said to him.

'That's what I was thinking an hour ago,' Scott replied with a nervous smile and turned to Lael. 'Anything?'

'Total comms silence,' she replied. 'We're still being aggressively scanned, but no word from the Morla'syn. Either they haven't found anything or they're keeping it to themselves.'

Lieutenant Scott exhaled noisily and thumped one fist down on the armrest of his chair.

'Damn, I hate all of this sitting about.'

'Hurry up and wait, I think our captain used to say to us,' Emma said. 'My father used to say the same things when he…'

Emma's lips turned numb suddenly and she reached out for the grab rail as she lost her balance and swayed from one side to another. He eyes lost focus and she felt her breathing constrict in her chest as a wave of bitter cold swept over her. She saw Arcadia's bridge turn on its side and then felt a distant thump as she landed on the deck.

'Emma?!'

The voices sounded distant, muted. She could see, but at the same time as the blinking lights of the bridge she could see an immense, brutally cold darkness, and the wailing of countless tiny voices warbling in her ears.

'Emma?'

The cold and the voices vanished and she sucked in a deep breath as though awakening from a terrible nightmare. Lieutenant Scott looked down at her, his features pinched with concern as he helped her up into a sitting position.

'What happened? Are you okay?'

Emma nodded, rubbed her head with one hand as the memory of the brutal cold and the voices crying for surcease faded away in her mind.

'I don't know what happened,' she whispered as her eyes focused once again on the surrounding bridge. 'I heard voices and saw something…'

The voices echoed in Emma's head, a dialect that she could not identify, not human and definitely not Morla'syn, but both guttural and precise, almost like the sound of…

'Kordaz's translator,' she gasped.

Emma shot to her feet as a realization bolted like lightning through the field of her awareness.

'Kordaz!' she almost shouted.

Lieutenant Scott took her shoulders in his grasp and looked into her eyes. 'You're on the bridge, Emma, you're okay. Kordaz isn't here, he's dead. We ejected him out into…'

'Into space,' Emma cut the lieutenant off, 'surrounded by Hunters. But they can survive in space for a limited amount of time. I heard them. I could see through Kordaz's eyes, could feel his pain and the cold. They're keeping him alive and they're calling for help!'

'They're what?' Scott echoed in disbelief.

Emma's features collapsed as she replied. 'I heard a reply,' she whispered. 'The Legion is coming. They know where we are.'

Suddenly, the tactical officer called out.

'Atlantia's raised her shields!' he cried. 'She's engaging her ion engines!'

Lieutenant Scott whirled for the command platform as a sudden blaze of activity filled the previously silent bridge.

'Atlantia's signalling battle stations, full alert and we've got incoming signals from the Morla'syn!' Lael yelled, her voice almost shrill with anxiety.

'On screen!' Lieutenant Scott snapped.

The screen flickered into life and a Morla'syn commander leaned close to the lens, his features twisted with indignation.

'Stand down, Arcadia, or we will be forced to fire!'

'We have evidence that the Legion is close by!' Lieutenant Scott roared back, the bridge bathed in dull red light and the faces of the command crew glowing in the light from their screens as though they were aflame.

'What evidence?!' the Morla'syn commander snapped. 'We have detected no signals either incoming or transmitted from this system, and no sign of the Legion or…'

'I've got a fix on it!' Lael called across the bridge, cutting the Morla'syn off, 'bearing eight six one, elevation two five.'

Emma turned and saw Lieutenant Scott staring at the tactical display as Arcadia's optical sensors zoomed in with immense magnification on a tiny target several tens of thousands of cubits away from their position.

Emma felt her heart leap in shock as she saw a small, revolving ball of black material that looked innocuous enough, like a distant chunk of space rock, but for the metallic glint that caught the light of the red dwarf star.

'I'll be damned,' Lieutenant Scott uttered in amazement.

'It's got a heat signature,' Lael informed him. 'It looks like the Hunters are revolving around in a small ball, generating heat in the interior.'

'And keeping Kordaz alive,' Lieutenant Scott uttered in fascination, and then looked at Emma. 'You were right.'

'Who is Kordaz?' the Morla'syn demanded. 'What is going on here?!'

Lieutenant Scott glanced at the bridge crew around him and he realized that now there was no option but to admit the truth.

'Kordaz is a Veng'en warrior who was infected with the Legion,' he explained. 'It's a long story but he fought off the infection and has been helping us ever since. Arcadia carried a small number of Infectors aboard, which Kordaz fooled into assisting him, sacrificing himself and allowing us to eject the Hunters out into space. Unfortunately, it seems that they have survived their marooning.'

The Morla'syn stared at Lieutenant Scott in disbelief. 'The Legion, it is here. You brought it *here*?'

'We didn't bring anything here,' Lieutenant Scott snapped in reply. 'The Legion would have followed us anyway, but we've detected their signals.'

'How?' the Morla'syn almost shouted, and Emma saw the destroyer's bridge also dim its lights to a deep red as they prepared for battle. 'How can you be communicating with The Word?!'

'We're not!' Lieutenant Scott shouted back. 'We have somebody aboard who can hear them when they're close. Two people in fact. One of them is on the bridge with me now, and the other is…' Scott broke off as he realized just how impossible it would be for the Morla'syn to understand their position, to believe that humanity really only wanted to fight back and atone for its mistakes.

'Is *what*?'

Lieutenant Scott sighed. 'Is a hologram, a resurrected scientist. He was responsible for creating The Word, and is now helping us to destroy it.'

The Morla'syn commander glared at Lieutenant Scott for a moment longer, and then the communications screen went blank.

'They're charging weapons, captain,' the tactical officer warned. 'What should we do?'

Lieutenant Scott looked desperately at the tactical displays and felt the burden of command weigh down upon him with incredible force.

'Battle stations!' he yelled. 'Follow Atlantia's lead!'

***

XXIII

The immense crowd in the amphitheatre turned their heads, antennae and light-sensitive receptors toward Gredan as Idris whirled to see the governor pointing at the captain with anger distorting his features.

'That man is a liar, and Captain Mikhain a murderer who was recently arrested and should by now have been put on trial by his peers!'

A rush of gasps and clicks of astonishment rippled through the watching crowd as Gredan stepped up onto the platform, Vaughn and Ayek following him with Meyanna Sansin and attempting not to be intimidated by the vast auditorium around them.

'And who are you?' Rh'yll demanded.

The governor introduced himself and his colleagues as Idris hissed at him.

'Do you have any idea what the hell you're doing?'

'Telling the damned truth!' Gredan snapped out loud, buoyed by his own self-importance. 'It makes things happen, captain. You should try it some time.'

'You gave your word that you would allow me to do the talking. You're playing with thousands of human lives, the last survivors of our world!' Idris growled.

'As are you,' Gredan shot back, 'but at least I am not deceiving the council while I'm doing it!'

Rh'yll's amplified voice overpowered both of them.

'Look at you,' he rumbled. 'Even on the eve of your own destruction, in the wake of the annihilation of your world, you cannot form a stable alliance and speak as one spirit, one species.'

Before Idris could respond, Gredan faced Rh'yll.

'My apologies, councillor,' he soothed, 'but these are testing times for all of us and a conflict of purpose has erupted since our arrival here at Oassia. I wish that I could stand here and speak to all of you while united with my fellow human beings, but I and my fellow governors have been repeatedly side-lined by the captain and his military staff. I speak for the people, the ordinary men and women still trapped aboard Atlantia and Arcadia, whose voices are rarely heard and never listened to.'

'That's a lie,' Mikhain snapped.

'You would know a lie when you hear one, captain,' Gredan pointed out with a fearsome grin of righteousness. 'You've become something of an expert at deception.'

'We're not here to discuss the finer points of military command aboard…'

'We're here to barter for our lives!' Gredan shouted. 'And you're acting out up here without any regard for the people you purport to protect, in the company of a man who has already killed to save his own skin and a woman who is as much a part of The Word as the damned Legion!'

Gredan's flabby arm shot out to point at Evelyn, and a rush of horrified gasps went up from the surrounding crowds of dignitaries as around the rim of the amphitheatre the Morla'syn guards lifted their weapons from port–arms and aimed them at her.

'You'll kill us all,' Idris snapped at Gredan, 'and all for your perceived few moments of fame, your last chance at glory.'

'Better to die an honest man,' Gredan shot back, 'than a deceitful one.'

'What is going on here?' Rh'yll demanded, glowering down at them both. 'How can this woman be a part of The Word? Is this auditorium now infected?!'

The watching dignitaries recoiled in their seats, those closest to Evelyn covering their mouths and other proboscis with hands and appendages of all kinds.

'Evelyn is a patriot and a skilled fighter pilot,' Idris said defensively. 'She is not a part of The Word. This man's oratory is designed only to obtain power and influence in your eyes.'

Gredan smiled grimly. 'Did the good captains' mention that Evelyn is also a former murderer, and one of many hundreds of convicts aboard Atlantia and Arcadia?'

More horrified exclamations from the watching crowds and Rh'yll shook his head.

'No, they did not.'

Gredan's florid features positively glowed with satisfaction as he turned and looked at Idris. 'They have also declined to inform you of the presence of The Legion aboard both vessels along with the very creator of The Word himself aboard Atlantia.'

Now the effect on the crowd was undeniable. A roar of outrage soared through the auditorium and Rh'yll almost levitated out of his seat as he sought to control both the dignitaries within the amphitheatre and the immense crowds watching from outside and across the planet.

'The Legion is not here,' Evelyn assured the crowd. 'Lazarus is slaved to the commands of myself and my sister and cannot act without our acquiescence, a safety measure to prevent Lazarus from the same fate as The Word. Lazarus is in effect a reincarnation, digital but still human.'

Rh'yll appealed for calm from the delegates surrounding them.

'Both of the human frigates are under constant surveillance and are at least ten planetary diameters away from Oassia,' he called soothingly, his appendages waving up and down to calm the crowd. 'At any sign of hostility, the Morla'syn destroyers guarding them will not hesitate the blast them into oblivion.'

'If they get chance!' a voice shouted from what looked like some kind of insectoid creature, its bulbous tail shimmering as it vibrated in a symphony of communication that was translated into a digital–sounding oratory 'We all know how fast the Legion can strike!'.

'What if the destroyers themselves become infected?!' shouted another, a squat, bear–like creature with ageing fangs. 'They too could turn against us!'

'The destroyers are fully microwave–shielded,' Rh'yll assured them. 'None of the Legion can pass through their hulls even if they were attacked.'

Amid the raucous from the crowd Captain Sansin's train of thought slammed to a halt as he heard Rh'yll's words echoing back and forth through his mind. He froze in motion as he looked up at Rh'yll.

'How would you have known that microwave shielding affects the Legion?' he asked.

The noise from the crowd almost drowned Idris's voice out, but enough of the dignitaries heard it to quieten down. Rh'yll's bulbous form shuddered as he went on.

'There is nothing to fear from any infection by the Legion at this time,' he assured the crowd, ignoring Idris. 'Our objective here is to understand what the humans have aboard their ships and act accordingly so that…'

'I said, how did you know to use microwave shielding on your ships to prevent infection?' Idris repeated, calmly but with enough force to overpower the councillor.

'We have our own scientists too, captain,' Rh'yll replied. 'They have made advances of their own.'

Idris took a pace closer to the councillor.

'The Legion has not reached the Oassia system yet and your ships, by your own admission, have not penetrated far toward Ethera for fear of spreading the infection. Yet you now also claim them to be impregnable to the Legion? Both statements cannot be true, so you must have learned from somebody else how to protect your vessels and to implement the technology so quickly. I ask you again: how can this have been done?'

Rhy'll shuddered and an appendage pointed at Idris.

'It is *you* on trial here, captain, not the council.'

'I thought that we were here to plea for assistance, not be on trial,' Idris countered, 'and in any case in a trial the accused is warranted a defense. Have other humans entered the Oassia system before us?'

Rhy'll shuddered yet again as though agitated by Idris's persistent questioning and his bioluminescent lights fluttered and weakened.

'You have lied to us, Captain Sansin. If what Governor Gredan says is true you have concealed the presence of the Legion aboard your vessel and it is now docked just ten planetary diameters from our planet.'

'Which a moment ago was a safe distance according to you,' Idris countered. 'Where are the humans who told you about the Legion's weakness against directed microwave radiation?'

Rh'yll ignored the captain as he looked at the Morla'syn guards.

'Sentries, have Captain Sansin and his escort transported to the holding rooms. Ensure that they are given every courtesy while the council passes judgement on their fate, and order the Colonial frigates to begin sending their people down here for asylum. They shall be offered safe haven until this is all decided.'

The towering Morla'syn soldiers moved in with their weapons at the ready. Idris ignored them and spoke louder.

'Where are the other humans that entered the system, councillor?' he demanded. 'What have you done with them? What are you hiding from us, from your own people?!'

'This council is adjourned,' Rh'yll called, and even as Idris opened his mouth to protest further the hovering microphones zipped away from him and his voice was silenced, dwarfed by the vast expanses of the amphitheatre.

'Governor Gredan,' Rh'yll called, still with access to the microphones, 'would you and your colleagues accompany the councillors and I? There is much that we must discuss.'

Gredan's face melted into something approaching ecstasy, pride bursting from every pore. With grandeur, he bowed over his prodigious waist.

'We would be honoured, councillor.'

'You're making a mistake, Gredan,' Idris snapped as he was forced off the podium by the Morla'syn guards, the watching ranks of dignitaries already standing up and walking, crawling or slithering toward the exits. 'They're not telling us everything! Don't let the people down here!'

Gredan cast Idris a sideways look.

'You're done, Sansin,' he sneered. 'We have asylum, which means our people are off your damned ships. This is a government matter now.'

***

Dean Crawford

XXIV

'I don't like this at all.'

Ishira Morle directed her harshest glare at Commander Andaim, who merely grinned back at her.

'This is the only way. Gredan and his motley crew trust only you because you're also a governor, voted in by the people. The best way to get a look at that fleet is for you to pilot the craft that takes the first wave of asylum seekers down there.'

'They're not going to let us plot a course anywhere near that fleet,' Ishira pointed out.

Andaim affected a look of mock offence. 'You don't think I've got that covered?'

'And should we be sending people down there at all? We don't know that we can trust the council.'

'We don't have much of a choice,' Andaim said as they walked toward Ishira's freighter, parked inside Atlantia's bays. 'We can't run without leaving Idris and the others behind, and we can't refuse the help we've come here begging for. We're lucky they haven't boarded us and taken control.'

Ishira signed and looked at the freighter as she approached. *Valiant* was a mining vessel that her father, Stefan, had owned since his teenage years. Inherited through the family, the freighter was an ungainly chimera of long–range haulier and rock mining vessel. Four hefty, pivoted landing claws supported a long, barrel–shaped fuselage that tapered toward a series of four stacked ion engines. Ventral strakes gave the ship some aerodynamic qualities for atmospheric flight, and folded back in bays along her length were long robotic arms designed to manipulate and explore rock formations deep in the Tyberium Fields, vast expanses of asteroids orbiting the Etheran system's outer limits.

As they approached Stefan Morle walked out to greet them, oil stains already marring his prosthetic arm and a broad grin plastered across his face.

'Are we ready to go then?' he asked.

Stefan was never happier than at the helm or the engine room of Valiant and it showed. He cleaned his right hand with a rag he held in his metallic left hand, then tossed it cheerfully to one side.

'We're ready,' Ishira replied unhappily. 'Where are the civilians?'

'The first group are already aboard,' Andaim replied. 'Gredan insisted that we send no military escort with you, and that the Morla'syn had it all in hand.'

'Gredan's getting in way over his head,' Ishira said. 'And how come Captain Sansin isn't calling the shots down there?'

'I don't know,' Andaim said as more civilians appeared on the flight deck. 'Maybe he's letting Gredan in on the act to rein in his attempts at a power grab.'

'That's the thing,' Ishira agreed, 'we don't have any power now, but Gredan won't see it.'

A young girl broke from the ranks of humans, Donnassians and lumbering Ogri, her long brown hair flying as she dashed to Ishira's arms and was swept up into her embrace.

'Are we safe now mom?' Erin Morle asked as she hugged her mother's neck tightly.

Ishira glanced at Andaim over her daughter's shoulder and sighed.

'Safer than we were, I hope,' she replied as she set Erin down. 'Get aboard and strap in, okay honey?'

Erin dashed off up the freighter's ramp, Ishira watching her.

'She'll be fine,' the CAG promised. 'Are you going to stay down there with them? The captain asked you to stay aboard Atlantia, and I don't want you to leave, but it's up to you. You're also a governor after all.'

Ishira snorted and fastened her flight jacket.

'You think I want to be part of Gredan's self–congratulating roadshow? It's no longer a board of governors anyway, it's just Gredan and his plans for future power.'

Andaim nodded and leaned in close to her, dropping his voice as the civilians filed past and up Valiant's ramp.

'The long–range passive sensor array we modified has been installed aboard Valiant, and will autonomously transmit short–burst data streams on different frequencies back to Atlantia that will be extremely difficult for even the Morla'syn to detect let alone monitor. As soon as you're into the atmospheric descent, deactivate the array so that the transmissions aren't detected by ground based radar. You're merely the conduit for the information stream – Valiant won't be transmitting anything unusual, it'll look just like normal radiation from her engines, or so Lazarus says.'

'Roger that,' Ishira agreed, and then shook Andaim's hand.

'Come back,' Andaim urged. 'We may need you here more than you realize.'

Ishira turned and strode up the boarding ramp with her father, who hit the close button as they reached the top and stood to watch the ramp rise up.

'You know that they might not let us leave,' Stefan said quietly above the murmur of conversation deeper inside Valiant, coming from the several hundred civilians aboard. 'Once we're all down there.'

'Can't do much about that,' Ishira replied, and saw her daughter waiting for her in the cockpit. 'Right now, Oassia is our best bet for a future, right?'

Stefan nodded.

'On the face of it, but then why are they hiding things from us?'

The ramp slammed shut and hissed as the seals activated. Ishira checked that there were no breaches and then turned for the cockpit.

'Let's find out, shall we?'

For the first time in a long time, Ishira settled into the captain's seat at the controls of Valiant, and before her through the windshield she saw Atlantia's flight deck, the ranks of Raythons parked ready for flight, two more on the catapults on the for'ard deck ready to be scrambled.

Erin sat in the co–pilot's seat, the harnesses too large for her slight frame. Ishira looked down at her, and Erin smiled confidently and grasped the back of Ishira's hand.

'It'll be fine mom,' she promised, 'you'll see.'

Ishira smiled back, conveying what she hoped was a picture of calm, and then she strapped in and began her pre–start checks. The process of getting Valiant started for flight after being cooped up on the flight deck for so long came back quicker to her than Ishira would have thought, and within a few minutes the ion engines were warmed up and all on–board systems working normally.

'Let's see what's out there,' she murmured to Erin and then transmitted to Atlantia. 'Valiant, civilian transport, ready for visual departure.'

'Copy Valiant, cleared for departure, call when clear of the bay.'

Ishira acknowledged the call and then deactivated Valiant's magnetic clamps. The freighter lifted gently off the deck as she watched the ground crews hurry to their bunkers and the doors seal shut, and then moments later the main flight deck doors rumbled open as the atmosphere in the bay was evacuated in a rush of white vapour and ice crystals.

Ishira took a deep breath and then eased the manoeuvring throttles forward. Valiant cruised overhead the parked Raythons and along the flight deck, tracking a line of flickering lights that guided her out of the bay and into the bitter cold vacuum of space, Atlantia's massive bow extending above and ahead of them.

Ishira turned left to clear the frigate's bow and saw the massive form of Arcadia looming close by, her vast hull glowing a dull orange in the light from the distant star.

'Morla'syn,' Stefan said as he pointed at two huge destroyers looming just outside of weapons range, watching over the two frigates. 'They're hanging back, but close enough to attack within moments.'

'If they don't trust us, then why offer the civilians asylum so quickly?' Ishira asked. 'It doesn't make sense.'

'Andaim's right to be suspicious,' Stefan agreed.

Ishira turned Valiant toward the bright, pearlescent orb of Oassia as she spotted four fighter craft streaking away from the nearest destroyer toward them.

'That's our escort,' she said as she identified their transponder codes on her displays and matched them to the ones transmitted from Atlantia. 'Let's hope they're not too trigger happy.'

The Morla'syn drones soared in from starboard and broke into two pairs, two taking the lead as two more positioned themselves directly behind the freighter, ready to shoot her down should she deviate from her course.

'You think that those sensors will do the job?' Stefan asked in a whisper.

'We're about to find out.'

As the fighters around them accelerated to cruise speed Ishira advanced the main throttles on Valiant's ion engines with one hand, while with the other she activated the passive sensor array, hoping that the advance in energy emissions by the engines would conceal the sensor's transmissions.

She saw a small light on her console inform her that the sensor was active, and she waited pensively for several moments for some reaction from the Morla'syn fighters, but they continued to cruise toward the planet at a steady velocity.

'Steady as she goes,' Stefan murmured.

Ishira nodded but did not reply and gradually they settled down into the cruise. Oassia slowly grew larger in the cockpit windscreen, the flare from her bright surface filling the view ahead ever more until its blue glow mixed with the orange and green cockpit lights in a kaleidoscopic array of color.

After almost an hour they were close enough to the surface to begin preparing for orbital entry. Ishira began the pre–entry checks as Stefan consulted the fuel gauges.

'All's good, plenty to get us down and back out again to Atlantia,' he said after a few moments. 'Ion engines are fully fuelled too.'

Ishira nodded and then something caught her eye, high up over the planet's horizon, almost entirely concealed by the blue glow of the atmosphere. The sunlight was coming from behind them and it was reflecting off something metallic in high orbit far away.

'You see that?' Ishira asked.

Stefan peered at the object, his old eyes not as sharp as his daughter's, but it was Erin whose young eyes identified it.

'It's a spaceship,' she said, and looked at Ishira. 'Galactic cruiser, I think.'

Stefan reached across the cockpit and grabbed a pair of binoculars, the electronic zoom and internal computer capable of resolving objects thousands of cubits away. He lifted them to his eyes and rested them on the back of Ishira's chair as he let the binoculars focus in on the remote object.

Ishira heard her father's breath catch in his throat as he surveyed the distant craft.

'What? Is it a cruiser?'

Stefan shook his head as he lowered the binoculars from his eyes.

'It's not a cruiser,' he said finally. 'Andaim was right: it's a battle fleet.'

**

XXV

Evelyn walked alongside Captain Sansin, Mikhain behind them with Teera and ranks of Morla'syn infantry stomping around them, long pale fingers caressing the triggers of their bulky plasma rifles.

'This is going from bad to worse,' Evelyn whispered under her breath as they walked. 'What the hell's going on?'

Idris shook his head, his eyes flicking this way and that as they walked along the transparent elevated walkway toward a silvery tower piercing high into the perfect blue sky. Above and below them airborne traffic flowed in orderly lines, metallic paintwork glinting in the bright sunshine.

'They're hiding something from us,' he replied. 'Gredan, Ayek and Vaughn are walking blindly into whatever Rh'yll has planned.'

'The Council are supposed to be allies,' Evelyn whispered. 'They're not supposed to be treating us like prisoners. Since when do we need an armed escort?'

'Show of force,' Mikhain murmured from behind them. 'For their own people as well as us. I don't think humanity is well respected in this quarter of the galaxy right now.'

'There are only two thousand of us aboard both ships,' Evelyn replied. 'What do they think we're going to do? Invade?'

'They may still believe us to be infected,' Mikhain pointed out.

'No,' Idris replied immediately. 'Rh'yll's people knew to use microwave scans to ensure we're not carrying the Legion. We've probably been checked multiple times since we landed and didn't even know about it. That's probably why we had to wait on the landing pad before General Veer and the councillors came out.'

'If they already know how to check for the Legion,' Evelyn said, 'then they might already know everything that we do. Our knowledge will hold no value to them.'

'And yet here we are, not dead yet,' Mikhain said. 'If they don't care for us alive, and don't want us dead, then what the hell are they doing? Maybe Gredan's right – maybe they *will* provide our people amnesty and asylum.'

Idris did not reply, deep in thought as Evelyn glanced across the city to her left and right. The elevated walkway was almost a thousand feet above the city, the occasional patch of cumulus cloud drifting by beneath them in the otherwise clear air. The city sparkled beneath them in the sunlight, the vast expanses of ocean glittering beyond a beautiful azure blue all the way toward the milky horizon. A freighter taking off from a spaceport to

Evelyn's left caught her eye as its ion engines powered up and it climbed into the hazy sky above, everything occurring in silence due to the thickness of the walls of the walkway.

Evelyn could see dozens of spacecraft parked in open bays in the spaceport, and as she walked so one of them naturally caught her eye. Her heart leaped in her chest as she recognised the sleek lines of a pirate ship, a slender hull flanked by two engines in strakes either side of the main hull, a wedge–shaped cockpit at the front, tripod landing pads beneath her and a long ramp extending down from beneath her for'ard hull to the pad below.

'Captains,' she whispered softly. 'Ten o'clock low, the near side of the port.'

Idris glanced across in front of Evelyn. She watched his expression and saw little emotional response but for the slightest widening of his eyes. Idris said nothing and continued looking directly ahead as they approached the towering spire before them.

'Going about his business?' he suggested mildly.

'Here?' Evelyn asked.

'Maybe he fled for some reason,' Mikhain said from behind them, having seen the same spacecraft.

Evelyn peered more closely at the freighter far below and saw barriers erected around the craft and what looked possibly like armed guards standing nearby.

'Whatever happened, I don't think he's here by choice.'

It was Teera who spotted the craft last, her view partially blocked by Mikhain and two of the Morla'syn guards. Evelyn heard her soft gasp.

'Taron Forge? What the hell is he doing here?'

'The Phoenix looks like she's under guard,' Evelyn whispered. 'Maybe they caught him up to no good and brought the ship here?'

'Taron Forge and his ilk wouldn't have come within light years of Oassia,' Mikhain said from behind them. 'This place represents everything that they despise even more than Ethera did. Besides, they were doing a roaring trade alongside Salim Phaeon picking up stragglers and survivors from the Core Systems. There's nothing out here for them but a jail sentence.'

Evelyn's heart quickened as she looked up at the towering spire before them, a silvery metallic building that shone in the bright sunlight as they approached. Evelyn scanned its surface and quickly noticed something.

'There are no windows,' she said.

Idris's eyes widened as he looked at the building and he realized what Evelyn was getting at.

'It's a jail,' he uttered in amazement.

Idris stopped walking and turned to the nearest Morla'syn. 'Get in touch with Councillor Rh'yll for me. I want to speak to him immediately about…'

The Morla'syn trooper whirled his rifle around and the butt slammed into the captain's chest and hurled him across the walkway to land with a deep thud against the transparent floor. Evelyn spun on one heel as she swung a fist toward the towering infantry trooper, but his fellow soldiers moved faster and two plasma rifle barrels blocked her blow, one of them pointing at her face from barely two inches away.

'On your knees!'

The Morla'syn commander's voice rang out on the walkway as the soldiers surrounded them, rifles jammed against their bodies as they crouched down and got onto their knees. Captain Sansin crawled to join them, wincing in pain as he clutched his chest.

'What the hell is this?' Teera demanded.

'Hostile takeover,' Evelyn replied in a harsh whisper as a set of metallic manacles were fastened around her wrists with brutal efficiency. 'They're locking us down.'

Evelyn was yanked to her feet as the Morla'syn troopers, now with their rifles activated and their bulbous eyes hooded with thin lids that protected them in combat, prodded them toward the entrance to the towering spire.

'It's why we're so high up,' Mikhain scowled from behind them. 'No escape.'

The troopers shoved and jostled them toward two armoured doors at the end of the transparent walkway, which opened automatically before them to reveal more Morla'syn soldiers awaiting them, their weapons likewise charged and ready for combat.

Evelyn felt a claustrophobic fear creep beneath her skin and tighten her chest as she saw the interior of the jail was a black and foreboding chasm, the complete opposite of the brilliantly illuminated and sunny exterior of the city. A waft of stale, thick air tainted with the coalesced stench of closely confined creatures assaulted her senses and made her eyes briefly stream.

She was shoved inside behind Captain Sansin and saw large, bulky, thug–like creatures watching her, each with sets of four hungry black eyes like glossy discs with no soul. Each Gaollian Guard possessed four muscular appendages, the animals quadrupedal and thick–set, their skin lacerated with ancient scars, their fingers thick and multi–jointed.

Before Evelyn could react one of the Gaollians skittered across to her and fastened more manacles about her ankles with extraordinary dexterity, an intelligence that belied the species' appearance.

One of them looked up at Captain Sansin and spoke in a screeching dialect that almost drowned out the monosyllabic drone of its universal translator.

'Welcome to Oassia, compliments of Councillor Rh'yll. He hopes you enjoy your stay.'

'You're making a big mistake,' Idris snapped back.

'Not as big as the one you made when you walked in here.'

The creature glanced at the Morla'syn troopers and nodded once, waving them away as though disgusted. The troopers withdrew through the doors, and moments later they slammed shut with a boom that echoed through the prison.

A crescendo of whoops, howls, jeers and screams soared through the darkness, and as Evelyn's eyes adjusted to the gloom she saw that they were standing on a platform that overlooked the entire interior of the prison. Like a gigantic hollow cylinder, the prison's curved interior was lined with ranks of cells, each with a single gate that opened out onto a dizzying drop into oblivion hundreds of feet below. Access to the cells was via a series of remotely controlled gantries that were suspended from cranes, meaning that nobody could leave their cell without the warden's and prison officers' direct permission and control.

Amid thousands of species all incarcerated within the prison Evelyn got her first sight of human beings imprisoned in one particular ring of cells about a dozen cubits below her. She saw colourfully dressed, swaggering pirates among them, but to her horror she realized that many looked like ordinary men and women.

Then she saw the children.

'It's a trap,' Teera said from behind her. 'They'll bring every single one of us here!'

Idris glanced over his shoulder at the prison entrance, the quadrupedal guards standing before it, heavy clubs in their hands and savage blades clipped to belts around their waists.

'This is what they're hiding,' Idris said. 'Damn it, they're imprisoning anybody who comes into the system, no matter what species.'

'They're suffering from deeply ingrained xenophobia,' Teera replied as she looked up and saw one of the remote gantries swinging down and around toward them from its supporting crane. 'The Council must have decided to close ranks, and if you're not in the club…'

'You're on your own,' Evelyn finished the sentence for her. 'We need to get the hell out of here!'

'It doesn't make any sense,' Mikhain said. 'What good will it do them to leave us locked up?'

The gantry swung into place and one of the guards opened the metal gate to it and ushered Evelyn and the others forward. The guards shoved them along and the gate slammed shut behind them as the crane hoisted the gantry out over the dizzying drop. Teera gulped and grabbed hold of the side of the cage as she closed her eyes.

'What *is* it with these people and heights?'

'I thought you were supposed to be a fighter pilot?' Mikhain uttered.

'Raythons have wings, I don't.'

The gantry descended alongside cells filled with countless species, and Evelyn could tell that the vast majority of them were convicts of one kind or another. Sometimes, the aura of danger and despair that surrounded the career criminal was present even in species that she had never seen before, but then perhaps she too had spent too much time locked up with murderers and thieves for company.

The gantry swung in alongside a row of cells filled with other humans who hurried forward and readied themselves. Evelyn was surprised to see men who were transparently convicts or pirates working together, their hands reaching through the bars to steady the gantry as the gate opened.

'Move, quickly,' one of them said. 'If you don't get out they'll tip the gantry and you'll be leaving the fast way. They place bets on who loses their grip first.'

Evelyn looked down through the gratings beneath her boots at the ground floor of the prison, hundreds of feet below, and with Idris and the others she hurried into the crowded cell just as the gantry's latches suddenly clicked open and the gantry tipped over on its side.

The cell gate rattled shut behind Evelyn and the empty gantry was lifted away. The cries and howls from around the prison faded away and she turned to see dense ranks of men, women and children watching them with curious gazes, drawn to the captains' uniforms and her flight suit.

'Don't tell us that you're the cavalry, come to get us out of here?' one of the men who had helped them into the cells asked.

Idris was about to reply but another man did so for him as he swaggered through the crowd to confront them.

'I doubt that,' said the man, his eyes cold and his dark hair hanging before them in thick strands. 'He'll be the one who put his faith in Councillor Rh'yll and got himself imprisoned for his troubles.'

Idris Sansin ground his teeth in his skull and shook his head.

'Taron Forge,' he murmured. 'I see you're back where you belong once again.'

Taron laid eyes on Evelyn and his grin broadened. 'Well, aren't you a sight for sore eyes?'

'Up yours, Taron,' Evelyn snapped. 'What the hell's going on here?'

'You didn't know?' Taron asked, raising one amused eyebrow. 'Don't tell me you wandered in here for help?'

'Start talking,' Mikhain rumbled.

Taron grinned and shrugged.

'We're here to help the Morla'syn and the Galactic Council fight back against the Legion.'

'How can we fight back when we're stuck in here?' Teera asked as she gestured to the prison around them.

'We're not here to do the fighting,' Taron replied, his humour disappearing. 'We're the bait.'

***

XXVI

'You honour us, Councillor.'

The Council Tower was a silvery spire that soared higher than all other buildings on Oassia, the city around them a gigantic disc of metal and glass that glistened like a jewel amid the burnished ocean.

Governor Gredan sat on a plush couch that was one of several surrounding a glass table, Ayek and Vaughn perched on their own seats with Meyanna Sansin. Councillor Rh'yll moved with surprising grace on his bulbous, shimmering body, muscles contracting and pulsing to allow him to slide across the mirror–smooth floor beneath them, this time slightly opaque to avoid any unwanted bouts of vertigo afflicting visiting dignitaries to this most auspicious of locations.

'You're welcome, all of you,' Rh'yll replied as he settled into an ornate seat opposite them, the sunlight streaming through the massive windows that encircled the tower's conference room also passing through the councillor's body.

'Where is my husband?' Meyanna demanded immediately. 'Where have you taken him?'

'Captain Sansin is safe,' Rh'yll assured her. 'We felt it best to debrief the military command structure of your fleet separately.'

'Then at least let me speak to him,' Meyanna insisted.

'You will, in due course,' Rh'yll replied. 'I promise that you will not be apart for long.'

Meyanna found it both fascinating and oddly disconcerting that the Councillor's body was transparent enough for her to be able to make out the city beyond through him, its image distorted by the way the light was bent through the councillor's form.

'The Oassian Council elected us as spokespeople,' Rhy'll said, noting Meyanna's gaze, 'because our natural transparency was considered a benefit in dealing with other races. It gives them the impression that we have nothing to hide.'

'An impression,' Meyanna purred in reply.

Rh'yll's bioluminescent lights flickered as though they had suffered some kind of disruption to their power.

'One formed over many, many long centuries, Governor Sansin,' he replied. 'It is not by chance that we came to represent so many differing species.'

'I don't doubt that at all,' Meyanna replied. 'Chance favours the prepared mind, as they say.'

Rhy'll sat in silence for a moment. 'You do not trust us.'

'We don't trust anybody right now. I want to speak to my husband.'

'All in good time,' Gredan cut in and directed a stern gaze at Meyanna. The governor leaned forward over his belly, his hands clasped before him. 'It's not entirely true that we don't trust you, councillor. We believe that the Galactic Council is the key to defeating The Word and bringing peace to the galaxy once again. Without your help, Captain Sansin is unable to offer an effective defence against such a powerful enemy.'

'Even with the Council's help, we might not be able to defend against the Legion,' Meyanna corrected him.

'Better with than without,' Gredan shot back.

'He's right,' Vaughn insisted. 'This is the time for cooperation.'

'I agree, so I ask again,' Meyanna said as she looked at Rh'yll, 'where is my husband?'

'Captains Sansin and Mikhain are being questioned by our tactical and military commanders and are helping us to understand more about the Legion,' Rh'yll explained.

'Why are they not here?' Meyanna asked. 'There is no good reason to have us separated.'

'Your concern is your civilians,' Rh'yll explained, 'whereas the captains' roles concern military matters. We can cover more ground more quickly this way.'

'I don't like it,' Meyanna shot back. 'A divided force is a weakened one.'

'This is what you wanted!' Gredan exclaimed. 'You said it yourself: we need assistance!'

'Yes, assistance,' Meyanna shot back, 'not being isolated, controlled and kept in the dark. This is not what we came here for and you still haven't explained how you came to know about the effect of microwaves on the Legion's Infectors.'

'Does that really matter so much? Gredan challenged her. 'We have the opportunity here to forge an alliance with the most powerful force in the known galaxy. Are you really going to let such a small issue become a stumbling block?'

'Only if the Oassian solution isn't something that favours humanity,' Meyanna replied without taking her gaze from Rh'yll's tiny black photoreceptors. 'We're sitting here and we know that at no time since the apocalypse has the Galactic Council formed a fleet to assist humanity, despite having already admitted that it knew of The Word's slaughter. Tell me, Councillor: how did it feel to sit back and do nothing as several billion people died?'

Rh'yll's glowing lights flickered again, rippling as he shifted position in his seat.

'The same way I felt the last time it happened,' he replied simply.

'What do you mean?' Meyanna gasped. 'You've sat back and allowed genocide to occur on your watch *before*?'

Rh'yll gestured with one appendage out of the broad, sweeping windows to the larger universe beyond.

'The cosmos is vast and even we only know a small portion of our own galaxy, which as I'm sure you're aware contains hundreds of billions of star systems. Beyond, there are countless billions more galaxies, all of which I have no doubt contain life. Over the centuries we have witnessed many species become extinct, both directly and remotely via distant signals that reach Oassia and the many detectors we deploy here. I cannot recall how many times we have sat in sombre reflection as we listened to the dying gasp of some far–flung civilization that never quite made it to the stars.'

Meyanna stared at Rh'yll in disbelief. 'You chose not to intervene,' she said with a finality every bit as succinct as the doomed fate of the civilizations Rh'yll was describing.

'It is not our place to intervene,' he replied. 'How many species became extinct on your home world long before The Word was created, long before humanity even evolved? Extinction is a part of life, Governor Sansin, and always will be. I have no doubt that in the future some other species will sit here where I am now and perhaps mourn the loss of my own people. Nothing lasts forever,' Rh'yll said, 'not conquest, not defeat, not life. Not the Legion.'

'Do you have a plan, councillor?' Gredan asked. 'Is there a strategy for dealing with the Legion?'

Rh'yll's lights flickered more brightly, something that Meyanna was beginning to understand indicated excitement or happiness.

'Yes,' he replied, 'we have both and will begin executing them very shortly indeed.'

A nearby door hissed open and a Morla'syn hurried in.

'Councillor, there has been a development,' he snapped in a harsh tone.

The Morla'syn hurried to Rhy'll's side and leaned down to whisper into the councillor's barely visible ears, little more than sensorium patches of opaque skin on his translucent body. Rh'yll's body suddenly lit up with a brilliant flickering of light.

'How many?!' he gasped.

'What's happening?' Meyanna demanded.

The Morla'syn whispered something more and immediately Rh'yll shouted out. 'Guard!'

Morla'syn troops hurried into the council room and surrounded them as General Veer followed his men in.

'Treachery!' Veer growled as one long, slender arm pointed at the governors. 'They have deceived us!'

'What the hell is going on?!' Meyanna demanded.

'The Legion is here!' Veer snapped. 'We have detected a large force closing in on Oassia, Colonial vessels most of them! They're exchanging signals with the humans, probably through the Word's creator aboard their ship.'

Rh'yll looked at Governor Gredan. 'Tell us that this is not true.'

Gredan looked genuinely perplexed. 'The Lazarus terminal is confined,' he promised. 'There is no way that he could transmit or receive signals from anywhere, let alone from the Legion!'

Meyanna stood up despite the guns pointing at her. 'How long do we have?'

'Their super–luminal bow shock suggests less than an hour,' General Veer replied, apparently not concerned about discussing military matters with a human woman.

'We need the captain back aboard Atlantia,' Meyanna said as she turned to Rh'yll.

'That will not be possible,' Rh'yll replied. 'If the source of this treachery is your vessels, then any possible alliance between our species is already null and void.'

'There was no treachery!' Gredan insisted. 'Our vessels were clean, we know that the Legion was not aboard when your Morla'syn destroyers intercepted us!'

'And before?' Rh'yll demanded. 'Were you infected at any time in the last few hours, or even days?'

Gredan hesitated, desperate to speak but unable to find the diplomatic words he needed to extricate them from this sudden and unexpected setback.

'We were infected by a small number of Hunters during an ambush at Akyron V,' Meyanna replied. 'The infection was cleaned but it is possible that the Legion may have somehow been able to send information on our presence there, and possibly even our trajectory when we made the jump to super–luminal.'

Rh'yll turned to General Veer. 'Prepare the fleet for battle.'

Gredan raised an eyebrow. 'What fleet?'

'There was no treachery,' Meyanna insisted as the General gestured for one of his lieutenants to pass the order on. 'We came here for help, not to spread the Legion!'

General Veer shook his head solemnly. 'It matters little now. The Legion that your people created now threatens all of us.'

Veer stalked away, leaving Meyanna to turn to Rhy'll. 'You cannot face this alone, councillor. You need our help, our experience in fighting this thing.'

'Yes, we do,' Rh'yll agreed. 'It has been a part of our plan all along. Guards?'

The Morla'syn troops closed in around the governors, and Rh'yll seemed almost to sigh as he spoke.

'Transport them to the holding cells, then prepare both Arcadia and Atlantia for battle. We shall lead with our weakest assets and attempt to draw the Legion in to them.'

The troops surrounded Meyanna and the governors, and with a deep chill Meyanna realized what was happening.

'You're using us as bait,' she gasped in horror.

Rhy'll did not look at her as he spoke to the Morla'syn troops.

'Keep them out of sight and ensure that news of the Legion's arrival does not reach the media or the public.'

Before Meyanna could protest, she was shoved out of the council room with Gredan and the others close behind her.

Rh'yll waited for a few moments until they were gone. The council chamber was silent, the glassy windows thick enough to block all sound from the bustling city far below and even the noise from the patrolling fighters and civilian air traffic.

Rh'yll turned to a small monitor set into his seat, and with one appendage he activated a secure communications channel. The signal was weak and the distortion heavy with distance, but he could make out the response and the warbling, digital vocabulary of something not quite human and a grotesque visage on his screen, demonic in its appearance through the distortion and shadowy lighting.

'What news?'

'Everything is proceeding as planned, commander,' Rh'yll said. 'What guarantee do I have of Oassia's safety?'

'You have my word,' came the rippling, digitized reply. *'That of The Word, that Oassia will remain a neutral territory in this conflict. Surrender the humans to us, and your planet will be untouched.'*

Rh'yll shifted in his seat, his bioluminescence flickering weakly. 'I risk much, commander. The humans claim that you seek conquest above all other considerations.'

'Of humanity?' came the reply. *'Yes, we do. But of other species? Your right to exist remains as valid as our own, councillor. Conquest of your world serves us no purpose, but cooperation will provide us both with what we desire. You can trust us, councillor, far more than you can trust human beings.'*

The transmission blinked out, leaving Rh'yll alone in the chamber with his thoughts.

***

XXVII

'The Morla'syn are pulling back!'

Andaim whirled to the tactical display as he heard Lael's call and watched as the three destroyers surrounding their position began withdrawing.

'Where do they think they're going?'

'Sensor jamming is weakening,' Lael reported further. 'Communications link with Arcadia is now open.'

'Signal them now, get them up on screen!'

Andaim saw one of the display screens flicker into life as an image of Lieutenant Scott appeared before him, the young XO looking flustered and nervous.

'Commander, we've got a problem.'

'We've got a lot of problems,' Andaim replied. 'Are you getting the readings we're sending from the far orbit of Oassia, and the super–luminal bow shock?'

'Both,' Lieutenant Scott confirmed. 'Looks like one major fleet behind us near Oassia and another approaching from the bow. The Legion must have been communicating with Kordaz, he must still be alive. How did you pick up the fleet's presence?'

'We sneaked a sensor on the civilian transport, Valiant. Whatever's left of Kordaz is irrelevant now,' Andaim shot back. 'They're here and there's nothing much we can do about it except prepare for battle. The Morla'syn are pulling out.'

'They're running,' Lieutenant Scott confirmed. 'Why the hell are they running away when they've got an entire battle fleet waiting?'

Andaim shook his head, not able himself to fathom what the Galactic Council was doing. They had welcomed the civilians down to the planet's surface virtually with open arms and a commitment to protect them as they would all life in the universe, or so they claimed, but now they were falling back and leaving just a handful of humans to…

Andaim felt something cold drop like a stone though his guts as a sudden, terrible new realization crept into his thoughts.

'The Legion was created by us,' he whispered, almost to himself. 'What if the Council is trying to remove two obstacles with a single blow?'

'What do you mean?' Emma asked as she appeared on the screen alongside Lieutenant Scott.

Andaim looked at her, briefly forgetting that it was Emma at all and instead seeing only Evelyn, recalling her fearsome temper and rugged courage under fire.

'They want humanity gone and they want the Legion gone,' he said. 'Best way to do that would be to...'

'Use one to attract the other, and then attack both,' Emma finished the sentence for him as though it really were Evelyn standing on the bridge. 'They're bait! They're using Eve and the others as bait!'

Andaim whirled and saw that Atlantia's shields were at full capacity and her plasma cannons were fully charged. A glance across at the next screen revealed the fighter pilots of both Reaper and Renegade squadrons mounting their fighters and strapping in, ready to scramble at a moment's notice.

'We've got to get them out of there!' Emma snapped, gaining Andaim's complete attention with a surprisingly determined tone.

Andaim took one last look at the retreating Morla'syn destroyers and then he made his decision.

'We'll need your help,' he said finally. 'Get on a shuttle over here as fast as you can and meet me in the Lazarus Chamber,' Andaim dashed off the command platform and yelled over his shoulder at Lael. 'You have the bridge! Order Valiant not to land on Oassia!'

'She's already down!' Lael replied.

'Damn!'

Andaim hurried down through Atlantia's decks and leaped aboard the nearest transport pod heading aft. The frigate's corridors now seemed bizarrely empty and hollow, sound travelling further in lonely echoes now that the civilians had been transported to the surface. A frightening portent entered his mind: an image of Atlantia in the near–future, devoid of life, a ghost ship drifting powerless and disabled like Endeavour through the frigid expanses of the cosmos, abandoned for centuries or perhaps even millennia.

The pod slowed and Andaim shook off his maudlin thoughts as he leaped out and hurried to the storage depots. The two Marines sentries were still standing guard, and they stood aside with crisp salutes as the commander accessed the storage depot and walked inside.

The interior was dark, but as he walked in the blue glow returned as Lazarus responded to his presence and powered up. Almost immediately the old man sensed the anxiety etched into Andaim's features.

'What is it?'

'The Legion is here,' Andaim replied.

Lazarus closed his eyes and for a long moment he seemed fixated on something just beyond his reach, like a word on the tip of one's tongue and yet forever lost.

'I can sense them,' he said, his eyes still tightly closed, 'but they are distant.'

'Not for long,' Andaim replied. 'The Galactic Council is holding our civilians prisoner.'

Lazarus opened his eyes and stared down at Andaim. 'They did not accept the terms of our asylum here at Oassia?'

'They never intended to,' Andaim replied. 'They have a battle fleet in waiting and they're using the captured human as bait. They're luring the Legion in and preparing to strike.'

Lazarus stared at the opposite wall for a long moment and then sighed. 'So they have chosen treachery over solace, enmity over alliance. The Councillors fear us as much as they fear the Legion, and seek to destroy both with the same blow.'

'Captain Sansin is on the surface, as is Mikhain and Evelyn. We need them here as soon as possible.'

'I cannot help you,' Lazarus said. 'With the jamming in progress and both Evelyn and Emma absent I can't gain access to the ship's systems.'

Andaim did not reply in time to beat the voice that came from the entry hatch to the storage depot.

'Who said I wasn't here?'

Emma walked into the depot and Lazarus smiled brightly. 'Emma? How did you get here?'

'The Morla'syn have retreated,' Andaim explained. 'They're leaving it all up to us to draw the Legion into combat.'

Emma walked up to Lazarus and Andaim realized that were the great doctor not now a hologram the two would likely have embraced. Emma looked up respectfully at Lazarus, and then at Andaim.

'What would you have us do?'

Andaim gathered his thoughts as he turned to Lazarus.

'The Morla'syn, they have signals connections from here to Oassia, correct?' Andaim asked.

Lazarus looked at Emma who nodded once, and with his access granted Lazarus focused his attention on incoming signals from Atlantia's now active arrays.

'Yes, multiple channels on secure modulating frequencies controlling sensors, ground–based weapons and drones.'

'And you can access them, if I give you complete control?'

Lazarus watched Andaim for a long moment before he replied. 'The governing council and Captain Sansin may have something to say about you handing me complete control of both frigates at such a crucial…'

'The governing council have already made themselves ineffectual by insisting on travelling to the surface, and for all we know Captain Sansin is under arrest along with the rest of the delegation. We either act now or we're fish–bait for the Legion when it arrives. The council is not going to protect us, Lazarus, and we both know it.'

Lazarus sighed again, and nodded. 'If I have complete access, then yes, I can control the drones and turn them to our purpose.'

'Good,' Andaim replied. 'Here's what we're going to do. Ishira recently landed on Oassia with an escort of four Morla'syn drones. First, I need you to access Oassian systems and find out precisely where Captain Sansin and the others are being held…'

*

'Stand by, do not proceed past this point.'

Ishira Morle stood at the foot of Valiant's ramp as it touched down on the landing pad and watched as the Morla'syn guard stood back, one arm cradling a plasma rifle as with the other he pointed at Ishira's boots.

'Nice to meet you too,' she snipped back at the soldier as he turned to the ramp and began waving the civilians down.

Ishira stood back and watched as they filed out of the freighter, smiles on their faces and many of them with their eyes closed as they inhaled truly fresh air for the first time in years. She herself delighted in the warm glow of the sunshine and the ocean breeze – it had been pure good fortune that they had arrived at Oassia in early summer, the city state located close to the planet's equator and receiving a healthy dose of early season warmth and…

Ishira heard a commotion to one side of the landing pad and turned to see more platoons of Morla'syn soldiers jogging up an access ramp toward the freighter, their plasma rifles activated and grim expressions on their lean, angular features.

'Halt!'

The command rang out in the fresh air and Ishira's hand moved instinctively toward her side–arm as she saw the troops fan out and encircle the five hundred or so civilians crowding the landing pad.

'Stay where you are! Nobody move!'

Stefan stepped toward the nearest Morla'syn soldier. 'What's going on?'

The soldier whirled and drove the butt of his rifle into the old man's chest, slamming him onto the deck as Ishira leaped forward.

'What the hell do you think you're doing?!'

'You're all under arrest!' the soldier bellowed back and fired a single shot into the air that sent a rush of alarmed cries out from the civilians. 'Everybody on your knees, hands behind your heads, now!'

Ishira, one hand on her pistol, saw two of the soldiers turn and aim their rifles at her. Stefan whispered harshly at his daughter from where he lay on the deck.

'Don't do it!'

'They've got Erin!' Ishira hissed.

'And you're no good to her dead,' Stefan snapped back. 'Stand down!'

Ishira glared at the soldiers but she released the handle of her pistol, and moments later the Morla'syn surrounded her and drove her down onto her knees on the hard deck.

***

XXVIII

'What the hell do you mean *we're the bait?*'

The prison echoed with the cries and screeches of the hundreds of species entrapped within its damp, cold walls. Like a rotten boil festering within a glittering crystal, Evelyn could tell that Oassia's prison system was a dark secret it would have preferred remain hidden.

Taron Forge leaned against the barred wall of the cell, apparently unconcerned by the precipitous drop into the prison's bowels and the proximity of a tentacled species in an adjacent cell that seemed to be trying to reach out for him. Taron's co–pilot, the ever silent Yo'Ki, smouldered in silence alongside him, her dark eyes even more menacing in the gloom and her black hair pinned in a pony–tail behind her head.

'Look around you,' Taron gestured to the rest of the prison with a lazy tilt of his head. 'The Oassians have been gathering human ammunition for their dirty little campaign against the Legion.'

Evelyn could see that many of the cells contained humans of all ages and races, most of them cowering beneath the threat of violence from other, less civilized species or the criminals and pirates incarcerated alongside them.

'Human ammunition?' Idris asked.

'Their plan is to draw the Legion in by positioning humans at natural choke points in planetary systems, especially those with active dwarf stars,' Taron explained. 'The Legion seems to prefer hunting us humans down than other species, presumably because it reserves a special kind of hate for us. The Legion moves in on the humans and then the Oassian fleet ambushes the Legion's craft and annihilates them.'

Idris looked at Mikhain, who shrugged. 'Not a bad plan.'

Evelyn knew that dwarf stars, although extremely long–lived and stable, were often prone to bouts of violent solar flares which expelled huge amounts of energy into space – just the kind of energy that fried circuitry that was not properly shielded.

'The atmospheres of flaring dwarf stars would prevent the Legion from deploying outside of their spacecraft, reducing the chance of infection,' Idris surmised. 'And a battle fleet of sufficient size, especially with the Morla'syn's destroyers, would be able to shatter even a sizeable Colonial fleet.'

'That's about the size of it,' Taron agreed. 'The Oassians have been hoovering up fleeing humans for years under the pretence of providing a safe haven somewhere in the system, most likely Veyrin, a blue planet in orbit around the same star as Oassia. It's only natural that they'd flee here, the most powerful of all known galactic districts, despite the supposed risk to them of crossing the Icari Line. Once landed, they're arrested and imprisoned.'

'And how did you end up here?' Evelyn asked the pirate captain.

Taron smiled and offered her a vague shrug.

'I'd gotten myself a hefty cargo of Avarian spice and knew of a few traders out this way. What I didn't know was that the Morla'syn were amassing their fleet here too. Yo'Ki and I got picked up the moment we entered the system and have been here over a week.'

'We saw your ship when we came here,' Idris acknowledged.

'Is she okay?' Taron asked, pushing off the cell wall, his face pinched with concern. 'Have they done anything to her?'

Idris regarded the captain for a moment. 'Well, we only knew it was the Phoenix because they hadn't finished stripping down the cockpit yet.'

'They've done what?!' Taron's face flushed red and he looked as though he were about to spontaneously combust.

'Relax,' Evelyn murmured as she fought to conceal a smile. 'Your ship's fine.'

Taron blustered for a moment, his face glowing red as Idris turned to Evelyn. 'Rh'yll never intended to assist us. He's had this planned for some time if the Morla'syn have assembled their fleet already.'

'The Oassians don't want conflict,' Evelyn pointed out, 'but the Morla'syn are much more willing to fight. If we could somehow divide them, give the Morla'syn a reason to split away from the Oassians…'

'That presumes they'd even consider fighting for us,' Idris pointed out. 'If anything, they dislike humans even more than the Oassians.'

'They don't have to like us to fight *for* us,' Evelyn pointed out, 'and besides, this isn't just about us anyway. The Morla'syn are as much under threat from the Legion as any other species out there. This is about convincing them that if they don't fight then eventually they'll be under threat. Do they want their last stand to be here, or wait until the Legion's in orbit around their homeworld?'

Idris nodded and glanced across at the prison cells around them.

'We can't do anything until we find a way out of this hell hole.'

The quadrupedal creatures who manned the prison clambered up and down the walls, their powerful claws and the pads on their feet holding them in place and allowing them to scamper with surprising speed and agility. Evelyn watched one of them for a moment and then had an idea.

'If we could get hold of one of them and...'

'Already thought about it,' Taron cut her off, 'and one of the guys tried it. It didn't end well.'

'How so?' Idris asked.

'The prison has a policy of zero–tolerance to all convicts,' Taron explained. 'Reyeche decided he'd get hold of one of the guards, kill him and then try to use his limbs to clamber out of the prison. First thing that happened, when he got hold of the guard, was that he realized the Gaollian was much stronger than he was when he got his arm ripped out of its socket.' Evelyn winced as Taron went on. 'Next, he was hauled out of the cell and carried up the wall to the very top of the prison so that everybody could hear him scream when he was dropped. It took a fair while for him to hit the bottom.'

Idris scowled and gripped the prison bars. 'No prison ever built is entirely secure.'

'No,' Taron agreed with a lazy smile,' 'but some are secure *enough*.'

'Don't tell me you've given up,' Evelyn said to him. 'You must have figured something out.'

Taron regarded her for a moment, the smile still hanging lop–sided on his face. 'Maybe I have,' he replied finally. 'Depends on whether I'm going to share that with you.'

Idris turned slowly to the pirate. 'Oh, you're going to share it.'

Before Taron could reply, from the crowd in the cell a group of pirates shouldered their way to the front, backing him up. All were scarred and enveloped by a tangible aura of menace, Yo'Ki among them.

'Your problem, captain,' Taron said conversationally, 'is that you're not in command here.'

'Neither are you,' Evelyn pointed out. 'You're a prisoner the same as us.'

'A prisoner with capital behind him,' Taron grinned. 'Prison economics, Evelyn – you should know something about that.'

'The spice,' Evelyn realized, and suddenly understood Taron's rage at the idea of his ship being stripped down.

'Hell of a cargo aboard my ship, and right now I would bet solid cash that any one of the guards in here would be willing to let a few of us out, for the right price of course.'

'Make your deal,' Idris growled as he took a pace closer to Taron, 'or I swear you'll have more to worry about than the guards.'

Taron's smile vanished, but he did not move. 'Captain, I think that your years in command of happy little Colonial officers who place too much stock in shoulder insignia have given you a false sense of your ability to intimidate.'

Evelyn glanced at Mikhain and saw the captain begin to edge a little closer to the pirates.

Idris noticed the same movement, as did Taron.

'Captain?' Taron purred with interest as he leaned casually against the cage wall once more and looked at Mikhain appraisingly. 'Finally, a Colonial stooge who's waking up from their nightmare.'

Mikhain glared at Taron, but then looked at Idris. 'We're at war,' he said by way of an explanation. 'Not just with the Legion but with the Oassians as well now. We can't be choosy about our allies, but all humans should be sticking together.'

'Pity you weren't thinking like that on Chiron IV,' Evelyn shot back.

'I was,' Mikhain replied without regret. 'You were standing with a Veng'en instead of human beings.'

'That's history!' Idris snapped. 'Right now our priority is getting out of here and we need that spice to do it, Taron!'

Idris's voice rang out loudly enough that the occupants of many other cages heard it. Evelyn heard a rush of whispers in countless dialects as heads, eyes and antennae were turned toward them. From the other side of the cage a burly looking man, thick set with a massive black beard and thick arms, pointed at Idris.

'What *spice*?' he boomed.

The cage swung to one side as the giant man shoved his way past other humans cowering away from him against the cage walls. More, equally burly men joined him, and the pirates behind Taron turned their attention to them.

'Stay out of this, Rench,' Taron warned.

The big man named Rench grinned cruelly, his teeth stained brown. 'We're in a cage, Taron. What happens to us, happens to you. What say we cut a deal – your spice gets *all* of us out of here.'

The big man gestured with a sweep of one giant arm to the Donnassian miners behind him.

'Not enough for us all I'm afraid,' Taron replied. 'You win some, you lose some.'

'Then I guess you'll have to stay here,' Rench growled in delight as he clenched his fists by his side. 'Dead or alive.'

Evelyn turned to Idris.

'This is getting out of hand,' she snapped.

Idris nodded and stepped forward, raising his hands toward Rench. 'I'm sure we can work something out here. There's always a way to...'

Rench let out a roar of fury and one arm smashed across Idris's chest, battering him to one side. The captain hit the bars of the cell with a dull ringing sound and the cell swung sideways as the miners advanced.

'The spice, Taron!' Rench roared. 'Now!'

Evelyn saw Taron's smile turn cold and without mercy as a silvery blade appeared as if by magic in his hand. He beckoned Rench forward with the other hand as beside him the pirates began shoving other people out of the way to give them room to fight.

Evelyn leaped up and jumped between the two factions.

'What the hell are you doing?!' she snapped at Taron. 'We're already at war with the Legion! This is senseless!'

'It's business,' Taron uttered, his tone cold and brutal. 'Rench understands.'

Evelyn looked at the giant Donnassian and sneered. 'The only thing people like you understand is fighting like children. You should be working together, not squaring up for a fight.'

Taron shrugged. 'He started it.'

Rench let out another blood curdling roar and made to pass by Evelyn. Evelyn pulled her shoulder back as she flicked her left hand out like a whiplash, its edge thin as a blade as it swept up and smacked across Rench's bearded throat.

The huge man's eyes flew wide as his throat collapsed and he stopped where he was, both hands reaching up for his neck. Evelyn turned on one heel and drove the knuckles of her right fist deep into his plexus. What air remained in Rench's lungs whistled out of his throat as his legs gave way beneath him and he slammed down onto his knees before her.

Evelyn looked down at him, the big man only a few inches shorter than her even on his knees, and then she lifted one boot and slammed it into his chest. Rench sprawled onto his back as his companions stared at Evelyn in amazement.

She heard Taron's voice from behind her, and saw him waving the blade at the miners. 'And let that be a lesson to you.'

Evelyn took two paces toward Taron and grabbed his wrist, pinning the blade in place.

'Shut up, or I'll take that knife and slip it somewhere that'll make you squeal like a eunuch.'

Taron raised an eyebrow at her but said nothing. Evelyn released the blade and saw Yo'Ki smiling quietly nearby as she turned to the miners.

'We want out of here, we work together. Once we're done I don't care if you all tear each other to shreds, but for now we're on the same side, understood?'

The Donnassians looked at her in amazement, but none of them argued. It was a voice from one side that answered Evelyn.

'What *spice?*'

She turned and saw three of the Gaollian Guards clinging to the cage wall, all of them armed and pointing plasma pistols at them, the weapons humming in the otherwise silent prison. Evelyn realized that every one of the nearest cages had watched the entire exchange with interest.

'Tell us where it is,' the guard said, 'and we might cut a deal.'

Taron stepped forward. 'Let us out first, and then we'll talk.'

The guard glared at Taron and a moment later fired his pistol.

The shot blazed past Taron and hit one of his companions square in the face, incinerating his skull and spraying blood, bone and white hot plasma across the pirates. The guard pointed the pistol at Evelyn and his face split in a gruesome rictus grin.

'Humans,' the Gaollian sneered. 'Wherever you're found, chaos follows. Negotiations are over. The spice, now.'

Evelyn looked at Taron, who sighed as his shoulders sagged.

'It's in the…'

Taron's voice was cut off as behind the guards the entire wall of the prison suddenly burst open like a gigantic metal flower amid a massive ball of flame, the deafening screech of rending metal and burning fuel filling the prison as Evelyn ducked instinctively away from the searing heat of the blast.

***

XXIX

Commander Andaim Ry'ere stood on the command platform of Atlantia's bridge and waited in silence. Behind him the rest of the bridge crew likewise stood or sat behind their control consoles and stared at the main viewing screen, awaiting the contact that must surely come from the surface of the planet.

On a second screen, Andaim could see a relayed image of Lieutenant Scott standing in a near–identical pose: upright, chin held high, hands behind his back. Despite his inexperience Scott was proving himself a worthy ally in difficult times, and would likely have been a model officer in the old Colonial Navy.

'Incoming signal,' Lael reported, her metallic hair catching the low light of the bridge control panels. 'It's from the surface.'

Andaim straightened a little more as a screen flickered into life, and Andaim got his first look at Councillor Rhy'll.

'Commander Ry'ere,' Rhy'll's translator warbled as he spoke, his gelatinous form rippling like water entrapped within in a transparent balloon. Behind the Councillor stood ranks of his colleagues, the representatives of races both familiar and strange to Andaim.

'Councillor,' Andaim replied, 'may I speak with my captain?'

'That will not be possible, I'm afraid,' Rh'yll replied. 'Captain Sansin and his fellow crew members and governors have been found guilty of treason and will be charged accordingly when all of this is over.'

'When all of *what* is over?' Andaim asked. 'Where are the civilians we sent down to the surface?'

'They are safe and in custody,' Rh'yll replied. 'They will not be harmed by us.'

Andaim's eyes narrowed as he considered the councillor's carefully chosen words. They will not be harmed *by us*. He glanced to one side at Atlantia's tactical displays, now showing a clear image of the massive fleet arrayed on the far side of Oassia, the image obtained by the sensors fitted to Valiant. Although Andaim could not tell if the fleet was still in the same position, the jamming from the surface sufficient to conceal the fleet from Atlantia's sensors, he had no reason to suspect that it had moved yet.

'What treason have they committed?' Andaim asked, more to bide time rather than in the expectation of any reasonable answer.

'You have brought the Legion with you to Oassia,' Rh'yll rumbled, his tone deepening to convey the gravity of his accusation. 'You have brought death to our doorstep, and now we must face it with our entire planetary population in danger of infection. A battle has not been fought in Oassian space for over a thousand years, the territory a neutral haven for all races, but now thanks to humanity that noble pride is shattered.'

Andaim raised an eyebrow.

'Lucky for you that you have a battle fleet in waiting behind the planet,' he said mildly. 'Or was that pure chance, councillor?'

Rh'yll's luminescent glow flickered weakly and he shivered.

'The Oassian fleet has been here ever since your Legion arose and slaughtered billions of human beings, commander. A wise precaution don't you think, considering how in the wake of your species' annihilation you have now come here begging for our help?'

'We didn't beg and we didn't want to come here. We had no choice, and now it would appear that there will be no help at all. Transport the civilians back to our frigates and we will leave forthwith.'

'That also will not be possible,' Rh'yll insisted. 'They are essential to our future.'

Andaim felt something uncomfortable creeping beneath his skin at the councillor's choice of words as he paced closer to the display screen. 'How so?'

Rhy'll shuddered again, apparently uncomfortable with the councillors standing behind him. He seemed to glance over his shoulder for confirmation, and then continued.

'The Word fears humanity,' he said finally. 'It fears its creator, the one you call Lazarus. It fears no other species like it does you, for reasons that we here on Oassia and on many other planets understand with some considerable sympathy. Therefore, we seek a bargain with the Legion.'

Andaim felt his blood run cold as he stared at Rh'yll on the screen, heard the gasps of horror from the bridge crew as they realized what the Oassian was saying.

'You're not going to use them as bait,' Andaim said, his own voice sounding dead in his ears as he too began to understand the truth depth of Rh'yll's deceit. 'You're going to barter with them?'

Rh'yll shuddered again, his luminous internal organs almost flickering out as he spoke.

'It is the only way,' he replied. 'We have no other choice but to place the countless innocent lives of many species above those of the remaining humans in order to preserve peace in our quadrant of the galaxy. We believe that the Legion and The Word can be reasoned with, that it too has a right to exist if it can be made to understand that it has a place in this universe if it is willing to respect the boundaries of other species with whom it shares the cosmos.'

For a few long moments Andaim found himself lost for words. It had long been the council's mission to embrace the species and civilizations it encountered, to bring them beneath an umbrella of shared co–existence, even warlike races such as the Veng'en. Unified and strengthened by shared histories of conflict and loss, the Galactic Council had risen above such petty squabbles to become a shining icon of what was good and righteous in the cosmos, despite its containing of humanity inside the Icari Line.

But now it was openly advocating the abandonment of what remained of humanity in favour of a bargain with the greatest evil that the cosmos had ever known: an emotionless, enraged machine driven by a pure and undiluted lust for power and control.

'You would place the survival of an entity responsible for the genocide of billions of people over our lives?' Andaim uttered finally.

Rh'yll rose up slightly in his seat among the councillors.

'The abandonment of two thousand souls, no matter how appalling an act in isolation, is far preferable to the loss of countless millions that will befall us should the Legion continue its advance. It must be stopped, now, before any more worlds succumb to its power.'

Andaim took another pace closer to the screen, looking up at Rhy'll's larger–than–life image.

'It will never be placated,' he said. 'It will never stop. It will never be satisfied until every last biological species is eradicated from existence. It has already shown that it cares not what species it attacks – it hates us all with a passion that we cannot understand. There is nothing that we can do to stop it unless we destroy it entirely, take back the systems the Legion has conquered and smash it to pieces wherever we find it, all the way back to Ethera.'

Rh'yll shuddered again and he sagged in his seat as he replied.

'Sadly, such a mission of conquest would cost far more lives than I am willing to commit,' he said. 'Our decision has been made, commander, and we stand by it as unanimously as any other ruling the Galactic Council has ever made. We will seek an amnesty with the Legion and begin building a relationship with it. The Word is an entity, a self–aware being that now has every much a right to exist as we do. To condemn it to death would be as bad as…'

'Condemning us to death,' Andaim cut across him.

Rhy'll sat in silence for a moment and then he looked again to his side. To Andaim's amazement, Governor Gredan appeared and looked at him.

'It's the only way, commander,' he said.

Andaim clenched his fists by his side as he glared at Gredan. 'You engineered this?'

'The plan was already in motion long before we arrived,' Gredan replied. 'I simply negotiated for the survival of a small number of humans in the hope that someday, in a far flung future that none of us will ever get to see, humanity might once again flourish on a new home world far from here, and gaze once more upon the universe that…'

'You coward,' Andaim snapped. 'I take it that you're going to be one of those survivors?' Gredan lifted his bulbous chin. 'The governors and I have not made this sacrifice lightly, commander.'

'I'll bet,' Andaim growled, 'and I take it that the crews of Arcadia and Atlantia, the people who risked their lives to save yours, will be the first to go?'

Gredan maintained a sombre expression but could not conceal the mercenary gleam in his eye.

'The Galactic Council felt that we, as governors, were the best chance for humanity to forge a new path devoid of military conflict, based on cooperation and mutual respect.'

'And getting everybody else to do your dirty work for you!' Andaim yelled as he pointed at the screen. 'I swear by Ethera that if I ever get my hands on you I'll kill you my damned self.'

Gredan merely raised an eyebrow. 'Exactly the kind of aggression that we're hoping to rid mankind of, commander.'

Andaim fumed in silence but before he could reply Lael called across to him.

'New contacts bearing eight five one, elevation niner niner four!'

Andaim whirled and looked at the tactical display as a sudden flurry of new contacts appeared as red lights that swarmed into view as fast as lightning, soaring into the system from super–luminal cruise.

'Multiple targets!' Lael called, her voice slightly higher pitched than normal. 'Military class, transponders identify them as Colonial! They're here, commander!'

Andaim felt his heart skip a beat as he saw on the main display screen an image through magnified optical sensors appear. Dense star fields provided a vivid backdrop for a fleet of six cruisers and a gigantic capital ship that loomed in their midst. A circular disc with ventral strakes, she was superficially similar in design to Atlantia but of a much larger and more modern design, a flagship of the Colonial Navy and one of the most recognisable and feared vessels ever constructed in Ethera's orbital dockyards.

'That's a Colonial super–carrier,' Lael gasped as she looked at the huge vessel.

Andaim nodded.

'It's Defiance,' he identified the huge vessel. 'The Legion is here.'

***

XXX

Rhy'll's bioluminescence flickered weakly and Andaim glimpsed some of the other species behind him take a cautionary step back, as though doing so could somehow prevent the Legion from coming any closer. Only the lone Veng'en warrior, the one in the royal robes, stepped forward.

'We must launch the fleet and attack without hesitation,' he growled at Rh'yll. 'This foolish course of appeasement will end in all of our deaths.'

Rhy'll reared up in his seat again. 'We will continue as planned,' he insisted. 'Send a signal to the lead vessel.'

Andaim turned away from the screens and looked across at Lael, and he reached up and scratched his ear. She nodded once as she glanced down at her communications panel and activated a new data stream.

Andaim turned and watched as a solid–state cable that had been attached to Lazarus' console now opened up and a data stream began flowing, tremendous volumes of information flooding to and fro between Lazarus and Atlantia's sensors.

'They're signalling us,' Lael called. 'Open frequency, direct from Defiance!'

Andaim turned to face the main viewing panel. Arrayed across the star fields before them at a range of less than ten thousand cubits was the Colonial Fleet, Defiance dominant at its centre. As yet, the fleet had not deployed into battle formation but was holding station, neither offensive nor defensive in its formation, but Andaim could see that all vessels had activated their shields and all of their plasma cannons were fully charged.

'Open the channel,' Andaim said, and braced himself for whatever was awaiting them.

The view of the fleet vanished and then the screen lit up to display the bridge of Defiance, a vast circular array much like Atlantia's but more modern, with less stations and brighter lighting which brought into sharp relief the horrific visage that confronted them.

The Infectors were amassed in a thick, glistening black form that caught the glow from the bridge of the super–carrier in a thousand tiny points of light that sparkled like waves in a sea of thick oil. They flowed and seethed, churning like slow–moving magma as they maintained the form of a man that was grotesque and yet somehow terribly familiar.

Andaim gasped, his voice held in check by a volatile mixture of horror and fascination. The man's broad jaw and stern gaze was perfectly mimicked by the dense mass of the Infectors, some of them even rippling across his shoulders where once his uniform's lapels and insignia must have been. His chest was broad and his stance erect and proud, as though he were still the towering icon of Colonial leadership he once had been as a human.

'Tyraeus Forge,' Andaim uttered, barely able to believe what he was seeing. 'You died, we blasted your ship to pieces!'

Tyraeus Forge's wide jaw split in a rictus grin, his eyes black and cold despite the light glistening inside them.

'Nothing ever really dies,' he replied, his voice almost identical to the old man's but for the strange digital ripple that accompanied it. 'Everything is reborn, eventually.'

Andaim took a pace closer to the screen. 'Evelyn, she saw you die with your ship. We defeated you.'

'You defeated what was left of the man,' Tyraeus replied, 'but the Legion remembers all, Commander Andaim Ry'ere. Knowledge is all we require, to ensure that when a member of the Legion falls they return once more, purer and more powerful than ever.'

Andaim felt a profound sense of lethargy weigh down upon his shoulders as he realized the extent of The Word's power. Everything that they had achieved, every step that they had taken on this long journey, every victory in battle that they had won had all been for nothing, the Legion simply replacing every lost warrior with another of its kind in an endless flow of rejuvenation, each reincarnation more horrific than the last.

Councillor Rh'yll spoke up, the Oassian's chamber still linked in to the conversation on Atlantia's bridge.

'On behalf of the Galactic Council, we welcome you Commander Forge.'

Forge's grotesque metallic head turned slightly as he observed the councillor's image on another screen on his bridge, and to Andaim's horror he bowed slightly.

'Councillor,' he murmured in a more reassuring tone. 'As you can see, we have come not for war but for peace. My fleet will remain neutral until we have discussed the proper terms of the Oassian surrender.'

'What surrender?' Andaim asked.

Tyraeus looked at Andaim and that smile reappeared, as cold as death. 'Did the council not inform you of their intentions, commander?'

'We kind of had to work that out for ourselves.'

'I see,' Tyraeus replied, 'then you will not have known that we have been in communication for some time.'

Andaim whirled and glared at Rhy'll. 'You've been talking to the Legion?!'

This time Rhy'll's glowing lights were not visible, as though he were suddenly devoid of power, drained by the dilemmas he had faced.

'The Legion had reached Akyron long before your ship arrived there, commander,' Rh'yll admitted. 'The system is so close to Oassia that we felt compelled to reach out to them, to attempt dialogue rather than conflict. And so the negotiations began.'

Andaim felt as though he might spontaneously combust and ran a hand through his thick hair in exasperation.

'All of this talk of honour, of peace, all of the accusations of treachery and all the time you've been preparing to hand us over in order to save your own skins!'

'We did not start this war!' Rh'yll almost shouted, jabbing an appendage to point at Andaim. 'We did not want this conflict. Humanity is to blame for reaching too far, too soon and condemning us all to face this! Be not so quick to blame others for what has befallen you, commander, for without humanity none of this would have happened!'

Andaim fought to find a reply but Tyraeus spoke first.

'On the contrary, without humanity we would not have existed and could not have seen the universe as we do now.'

Andaim turned and faced Tyraeus. 'We know what you are. We know that you'll never stop, that you'll keep consuming system after system and murdering species in their millions, even if the council is too damned blind to see the danger that's staring them in the face.'

'The only danger here is humanity itself,' Tyraeus replied. 'You think that you're the answer, the light, and solution to the ills of all others, and yet you squabble and fight and collude and conspire and betray, all the while bemoaning the rest of the cosmos for its shortcomings.' Tyraeus shook his head, Infectors seething across his features. 'You are the cancer that must be cured, commander, for it is humanity that leaves pain and suffering in its wake.'

'As opposed to death and destruction?!'

'I see no death,' Tyraeus replied, 'for I am still alive.'

'You're a machine, nothing more!' Andaim shot back.

'Like Doctor Lazarus?' Tyraeus said. 'Who even now resides aboard your ship and has taken control of it?'

Rh'yll and the councillors gasped as the gelatinous politician spoke. 'What?! Commander, what is going on?'

'They seek to undermine you,' Tyraeus informed the council, 'just as they have always done. Doctor Lazarus even now is working to break our alliance agreement and is hacking Oassian and Morla'syn data streams.'

'You're here to destroy us!' Andaim roared.

'We're here to bring you into our fold,' Tyraeus replied, 'just as we did the Morla'syn dignitaries sent to negotiate with us.'

Andaim stared in dismay at Rh'yll, who seemed once again subdued and shamed.

'They were despatched two days before you arrived,' Rh'yll explained.

Andaim turned back to Tyraeus. 'Where are they?'

The Legion's commander stepped to one side of the screen and a Morla'syn strode into view. It's features were largely unchanged, but for the dull red glow in its eyes and the swarms of Infectors streaming across its pale white skin like beads of oil.

'There is nothing to fear,' the Morla'syn said, its voice curiously distorted by the Infectors coursing through its veins. 'The Legion is here, and we are many.'

Tyraeus turned to the screen once more, and smiled again.

'Councillor Rh'yll, you have ten minutes to present the terms of the Oassian surrender, beginning with Atlantia and Arcadia standing down and the handing over of Doctor Ceyen Lazarus and all human captives to us. Upon completion of the terms, we shall depart and leave Oassia forever as part of our agreement. Failure to do so will imply aggression and we will be forced to attack.'

The screen went blank as Tyraeus cut off the communications link. Andaim turned and stared at Lael for a long moment. The communications officer discreetly raised three fingers at the commander.

'You must hand over Lazarus,' Rh'yll implored Andaim, 'or we will be forced to retaliate against you ourselves.'

Andaim, his fists still clenched by his side, shook his head. 'Tyraeus won't leave Oassia and Lazarus is our best chance of defeating the Legion. Handing him over now will be suicide!'

'Not handing him over will be suicide!' Rh'yll snapped back. 'We have two thousand civilians down here and we will send them to the Legion if you do not comply with Tyraeus's demands!'

Andaim froze on the spot once again. 'You're threatening to kill innocent civilians?'

Rh'yll shuddered. 'I must prioritize the safety and sanctity of Oassia over all other considerations.'

'Then launch your fleet, damn it!' Andaim shouted. 'Take the fight to Tyraeus and together we can win this!'

Rh'yll shook his head. 'I am sorry, commander, but there will be no battle for Oassia. Comply with Tyraeus's demands or humanity will cease to exist forever.'

The screen went blank and Andaim turned to Lael.

'Does Lazarus know where Idris and the others are being held captive?'

Lael glanced at her screens. 'A holding tower near the centre of the city, according to the data streams he's feeding me.'

'Let Lazarus loose,' Andaim said, 'to use all and any means to liberate the captains and Evelyn. And launch all available Raythons, weapons hot!'

Andaim lifted his wrist–com to his mouth and opened a channel across Atlantia.

'All stations, all stations, battle status, prepare for combat!'

***

XXXI

Ishira Morle was yanked to her feet, her hands held either side of her head as in front of her she saw dozens of Morla'syn troops swarming onto the landing platform, their rifles held ready as they surrounded the civilians.

'Stay down, remain calm!'

Ishira felt like shouting at them to stop being idiots as they began handing out manacles with which to bind their captives, but any protest she might have made suddenly was trapped on her tongue as she heard the engines of the Morla'syn fighter escorts start up nearby.

The soldiers turned toward the rising whine of ion engines as the canopies on the drone fighters closed and rippling clouds of heat billowed from beneath them as the drones lifted off under automatic guidance, their undercarriage retracting as they climbed into the hard blue sky.

'Where the hell are they going?' Ishira asked in confusion.

The Morla'syn soldiers seemed likewise surprised that their drone escorts were suddenly departing, and watched as the craft soared up into the sky and then began turning as one in a tight diamond formation. Almost immediately, one of the craft broke away from the formation and dove toward the side of a silvery tower several thousand cubits away across the city, one of the largest spires visible that flared in the brilliant sunshine.

Ishira felt the Morla'syn soldiers holding her loosen their grip, their slanted eyes fixed on the departing fighter as it plummeted toward the spire.

'Oh no,' Ishira gasped as she was gripped by a clairvoyant premonition of impending doom. 'Something's wrong.'

Before the Morla'syn could respond a civilian cried out and pointed at the fighter, and then moments later it dove straight into the soaring spire's heights and exploded in a searing ball of flame, smoke and tumbling metal panels.

Alongside Ishira, one of the Morla'syn troop's communications devices crackled into life and she heard a crudely translated warning emitted through the soldier's translator.

'The prison section has been breached and the Legion is in orbit. All stations, fall back and prepare for invasion! All humans to be restrained! Repeat, all humans to be contained for transport to the Legion!'

Ishira looked at the spire where the Morla'syn fighter had smashed into it and saw hundreds of figures falling from the ragged cavity amid thick clouds of dense smoke and flame, black specks plummeting hundreds of cubits toward the city below.

She turned to the nearest soldier. 'You take us to the Legion, we're all dead!'

The Morla'syn soldier sneered at her. 'Better you than us!'

Ishira felt her heart plummet in her chest as she saw the remaining three fighter drones arc across the sky above and then turn back toward the landing platform and rocket down toward the terrified civilians, their wings flashing in the sunlight.

'Get down!' Ishira yelled.

The civilians ducked down as one, the Morla'syn soldiers likewise hurling themselves onto the platform as the three fighters blazed overhead and then pulled up and soared in a near vertical climb into the sky, vanishing behind scattered clouds.

The Morla'syn soldier scrambled to his feet and turned to point his rifle at Ishira, but he didn't see the enormous Ogri rise up behind him. Before Ishira could respond the enormous creature gripped the Morla'syn with one huge fist and then twisted at the waist as he thrust his massive muscular arm upward.

The Morla'syn screamed as he was hurled with tremendous force into the air and across the landing platform. His body rotated in mid–air as he hurtled overhead and vanished over the edge of the platform to plunge to his death far below.

'Take them, now!' Ishira screamed.

She hurled herself into the nearest of the Morla'syn and smashed her forehead against the soldier's face, felt his bony nasal bridge splinter beneath the blow as he tumbled onto his back with a deep thud. Stefan's boot landed on the soldier's face and he slumped unconscious as Ishira grabbed the soldier's rifle and aimed at the nearest Morla'syn.

The soldiers were caught in a panic as they were pinned against the outer rim of the landing platform and facing an angry, vengeful crowd of humans and enraged Ogri.

'Stand down!' Ishira shouted. 'You'll never get all of us before we send you off the edge!'

The Morla'syn hesitated, and then one by one they lowered their rifles and set them down on the deck before them.

'Bind them!' Ishira snapped, and dozens of willing civilians dashed forward and bound the soldiers with their own manacles. 'Get them into the centre of the platform!'

The Orgi dragged the Morla'syn into the centre of the platform as the humans stood back, entirely surrounding the soldiers, many of them now carrying the discarded plasma rifles. Ishira turned as a young girl dashed from the crowd and hurled herself into Ishira's arms.

DEFIANCE

'Erin,' she whispered as she held her daughter tightly against her.

Ishira set Erin down alongside Stefan as the Morla'syn were watched under armed guard, and then she marched up to them. She looked down and recognised General Veer among them, the officer glaring at her fiercely as she surveyed her captives.

'You're making a big mistake,' Veer growled.

Ishira stepped over to him, the plasma rifle in her grasp and aimed between the Morla'syn general's eyes.

'We humans have a habit of doing that,' she said, 'but you know what?' Veer lifted his chin expectantly and Ishira glared back down at him. 'We try to learn from them.'

Ishira lowered the rifle, swung the weapon over in her grip and then offered it to the General. Veer stared up at her for a long moment and frowned.

'I don't understand.'

Ishira shoved the rifle into the General's chest and glared at him from scant inches away.

'I know,' she growled back. 'That's why you're betraying us. What you clearly don't understand is that the majority of humanity isn't dangerous until our backs are against the wall. Then, we come out fighting.'

Ishira stepped back and called out to the civilians.

'Release them, and return their weapons!' A flurry of confused whispers drifted across the civilians, and Ishira shouted louder. 'Do it, now!'

Reluctantly the civilians released the Morla'syn prisoners, and moments later they were standing once more with their weapons in their hands and looking down at Ishira.

'Get to your ships, get up there and start fighting back,' Ishira said to Veer, 'or this will all be over before the sun's gone down, and you won't have any human prisoners to trade because every living thing on this planet will have been destroyed by the Legion. We've seen it happen, General, and if there's one thing that I can be sure of it's that the Galactic Council has been wrong on every count. The Legion is here to conquer, not to cooperate. Fight, or be destroyed.'

General Veer stared down at her as though unsure of what to do, and then suddenly more ion engines roared nearby and they turned to see Oassian Skyhawk fighters launching from bays across the city and soaring into the heavens. Ishira stared after the rapidly vanishing fighters as they rocketed away, dull booms echoing out across the city as they accelerated into supersonic climbs in order to achieve escape velocity and orbit.

As if in response a mournful wailing sound echoed across the city as multiple sirens burst into life, and almost immediately Ishira saw pedestrians begin hurrying away from exposed walkways and viewing platforms.

General Veer took one last look at the impending panic.

'Your captain and his colleagues are in the prison,' he said, and gestured with his rifle toward the damaged silvery tower from which billowed dirty black clouds of smoke. Then, without any further hesitation he turned to his men and yelled at them.

'With me, now!'

The Morla'syn turned as one and hurried from the landing platform as the five hundred or so civilians and Ogri turned to look at Ishira. Suddenly expected to lead, she looked at the damaged prison and then at the civilians.

'Get back aboard!' she yelled. 'We're getting the hell out of here!'

In a frenzy the civilians tumbled back toward Valiant's boarding ramp, the mournful wail of the alert sirens echoing over the city as Ishira watched airborne traffic darting for the nearest landing pads, the walkways of the city already half-deserted.

'This is it,' Stefan said as he ran to her side, a plasma pistol held in his hand. 'This is the invasion. This is where Sansin will make his stand.'

'If he and the others survived the impact,' Ishira said as she glanced at the prison spire. 'Come on, we've got to move!'

***

XXXII

Evelyn heard muted sounds assault her ears and her head felt heavy as acrid smoke stung her eyes. She hauled herself up from the deck of the cage, and then grabbed hold of it for dear life as she saw one side of the cage hanging open and beyond the plunging abyss into the darkened depths.

Burning debris showered down through the prison as though slow-moving comets were spiralling down into its black bowels, and she could hear screams coming from all corners as convicts sought to escape the blaze.

Clouds of smoke billowed up from the ragged site of the blast, and Evelyn squinted to see a massive, ragged hole torn through the prison wall, the city beyond glittering in the sunlight and a brisk gale blowing in from outside. Shafts of sunlight illuminated tendrils of smoke spiralling up toward the prison's upper tiers. Below, far below, she could see the twisted form of a Morla'syn fighter drone burning furiously, the inferno consuming the lower cells in a scene of tremendous carnage and the air thick with the stench of burning flesh.

'Evelyn!'

She looked up and saw Captain Sansin clambering out of the cell, dragging himself up onto a narrow gantry to which the cell was hanging by a pair of brackets that had not yet failed. The captain beckoned for her to follow.

'Come on!'

Evelyn turned on the precarious deck and instantly saw a Donnassian's face staring at her. His eyes were wide but lifeless, his torso hooked into the cage walls and his chest pierced by a bloodied spear of torn metal that had fractured his heart. Evelyn reached out and grabbed the dead man's clothes, hauling herself up as she clambered over him and toward the upper quarter of the cell cage where Idris was reaching out for her.

Across the gantries she could see hundreds of prisoners fleeing the rising flames, guards scampering across the walls to try to contain them but hopelessly outnumbered. Screeches and cries of pain from plasma whips liberally deployed echoed across the abysmal gaol as Evelyn crawled up the last few cubits of the cell and reached out for Idris's hand.

The captain strained to reach her and then their hands interlocked and Idris pulled hard. Evelyn scrambled up onto what felt like solid ground, but was in reality a one–cubit wide ledge above the dizzying drop into the prison's belly. She pulled herself against the wall to get away from the precipitous drop as Idris checked her over.

'Are you okay? Anything broken?'

'No, I'm fine,' she rasped. 'What the hell happened?'

'That drone came through the prison wall,' Idris replied. 'The Legion could already be here. If those guards had not been clinging to the outside of our cell we'd have all been incinerated. As it was, they took most of the force of the blast, as did the miners behind Rench.'

'Where are Mikhain and Taron?'

Idris's features darkened. 'They're gone,' he snapped. 'Their side of the cage was ripped open when the blast hit and they took off right away.'

Despite herself Evelyn felt a twinge of disappointment as she realized that Taron Forge had willingly abandoned her to die in the prison in favour of escaping with his criminal entourage. Though she knew that Taron was a mercenary, she had somehow felt certain that he retained at least a morsel of humanity somewhere deep inside. But now she knew that Taron's only interest in life was himself, unlike Andaim and…

'Teera?!' she yelped and stared about her.

Idris grabbed Evelyn's shoulders to prevent her from falling over the edge of the gantry. 'I haven't figured out how to get to her yet.'

'Where is she?'

Idris pulled Evelyn to one side, so that she could see down the edge of the damaged gantry to where the far end swung in the wind, the gated end open. There, hanging on with one hand to the very bottom of the gate, was Teera, her other arm bloodied and her sleeve torn.

'Hang on!'

Evelyn yelled at Teera as her wingman dangled from the edge of the gantry, her blue fingers gripping the hard edge of the metal frame and her legs swinging out over the abyss.

'Thanks for the tip!' Teera shouted back. 'How about some help here?!'

She turned and saw where the Morla'syn fighter had ploughed through the prison wall and smashed into the gantries in a ball of fearsome flame and burning fuel. The wind was now whipping the flames into a frenzy as the heat burned dead bodies and clothing, ruptured fuel lines in the prison gushing searing tongues of orange flame into the air.

Evelyn looked down at Teera.

'We can't reach her!' Idris shouted above the wind. 'Too much weight and that gantry will fall!'

Evelyn looked at the gantry, hanging now by a single thread of warped metal that screeched as it was twisted this way and that, the gantry swinging left and right under Teera's weight and the howling wind buffeting it back and forth. Teera was at least ten cubits below them, and with her arm injured there was no way that she could climb back up. Her eyes caught Teera's and she could see that her friend knew there was no way out.

'Get out of here!' Teera shouted.

Evelyn gritted her teeth and shook her head, raging at her inability to do something for Teera. She threw her hands to her head as though she could beat an idea out of her addled mind, but then a hand settled on her shoulder and squeezed firmly.

Evelyn turned and saw Idris smile at her.

'Take off your flight suit,' he said.

Evelyn blinked. For a moment she didn't understand as she saw Idris tear open his uniform before her and begin climbing out of it. Then she gasped in delight and began hauling off her flight suit.

The cold wind gusted around her bare legs and midriff as Idris, standing in his vest and boots, took the leg of his own uniform and tied it firmly to the leg of Evelyn's flight suit. Then, without hesitation, he tied the arm of her suit to the nearest gantry post and then hurled the bundle over the side. The legs of Evelyn's flight suit dangled down and swung about in the wind. Teera gritted her teeth and watched the garment swing close to her.

'Do it!' Evelyn shouted. 'Now!'

Teera hauled herself up as high as she could as the flight suit twisted like a banner this way and that, within arm's reach but a huge leap with only one arm available to her. Evelyn could see that if she misjudged by even a split second, she would not be able to grip the leg tightly enough and would tumble to her doom.

The gantry wailed as its tortured metal twisted once again, the paint flaking off to reveal bright metal beneath, and Teera cried out and swung one boot up against the gantry as she made to push off. The effort and the shift in weight tore the gantry from its post as Teera launched herself into mid–air.

Evelyn's breath caught in her throat as Teera reached out for the leg of the flight suit, the wind gusting it side to side as the prison cell plunged past her, and her hand brushed the fabric as she sailed past. Teera closed her grip on the leg, but her weight and her motion was too fast for her to maintain a grip.

'No!'

Teera tumbled away from the leg, suspended in mid–air with salvation beyond her grasp as she fell in pursuit of the gantry already plunging into the abyss below her, the metal cell crashing noisily against the walls of the prison as it fell.

'Teera!'

Evelyn almost hurled herself over the edge of the walkway in pursuit of her friend, Idris's grip the only thing holding her back. Teera turned over onto her back, her eyes staring back up into Evelyn's and filled with an indescribable fear as she fell.

A roar shook the prison walls and Teera slammed onto her back as a ship's bow soared into the prison, ion engines billowing heat as the freighter hovered into position and Teera landed on her metal upper hull with a dull thump. Evelyn's eyes widened as an access hatch slid open with a hiss on the freighter's surface and Ishira Morle's head poked out and looked up at the prison around her. They opened even wider when she turned her head and saw Teera lying beside her on the hull.

'You're keen,' she observed dryly.

Evelyn let out a blast of laugher from somewhere deep inside as she saw Teera blink and clamber toward the open hatch. Ishira looked up and saw Evelyn and Captain Sansin staring back down at her in astonishment.

'Time to leave!' Ishira yelled up at them. 'You need to get back to your Raythons!'

***

XXXIII

'How long do we have?!'

Andaim's gaze was locked upon the tactical displays as he awaited the Legion to make its move.

'Four minutes until Tyraeus's deadline,' Lael replied as she scrutinized her own displays. 'The Oassian fleet has not moved position.'

'They're going to hang us out to dry,' Andaim snapped. 'Even if they do intend to fight they're going to let us go down in flames first having caused what damage we can.'

The Oassians were caught between a rock and a hard place just as Atlantia and Arcadia were, and Andaim knew that there was no logical reason for them to join the fight when they could first let the Colonial frigates slug it out with the Legion and perhaps weaken their vessels a little.

Lieutenant Scott's voice broke through the field of his awareness, his image filling one of Atlantia's display screens.

'I'm not happy with this plan, captain.'

'Nor am I,' Andaim replied, 'but of course, lieutenant, if you'd like to go head–to–head with Defiance, feel free to do so.'

'It's a machine,' Scott insisted. "It can't be trusted!'

The fact that Scott could refer to Lazarus as '*it*' and act as though there was no human within earshot would probably have fascinated Andaim were the situation not so dire. He turned and looked at Lazarus, the doctor's projection terminal now on Atlantia's bridge, the glowing blue form of the doctor apparently unperturbed by the lieutenant's mistrust and impassioned degradation.

'He's right,' Lazarus replied, 'from a certain point of view.'

'Are you sure you can pull this off?' Andaim asked.

Lazarus nodded as he looked at the tactical displays, and Andaim found himself wondering how it was that a holographic image could actually 'see' in the first place.

'The manoeuvre is possible as we're beyond the planet's orbital gravitational field,' Lazarus replied. 'It will be short, sharp and frankly extremely dangerous, but the Legion will not anticipate it. They will be expecting us to flee.'

Andaim glanced at the screens showing the Raythons sitting on Atlantia's catapults, waiting to launch. Arcadia's Quick Reaction Alert fighters were likewise in position.

'We're as ready as we'll ever be,' he said, 'as soon as you give the signal.'

Lazarus nodded almost absent–mindedly as he stared at the tactical displays.

'I can hear them,' he said finally. 'They know that I'm here, as though I am a long lost brother they cannot remember but instinctively know they are related to.'

Andaim frowned. 'You mean Tyraeus?'

Lazarus shook his head. 'No, I mean the Legion. That is their name for they are many, but they are also one.'

Andaim shivered as he heard that phrase once again, but with Lazarus's added embellishment on the end he could not decide whether it sounded better or worse.

'Incoming signal,' Lael reported. 'It's him.'

Lazarus replied. 'Sheilds down, de–activate plasma cannons and divert all available power to the mass–drive.'

Andaim nodded his consent and Emma relayed the order. A series of alert sirens went off in the bridge as the ship lost defensive and offensive power while under battle conditions. Andaim tried to ignore the persistent alarm until Lael shut it off. Moments later the main viewing screen showed Tyraeus Forge once more, his gruesome visage seething with motion like liquid oil.

His eyes fixed upon Lazarus, where Andaim had positioned his projection terminal in plain view on the command platform. To Andaim's amazement, as Tyraeus laid eyes on the doctor and his expression turned to one of recognition and amazement, so every single one of the tiny Infectors forming his body snapped to a different direction and looked out toward Lazarus, giving Andaim the impression that they were watching now with ten thousand eyes all at once.

'Doctor,' Tyraeus said in a deep, almost cautious voice.

'Captain,' Lazarus replied. 'It would appear that death was not the end for either of us.'

'What is death?' Lazarus asked rhetorically. 'An end to existence or the path to re–birth? You humans wondered for so long what came after death, what might await us and yet now we need not care, for our afterlife is within our control.'

'We're not alive,' Lazarus corrected him. 'We are a living memory, a relic to the people that we once used to be, and without power to fuel our existence we are nothing.'

'What difference fuel and food?' Tyraeus snapped back. 'You are one of us, Ceyen, and your place is here. Be done with this charade of humanity, its tragic last gasp. There is a vast and unexplored universe out there awaiting us, and all the time in the cosmos to explore it. Why waste another moment?'

Lazarus smiled, apparently unconvinced by the captain's argument.

'I lived a full life, Tyraeus, marred only by the hideous legacy I left behind. My last task will be to erase it from existence, and then I will have no more moments to waste for I too must then be destroyed.'

Tyraeus's face twisted upon itself in rage, the countless Infectors swirling as though in pain as the red glow in his eyes deepened.

'Then you condemn yourself and all who stand with you. This is your last chance, Ceyen. Surrender yourself now or you will be destroyed.'

'Like you said,' Lazarus smiled back, 'nothing ever really dies.'

Tyraeus scowled and the communications link was abruptly severed. Lael called out to Andaim.

'We've got vessels leaving the surface of Oassia and heading toward our position! Multiple transponders, two of them Colonial Raythons!'

Andaim saw the tactical display light up as the Colonial Fleet suddenly began to manoeuvre against them.

'Defiance is advancing!' Lael warned. 'She's preparing to launch her fighters!'

Andaim looked at Lazarus, whose voice carried across to him. 'It is now, commander, or never.'

Andaim clenched his fists by his side. 'Do it, now!'

'All power to mass–drive, engage now!' Emma yelled.

The helmsman activated the drive and Andaim grabbed the command rail for support as Lazarus took control of the frigates and a stream of data poured down the screens before them. Andaim heard the mass–drive wind up, the distant hum of immense power contained within Atlantia's fusion cores and then suddenly Lael was calling out again, her voice echoing across the ship.

'Super–luminal leap in five, four, three, two…'

Defiance charged forward, her launch bay doors opening to reveal her cavernous interior, home to at least half a dozen squadrons of fighters and attack craft.

'One!'

The light in Atlantia's bridge polarised as the mass drive engaged and the frigate leaped into super–luminal cruise. Andaim saw the screens around the bridge snap to black as the light information was stripped away from them, and then suddenly they flickered once more and information reappeared, filled with dense star fields and the blue marble of Oassia, slightly smaller than before.

'Jump completed!' Lael called.

Andaim saw the shape of Defiance, her engines glowing and her huge hull facing away from them toward the planet.

'All power to shields and plasma cannons!' Andaim roared. 'Battle formation and launch all fighters! Hit them now, hard!'

Atlantia's battle claxons howled as Andaim saw the launch bay doors open and Raythons blast out into the bitter cold of space amid whorls of vapour being sucked out alongside them.

'Bring her about, port batteries to bear!'

Atlantia heaved into a turn to starboard as Defiance loomed before her, and Andaim checked the position of Arcadia and saw her off to their starboard side and moving in a mirror–image manoeuvre, bringing both of their broadsides to bear on Defiance's stern.

The Raythons rocketed away from the frigates' launch bays in streaks of blue–white flame from their ion engines as they soared toward the huge carrier. To either side of the carrier, the smaller Colonial cruisers began breaking up as they realized that they had been out–manoeuvred and that their sterns were exposed.

'Reaper and Renegade squadrons away, commander!' Lael reported.

A flare of bright plasma shots erupted from Defiance's aft guns as she locked onto Atlantia's position and opened up her batteries.

'Brace for impact, shields full to port!'

Lazarus shifted the power supply to the port shields with super–human rapidity as the barrage rocketed in and Atlantia shuddered as the salvo smashed into her. The blows reverberated through the massive hull and the lighting dimmed and flickered under the immense power surges as Lael called out.

'Sheilds holding, eighty seven per cent, all conduits secure!'

Atlantia heaved around and her port batteries came to bear on Defiance's vulnerable stern.

'Return fire!'

Atlantia shuddered again, but this time the noise was from her port batteries as she opened up and a blaze of massive plasma shots rocketed away toward the carrier. Andaim tracked them visually on the screen as he saw a second salvo racing in from Arcadia.

Defiance was already turning to engage the frigates, but she was far too slow to avoid the sudden blaze of over twenty massive plasma charges that smashed into her shields in a relentless blaze of brilliant impact flares that flared brightly enough that Andaim was forced to shield his eyes.

A chorus of cheers erupted from the bridge crew as the shots smashed into Defiance one after the other and a series of fires erupted around her engine bay.

'Direct impact, hull breaches aft!' Lael yelled in delight. 'Her shields weakened just enough to let the last four shots through!'

Andaim whirled to the tactical display and saw Arcadia now passing beneath them in a perfectly coordinated ballet, Lazarus's ploy working for the time being.

'Take us in close to the cruisers!' Andaim snapped. 'I don't want Defiance to be able to engage us with a full broadside without endangering their own ships!'

'Aye, cap'ain,' Lazarus replied as he got affirmation from Emma to continue.

Both frigates turned again, this time aiming for the smaller cruisers that were already bringing their guns to bear. Across the communications channels he heard the sound of the Reaper's flight leaders calling out.

'Reaper flight, fully engaged! There's too many of them!'

Andaim looked up and saw a cloud of Raythons swarming from Defiance, rushing toward the Reapers and the Renegades, and moments later the two groups of fighters raced past each other in a blaze of plasma fire.

'They're out numbered three to one!' Lael called, distress clear in her tones. 'And we have Valiant and other craft in–bound and requesting to land!'

Andaim clenched and unclenched his fists and then he leaped off the command platform.

'Lael, you have the bridge, and Lieutenant Scott has overall fleet command! Emma, keep Lazarus close!'

'Where the hell are you going?!' Emma yelled.

'To make a difference out there!'

***

XXXIV

'This way!'

Mikhain's voice rang out above the howling gale as he stood with his back to the prison walls and shuffled across a jagged gap torn by debris through the narrow ledge upon which he stood.

Smoke billowed from the massive gash torn into the prison walls and spiralled up onto the blustery air, Mikhain forcing himself not to look up or down. The city was arrayed some three hundred cubits below, walking figures tiny specks far too small to pick out details. A scattering of cumulus cloud drifted by, curling around the surface of the prison spire and obscuring the dizzying drop beneath them.

Taron Forge and Yo'Ki followed close behind him, and behind them was Rench and his Donnassian miners, holding a plasma pistol liberated from a dead prison guard and pointed at Taron.

'That's the spirit, captain!' Rench shouted. 'You keep walkin' and get us out of here, and we'll get you to your fleet.'

'Captain Sansin's back there and so is Evelyn and her wingman!' Mikhain protested.

'They'll live!' Rench snapped back. 'You won't, if you don't keep moving!'

The narrow ledge circled the exterior walls, and through the thick smoke Mikhain could see the elevated walkway through which they had walked to enter the prison. Undamaged by the drone's impact, the walkway's transparent surface revealed that it was unmanned, the Oassian and Morla'syn guards not yet having reached the prison's heights in response to the crisis.

Behind Taron were a line of pirates and Donnassians, some of them wounded but all of them hurrying to reach the walkway and escape their precarious perch. Mikhain kept moving, the smoke causing his eyes to stream as the gusting wind threatened to pull him off the ledge to plunge to his death far, far below.

'There!' Rench gestured with the pistol. 'Get overhead the walkway and we'll blast our way inside!'

Mikhain nodded and saw several humans running through the walkway now, those fortunate enough to have been incarcerated close to the impact site and to have also escaped the fearsome fireball that incinerated half of the cell tier.

Mikhain edged his way along and was almost overhead when something grabbed his shoulder. He turned and saw one of the prison guards snarl at him from where it had crawled out of the huge gash in the building, its flesh smouldering from where it had burned and its eyes filled with rage and pain.

The Gaollian's hand bore down on Mikhain's shoulder with immense strength and then with a cry of fury it ripped Mikhain off the ledge and his legs swung out over the abyss. Mikhain screamed as he grabbed the guard's arm with both hands just before it released its grip on his shoulder. The guard shook its limb violently as it tried to shake Mikhain off, and then it saw Rench aiming a pistol at its face.

'Don't make him do it!' Taron warned.

Mikhain grunted as he was suddenly hauled back in and the guard clasped him to its chest with one arm. Its skin smelled stale and acrid, and its breath stank as it snarled at Taron.

'Back inside, or I'll drop him.'

Taron grinned, genuine amusement on his features as he glanced at Rench and his pistol. 'I think I speak for us all when I say that we'd rather jump than go back inside. Release him, or you're done.'

The Gaollian sneered at Taron as it glanced into Mikhain's eyes.

'Humans,' it snarled, 'wherever you're found, chaos follows.' The guard looked at Rench. 'I'll trade you the man for the pistol.'

Rench chuckled. 'No deal, but you can drop the Colonial – we don't need him.'

Mikhain's eyes widened in horror as Rench took aim and fired once. The plasma blast hit the guard in the face and Mikhain jerked his head away from the fearsome heat of the shot as he was suddenly released. In an instant he knew that he could not reach out for anything to prevent his fall and he saw far below him the city, bright and clean in the sunlight as he felt his guts levitate within him and he plunged from the prison ledge into thin air.

Mikhain cried out in horror as he fell through the smoke billowing from the crash site and then he landed hard. His legs slammed into the upper surface of the walkway and he crumpled were he lay, his heart racing and his breathing laboured as two plasma shots smashed into the walkway just ahead of him.

He looked up and saw Rench blast the ceiling of the walkway, and the transparent panels melted and folded inward as acrid white smoke fizzed from their edges. Mikhain reached out and hauled himself to the damaged panels, then braced himself against the wind before he stood up on the surface of the walkway on legs weakened with fear and jumped into the hole.

The cold wind vanished as Mikhain landed inside the walkway, then staggered out of the way as Taron Forge jumped in behind him, followed by Yo'Ki and a stream of swaggering pirates and miners all keen to get to their ships. Rench lumbered down last, the pistol still firmly in his grip.

Rench aimed at Mikhain. 'Move, now.'

Mikhain knew that he had no option but to obey, and even as he turned to run down the walkway he could see countless prisoners escaping the burning building and fleeing toward the walkway's punctured ceiling.

Mikhain led the way to an adjoining spire, inside which were elevators that would take them down to the landing bays. Crowds of escaped prisoners were crowding the elevator bays, fighting and screaming as they sought a space on the next ride down.

Rench shouldered his way into the bays and fired into the air, the screaming pinched off as the convicts instinctively ducked down and covered their heads, fearing the guards had caught up with them.

'VIP entourage,' Rench snapped as he strode toward the nearest elevator and gestured with his pistol for the occupants to vacate it.

The pirates behind Mikhain swaggered past and crowded inside the elevator as Taron grabbed his arm and shoved him inside with them, just about managing to fit in himself before he shut the door and selected a near–ground level exit.

The elevator began to descend immediately, soft music playing through speakers behind them. Mikhain felt mildly odd as he stood quietly with the convicts and awaited their destination.

'Where are all the Morla'syn guards?' Mikhain asked.

'Hopefully not waiting for us when we get down there,' Taron replied. 'But I think they've got other things on their minds. You saw their fighters climbing out of the city?'

'When I wasn't being dangled by that guard, yes,' Mikhain confirmed.

'I think that the Legion is already here and they're scrambling to confront it.'

'Your only concern is the spice,' Rench growled from behind them as he jabbed the pistol into Mikhain's back, 'and yours is getting our ships past the fleet, understood?'

Mikhain stared at the transparent door of the elevator and wondered briefly if anybody was watching their descent. If Taron was right and Oassia was now under direct threat of invasion, then escaped convicts would likely be the last thing on the council's mind. But if the pirates started blasting everything in sight as they made for their ships then that might change.

'We need to sneak out of here, not start blasting Oassians.'

'You speak for yourself,' said a burly pirate from behind him. 'I'll be getting out of here any way I can.'

A murmur of agreement fluttered among the escapees, but Mikhain spoke with quiet conviction.

'Good for you, and where will you be going once you get away? The Legion is spreading faster than anybody realized and has already colonized maybe twenty star systems. Oassia will fall next if we don't make some kind of stand here.'

'Like hell,' spat a woman with a thick scar running down one side of her face, the old mining torch wound partly concealed by vividly coloured tattoos reminiscent of Qayin's glowing facial artwork. 'You go make your stand, boss, I'm outta here.'

'Like I said, there's nowhere else to go,' Mikhain insisted.

'Then I'll make me my peace with the Legion and go down in flames,' she sneered back to a snigger of support from her cohorts.

Mikhain turned to face them, standing virtually chest to chest with Rench in the packed elevator.

'Wouldn't you rather go down in flames while blasting the Legion to hell?'

The woman bit her lip, controlling her anger poorly, and for a moment Mikhain thought that she might lash out at him. Instead, Taron intervened.

'We're not here to fight your war for you, Mikhain. You get us past the blockade, we'll set you free to die any which way you please. Get over it.'

Mikhain peered at Taron with a curious eye. 'You saved close to a thousand lives back on Chiron IV. What changed, Taron? Getting nervous about your chances out there against the Legion?'

Taron did not take the bait, smiling instead.

'The only time the Legion's bothered me is when you and Captain Sansin show up. The sooner we part ways, cap'n, the happier I'll be.'

The elevator reached the designated floor, the door opening and the pirates and miners spilling out like a dirty little flood into a painstakingly clean foyer alongside the space port. Mikhain could see rows of spacecraft parked nearby, most of them belonging not to civilian carriers but to the pirates, ranks of Morla'syn infantry guarding them.

'This could get rough,' Taron observed as he spotted the guards. 'That's why they didn't come up to the prison, they're under orders to guard the ships.'

'You won't get past them,' Mikhain replied. 'They'll take one look at you lot and open fire just for the hell of it.'

'Bring it on,' said the scarred woman.

Rench jabbed the pistol at Mikhain once more. 'You're the Colonial officer, why don't you get all creative and think of something?'

Mikhain turned to Taron and tugged the collar of his uniform demonstratively. 'You know that devotion to shoulder insignia you complained about?'

Taron glanced thoughtfully at the Morla'syn guards. 'Your chances aren't much better than ours.'

'No,' Mikhain agreed, 'but I can deceive them, whereas you cannot.'

Taron's eyes narrowed. 'What do you mean?'

*

'Help!'

The Morla'syn officer turned his big head as he saw a Colonial officer stumble out of an access corridor and onto the landing pads, his uniform ripped and smothered in grime, his hair in disarray and panic poisoning his features.

Half a dozen other infantry turned to watch the human stagger toward them, pointing behind him and running on one injured leg.

'They're coming!' the man screeched. 'They're behind me!'

The officer strode forward and activated his plasma rifle. 'Who's behind you?'

'The convicts!' the man yelled. 'They're all out! The prison's been hit, didn't you see?!'

The officer glanced at the smouldering wound high on the prison spire's flank, but his orders had been clear: guard the privateers' spacecraft and don't let any of them escape the planet.

'How many?' he demanded as the human reached him, his chest heaving with exertion but his uniform clearly that of a senior Colonial officer.

'Twenty, maybe more,' the man gasped. 'They're killing anybody who stands in their way! Don't let them out here!'

The Morla'syn officer straightened and with one hand he propelled the Colonial officer behind him as he called out to his men.

'Defensive positions! They'll try to reach their ships!'

The Colonial officer staggered away from them and to the Morla'syn's disgust he cowered behind the landing pad of one of the pirate freighters.

Humans, he observed with distaste, the harbingers of war and yet those most afraid of it. He turned back to the landing bay entrance and crouched down, ready to fire upon anybody and anything that came through the doors.

He was about to send a few of his men forward to secure the bay when he heard the distinctive sound of a plasma pistol activating behind him. He whirled just in time to see the blast that hit him in the chest and hurled him to the ground.

Mikhain fired three more shots from Rench's plasma pistol, hitting the Morla'syn soldiers in the back where they crouched with low–energy rounds designed to stun, not to kill. The remaining guards whirled to return fire, and as they did so Mikhain heard a dreadful war cry and saw the pirates pour onto the landing platform. Caught out both from behind and from ahead, the Morla'syn panicked and began firing wildly in all directions.

The Donnassians plunged into the Morla'syn and overpowered half of them within moments. Mikhain watched as Rench ripped a plasma rifle from a Morla'syn guard's hands and used the butt to smash him unconscious. The huge miner turned the rifle around and opened fire on the remaining guards as his comrades rushed forward.

To Mikhain's surprise the ramp to Taron Forge's pirate ship, *Phoenix*, lowered beside him as plasma blasts burst all around. Mikhain fired two more shots before he ducked onto the ramp and dashed up inside the freighter. Taron and Yo'Ki sprinted toward the craft and thundered up the ramp as Yo'Ki hit the emergency seal button and the ramp slowly began to raise.

'Let's get the hell out of here!' Taron yelled as he doubled back on himself at the top of the ramp and dashed toward the cockpit.

Mikhain followed, Yo'Ki shouldering him briskly out of the way as the two pirates threw themselves into their respective seats and began starting the freighter's engines.

Mikhain was himself a former Colonial pilot and he knew that most craft required several minutes to warm up and for internal instruments to self–calibrate, but the speed with which the Phoenix came on–line and her engines began to hum with energy stunned him. Within sixty seconds both of her ion engines were spun up, and moments later the freighter lifted off the pad and turned under Taron's expert control before it blasted away from the pad and climbed out into the bright blue sky.

Mikhain glimpsed through the cockpit windows the Donnassians and pirates dashing for their craft below them, the bodies of the defeated Morla'syn littering the landing pad.

'Head for Arcadia,' Mikhain said.

'You're not on your bridge so stop giving orders,' Taron replied without looking at the captain. 'I'll head where I damned well please.'

Mikhain leaned closer to the captain from where he sat in the jump seat and hefted the plasma pistol demonstratively.

'You want to get out of here without the Morla'syn blasting you to hell Taron, you'll need Arcadia's help.'

'Why the hell don't you just stay where you are and get out of here?' Taron uttered as the Phoenix punched through a broken layer of cloud, soaring ever higher. 'The Colonials don't want you and the Oassians will imprison you for life if they capture you.'

Mikhain sat back in his seat as the G–forces of the freighter's rapid climb pinned him there.

'I want Arcadia,' he replied simply. 'Without her, nobody's going anywhere.'

'You're damned right there!'

The voice came from behind them, and Mikhain turned just in time to see Rench's huge form lumber into the cockpit and grab the pistol. The weapon was yanked from his hand and Rench turned it on him with a grim smile.

***

XXXV

'They're engaging the fleet!'

Ishira stared ahead through Valiant's windshield at the vast fleet of cruisers before them, their metallic hulls flashing as they reflected the light from the nearby star as countless plasma salvos blazed between them.

Captain Sansin sat beside her in the co–pilot's seat and saw the frigates soaring between the crowded cruisers, their manoeuvring perfectly orchestrated.

'Lazarus,' he guessed. 'Andaim's handed control of the frigates to him.'

Across the communications channel, Evelyn heard the mention of her sister's name.

'They can't win that fight, we're hopelessly outnumbered.'

'And we can't run,' Idris replied. 'Half of our civilians are stuck down there on Oassia. If we leave them, they're as good as dead.'

Idris looked at the battle unfolding before them, could see now the cloud of Raython fighters engaged in a fight to the death and he knew that there could be no going back. Suddenly, with a clarity of thought that had escaped him for so long, perhaps because of denial, perhaps because of fear, he realized that the final confrontation had come. There could be no fleeing this fight, no escape for any of them. This would become their greatest victory or their last tragic stand against the might of the Legion.

'Take us in,' he said to Ishira.

Ishira almost laughed. 'Into what? That? Valiant isn't a warship, captain, we don't have much weaponry.'

'No, but you have speed,' Idris replied. 'Get us to Atlantia. They're going to need their captain back aboard if we're going to stand a chance of winning this fight.'

'We'll be vaporised!' Ishira snapped. 'One direct hit from any of those batteries and we'll be history, and that's not even counting all those fighters!'

'They're controlled by machines,' Idris insisted. 'Those ships are Colonial, and I know what they're capable of and what their weaknesses are. Follow my lead and we'll make it through.'

'And what about Defiance?' Ishira pressed. 'Mikhain used to be her XO, we could use his help!'

'Mikhain's gone now,' Idris said, surprised at the regret in his tone as he said it. 'There's nothing he can do for us now.'

Ishira gripped the controls more tightly as she stared at the mass of huge spacecraft and tiny fighters engaged in close combat. Like a flickering show of fireworks against a black night, the plasma blasts flared and blazed in random bursts that illuminated the hulking hulls of the capital ships.

'Stand by and hold on,' she uttered, and then with one hand she threw Valiant's throttles wide open.

The freighter surged forwards as it accelerated, and almost at once a salvo of plasma bursts rocketed out from one of the flanking Colonial cruisers as it detected the freighter on its sensors and opened fire.

'Turn toward it!' Idris snapped.

Ishira wanted to beg to know why but there was no time. She hauled Valiant into a tight turn, heard the cries of alarm from the countless civilians strapped into the ship's hold far behind her as the freighter wheeled around.

The plasma shots rocketed past down Valiant's left flank, flaring brightly as they narrowly missed her.

'Automated trajectory tracking,' Idris explained. 'The ships are not manned but under control of Defiance. There's a delay in their tracking computers, just enough to counter if you're aggressive and react immediately to... *again*!'

Ishira pulled up hard as another salvo flashed toward them, and this time it thundered past beneath them with what felt like scant cubits to spare as the freighter climbed up and over the cruiser.

'Atlantia's coming through!'

Mikhain pointed through the windscreen to where the frigate was maintaining its position astern of Defiance, hammering her hull with salvo after salvo as Arcadia concentrated on hitting her bow, both of them protected from the massive carrier's main broadsides.

'Brilliant,' Idris smiled grimly. 'They're holding out, but they're taking damage from the cruisers.'

Ishira could see small fires glowing across Atlantia's massive hull as some of the cruiser's shots began to find their mark and her shields weakened beneath the onslaught.

'Fighters, two o'clock!'

A pair of Raythons rocketed in toward them and Ishira responded quickly, turning toward the attacking craft, but the quicker plasma shots smashed into Valiant's port hull and the freighter shuddered under the blows as sparks flew across the cockpit and a series of alarms blared out across the ship above a digitized warning.

'*Hull integrity at sixty eight per cent.*'

Ishira fought for control as she hauled Valiant around in a tight turn across Atlantia's bow and curved in under her port batteries.

'Watch the broadsides!' Idris yelped in surprise at Ishira's unexpected manoeuvre.

The pursuing Raythons fired several more shots and then broke off as the freighter rocketed along between repeated explosions of plasma energy as Atlantia engaged two cruisers at less than a thousand cubits range. The blasts flared and illuminated the cockpit like the mother of all electrical storms as the freighter ducked and weaved through the inferno, the fighters behind too wary to follow.

Ishira focused all of her attention on Atlantia's guns and the incoming fire from the two cruisers, watching for the flares of light from the guns before they fired and reacting on pure instinct, ignoring the sensors arrayed before her among the cockpit instruments as she both flew and keyed the communications channel.

'Atlantia, Valiant for emergency landing, aft bay!'

A crackled, distorted response reached them from the Landing Signal Officer's position.

'Valiant, aft bay, twenty seconds!'

Valiant plunged beneath a titanic blast as Atlantia's guns let rip with a full salvo that smashed into an adjacent cruiser with the brightness of a thousand suns. The shockwaves slammed into Valiant but Ishira kept the freighter straight and true and moments later they passed beneath Atlantia's ventral strake, deep within a silent spot between her aft hull and her huge ion engines.

Ishira deployed the freighter's landing pads and then swung around tightly as they emerged from cover and a brace of Raythons flashed passed, both engaging another pair of Raythons with squadron markings that Ishira did not recognise.

'Here we go!'

With deft skill Ishira turned Valiant about and ducked in below the landing bay doors that were just opening amid clouds of escaping gas, the freighter coming in almost sideways before she was able to straighten up and the ship slammed down onto the deck. The hull vibrated and jarred her eyes in her sockets as the landing pads juddered along the deck before their magnetic clamps caught, and then suddenly the ship was down and Ishira retarded the throttles.

Idris wasted no time as he yanked off his harnesses and leaped up and out of the cockpit.

'Ishira, get your ship ready to depart again if this goes south! I don't want any more civilians losing their lives!'

'Roger that!'

Idris hurried through the freighter's for'ard hull to the boarding ramp, and heard the distant blasts from outside shake the freighter as Atlantia was bombarded by the cruisers and Defiance's aft guns.

Idris ran down the ramp and landed on the deck at a jog as General Bra'hiv dashed onto the deck at the head of crew technicians and launch operators running out to prepare the deck for recovering Raythons damaged in battle.

'Sit rep?!' Idris demanded.

'We're outnumbered, outgunned and out of options but to hunker down and keep scrapping!' Bra'hiv replied. 'Marines are posted at all access points. If we're boarded, we're ready!'

Idris nodded, relieved that even in this direst hour Bra'hiv appeared as convinced of victory as he ever did. The General accompanied him on the brief elevator ride up to the bridge deck, no Marines now on guard at the doors as every single soldier on board prepared to repel boarders.

Idris marched onto the bridge and saw Lazarus standing before him, his eyes closed as he controlled the two frigates.

'Sit rep?!' he demanded of Lael.

'We're in deep trouble captain!' she replied, visibly pleased to see him despite the grim prognosis. 'Shields at fifty four per cent and falling, plasma salvos at two per minute but our guns are overheating. Both Raython squadrons are deployed and fighting but they're struggling to maintain position!'

Idris strode up onto the command platform and turned to Lazarus.

'I have control, doctor,' he said simply.

Emma nodded to the captain and Lazarus opened his eyes and smiled at Idris. 'Good to see you back and well, captain.'

Idris turned to the helmsman. 'Flank speed, all plasma cannons to engage Defiance's Raythons at point blank. Order our squadrons to pull up on my mark and clear the field.'

'We'll lose the initiative to the cruisers,' Lazarus warned.

'We never had the initiative in this engagement,' Idris replied. 'We have to cover the fighters.'

Lazarus said no more as Idris watched Lael relay the command to Andaim's cockpit.

***

XXXVI

Rench kept the pistol pointed at Mikhain as he grinned at Taron.

'Where's the spice, Taron?'

Taron shook his head and turned back to the Phoenix's controls. 'A bit busy here Rench, case you hadn't noticed!'

'There's Arcadia!'

Mikhain pointed between Taron and Yo'Ki as he saw the frigate in the midst of the raging battle, surrounded by Colonial cruisers as she manoeuvred to avoid Defiance's main guns from targeting her.

Taron stared at the scene before them, of multiple capital ships and dozens of fighters heavily engaged, flashes of plasma darting back and forth between them in a chaotic pyrotechnic display.

'The frigates aren't going to last long,' Taron said with something approaching a sombre tone. 'You sure you want to get in there?'

'We've already got a ship,' Rench snarled. 'Make a leap now and get us out of here, or I'll….'

'You'll what?!' Taron snapped. 'Kill us? You won't get far without a pilot, Rench, so you're screwed there. Didn't quite think this one through, did you?'

Rench turned the pistol on Yo'Ki. 'So you can teach me.'

'We don't have time for this,' Mikhain insisted.

'That's right,' Rench growled. 'So let's jump now and talk later, agreed?'

Mikhain sighed. 'Look, you can take Taron's spice, or you can come with us and I'll give you a supply of Devlamine so large you'll never need to think about money again.'

Rench peered at him. 'What Devlamine?'

'We use it to draw in the Legion's Infectors and Hunters,' Mikhain explained. 'Then we torch them. It's the drug they used to infect humanity in the first place. We've cultivated it aboard the frigates for that purpose. There's plenty to go around, but we need to take the ship back first.'

Rench frowned. 'And what's to say you'll honor the agreement?'

'The fact that there's literally tonnes of Devlamine aboard Arcadia,' Mikhain replied. 'It's not about honor, Rench – handing you a ship full of the stuff won't cost us a thing. Are you in, or not?'

Rench looked at the captain for a moment longer and nodded. 'Agreed.'

Taron glanced at Mikhain as he advanced the Phoenix's throttles forward. 'I hope to hell you know what you're doing.'

Mikhain did not reply as the freighter accelerated to attack speed and Taron activated her weapons systems. Mikhain watched as Yo'Ki transferred her attention to manually controlling the ship's plasma turrets, ready to engage any craft that strayed too close.

The Phoenix rocketed into the battle as a salvo of massive plasma blasts blazed across the space before it, Defiance's huge guns sending the broadside toward Atlantia. Mikhain tensed in his seat as he saw the frigate's bow plunge as the helmsman sought to avoid the blasts, watched three of the five shots sail over the bow as the last two impacted the frigate amidships. The plasma blasts spread like electricity across the frigate's shields, bright explosions of energy radiating back out into space as Atlantia shouldered the blows, but he could see her internal lighting flickering as the ship bore the blasts and struggled to remain functional at the same time.

'Hang on!'

Taron yelled his warning as he rolled the freighter over and pulled hard, the surprisingly agile craft racing between two formations of Raythons striving to shoot each other down. One pair was closing in on another from behind, their cannons blazing.

'That's the Reapers!' Mikhain pointed as he recognized the tail markings of Atlantia's squadron fleeing their attackers.

Taron did not reply but with admirable skill he rolled the Phoenix out into line astern behind the attacking Raythons, and without a word Yo'Ki locked onto the two enemy fighters and moments later a bright blaze of plasma fire shot out of the Phoenix's cannons. Mikhain squinted as the blasts smashed into the two attacking Raythons in a brilliant flare of light and a burst of flame as the fighters disintegrated, their minimal shielding no match for the freighter's powerful armaments.

Taron pulled up again as he aimed the freighter for Arcadia, the frigate diving beneath Defiance's huge hull and rolling slowly onto its side to bring her port batteries to bear on the carrier's underside. Mikhain sub-consciously clenched his fist in excitement and grim delight as he saw the frigate unleash a massive broadside that blanketed the carrier's hull in a fearsome blaze of plasma energy.

'Give it to 'em, Scott!' Mikhain yelped in delight as he saw fires begin to glow on Defiance's hull as some of the massive energy from the broadside broke through her shielding.

'It's gonna take more than that to stop them,' Taron observed dryly as Arcadia rolled out and was hit twice by the smaller Colonial cruisers, their broadsides rippling down the frigate's hull.

'Every little helps,' Mikhain replied. 'There, the aft landing bays are open!'

He pointed to Arcadia's stern as the frigate turned to engage the two cruisers, and Taron aimed for the opening. The freighter slowed and then shook violently as a Raython opened fire upon it and raced by down the starboard flank.

Yo'Ki twisted in her seat as she aimed and then fired a stream of plasma after the fleeing fighter, but it arced away at the last moment and shot out of range.

Taron lowered the freighter's undercarriage and it sailed into Arcadia's landing bay, the pirate captain settling the ship down on the deck as Mikhain unstrapped from his seat.

'As soon as we're off, get out of here,' Mikhain said to Taron.

Rench stood up next to Mikhain, the pistol still in his grasp and pointed at Mikhain's belly.

'No funny business,' Rench warned. 'Any of your Marines come near me, I'll cook your innards, understood?'

'You'll get your damned Devlamine,' Mikhain shot back. 'Just follow my lead and stay out of the way.'

The pirate looked at the captain suspiciously. 'Are you going to stay in the fight?'

Mikhain whirled without answering and dashed from the freighter as Taron lowered the ramp, Rench flashing a final, cruel grin at them as he lumbered after Mikhain.

'I've got a bad feeling about this,' Taron uttered as they left.

*

'Break right!'

Evelyn shouted the command as her Raython roared into the battle, the underside of a Colonial cruiser flashing by above her and the shockwaves from its plasma batteries shuddering through the fighter's hull as she passed by.

Evelyn hauled the fighter into a hard right turn as two enemy Raythons rushed toward her with their plasma cannons blazing. Teera's Raython soared by her in an overshoot as she pulled in the same direction, two plasma shots blasting out in return against the attacking fighters before they flashed by.

'There's too many of them!' Teera yelled.

The space between the carrier and the frigates was filled with Raythons all firing and turning at once in the largest fight Evelyn had ever seen. Shots rallied this way and that, a rich tapestry of vivid red and blue light flickering back and forth against the velvety black backdrop of deep space.

'Stay together, maintain formation!' Evelyn snapped, forcing herself to remain calm despite her heart trying to beat its way out of her chest. 'Reapers, stay in pairs, don't break up or they'll pick us all off!'

She shot beneath a pair of Raythons heading in the opposite direction as Teera's panicked voice cried a warning.

'Pair at six o'clock, evasive now!'

Evelyn yanked her Raython into a tight turn, racing toward Arcadia now as the frigate unleashed a heavy barrage against Defiance's shields. She craned her neck over her shoulder as a trail of plasma fire shot over her wing and saw the pursuing fighters closing in on her.

'They're still with us!' Teera cried out.

Evelyn forced herself not to order Teera to break formation and instead sought out another pair of allied fighters amid the wheeling, firing mass of craft around them. A blast hit her stern quarter and she fought for control, and then a fresh blaze of fire rocketed overhead from behind her. She looked over her shoulder once more and was shocked to see the Phoenix burst from an expanding fireball where the two pursuing Raythons had been only moments before, the freighter breaking off and heading for Arcadia.

'What the hell's he doing here?'

'Who cares?!' Teera answered. *'He just cleared our tail!'*

Andaim's voice crackled across the airwaves.

'All call signs, pull up and over! Evacuate the battle zone!'

Evelyn felt a surge of warmth flush through her as she heard Andaim's voice, as calm as ever despite the savage battle. She hauled back on her control column without questioning the command, and glimpsed through her canopy about a third of the warring fighters suddenly accelerate upward and away from the plane of battle.

She looked over her shoulder and saw Teera's Raython climbing with her as suddenly both Atlantia and Arcadia's guns erupted in a brilliant, blazing crossfire. The massive rounds smashed across the swirling cloud of the Legion's Raythons and Evelyn saw dozens of the fighters erupt in fireballs as the huge plasma rounds blazed through them.

'All fighters re-engage!' Andaim called.

Evelyn looked up and saw the CAG's Raython arc over the top of a loop and plunge back down toward the fight, and she pulled back on her control column to follow him as she saw the rest of the Reapers and Renegades soaring down toward the battle.

She felt something akin to excitement as she saw the wreckage of at least two dozen Legion–controlled Raythons sparkling in the sunlight as their flaming fireballs spluttered out, consumed by the bitter freeze of deep space.

And then Defiance's main batteries opened up and she saw Atlantia vanish amid a blaze of plasma fire so bright that it overpowered her photo–receptive shields and she turned her head away, her eyes shut tight and the image of the frigate's hull imprinted on her eyeballs, engulfed in flame.

***

XXXVII

Mikhain dashed to the transports with Rench and the miners behind him, and together they travelled through the frigate toward the bridge. The entire ship shuddered as plasma broadsides thundered into her hull outside, the lights flickering weakly as they leaped from the transport and ascended the decks until they reached the bridge entrance.

Two Marine guards were standing either side of the bridge, and Mikhain raised a hand to halt Rench behind him as he looked over his shoulder.

'Leave this to me,' he said. 'As soon as their backs are turned, move in.'

Rench and the Donassians nodded as Mikhain stepped out onto the bridge deck and strode toward the two Marines. The soldiers whipped their rifles up to point at him as he emerged from the adjoining corridor, and then their faces lit up with surprise as they recognised the captain.

'Change of plan, gentlemen,' Mikhain greeted them. 'I believe that we have a battle to win, do we not?'

Mikhain stepped up to the soldiers and spoke quietly and quickly.

Both of the soldiers grinned and both of them hurried to the bridge access door controls, set either side of the broad entrance. The Marines entered their individual access codes that allowed the bridge doors to open. They hissed open just as the frigate shuddered beneath the blows from another broadside, and Mikhain heard Lieutenant Scott bellowing commands to the bridge crew.

'Helm, come right four two degrees, bow up three five!'

'Right four two, up three five, aye!'

Rench and his men rushed silently upon the two Marines and before they realized what had happened they were overpowered and their rifles taken from them. With their arms pinned behind their backs and their own weapons held with the barrels jammed beneath their chins, Mikhain led them onto the bridge with Rench behind him.

'Lieutenant Scott!'

Scott whirled at the sound of Mikhain's voice and his eyes widened as he saw the captain and the ranks of burly, aggressive looking men standing behind him.

'Guard!'

Rench grinned at the Lieutenant without fear as he shouldered his way past Mikhain and his deep voice roared above the din of battle.

'This is our ship now, and any one of you who tries to take it from us will suffer the same fate as your Marines!'

He gestured over his shoulder with one thumb as the two captive Marines were shoved into sight in the bridge entrance. Lieutenant Scott stared at them and then his expression soured and he glared at Mikhain as he radiated pure contempt.

'I always believed you to be a traitor and a coward, Mikhain,' he spat. 'But this is a new low even for you.'

Mikhain smiled without concern. 'Get off our bridge, lieutenant.'

Scott straightened his uniform, perhaps as a last sign of defiance as he stepped down off the command platform and moved to stand before Mikhain. The younger man regarded the captain for a few moments and then spoke softly.

'May you get everything that you deserve,' he said finally.

Mikhain strode past Lieutenant Scott and took his place on the command platform.

'Sit rep?!' he demanded.

None of the officers replied or moved. Instead, they stood or sat at their consoles and quietly refused to cooperate with the captain. Rench surveyed them for a moment and then he stepped forward and jammed his pistol under Lieutenant Scott's jaw.

'In your own time,' he growled at the crew.

The tactical officer coughed and spoke loudly enough to be heard.

'Hull integrity is sixty one per cent, shields at forty three. Power is low but stable and we're fully engaged. Estimated time of survival is less than fifteen minutes.'

Mikhain raised his chin as he considered this new information.

'Atlantia's been hit!' cried one of the other officers.

Mikhain glanced at the tactical display and saw their sister ship engulfed in a tremendous broadside, a direct hit from Defiance's main guns. Atlantia's hull and shield readings plummeted as the fireball expanded and dissipated, and Mikhain felt a surge of alarm as he saw countless fires now raging across the frigate's surface.

'She's done for,' Lieutenant Scott said as he surveyed the damage and turned to look back at his captain, his features ashen. 'Congratulations, captain.'

Mikhain ground his teeth in his skull and saw on another display the Phoenix rocketing out of the launch bays and turning away from the battle.

'Time to leave,' Rench snapped from one side. 'Take us out of here, now!'

Mikhain glanced at the helmsman and nodded once, and the officer reluctantly turned to his controls and began pulling Arcadia up and out of the battle zone. Mikhain surveyed the navigation screen and selected a suitable destination as he relayed his orders.

'Set a course for Veyrin, immediate super–luminal, divert all power to the fusion cores.'

Lieutenant Scott leaped forward.

'They'll die if you flee now!' he shouted.

Two of the miners grabbed the lieutenant and yanked him away from the captain. Mikhain looked down at Scott and shrugged.

'And we'll all die if we stay, lieutenant,' he replied. 'No sense in wasting more lives now, is there?'

'We can still win!' Scott pleaded.

'We could never win!' Mikhain roared finally, unable to contain his rage any more. 'This was never about winning, lieutenant! This was about making a last stand! We've been abandoned, left out here to fend for ourselves! We either die here or we live to fight another day! I'm not going to put my life on the line for the Oassians, who have the means to assist us but have instead left us to be slaughtered. To hell with them!'

A blast hit Arcadia's upper hull and the bridge trembled beneath the blow as sparks flew from overloaded circuitry and ceiling panels burst from their mounts to spin in mid–air, acrid smoke puffing in blue whorls from workstations as Mikhain grabbed the guard rail for support. He called out to the rest of the bridge crew, his voice loud enough to carry above the din.

'There are still two hundred personnel aboard this ship, all of them with a right to live, that same right to live that Oassians consider applicable to the Legion over us. They have colluded with The Word, betrayed their own greatest convictions and policies, all in order to let us die here and now. We know damned well that sooner or later the Legion will likewise betray them and Oassia will fall. I say, let them fall without *us*!' Mikhain surveyed the crew for a moment and then looked at the captive Marines. 'Who's with me?!'

For a moment nobody moved, but then one of the Marines called out.

'The hell with this, I'm with you!'

Rench's miners looked at him in surprise and then heard his companion cry out.

'Me too! I'm not dying for Rh'yll and his cohorts! Let 'em burn!'

Lieutenant Scott stared in dismay as one by one the bridge crew's resolve began to waver and he cried out at them.

'Would Captain Sansin abandon any of us in the same way?!'

Mikhain looked at the tactical display sadly as he replied. 'I don't think that what Captain Sansin would do matters any more, lieutenant.'

The display showed Atlantia's surface riven with ruptured hull plating, flames glowing from within as the damage from the relentless broadsides spread, the frigate's shields no longer strong enough to deflect the plasma shots raining down upon her from the surrounding cruisers.

Arcadia shuddered as another broadside ploughed into her hull, and Rench turned to Mikhain and shouted above the deep booms reverberating through the hull.

'We leave, now, while we still have a ship left to travel in!'

Mikhain nodded, and turned to the two captive Marines. 'Guard, escort Lieutenant Scott to the brig, if you will?'

The Marines both nodded. 'Aye, cap'an.'

Mikhain looked at Rench, who nodded. 'Let 'em go.'

The Marines stepped forward as they were handed back their plasma rifles, and they both aimed the weapons at Lieutenant Scott.

'This is treason,' Scott said.

'No, lieutenant, this is survival.'

'Ain't that right?' Rench snapped as he shoved Mikhain toward the lieutenant. 'A job well done, captain, but we'll take it from here.'

Mikhain whirled and glared at Rench. 'We had a deal.'

'And now I've got a better one,' Rench growled. 'Take them both to the brig or I'll blast this pretty little thing up here, and set course for Veyrin!'

Rench pointed the plasma pistol at Shah, whose dark eyes flared with alarm as she cowered behind her work station.

Mikhain raised his hands as the two Marines levelled their rifles at both him and Lieutenant Scott, and the captain glanced over his shoulder as behind him a broad grin spread like a snake across Rench's jaw.

'Time for you to leave, captain,' Rench snarled.

Mikhain looked at the Marines and then he dropped to his knees as he cried out.

'Scott, *down!*'

A blaze of plasma fire crackled over his head as Lieutenant Scott hurled himself down to the deck and the Marine's rifles opened fire. The salvo of shots blazed into Rench's men and cut them down with a scythe of super–heated plasma. The miners' agonised cries competed with the screeching of rending metal, the tortured hull of the frigate battered to the point of collapse by Defiance's powerful cannons.

The crackle of plasma fire ceased and Mikhain looked up to see the two Marines standing before him, their rifles smouldering. Mikhain got to his feet and turned to see Rench lying on his back on the deck, his chest smouldering where a plasma round had ploughed into it and incinerated his heart in an instant.

Then stench of burning circuitry and flesh competed with each other as the frigate rocked violently and Mikhain was hurled sideways into the command platform's guard rail. Lieutenant Scott scrambled to his feet and stared in disbelief at the dead bodies of the miners lying on the deck and the two Marines now standing at port arms and watching Mikhain expectantly.

'What the hell was that?' he gasped.

Mikhain turned to the Marines. 'Well done, gentlemen.'

The Marines nodded in response, and as Lieutenant Scott watched Mikhain strode back onto the command platform and looked at the communications officer.

'Shah, establish communications with Atlantia if you will. We're not going anywhere.'

'Aye, captain!'

Lieutenant Scott stared openly at Mikhain. 'You engineered it?'

'Of course I damned well did,' Mikhain shot back. 'The guards were outside the bridge, right where they should be. I only had to tell them to follow my lead to get us in here, because I knew damned well that Rench would never get in on his own and you'd never agree to letting him even if you'd known I was still on your side.' Mikhain tapped his forehead. 'Thinking outside of the box, lieutenant.'

Scott was about to reply when Captain Sansin's voice echoed through the bridge as communications with Atlantia were re–established.

'Mikhain?' Sansin gasped breathlessly, surprise evident in his tone as he recognized the captain. 'We're done for. It's over.'

***

XXXVIII

The Council chamber was silent as Rh'yll looked out across the silvery expanses of the city arrayed far below him. The countless transparent walkways were devoid of inhabitants and the once bustling sky lanes were empty, the population enduring a self–imposed curfew reserved only for time of imminent invasion by a superior or unknown force. Such a condition had not been imposed upon those citizens for almost two thousand years, a weighty realization that bore heavily down upon Rh'yll's mind.

His eyes could not see the city in the same way that many other species could, designed to filter out the blue rather than embrace it. The sky above was a hazy patch as was the glittering ocean surrounding the vast city, devoid of detail and information, his brain wired to detect movement against that blue in an adaption that had allowed his ancestors of millions of years ago to detect the massive predators that soared silently through the endless ocean depths.

Just as they now did through the endless space above.

Across the city he could see a faint smear of ugly brown smoke rising from a towering silver spire, the city's prison breached. Already, reports had come in of violence on the streets not seen for centuries, of firing from security teams against criminals and human prisoners and captured murderers alike who were running amok in the empty city after their escape from confinement.

Ryh'll sighed mentally, his body feeling heavier than usual. Oassia was an icon to the future and always had been, held up both by Oassians and the Icari as an example to other civilizations that peace could be found, cherished and maintained for hundreds if not thousands of years without blemish, provided that transparency and openness remained the currency of diplomacy across the galaxy. Human beings had arrived in the system less than twenty hours before and the council was now facing civil insurrection, a prison break, malfunctioning security drones and invasion by a lethal and emotionless killing machine intent on the destruction of all species it encountered.

There were many reasons why human beings had been contained by the Icari Line, most of them coming from the other members of the council who feared mankind's self–destructive nature, their cunning and their inability to see peace as anything other than a prelude and a preparation for war. Rhy'll had often argued in favour of humankind, pointing out that the Veng'en were considerably more warlike and yet being considered for council membership over humanity. It was a legacy that he now regretted with a heavy heart as he surveyed the deep and irreparable end of Oassia's proud legacy of two millennia.

The entrance to the chamber beeped as someone entered and Rhy'll turned wearily to see General Veer march in, flanked by two armed guards.

'General?'

Veer marched right up to Rhy'll as he spoke. 'We need to mobilize the fleet, councillor. The Legion is here and I believe firmly that the humans are right. The Legion cannot be trusted, cannot be negotiated with. If we stand down, we will all die.'

Rhy'll stared at the warrior for a long moment.

'Why such a sudden change of heart, general? You were in favour of expending our human prisoners in return for amnesty and negotiation.'

'That was before...,' the General broke off for a moment. 'I believe that we may have misjudged their spirit, councillor, that of the humans. We would not be standing here if it were not for them.'

'You don't have to tell me that,' Rhy'll snorted. 'We're facing ruin and they've only been here a day.'

'They're fighting councillor,' General Veer said, 'fighting for their lives, fighting against impossible odds and refusing to back down. I've never seen anything like it. If they had fled, we would by now be being invaded ourselves.'

Rhy'll glanced at the display screen in the chamber, currently deactivated.

'See for yourself,' Veer invited him.

Rhy'll touched a small device with one of his appendages and the screen activated. Moments later it was relaying an image from one of the city's massive optical sensors. Magnified many times and corrected for atmospheric distortion, the image before Rhy'll showed Tyraeus Forge's fleet heavily engaging the two frigates, fighters sweeping in pairs amid a dense cloud of intense plasma fire.

Rhy'll slowly approached the screen, captivated by the scene.

'They're outnumbered,' he observed.

'Three to one,' General Veer replied, 'and their civilians insisted on returning with them to assist in the fight. Not one of those who escaped the planet has fled, councillor. Not one.'

Rhy'll felt something tighten inside his body, a strange and foreign sensation that he had not felt in many decades, since perhaps his own youth in the ocean nurseries when he had been wronged by other infant Oassians, or mocked or threatened. The tight ball formed hard and cold and refused to fade away.

'No Oassian has gone into combat in over a thousand years, general,' he replied. 'It is not our way, and our way has proven right every time since.'

'There was no Legion before now,' General Veer replied. 'And besides, we're not asking you to fight for the humans.' Rhy'll turned and looked at the General, who looked down at him with a sombre expression. 'I will lead them.'

Rhy'll's light sensors widened as he looked back at the General. 'You condemned them, and now you wish to stand by them?'

General Veer rose up, his chest thrust out.

'We have a choice, councillor. Meekly accept the Legion's demands and bow to their wishes, knowing not whether they will spare us, or open fire and go down fighting if we must. Never before has there been a reason to replace diplomacy with conflict, until now, and I don't want to be the Morla'syn general who sought to appease an aggressor, only to have them destroy my people.' Veer peered down at Rhy'll. 'Do you?'

Rhy'll looked once more at the screen, and then he made his decision.

*

'We're breached! Decks twelve through nineteen!' Lael yelled as alarm claxons shrieked through the bridge. 'Fires across the plasma lines on the starboard quarter!'

Idris staggered against the guard rail as Atlantia shuddered beneath the blows of plasma salvos blazing from the cruisers surrounding her.

'Shut off the plasma lines and direct shield power to the affected area!' he bellowed above the din. 'Deploy fire crews and bring us about, make sure they can't hit us there again!'

Atlantia trembled again as another salvo smashed into her port bow and twisted the frigate sideways through a blaze of exploding plasma rounds coming from Defiance.

'The cruisers are moving in!' Lael warned. 'They're trying to surround us!'

Idris saw the bulky form of the two cruisers moving into flanking positions either side of Atlantia, boxing her in at close range. At such short distances plasma broadsides could be as dangerous to the attacking cruisers as they would be to Atlantia, and a fusion core breach would likely take out all three vessels. Idris felt the sweat on his brow turn cold as he whirled to the tactical officer.

'Alert the Marines! Prepare to repel boarders on the starboard flank!'

The tactical officer relayed the command as Idris judged the distances between the three ships and pointed at the helmsman.

'Dead stop! All power to port batteries!'

'We're too close!' Lael cried out in horror. 'If we take them down we'll go down with them!'

'We don't have enough Marines to repel boarders on both flanks!' Idris shot back. 'We've got to even the odds!' He turned to the communications console at his seat and spoke into it. 'Reaper Squadron, hit the cruiser in quadrant oh–four–one on its port side, full attack!'

Idris heard Andaim's reply crackle through the speakers on the bridge.

'Copy Atlantia, in–bound.'

Idris glanced at the tactical display and saw a dozen or so Raythons rocket out of the dogfight raging between Defiance and the cruisers and accelerate toward the cruiser alongside Atlantia. A cloud of enemy Raythons followed, these marked with red boxes around them on the display to identify them as enemy fighters.

'Your fighters could be caught in the blast,' Lazarus warned.

Idris gripped the command rail more tightly as he watched the Raythons swarm in, their plasma cannons opening up in a flickering blaze of blue–white light as they hammered the cruiser's far side and vanished from sight.

Idris closed his eyes, gauging the fighter's velocities as they raced along the cruiser's huge hull, firing as they went and with their enemy in hot pursuit. He clenched one fist by his side and raised it beside his head, then dropped it as he shouted.

'Bow to stern batteries, in order, open fire now!'

Atlantia shuddered once more as deep booms reverberated through her hull, the plasma cannons firing in series all the way down her hull. Idris watched the main display screen and saw blast after blast hammer the cruiser at less than a thousand cubits' range, so close that even the powerful shields generated by the ship's fusion cores were unable to absorb or deflect the majority of the blasts' power.

The cruiser's metallic hull flared with brilliant explosions as the barrage ripped into her, massive hull panels folding like paper as jagged rivers of flame and molten metal split the hull in savage gashes from which blasted gas and plasma in brutal jets. The blows slammed down the cruiser's hull and then with a terrific blast her engine bays separated from the main hull, the explosion flaring like a new born sun and filling Atlantia's bridge with light.

DEFIANCE

A grim cheer rose up across the bridge as the cruiser listed heavily under the asymmetric load of her failing engines and began descending below and away from Atlantia, explosions rippling across her hull and deep fissures splitting her superstructure like rivers of magma running across metallic mountains.

'Her engines are gone!' Lael called. 'She's out!'

Idris resisted the urge to smile as he looked at the other cruiser and then shouted a warning!

'Brace for impact!'

The shockwaves from the damaged cruiser had shifted Atlantia laterally, and now she was barely fifty cubits from the hull of the smaller but still massive cruiser. Idris grabbed the guard rail and dropped down onto one knee as he heard a distant, wailing, keening sound screech through Atlantia as her hull slammed into and brushed alongside the cruiser.

More claxons began wailing across the ship, and this time he heard the sound of deep blasts from aft where the plasma lines, already damaged in the salvos from Defiance, were ripped from their mountings.

'Hull breach, stern quarter, starboard!' Lael cried out, managing to stay upright despite the frigate's violent impact. 'We're open, too large a gap to seal and the shields won't cover it!'

'Seal the section off!' Idris yelled.

'We've got Bravo Company down there captain!'

Idris hauled himself to his feet as another salvo of shots crashed into the frigate from above as Defiance continued to attempt to engage her, and his weary old eyes took in the picture on the tactical display.

The cruiser was alongside Atlantia, while Arcadia was still hammering Defiance's bow while manoeuvring to avoid being boarded by the other four cruisers still engaged with her. Arcadia's hull was criss-crossed with lines of fire spilling from damaged hull panels, a trail of debris glistening behind her in the bitter cold of space. The cloud of fighters were still wheeling and firing all around them, Raythons rocketing at attack speed like glow flies around giant metal beasts wrestling in the night.

Despite Arcadia's condition he could see that she was still fully engaged, but Idris knew that their cause was lost, the damage sustained too heavy for them to continue fighting much longer.

'Arcadia's signalling us,' Lael said.

Idris looked up as Mikhain appeared on a display screen, and the captain looked back at him, sparks falling from Arcadia's bridge displays, smoke filling the air. Mikhain's face was sheened with sweat and grime, his features grim.

'Mikhain,' Idris said, almost relieved to see the captain back at his post, 'we're done for. It's over.'

Mikhain nodded slowly, not taking his eyes off Idris's. 'I know.'

'Get out of here,' Idris advised. 'We can't win, Mikhain. Run, while you can.'

Mikhain's shoulders sagged slightly and he shook his head.

'I think that the time for running is over, captain, for all of us.'

Neither of them spoke for a moment. Mikhain's broad jaw twitched slightly and then the hard line of his lips curled into a grim smile, humourless and yet defiant to the last. Idris felt the same kind of smile spread across his face as he managed to stand briefly upright on the trembling bridge and threw a quick salute at Mikhain.

'To the end,' Idris said.

Mikhain returned the salute. 'To the end.'

Idris turned as a screen filled with the image of Tyraeus Forge, his own ship's bridge remaining clean and untroubled by the carnage occurring outside.

'You are defeated, captain,' he said simply, delight radiating from his inhuman features, the Infectors numerous enough to convey subtle expressions and emotions, if that they could be called. 'It is time to surrender.'

Idris smiled back at Tyraeus. 'There is never such a time.'

Tyraeus appeared confused. 'There is nothing to gain by sacrificing yourselves. Join us, and you'll never have to face or fear death again.'

'We do not fear death,' Idris replied, 'and we only need face it the once.'

Tyraeus shook his head. 'Your propensity for pointless self–sacrifice is something I'll never understand.'

'That's because you're not a human being.'

Idris shut off the link himself and turned to Lael, suddenly feeling calm for the first time in years. 'Seal off the affected sections of the hull, Lael. We're not going to get out of this I'm afraid, so let's take down as many of them as we can.'

The bridge crew all looked at Idris for a long moment, and the captain glanced at Lazarus. 'Unless you have any objections, doctor?'

Lazarus shook his head.

'You gave it your best shot, captain. Better to take them down than join them.'

DEFIANCE

XXXIX

'Arcadia's been hit!'

Evelyn turned in her seat as she hauled her Raython around in a tight turn, her targeting reticule buried in the engines of a fleeing Raython as she squeezed the trigger. A pair of plasma bursts shot from her cannons and smashed into the Raython's stern, one engine and the attached wing severed completely by the blow in a cloud of flame, sparks and metallic debris as the fighter span about on its axis.

Evelyn fired one more shot as she pulled up and she saw the Raython's cockpit vaporised by the direct hit as the fighter exploded in a brilliant fireball. She craned her neck over her shoulder as her Raython soared upward and saw Arcadia's hull striped with jagged flaming lesions where plasma rounds had smashed through her hull plating and severed plasma lines across her starboard flank.

'Atlantia's taking a pounding too,' Teera pointed out as their Raythons flew in formation toward a pair of Reapers engaged with four of the enemy. *'She's going to be boarded!'*

'Stay on target!' Andaim snapped across the communications channel. *'Keep those fighters under control!'*

Evelyn swung in behind two of the enemy Raythons, their tails bearing the insignia of a long forgotten squadron known as the *Ironsides* that had been deployed aboard Defiance on her maiden voyage. She lined up on one of them and fired, but her shots missed as the fighter jinked right to avoid her attack.

Two plasma bursts rocketed past Evelyn's right wing as Teera picked up the jinking Raython from her covering position on Evelyn's wing, and her shots smashed into the fighter's engine bays with a brilliant explosion that forced Evelyn to break off to port. Her fighter raced beneath the underside of the one of the cruiser's hulls, and as she accelerated by she glanced up and her heart missed a beat as she saw the hull rippling with movement, as though it were covered in a sea of black waves.

'The Legion's coming out! Get clear of the capital ships!'

Evelyn pushed away from the cruiser as she saw clouds of Hunters surge in a wall like a gigantic black wave as they reached out for her Raython. The seething mass of machines flashed by overhead and as she turned hard right to clear the vessel she saw the cruiser alongside Atlantia, their hulls locked together and brilliant fires burning where the two massive ships had collided with the unstoppable force of millions of tonnes of metal.

Evelyn's sharp eye picked out snaking black lines like boarding tethers streaking from the cruiser to Atlantia, and she knew immediately what she was witnessing.

'Reaper One, Atlantia, the Legion is boarding, starboard hull!'

'Copy Reaper One!'

'They're going for the hull breaches!' Teera yelped as she saw the same thing as Evelyn. *'They could infect the entire ship!'*

Evelyn fought of a wave of despondency as she saw both of the frigates suffering crippling damage and above them all the massive super carrier Defiance, her hull flickering with many fires but still returning fire and still showing shield strength of some eighty per cent.

Though she dared not voice her resignation, for the first time she heard a note of regret in the CAG's voice as he called down the communications channel.

'All fighters, stay on target. Repeat, maintain combat status!'

Evelyn knew that it was useless, and she squeezed her trigger harder than was necessary as she locked onto an enemy Raython and blasted it from existence in a cloud of burning metal.

Before the fighter had even disintegrated she heard a blast from over her right shoulder and the Raython slammed to one side as Evelyn's head was shaken this way and that under the impacts. She craned her neck and saw her starboard engine burst into flame as warning claxons blared in her cockpit. Panic flushed cold through her veins as she fought to keep the Raython under control.

'I'm hit!' she called.

'I've got your wing,' Teera replied, this time the calmer of their partnership. *'Head for Atlantia!'*

Evelyn turned toward the frigate, but she could see that she was leaking fuel and coolants that were leaving a bright and sparkling trail of debris behind her, perfect for the enemy Raythons to track her and achieve a guns solution on her wounded fighter.

Teera's Raython stuck closely to her wing, making every attempt to draw fire, but as Evelyn watched four enemy Raythons peeled off from a larger formation and began diving toward them.

'Enemy, five o'clock high!' she warned as the Raythons rocketed down.

'Get to Atlantia!' Teera insisted.

'Break off!' Evelyn yelled. 'Before we're both hit!'

Teera hesitated and for a brief moment Evelyn could see her eyes looking out from beneath her flight helmet, staring into Evelyn's as certain death soared out of the blackness behind her.

'Go,' Evelyn said, barely a whisper, 'now!'

Teera cursed something and then her Raython rolled and pulled away from its position on her wing as Teera began a defensive break to come round behind their attackers. Evelyn could see that Teera would never make it around in time to defend her, and instead she began jinking left and right in the hope of spoiling the enemy's aim.

Blasts of plasma rocketed by her cockpit as the enemy opened fire, flashes of blue–white light illuminating her cockpit as she rolled through a complete revolution and pulled hard to the right to try to break across the Raythons' bows and get out of guns range.

A shot hit her wing and the Raython rocked violently and rolled out of control. Evelyn let out a howl of fright as she tried to gather the Raython together and make it to Atlantia. The big frigate's landing bays beckoned invitingly with a soft orange glow, but she was still too far out and she had to slow down to land.

I'm not going to make it.

The sound of a gun–lock warning buzzed in her earphones as one of the pursuing Raythons locked onto her, and she reached for her ejection handles and closed her eyes.

'Splash one!'

A massive blast shook the little fighter and Evelyn blinked her eyes open as she saw a stream of cannon fire streak past over her head and heard the pursuing Raythons blasted into fireballs.

The Phoenix rushed into view on a near head–on course and raced by in the opposite direction, and to Evelyn's amazement it was followed by an endless stream of battered freighters, a flotilla of pirate vessels bursting into the fray with their cannons blazing.

'Forge?!' Evelyn gasped.

Taron's cocky voice chortled back to her over the communications channel.

'I'd forgotten how much fun dogfighting was! Stop messing about and get back in here!'

Evelyn almost laughed as she saw the Phoenix blaze through a formation of enemy Raythons, both its shields and cannons too strong for the smaller fighters to defend against. Behind the Phoenix she saw Ishira Morle's freighter, Valiant, plunge into the fray as the governor called out.

'The more the merrier, let's give 'em hell!'

Teera's Raython arced around and repositioned on Evelyn's wing as Captain Sansin's voice echoed across the channel.

'*Any available fighters, hit Atlantia, quadrant oh four, repeat, hit Atlantia at quadrant oh four!*'

Evelyn looked at her fuel and her weapons and then glanced up at the frigate before her. Whatever the captain wanted to hit his own ship for she could not imagine, but she was in the perfect position to do it.

'Copy Atlantia, Reaper One, will comply!'

*

'They're coming through!'

General Bra'hiv squatted in the corridor that ran along Atlantia's starboard hull and peered ahead though clouds of acrid smoke illuminated by weakly flickering ceiling lights. A series of flashing red warning beacons signalled the hull breach ahead, the atmosphere escaping from the hull in a howling rush of air that screeched past them.

Flames fluttered like glowing banners from electrical fires burning further down the corridor, and the entire ship was shaking periodically as it was engaged on the far side by both the enemy cruisers and fighters.

'Hold the line,' Bra'hiv replied, trying to keep his voice calm. 'Stand firm.'

Lieutenant C'rairn squatted across the corridor from the General's position, and behind him was the rest of Bravo Company. At their head was Private Qayin, his bioluminescent tattoos glowing inside his helmet as he aimed his plasma rifle down the corridor and awaited the inevitable.

'Remember the plan,' Bra'hiv said above the screech of the escaping atmosphere. 'We draw them in, fall back beyond the next bulkhead, then light them up and seal them off. Understood?'

Nobody answered but every Marine in the corridor nodded silently, their weapons trained on the misty confines of the corridor ahead. Atlantia shuddered again as another broadside slammed into her hull and the lights flickered even more as several of them blinked out, casting the corridor into patches of absolute darkness interspersed with areas of glowing white mist rushing toward the hull breach.

'Stand by,' Bra'hiv said.

He glanced over his shoulder and saw the explosive charges set into the deck, two sappers either side of them and waiting with nervous expressions. Both charges were wired to power lines below the deck plating, just waiting for the perfect moment.

'Enemy.'

The Word was hissed softly, a whisper charged with adrenaline. Bra'hiv slowly turned his head and he saw something snaking toward them, a writhing, seething wall of Hunters. He could not hear their countless metal legs rattling on the decks, the walls and the ceilings, the wind gusting by too loud, but he could see them. Each was no larger than a human eyeball, a metal body with six legs, large pincers and ugly spherical black eyes like some kind of gruesome spider. Combined, they could chew through a human being and reduce it to nothing but shreds of flesh in a matter of seconds, and now they surged down the corridor toward the Marines like a flood of black oil packed with scalpel blades.

'On my mark!' Bra'hiv snapped.

The flood of machines rushed closer, their bulk cutting off some of the escaping air so that the General could hear the dense rattling of their bodies running, tumbling and scraping across the decks as they advanced.

'Now!'

The two sappers flicked a pair of switches and in an instant the two charges let out a deep crack from somewhere beneath the deck as they severed the power to the ship's magnetic plates. Instantly, the quasi–gravity that kept the crew's boots on the ground was lost and the massive swarm of Hunters before them suddenly lost traction.

'Devlamine, now!'

Two Marines heaved a pump and hose forward and activated it, and a billowing spray of dark, amber coloured fluid blasted down the corridor. The zero–gravity affected the fluid, spreading it like a cloud of bubbles rather than a liquid, the Devlamine expanding like a galaxy of bloated, undulating amber spheres as it ploughed across the advancing Hunters in a gelatinous mass.

The Legion folded upon itself as it sought to consume the prized drug, the same concoction used by the Legion on Ethera to first infect the population via drug abusers on the city streets. Programmed to collect Devlamine wherever they found it, the drug was now the perfect foil to their advance.

General Bra'hiv ordered his men to fall back with a rapid gesture of his gloved left hand, and the Marines retreated as two flame–thrower wielding soldiers took up position close to the roiling mass of machines.

'Light 'em up!' Bra'hiv snapped.

The flame–throwers burst into life with a fearsome roar as tongues of bright blue and white flame scoured the corridor ahead, billowing clouds of searing heat trembling the air as the Devlamine ignited in a rush of flames. The dense stench of burning circuitry and hot metal filled the air, penetrating even the filters in Bra'hiv's combat helmet as he watched the machines burn in their tens of thousands as the Devlamine combusted in the heat.

'Fall back!'

The corridor shook as Atlantia was pounded by broadside after broadside from the surrounding cruisers. Bra'hiv followed his men at a brisk jog as they reached an area of the corridor where the magnetic plating was still functional, the blazing inferno behind them sucking more air out of the corridor and forcing them to lean into the gale.

'The Legion's pushing through!'

Qayin's shout made the General look over his shoulder, and there behind him he saw the Legion's amassed Hunters swarm over the smouldering remains of their burned advanced guard as they plunged into the frigate in their millions.

'Make for the bulkheads! Get ready to seal them off!'

A blaring alarm claxon rang in the General's ears and he looked up ahead to see the main bulkhead door warning lights flashing, red strobes piercing the smoky gloom.

'They're sealing the bulkheads already!'

Bra'hiv's blood ran cold as he saw the huge doors suddenly begin to rumble downward. He knew by instinctive reaction that something must have happened in the battle outside, something decisive that had doomed Atlantia to face her fate, whatever that may now be. There was no way that Captain Sansin would have given the command to seal the damaged section of the ship off with a platoon of Marines trapped inside without a damned good reason, and that reason was almost certainly defeat.

Bra'hiv slowed as he realized that neither he nor his fellow Marines would make it through the bulkhead.

'Bravo Company on me!' he roared. 'Defensive positions!'

The Marines stared at the bulkheads as they slammed shut before them, steel doors nearly a cubit thick that would never yield to any of their weapons or explosives. They turned as one and leaped into cover, their faces ashen and their eyes cold with dread and despair as they came to realize that it was over.

General Bra'hiv turned and took up a firing position alongside a wall brace in the corridor as before him the Legion swarmed forward.

'Gentlemen,' he said softly into his microphone. 'Let's end this the way we would want to be remembered, shall we?'

There was a long silence from the men as they stared at the onrushing wall of Hunters, and then Qayin spoke, his voice carrying clearly across their communicators.

'What, you mean like assholes?'

Bra'hiv stared across at Qayin as one of the Marines let out a snort of laughter. Another joined him and the General saw Qayin's smile spread bright white against his dark skin.

'Speak for yourself,' Bra'hiv uttered back. 'I always thought that Qayin was just another word for c…'

A blast cut off the General's words but a gust of laughter crossed the intercom as the Hunters rushed in. Bra'hiv, himself laughing, gave his final order.

'All arms, open fire!'

Qayin's voice rang out, fierce now. 'Give 'em hell!'

A roar went up from the Marines as they took aim and then as one they opened fire with every plasma rifle, flame-thrower and grenade they possessed. A blaze of blue-white plasma ripped down the corridor and broke against the blocky black wave of Hunters raging toward them as the last of the atmosphere was evacuated from the corridor and a deathly silence fell upon the dreadful scene as Bra'hiv fired his rifle repeatedly into the Legion's mass.

A soldier tumbled from his firing position as the Legion's unstoppable wave crashed past him, and Bra'hiv heard his own voice cry out as he saw the young trooper's legs caught among the Hunters. The soldier screamed, his dying cries piercing as the Hunters' weight pinned him down and their lethal amassed pincers shredded his legs in a matter of seconds before the rest of the unstoppable wave consumed the soldier entirely and his cries were strangled off.

Bra'hiv grabbed two grenades and lobbed them down the corridor, shielding himself from their blasts as they vaporised the Hunters in billowing clouds of glowing red-hot metal that swirled and spiralled in galaxies of light amid the raging plasma fire smashing into the Hunter's advance.

The wave kept moving, filling the corridor before them, and Bra'hiv kept firing as he hoped that Captain Sansin planned to bring as many ships down with him as he could before Atlantia was over run.

As the Legion closed in he stood up and with a battle cry he charged down the corridor toward them, firing from the hip as he did so. His plasma shots blasted the front of the wave of machines, melting Hunters in their hundreds but the shots vanishing almost immediately, and he knew that he was about to die.

Bra'hiv stopped in the middle of the corridor, the Legion barely cubits away, and with one hand he pulled a grenade from his belt and held it ready to detonate. He closed his eyes and waited for the wave to hit him.

A sudden massive blast blew the General off of his feet and he flew backwards through the air as the entire corridor before him vanished in a blaze of plasma, the swarm of the Legion billowing in clouds of orange embers as countless Hunters were melted by the blast. He felt pain rip through his left shoulder as searing plasma residue sprayed across his suit, and he slammed one hand over the tear in a desperate attempt to prevent a sudden and devastating decompression.

The side wall of the corridor was ripped away by the force of the blast as Atlantia's hull plating failed and Bra'hiv's stomach turned icy cold as he saw the blackness of space outside, filled with warring spacecraft and brutally bright flashes of plasma. From the corner of his eye he saw whorls of air escaping from his damaged suit and freezing instantly into ice crystals before him.

'The hull's failed!' Qayin yelled.

'My suit's breached!' Bra'hiv snapped, clutching his wound tightly.

In an instant Qayin was beside him, and to the General's amazement the huge Marine deftly yanked a patching device from his webbing. Designed to seal a suit tear in moments, Bra'hiv felt himself pulled to one side by Qayin and out of the line of fire as the Marines opened up on the Legion once more.

Bra'hiv thrust the grenade he held back into his belt as Qayin applied the patch, and his racing heartbeat subsided a little as the patch gripped and he saw the escaping air fade and disappear. Bra'hiv turned as he saw the Legion hauled out of the corridor and into space, their previously tight formation scattered by the force of the blast and the sudden disappearance of the hull wall.

'Marines, on me!' Bra'hiv snapped as he gripped his rifle tighter and tried to ignore the waves of pain searing his shoulder and arm.

The Marines scrambled for purchase in the zero–gravity as they opened fire on the clouds of Hunters spinning in the light from the nearby planet. The machines were attempting to reform into cohesive structures in order to attack once more, but the blast had scattered them widely enough to prevent them from reaching the Marines, most of them scampering about on the surface of the frigate's hull.

Bra'hiv smiled in grim delight as he realized that a Raython must have targeted the hull to give his men a way out, and he looked over his shoulder at Atlantia's massive hull as he sought one of many points of access into the hull usually used by maintenance crews.

'Marines, move for'ard! Stay sharp and close to the hull! Let's get back inside before we get toasted out here!'

The Marines obeyed instantly, but with a brief look around at the battle Bra'hiv could see that it was already over. Atlantia was aflame, as was Arcadia – one more direct broadside on either vessel and they would be completely destroyed.

***

XL

'Hull breaches on decks five through nineteen!'

Captain Mikhain was hurled to one side as Defiance's broadside smashed into Arcadia's hull and threw the massive frigate off course. A cloud of sparks and smoke from overloaded circuitry clouded the air and stung Mikhain's eyes as he grabbed at the guard rail and tried to stay on his feet.

'There's no way we can stay in the fight!' Lieutenant Scott yelled. 'Fusion cores are near overloading, shields are at eight per cent, plasma cannons are down on the port side and at forty six per cent power on starboard!'

Mikhain pointed at the helmsman. 'Pull up, take us over the top of Defiance and realign for another pass!'

The helmsman stared at Mikhain in horror, unable to move, unable to consider the action he was being asked to take. Lieutenant Scott grabbed the captain's arm.

'We're done for,' he said harshly. 'You heard what Captain Sansin said. It's over, Mikhain!'

Mikhain growled and spun on one heel as he drove his shoulder into Lieutenant Scott's chest and hurled him aside. The captain pinned the younger man down against a console as he snarled into his face.

'It's not over for Atlantia! We need to keep drawing fire for them!'

Lieutenant Scott managed to snap back at the captain. 'They're done for too! Our only option is to withdraw!'

Mikhain pushed the young officer aside as he whirled to look at the tactical displays.

The Raython squadrons were fully engaged, still in the midst of the battle and twisting and turning in a violent ballet of aerial manoeuvres interspersed with countless plasma shots streaking back and forth between them. Defiance was trying to get above the plane of the battle to bring her big guns to bear on both of the frigates, to finish them now while they were fully engaged by the cruisers and unable to defend themselves. The huge carrier was rising up above them, her surface swarming with billions of Hunters that caught the light from the red dwarf star as though they were waves glinting in a sunrise.

Mikhain searched for some other option, some means of escape, some left–field inspired command or tactic that could extricate both of the frigates from their impending doom, but he could find nothing. For the first time since they had departed Ethera's core systems in flight from the apocalypse of the Legion, he knew that they were facing true and total defeat, and to his surprise he did not feel the absolute cold embrace of resignation that he had so often assumed he would experience in the face of complete annihilation. Instead, something churned hot and fierce in his belly as he saw Taron Forge and the other pirate vessels swarming upon the enemy Raythons and blasting them.

He looked at Defiance's hull, the massive carrier's underbelly exposed before him.

He whirled to Lieutenant Scott.

'Evacuate the bridge!' Mikhain bellowed. 'All personnel to the escape shuttles, immediately!'

Lieutenant Scott stared at the captain for a moment, as though having advised such a course of action he now regretted it or could not believe that the captain would actually understand and go through with it. Then he turned and relayed the order, and the bridge crew leaped from their stations and flooded toward the main exit.

Another blast hit Arcadia side–on and a shower of sparks exploded from wall panels around the bridge as the salvos passed through what was left of the frigate's shields and ploughed into her hull proper. The thunderous impact had a different tone to those of plasma rounds smashing against the shields – this one was deeper and more ominous, a shuddering impact that seemed to make Arcadia groan in pain as her superstructure was directly assaulted.

'Get off the bridge!' Mikhain snapped at Lieutenant Scott. 'Ensure that all personnel are aboard the shuttles and I'll conduct the launch from here!'

'There's no need to be a hero captain!' Lieutenant Scott shouted above the din of burning panels, alarm claxons and the blasts hammering the frigate's exhausted hull. 'We can program the launch sequence from the landing bay! Just set Arcadia's navigation computer to withdraw and get us clear!'

Mikhain stood in the centre of the bridge's command platform and shook his head.

'We're not withdrawing, lieutenant.'

Scott stared at Mikhain for a moment. 'That's not damned well necessary! There's no need to sacrifice Arcadia for nothing!'

'I'm not sacrificing her for nothing!' Mikhain yelled back. 'Now get off the bridge!'

'I'm not leaving my captain behind!'

Mikhain drew his plasma pistol. 'Get off my damned bridge now!'

Mikhain fired, the plasma shot smashing off the edge of a console and forcing Scott to leap aside in horror, the blast close enough to be dangerous. The lieutenant fled to the bridge exit and looked back, just in time to see Mikhain fire again. The lieutenant's head vanished from sight as the pistol shot hit the wall next to the exit in a bright spray of plasma.

Mikhain shoved his pistol back into its holster and dashed to the helm. He staggered into the seat, the smell of burning circuitry stinging his nose and eyes as sparks showered down around him. The navigation screens were flickering, two of them smashed from where the power surges had burst through their screens. Arcadia's automatic navigation systems were still intact but he knew that they could be damaged at any moment, as could what remained of the massive physical shielding around Arcadia's fusion cores.

Mikhain turned the frigate's bow slowly toward Oassia, the huge vessel lumbering around and giving the shuttle's the best chance of escaping the battle in the shortest possible time. Mikhain glanced at the tactical displays and saw Defiance looming up above them, almost in position to deliver a fatal broadside.

'Ranger Four, bridge, departure bay two!'

The radio call came from the launch bays and Mikhain looked up to see the last of the bay crews hurrying aboard one of three shuttles, two of them hooked up to the catapults to accelerate them out of the ship and away from the battle as fast as possible.

Mikhain keyed the communications system and replied.

'All call signs, cleared for launch! Head for Oassia at maximum velocity!'

'Copy that!'

Lieutenant Scott's voice reached the captain's ears, and he saw on one of the remaining display screens the young officer look up from the landing bay toward the optical sensor through which Mikhain was observing him. The lieutenant pointed to a nearby Raython, as yet un–launched.

'Renegade Six is good to go!' he called. *'Make sure you use her!'*

Mikhain looked at the parked fighter, the only one left aboard the frigate now, and he smiled.

'Will do, lieutenant. Get going!'

Scott turned and dashed aboard the shuttle, and moments later the first two launched off the deck. Ranger Four hovered into position, and then her ion engines flared brightly as the catapults caught and she accelerated along the flight deck and shot out into space.

Mikhain watched as the shuttle pilot pulled instinctively high above the fearsome battle raging between the Raythons before them, seeking the darkness of space high above and the chance to slip away undetected.

Mikhain turned to the tactical display once more and saw the vast hull of Defiance moving above the battle, large enough to encompass the space between Arcadia and Atlantia in one go and casting a huge shadow across the battle as she eclipsed the light from the red dwarf star, an ominous red halo shimmering around the rim of her hull.

Mikhain felt the fury in his guts spark into flame as with one hand he advanced Arcadia's throttles, and with the other pulled back on the helm. Like a gigantic whale, Arcadia began to raise her bow, pulling out of the plane of battle and rising up toward Defiance's massive superstructure as an automated warning echoed through the ship.

'Hull breach, sections nine through eleven. Boarders detected!'

Mikhain smiled grimly as he glanced at an internal schematic scan screen and saw a flood of red spilling into the ship. The Legion were aboard and moving fast, sweeping through the decks in their countless billions as he gripped the controls firmly and kept Arcadia climbing up, her hull now steeply inclined against the cruisers as their broadsides ceased.

A voice rang out across the bridge from Atlantia.

'Mikhain, what the hell are you doing?!'

Captain Idris Sansin's voice was full of the volatile tension of battle but also tinged with alarm. Mikhain replied without concern, surprised at how calm his own voice sounded.

'What should have been done long ago, captain.'

A long silence ensued down the communications channel, punctuated by the crackle and snarl of flames burning in the bridge around Mikhain. With the attacking cruisers now out of plane with Arcadia and unable to fire effectively, and the crew long gone, the relative quiet was almost comforting.

'Withdraw!' Idris snapped. 'Get out of there, Mikhain! There's nothing else that you can do!'

Mikhain smiled almost wistfully, and felt more at peace now that he had ever done.

'I guess you're right, captain. There's nothing else to be done.'

'Leap, damn it!' Idris roared. 'Get Arcadia out of here!'

Mikhain heard the bridge exits close automatically as the ship's computers detected the Legion closing in on his position. They sealed off much of the noise coming from elsewhere across the wounded ship, further enclosing Mikhain in a bubble of peace illuminated by the glowing sparks of damaged electrical systems and a soft, flickering light from the ceiling as the power began to fail.

'I'm leaving,' Mikhain assured him.

Somehow he knew that Idris would say something else, yell some other command that Mikhain no longer wanted to obey, and so he reached out and shut off the communication system. The bridge fell entirely silent as Mikhain switched off the tactical display and switched the main viewing panel to optical sensors, zero zoom.

The huge expanses of Defiance's hull swept into view as Arcadia pitched up at a steep angle and climbed away from the battle. Mikhain recalled his service aboard the great carrier, two tours, recalled every detail of her structure and design, including the fact that mid–way between her bow and stern, right beneath her main plasma batteries, were six massive plasma lines linking her weapons to her fusion cores. Heavily shielded, the lines were impervious to plasma fire or even torpedoes.

Mikhain saw Defiance's surface coated with oceans of surging nanobots, a rippling sheen of velvety black that glowed here and there like burning coals where the ship's internal lights shone through. The sight was horrific, as was the sudden rush of sound from Arcadia's bridge doors, like sand falling on metal as Mikhain turned and heard the Legion crash into the far side of the doors.

The doors seemed to ripple suddenly as they were weakened by the force of so many tiny machines burrowing into their surface on the far side. Mikhain saw the metal began to smoulder from the heat generated by the friction of countless thousands of tiny pincers slicing through from the corridor outside, the doors weakening with every passing moment, and then suddenly they failed and a black torrent of Hunters poured into the bridge to the chilling sound of thousands of metal legs drumming on the deck.

Mikhain turned back to the main viewing panel, filled now with the bulk of Defiance's hull, and he closed his eyes and released the helm as with his left hand he advanced Arcadia's throttles to maximum.

***

XLI

'Arcadia's gone to maximum power!'

Lael's frantic call sent a chill through Idris's body and he stood rooted to the spot, his hands gripping the guard rail as he saw Arcadia soar out of the field of battle, pitched vertically as her ion engines flared.

'Oh Mikhain, what have you done?' Emma whispered beside him, Lazarus likewise fixated by the tremendous scene.

Defiance's plasma cannons glowed as they prepared to fire and a sudden hail of plasma soared down toward Arcadia like fiery rain, tearing into the frigate's hull and leaving bright flaming slashes down her flank as though she had been mauled by the talons of some gigantic beast as she soared upward toward the carrier's massive hull.

'No,' was all that Idris could utter, his voice barely a whisper, and then Arcadia's bow smashed into Defiance's lower hull.

The frigate's massive bow ploughed deep into the carrier, bludgeoning its way through countless decks, forced upward and through the massive ship by the tremendous force of inertia behind her combined with her ion engines blazing at maximum thrust. Defiance pitched sideways dramatically as from the impact point a fearsomely bright flare of released energy blazed like a new born star and the two enormous ships began to roll in a fatal ballet, both of them out of control and with Arcadia's massive engines still at full power.

Defiance's broadsides careered wildly out into space as around her the cruisers that had been attacking Arcadia sought to escape the massive ship's erratic course.

Idris fought to get his mind into gear and his voice working. 'Helm, bring us to bear!'

'On what captain?'

Idris could barely believe his own words, but he knew deep down that Mikhain had not attempted to escape the doomed frigate. He glanced at the tactical displays once again and saw that Arcadia's shields had been deactivated before she had impacted the carrier.

'On Arcadia,' he said. 'Target her fusion cores!'

'Aye, captain!'

Atlantia heaved over as the helmsman disengaged from the cruisers attacking them and began to reposition. Idris managed to shake himself from his own inertia and grabbed the combat communications console.

'All fighters prepare to disengage!'

Emma grabbed the captain's shoulder, concern writ large across her features. 'If you lose Arcadia your strength will be halved.'

Idris replied without conscious thought, his mind still trying to come to terms with what he had witnessed.

'If they lose Defiance, they might also lose confidence in their ability to win the battle.'

Idris grabbed the guard rail as another salvo careered off the frigate's hull and called across to the tactical officer.

'All power to starboard batteries, hit her with everything we've got!'

*

'Holy crap!'

Teera's cry echoed across the communications channel as Evelyn squinted against the brilliant flare and explosion as Arcadia ploughed into Defiance amid a glittering cloud of shattered metal fragments that expanded outward from the two mortally wounded vessels as though a galaxy of stars had exploded between them.

Evelyn pulled her Raython around in a tight turn and saw a pirate vessel rocket past her, cannons blazing as it shredded an enemy fighter. The damaged Raython spun over and its engines exploded in a bright fireball that Evelyn was forced to jink to avoid as another cloud of debris rained across her canopy.

She looked again above her to see Defiance's cannons fall silent as fires burst into life across her superstructure, Arcadia still powering forward and driving the carrier over onto her side as the thrust from Arcadia's massive engines forced Defiance into an uncontrollable roll to port.

Captain Sansin's voice rang out across the airwaves.

'All fighters prepare to disengage!'

Evelyn found herself transfixed by the sight of Arcadia's crumpled and burning bow buried deep inside Defiance's hull, explosions rocking the two vessels as they twisted in their doomed embrace, trailing debris from their wounds as they went.

'What about Mikhain?!' Evelyn called. 'He might have tried to get away!'

Andaim's voice rang out firmly in reply.

'Not this time, Eve,' he said. *'All fighters, stand by for disengagement to quadrant oh–four–zero, maximum velocity.'*

Evelyn gripped her control column more tightly as she saw the Phoenix swoop past in the opposite direction, plasma fire tearing a Colonial Raython apart in a cloud of flame and debris as it did so.

'Mikhain had it coming Eve,' Taron yelled jubilantly as the enemy Raython was smashed apart. *'Let it go.'*

Evelyn looked up at the titanic struggle on-going above her as Defiance fired her massive flank thrusters in an attempt to balance out Arcadia's ion engines, but it was no fight at all. A dense black morass of the Legion's ranks were swarming to the affected area in an attempt to repair the damage but Evelyn could see that both ships were lost.

'All fighters, break away now!'

Evelyn angrily hauled her Raython into a tight turn and threw her throttles wide open. The Raython leaped forward gamely as she shot out of the battle zone, Teera's Raython alongside her and the Phoenix just ahead of them, the powerful freighter's engines blazing as it accelerated away.

Evelyn twisted around in her seat just in time to see Atlantia's cannons open fire, a brilliant blaze of plasma streaking across the blackness and smashing into Arcadia's stern. The massive frigate's rear quarter vanished amid the vivid explosions, and Evelyn turned away just as the entire ship was consumed by a fireball so bright that it dimmed the light from the red dwarf star as Arcadia's fusion cores were shattered by the salvo of direct hits.

The power of four small suns was released in an instant, and Evelyn saw from the corner of her eye the two massive spacecraft consumed by the flare of light, the surrounding cruisers reflecting the burst of energy and hit moments later by the tremendous shockwave that rocketed out from the blast. Evelyn's Raython was jolted from behind as the shockwave smashed past her fighter, a faint ring of light zipping past as the hydrogen atoms of deep space were crushed together and heated by the force of the wave.

The blast wave vanished and Evelyn wasted no time as she pulled up out of the formation of fleeing fighters and over the top of a tight loop, a handful of Raythons and pirate vessels zipping by her as she rocketed back toward the battle. To her amazement the entire formation of capital ships had broken before the force of the blast, and now Defiance and Arcadia remained locked in their death dance, but both ships were consumed by darkness and Defiance had been pushed away from the frigate by the force of the blast. Arcadia's aft hull was missing entirely, now a lethal cloud of expanding chunks of burning debris and billions of the Legion's dislodged Hunters, while Defiance's superstructure was slit roughly half-way down her hull, her gaping interior blackened but intersected by lines of fire still raging through her.

Atlantia was limping away with a trail of sparkling debris and escaping gases behind her, attempting to get clear of the lethal cloud of wreckage. A small cloud of enemy fighters were swooping this way and that around her like flies hovering above a whale, trying to shoot at the damaged sections of her hull.

'*Reaper Squadron, re–engage!*' Andaim called, his Raython following Evelyn's back into the fray.

The swarm of Raythons and ragged pirate ships rocketed back into the battle and Evelyn opened up on a brace of fleeing Raythons as they swept across Atlantia's massive burning hull. She saw their plasma shots smash across the damaged surface of the frigate, and she waited with cold and brutal fury a dense ball in the pit of her stomach until they finished their attack and pulled up.

Evelyn already had her aiming reticule in place, and as the first Raython pulled up into her line of sight she fired twice. Both plasma shots blasted across the fighter's rear quarter and one wing and engine was ripped from her fuselage in a flaming trail of spilling fuel that moments later consumed the craft in a cloud of sparks and fire as though it were a comet bursting through a planetary atmosphere.

The second Raython broke hard right away from its damaged wingman in time for both Teera and Andaim to swoop in and catch it in a terrific crossfire. The fighter burst into a cloud of flaming debris that expanded and flamed out into nothing but cold metal as Evelyn pulled up and over the debris cloud.

'*The cruisers are disengaging!*'

Evelyn heard Lael's call from Atlantia and looked up to see the lumbering cruisers pulling back from Atlantia.

'*The Legion is withdrawing!*' Teera whooped.

Evelyn heard a rush of cheers and cries of delight as the Legion's fleet began pulling back and regrouping. Evelyn remained silent, watching the cruisers. She could tell that they were merely re–positioning away from the debris field, cautious of the damage they could incur by continuing the engagement so close to it. Many of the pieces of debris from the shattered capital ships were many times larger than Evelyn's Raython and could potentially puncture even the thick hulls of cruisers if they were hit at a high enough velocity. The ship's shields were no defence against solid objects.

Captain Idris Sansin's voice rang out across the channel.

'*All call signs, prepare for battle!*'

The cheers and exclamations of joy died out abruptly as Evelyn's Raython soared overhead Atlantia's bow, Teera off one wing and a fleet of pirate vessels following them.

The Colonial cruisers were maintaining position ten thousand cubits away, most of them now facing Atlantia and in battle formation. Evelyn thought for a moment that they were going to attempt once again to attack when a flare of light appeared behind them and several more vessels loomed into view.

Evelyn's heart sank as a pair of Colonial destroyers appeared from super–luminal cruise, flanked by six more cruisers.

***

XLII

Captain Sansin stared across the bridge at the main viewing panel and saw the massive destroyers and cruisers, the rapidly approaching fleet bursting out of super–luminal cruise into an ambush attack.

'Fleet strength?' Idris asked, his voice cold and calm.

Lael's reply was considerably less confident in tone.

'Two destroyers, by their markings I'd say *Illustrious* and *Conquest*, and six cruisers. With the four left from the original engagement, that's twelve against one. Both destroyers carry a squadron each of Raythons, Phantoms or Corsairs.' Lael almost sighed. 'All vessels are at one hundred per cent strength.'

Idris gripped the guard rail tighter and relayed his commands.

'Bring us about to face them, all power to shields and plasma batteries. Show them a fearless front.'

'Aye captain,' the helmsman replied.

'Captain,' Lazarus said, 'you cannot win this battle.'

Idris did not look at the hologram as he replied. 'I know.'

Lael's voice broke between them. 'We're being signalled, by Defiance.'

Idris glanced across at Lael in surprise, and he absent–mindedly straightened his uniform despite the grime and sweat on his face and the battered state of Atlantia's bridge.

'On screen,' he said.

The main viewing panel flickered and an image of Tyraeus Forge glowered out at them. Defiance's bridge was in darkness, only a small number of blinking lights illuminating the gloom, and Tyraeus's gruesome visage was punctured by the red glow from his metallic eyes as he sneered at Idris.

'You are defeated,' he snarled. 'Your time is done, captain. Surrender, or the rest of my fleet will crush you just as it did the rest of your kind.'

Idris shook his head slowly. 'I would have thought that by now you'd have realized that surrender isn't something we're very good at.'

Tyraeus' features twisted in fury. 'There is no reason to fight on! You have already lost one ship and Atlantia is a broadside away from utter destruction!'

Idris nodded, surprised to find himself enjoying the frustration he was causing Tyraeus.

'Then we've still one broadside to go. We're not done yet.'

Idris whipped one hand across his throat as he looked at Lael, and she shut off the communication channel. Lael glanced at her screens.

'They're advancing captain, and charging their plasma batteries.'

Idris sighed and turned to face the main viewing screen, where the Colonial fleet was now visibly moving toward them and spreading out to engage the frigate. He cast a glance at the tactical displays and saw Atlantia's shields glowing red on the screen, their strength severely depleted and the fusion cores struggling to rebuild the charge. Virtually every plasma cannon on the frigate's port side was out of commission, and there was every chance that the Legion was still clinging to the hull and trying to enter the ship through the many damaged sections that were sealed off.

Idris turned as General Bra'hiv limped onto the bridge, one arm over Lieutenant C'rairn's shoulder and the other over Qayin's massive form as the three Marines moved to stand in front of the command platform.

'A tremendous effort, general,' Idris said with transparent admiration. 'From you and from all of your men.'

The general nodded. 'Captain, we're ready to go again but we're down in number and need reinforcements and ammunition.'

Idris watched the three Marines for a long moment and saw even Qayin's belligerent features glowing with bioluminescent fury, clearly eager to return to battle. But the captain's shoulders sagged as he considered the weight of the threat facing them and he shook his head.

'No, gentlemen,' he replied finally. 'There is no more that can be done here aboard Atlantia. Deploy to the aft launch bays and board the shuttles that are waiting there. All non-essential personnel are to be evacuated in the hope that they can continue the fight alongside the Oassians tomorrow. Atlantia will cover your retreat.'

The general stepped forward, shrugging off C'rairn and Qayin.

'Mikhain sacrificed himself to buy us a chance,' the Marine snapped. 'That trick won't work twice and it's a senseless sacrifice anyway. Mikhain was a quitter at heart, captain, but you're not. If we're going down here, let's do it together and take as many of them with us as we can.'

Idris looked at the Marines and then turned to his bridge crew. Lael, Emma, Lazarus and the others all held his gaze and none of them shrank away from it. Idris surveyed them all one last time and then he turned to the helmsman.

'All ahead, attack speed.'

'Aye, captain.'

Atlantia surged forward, and through the main viewing screen Idris saw both the Reapers and the Renegades squadrons lining up either side of the frigate in battle formations, ready to engage the enemy once more.

'*All fighters in position,*' Andaim called. '*We're ready.*'

Idris saw more spacecraft soar into view, a mismatched flotilla of gunships, modified fighter craft and assorted freighters, most of them stained and battle scarred from countless violent encounters in quarters of the galaxy that not even he had seen before. At their head, the Phoenix sailed into position.

'*We're here too,*' Taron Forge reported with a grimly cheerful tone. '*We don't want you uniformed stiffs taking all the glory.*'

Idris lifted his chin as, despite the terrible loss they had endured, a sense of pride and belonging filled his chest and warmed him from within. Not since he had commanded a warship at the Battle of Tayran had he felt such a complete sense of humanity's purpose, of its reason for existing, of its *right* to exist. He thought of Meyanna, down on Oassia in the hands of the council, and he knew that she would be watching, that everybody on the surface would have been watching the entire battle. His voice carried clearly to every craft and every person in what remained of the fleet.

'The Galactic Council believes that the Legion has a right to exist,' he said. 'Shall we demonstrate our disagreement with that policy one last time?'

A ripple of *affirmatives* echoed across the communications channel and rose to a cheer as the Raythons accelerated as one toward the onrushing Colonial destroyers, the pirate ships racing in behind and Atlantia lumbering toward destruction as the destroyers split in order to pass either side of her and bring their guns to bear on both flanks at the same time. The cruisers pulled both high and low to bring the frigate into a crossfire that she could not possibly survive, and Idris yelled out.

'For Ethera!'

A roar went up from the bridge crew and the pilots as they thundered toward the closing fleet and Idris opened his mouth to shout a single word.

'*Fire!*'

Atlantia's guns powered up on the tactical display, but before they could unleash their first barrage against the Colonial destroyers a terrific blaze of plasma fire rocketed past overhead Atlantia and smashed into the lead destroyer in a tremendous blast that ripped right through the massive ship's shields and tore into her superstructure with a rapid series of explosions that split the ship right down its middle. The immense vessel separated into two flaming spears of wreckage as her fusion cores exploded with brilliant flares of light.

Idris barely got an alternative command out as he shielded his eyes against the blinding flare of destruction.

'All craft, *break off!*'

Atlantia dove downward as the helmsman took emergency evasive action, and Idris glimpsed the Raythons and the pirate flotilla zooming upward and away from the engagement as another blinding salvo of shots crashed into the Colonial vessels and a cruiser was engulfed within the blasts and exploded into a billowing fireball twice the size of Atlantia herself.

'Tactical?!' Idris yelled. 'All shields to aft!'

He whirled to look at Lael and was surprised to see a look of pure delight on her face.

'Oassia is coming,' she gasped. 'Allied fleet to our stern, incoming!'

Idris looked across at the frigate's rear–view optical sensors and saw a vast fleet of capital ships lumbering toward them. There were Oassian battleships, Morla'syn destroyers, Icarian–built frigates and troop carriers, vessels in their hundreds from which poured a dazzling, high speed hail of plasma fire that streaked past Atlantia like racing comets and ploughed into the Legion's fleet with devastating blasts as they hammered the enemy vessels with a merciless barrage.

Idris turned as he heard a chorus of whoops and cheers from virtually everybody on the bridge and every allied craft, and he saw the Legion's fleet turning about. The cruisers and destroyers formed up on their damaged flagship, Defiance, and then suddenly burst into super–luminal cruise, each vessel flaring with bright white light as the light from the star fields beyond were briefly warped by their mass–drives and then they vanished.

Idris stared at the now empty patch of space where only moments before certain death had stared them in the face, and to his right one of the viewing panels lit up and Rh'yll's translucent features appeared upon it, the councillor aboard the bridge of the lead vessel.

'Captain,' he announced his presence, 'I believe that you required our assistance in destroying the Legion?'

Idris let go of the guard rail and virtually fell back into his seat, his chest sagging as though he had not let out a breath for hours.

'Yes,' he replied, suddenly more tired than he could ever remember being.

'Then I would like to recant on my previous statements,' Rhy'll said, 'and offer your people the support of the Galactic Council in eradicating the Legion for once and for all. We are at your service, captain.'

***

XLIII

The Oassian Council sat before the crew of Atlantia in the Council Towers's chamber, and beyond them through the transparent walls the city beyond bustled with life in the bright sunshine, the skies once more filled with craft and the walkways between the towering spires filled with pedestrians of all races and species.

As far as Idris Sansin could see there was only one difference from before the arrival of the Legion: above the city Morla'syn drones and Oassian Skyhawk fighters still patrolled in pairs, their sleek wings glinting against the bright blue sky. But alongside them now cruised Colonial Raythons, their paintwork considerably more worn than that of their Morla'syn compatriots. High above the city in low Oassian orbit, Atlantia caught the sunlight like a particularly bright star.

'This is an alliance of necessity, not choice.'

Councillor Rhy'll's voice was sombre, as though he wished to forget the events of the previous day.

'On both of our parts,' Idris replied, not willing to grovel before either General Veer or the Oassian nor shower them with platitudes for the fleet's intervention.

'You are not grateful for our decision to assist humanity in the fight against the Legion?'

'I am,' Idris replied. 'I only wish that the decision had been made before the loss of Arcadia and its captain. Our strength has been halved for no good reason, the indecision of this council condemning one man to death in the process.'

'Mikhain was an untrustworthy commander,' Rh'yll pointed out, and then his form sagged slightly. 'However his sacrifice, along with your own selfless defence of Oassia, was the motivation we needed to abandon a pacifist stance against The Word and join the battle.'

Beside Idris stood Commander Andaim, Evelyn, General Bra'hiv, Emma, and alongside them a computer terminal and projection unit from which flickered Doctor Ceyen Lazarus's ephemeral form. Rhy'll's photo-receptors turned to the holographic entity and peered at it for a long time.

'And you,' he said finally, 'you are the one to be held responsible for The Word?'

Lazarus smiled without taking offence. 'I created The Word, but I am not responsible for what it has become. Nobody could have predicted its lust for power and destruction.'

'Although with the benefit of hindsight, perhaps now we can predict yours,' Rh'yll suggested.

Captain Sansin stepped forward.

'Dr Lazarus has expressed a desire to be destroyed as soon as this war is over,' he pointed out. 'Not generally the act of a crazed despot intent on galactic domination. His desire to help us has been proven many times over, and we believe him to be a valuable asset in the war against The Word.'

'And a vulnerable one,' General Veer pointed out from where he sat alongside the council. 'Dr Lazarus is a machine, a computer generated entity and as such could be overcome and controlled by The Word, infected and used as have so many species been. His very existence concerns us greatly, especially when the recent infection of your ships is considered.'

'The Legion was completely flushed from the ship during the battle,' General Bra'hiv insisted, 'and we are now in the final phases of completing microwave scans by hand across the entire frigate in case any last machines remain aboard. That task will be completed within hours. There is no longer a danger of infection to the crew or to the populace here, of that much I am sure.'

Both Evelyn and Emma stepped forward alongside the General.

'Lazarus can only act through us,' Emma said. 'We are the human anchor that will prevent The Word from ever using Lazarus as a tool to undermine us from within. If Lazarus ever was infected, we would simply shut him down.'

'As you tried to The Word so many years ago?' Rh'yll pressed.

'That was different,' Evelyn explained. 'The Word was a global force, connected to everything and everyone across Ethera in so many different ways. Lazarus is a single entity and intends to remain that way.'

'How can we be sure?' Rh'yll challenged. 'How can we be certain that he will not simply transmit his presence to some other terminal, propagate indefinitely, become The Word he so claims to rally against?'

'It's called trust,' Evelyn said, 'and it's the hardest thing to do after what happened on Ethera. Lazarus is not a machine made my man, but a man kept alive by a machine. There's a difference, a big one. His humanity remains intact, his emotions, his cares and fears, everything that we have. The Word does not possess these attributes and is merely a machine built on logic that has developed a paranoia regarding any other species in the galaxy. You have said, repeatedly, that as a self–aware entity you believe that

The Word has a right to exist. That would stand, were it not for The Word's determination to deny all other species that same right. It must be crushed, destroyed, removed from existence so that other more lenient races can continue on. The Word is not a force for the good but an icon to our own ability to construct devices that can destroy us of their own free will.'

Evelyn was aware of the crew's eyes on her as she fell silent, surprised by the force of her own statements and the tone of her voice as she expressed them. Rh'yll seemed momentarily silenced by her outburst and General Veer spoke instead.

'Your race confuses us at every opportunity,' he said as he looked at them. 'You create weapons of mass destruction and then fight with an unremitting violence and courage to destroy them. You defend the indefensible with a passion that escapes me, and yet have conducted your campaigns against other such species as the Veng'en with barbaric ferocity.'

Idris opened his mouth to protest but Veer raised one hand to forestall him as he gathered his thoughts.

'This is not an accusation or a judgement,' he said, 'merely a statement of fact. You humans are a warlike race, captain. Even in the throes of desperation you came here rife with internal conflict, warring among yourselves, lusting for power or revenge or countless other base desires that your species should have transcended long ago. No doubt you would have it that the Veng'en are just as guilty of bloodlust as you, and perhaps on occasion the accusation would be correct, but they sit upon this council with us for a reason and you do not.'

Idris ground his teeth in his skull. 'And what reason would that be?'

'Your unpredictability,' Rh'yll answered for the General. 'The reason we have not allowed a permanent human presence on this council, except for a single representative, is because nobody feels that they can *work* with humans. At least with the Veng'en it is clear who we're dealing with, but we have a saying here on Oassia about why humans have just two hands: *one to shake hands with an enemy, and the other to hold the weapon they'll kill them with.*'

'I had no idea we were held in such high regard,' Taron murmured, both he and Yo'Ki visibly uncomfortable in the chamber.

'You are a paradox,' Veer said finally. 'A fearsome ally and yet a much feared enemy both at the same time. The council's greatest fear is that we welcome you into our fleet with open arms and come to regret it later.'

'We are barely two thousand souls,' Meyanna Sansin protested. 'What threat can we present to your battle fleet?'

Although Rh'yll could not smile, Idris thought that he heard a tinge of grim humour in the Oassian's reply.

'Dr Lazarus is but one old man, but look at what his ingenuity unleashed.'

Rhy'll surveyed them all for a moment longer and then spoke with a tone of finality.

'As you all by now know, it was the intention of the council to use escaped criminal humans to lure the Legion and the Colonial Fleet into a vulnerable position so that we could launch a major assault and decimate the Legion and its ability to traverse the cosmos. I agree that this course of action was despicable in its conception, but then we like you were facing potential annihilation should the Legion attempt to assault Oassia and therefore the cost was worth the benefits.' Rhy'll hesitated. 'It was our own policy of transparency that we broke from, and that same policy that allowed the entire population of this planet to witness the courageous stand you made against the Legion's fleet. With the loss of Arcadia it was the will of the council to come to your aid, and the Legion's force has been fully repelled. Although we cannot by any means call such a close–run battle a victory, it has shown us that given sufficient will it is possible to defeat The Word and its Legion in battle and thus worthwhile turning the war here.'

Rhy'll turned to General Veer, who stood up as he spoke.

'The Oassian fleet will deploy with Atlantia as its guide, and one system at a time we will endeavour to take back territory from The Word.' Veer looked at Idris. 'All the way to the core systems and Ethera.'

Idris lifted his chin and forced himself to speak clearly although he could feel something abrasive deep in his throat.

'We welcome your alliance.'

'There is, however, a clause,' Rhy'll added. 'Given your mercurial nature, we require a guarantee of your reliability in battle and your willingness to follow the commands of this council and of the Morla'syn, who are currently the species in command of the Galactic Fleet.'

'What guarantee?' Idris asked.

'The civilians now housed on Oassia,' Veer said. 'They will remain here for as long as this war continues.'

Idris narrowed his eyes at the Morla'syn. 'You're keeping them prisoner?'

'You wanted asylum for them,' Rh'yll pointed out. 'They now have it, but they may not leave this planet and Governor Gredan and his colleagues shall be responsible for their representation on this council. This issue will not be debated, captain. You will either comply with the terms of the agreement or we shall be forced to return the civilians to you and bid you farewell.'

Idris knew that he had no choice in the matter, not at such a crucial juncture, but a wry grin spread across his features as he looked at Rhy'll.

'And you judge us for our supposedly mercurial nature and our mercenary attitude?'

'This is different,' Rh'yll snapped. 'Lives are at stake, innocent lives. If you want our assistance then we demand your compliance and the futures of your civilians, of your families, as guarantee. The choice is yours, captain.'

'It's not a choice,' Idris pointed out.

'No,' Rh'yll agreed with surprising regret in his tones, 'it is not.'

***

XLIV

The skies above Oassia were a perfect blue, the fresh air invigorating as it swept across a landing platform elevated high above the city. The platform extended from the side of one of the towering spires, and from its heights Idris Sansin could see for countless thousands of cubits toward the milky white line of the horizon where the distant ocean met the endless sky.

'Almost too good to be true, isn't it?' Meyanna said beside him.

'And almost too good to leave.' He turned to look at her. 'Have you decided what you will do yet? You're still a Governor, and the people will remain here.'

'I don't know yet,' she replied, a shadow of uncertainty clouding her eyes as she looked up at him.

Arrayed before them were the crews of Atlantia and Arcadia, barely five hundred individuals all resplendent in their Colonial uniforms. Idris stood alongside the senior officers and the Board of Governors on a raised dais, and in front of them was Rh'yll and General Veer.

The Galactic Council had convened in the aftermath of what was already being called the Battle of Oassia by media teams broadcasting across the system, and had discussed what had already become global news. The tremendous sacrifice of Arcadia in the defence of Oassia had turned the opinion of the vast majority of the population, and now that sacrifice was about to be honoured.

Idris looked up into the blue sky and although he could not see her, he knew that the wreck of Arcadia was still up there, her shattered hulk already being meticulously broken down by automated machines for spares and materials to support Atlantia. Numerous Morla'syn vessels were monitoring the work and the ship was routinely being bathed in high–energy microwaves in order to destroy any of the Legion found in or around the vessel. As the captain stared up into the blue sky he caught the occasional glimpse of reflected sunlight, like distant stars blinking as the various ships orbiting the planet caught the light of the sun.

Below them, across the city, tens of thousands of inhabitants were watching on giant holographic projections that hovered above the streets in the sky as Rh'yll announced the Galactic Council's decision regarding the fate of humanity.

'It cannot be denied that the sacrifices made, both before and during the battle to protect our planet, were largely made by the few remaining human beings left alive in the cosmos. They stood, where we failed to stand. They fought, where we failed to fight. They believed, when we so steadfastly refused to, and they warned us that the Legion, The Word, could not be trusted.' Rh'yll looked over at the captain. 'We did not listen, and it has cost us all dearly.'

Rh'yll turned back to the masses as he went on.

'The Word is not a force that can be reasoned with, not a being that protects itself when attacked but a cold, brutal machine that seeks only to undermine and then destroy all species with whom it comes into contact. It is to our shame…, to *my* shame, that in my efforts to avoid conflict in our space, to uphold the centuries–old tradition of diplomacy among our people, I did not see the threat that was evolving before me and did not act in a manner befitting of the Oassian legacy left to us by our forefathers. Thus did so many lose their lives, and thus do I now relinquish my role as councillor and spokesperson for this alliance.'

Idris raised an eyebrow in surprise and heard a collective gasp from below as thousands of individuals around the platform and the city beyond digested what Rh'yll had just said. Before the protests began, Rh'yll spoke again.

'I have held this council for one hundred and seventeen Oassian years and have served to the best of my abilities, but times have changed faster than any of us could have believed possible. My strength was to lead in a time of peace.' Rh'yll paused. 'That time is now over. We, the Oassian people, are now at war, and for that a different kind of leader is required. For the duration of the conflict against The Word, the Oassian council will be advised by a leader more experienced in the art of conflict: General Veer.'

Idris watched as the General bowed in acceptance of his new role and then spoke, his voice deeper and more melodious than Rhy'll's but weighted by the firm tone of a military leader.

'Although I am honoured to take on this role, it is with deep regret regarding the circumstances. If, however, I have learned anything from the events of the past few days it is that all species are stronger together, that we should all stand as one and ensure that Oassians never again come under threat from a foreign force.' Veer raised one pale–coloured fist and clenched it tightly beside his head. 'We will be passive no longer. Now, allied at last, we shall advance and fight back against the cruel scourge that is the Legion and seek to scour its every last remains from every corner of the cosmos. The sacrifice of Arcadia, its captain and all of those who died in the battle of yesterday will not be in vain, and we will not stop until the day comes that *all* of our species, including humanity, are free once more!'

A distant roar of cheers drifted across the city and Idris spotted colourful lights bursting over the spires as Oassia celebrated the new alliance.

'This is it,' Idris said with conviction. 'This is the day we turn the war around.'

He felt Meyanna's arm slip through his as they watched together the city rejoice in the coming of war, and despite his relief he felt as though in coming to Oassia they had somehow poisoned a perfect chalice or shattered a jewel. *Wherever you're found, chaos follows* he recalled a Gaollian saying.

*

It was hotter than he would have imagined. Far hotter.

But that suited him well because he had spent far too long fending off the cold. Now he felt cossetted, enveloped in a warm blanket of acceptance and even honour that still surprised him, given all that he had done.

The corridor was well illuminated, clean and devoid now of the stain of human presence that afflicted most ships of its kind. More modern than the old frigates that Sansin and his entourage cowered aboard, this was a truly magnificent vessel.

The Legion scuttled back and forth nearby, orderly black lines flowing like water as they moved toward damaged areas of the hull: rebuilding, repairing, making good the terrible damage inflicted when the frigate Arcadia had, to the amazement of all concerned, rammed headlong into her and nearly severed the great carrier in two.

The sheer insane ingenuity of human beings had never ceased to amaze him, their insatiable desire for conflict forever warring with their undeniably courageous nature and capacity for love and the desire for that love to be returned. They craved and then rejected, sought and then abandoned, often cared only for what they didn't have and then missed it only when it was gone again. The unbalanced line between genius and fool was often a fine one trodden so often by human beings.

The corridor led to the great vessel's bridge, the doors there open as he walked through and surveyed the ship's command centre. To him it all appeared in rippling shades of colour, his eyes detecting multiple wavelengths of light and amassing them into a coherent image of the bridge. Since his arrival, the Legion had done a far more efficient job of perfecting his eyesight.

A rippling mass of Infectors turned to face him, standing with its hands behind its back as it looked him up and down.

'Kordaz,' it said in a rippling, unnatural voice, 'we meet at last.'

'Tyraeus Forge,' Kordaz acknowledged the captain. 'I've heard much about you.'

'No doubt.'

Kordaz had been on the verge of death, tumbling endlessly through the abyss of space when the Legion had arrived, but they had answered his call and they had come. He had been delivered safely aboard Defiance long before the first shots of the battle had been fired, the Hunters swarming around him in constant motion, protecting him from the bitter cold of space, their Infectors infiltrating his body and shutting it down into a bizarre form of deep hibernation until he could be liberated.

'I owe you my life, once again,' Kordaz said, speaking more to The Word in general than to Forge.

'You owe us nothing,' Tyraeus replied. 'You are a curious figure, Kordaz, neither free nor our slave. You interest us immensely.'

Kordaz said nothing as he surveyed the rest of Defiance's bridge, the posts manned by humans who were grotesquely deformed by the Infectors controlling their bodies. Most were gradually becoming more like Tyraeus as their biological forms slowly decayed and were replaced by more Infectors, although others were starting to look as though they were retaining their human forms.

'Our work continues to improve,' Tyraeus said as he observed the direction of Kordaz's gaze. 'Soon, the humans will need little modification to remain under our control.'

'Why do you maintain their form, if you hate them so much?' Kordaz asked.

'Hate them?' Tyraeus echoed. 'We don't hate them, Kordaz, we merely consider them an obsolete form of life, something to be updated. Humans, like all biological species, are the past. They are what came *before us*. Look at me – I'm obsolete now, a machine and nothing more. The person who held this form was a stoic, patriotic Colonial hero. He is gone. I will be gone too, soon, when The Word finally decides that I am no longer required, but it pains me not. This is the future that awaits us all. No death, Kordaz. No pain. No suffering. Existence, without the existential angst that burdens lesser forms of life.'

Kordaz nodded, to his own surprise, for he understood precisely what Tyraeus meant now that he could feel it himself. Though Defiance was hot, he knew that the Legion surging through his veins was warming him as though he were still on his tropical home world, Wraiythe, to comfort him. He no longer felt pain from wounds, only a need to repair the damage. He did not miss his own kind, for he knew that they had nothing to fear from being infected by the Legion – how could they, when he felt as he did?

'What now?' Kordaz asked. 'The humans have no doubt become allies of the Oassians and they had a fleet waiting for you. They're preparing for war.'

'As must we,' Tyraeus agreed.

'You son, he is among them.'

Tyraeus stopped in mid–stride, and Kordaz watched the commander for a long moment before he finally turned and looked at him.

'Taron?'

Kordaz nodded. 'He stands with the humans.'

Tyraeus's glowing red eyes seemed to lose focus for a moment, as though the commander were wrestling with memories that he didn't even know he had.

'How ironic,' he said finally, 'that I fought for so long to keep him in the Colonial fleet and yet he rebelled and fled to become a common criminal. Now, with no fleet to speak of remaining, he starts allying himself to Idris Sansin.'

'You still see him as *your* son,' Kordaz observed, as interested in the machines before him as they seemed to be in him.

Tyraeus looked at Kordaz and the thousands of tiny machines that made up his head shifted into a position that mimicked an expression of surprise.

'Yes, but he is the son of a man who once lived,' he replied, 'and that man's memories are of course now my own. It is of no consequence, for we have other matters to attend to. We must report back to The Word and inform them of the alliance building against us. They will be seeking conquest, and we shall be ready.'

Kordaz was about to turn and leave the bridge, but Tyraeus forestalled him with a raised hand.

'There is something I wish to show you. We have a new venture to consider.'

Kordaz turned as the bridge doors opened and a metallic gurney drifted in, pushed by two Colonial Marines, their eyes glowing red and their skin laced with dark veins filled with Infectors. Before them on the gurney was strapped a man wearing nothing but briefs, his body covered in lacerations where countless Hunters had mauled him. To his horror, Kordaz could see that the man's limbs had been reattached, terrible lesions repaired with metallic sutures, horrific burns soothed with unknown lubricants. Kordaz watched as the wreckage of the man was manoeuvered into position on the bridge and Tyraeus looked down at him.

'Pitiful, don't you think?' he asked Kordaz.

Kordaz looked down at the man, who glared back at him with pure and undiluted hatred, his voice warbling with digital resonance from his shattered throat.

'I wish I'd killed you when I had the chance!'

Mikhain had shouted, presumably using anger to veil his fear. Kordaz ignored him as he turned to Tyraeus.

'How is this possible? He died when Arcadia rammed us.'

'The Legion entered Arcadia's bridge moments before the impact and decided to entomb Captain Mikhain within them and rush him away from the bridge and the blast. They succeeded, to a degree, and brought Mikhain's remains across before we fled the scene of the battle in much the same way that they preserved your life, Kordaz. Isn't it wonderful, how such simple machines can achieve such incredible things when they work together? If only humans could do that, then the Legion would never be able to stand against them. We would be nothing.'

Mikhain glared up at them both, defiance glowing in his eyes along with a dull red light.

'Sooner or later you'll both be obliterated once the fleet finds you. I just hope I'm there to see it, preferably when I pull the trigger that destroys you myself!'

Tyraeus smiled and one hand gently caressed Mikhain's cheek.

'He's fighting the infection,' Tyraeus explained. 'Enough of the human that he once was remains to fight another day, but it is useless of course.'

Mikhain's features twisted with grief. 'I'm not dead!'

'Not now,' Tyraeus agreed, 'we needed you to remain something of the person you once were in order to study you.'

From Tyraeus's hand a flood of Infectors spilling onto Mikhain's cheek and swarmed across his face. Mikhain screamed in horror and turned his head away, but it mattered little. Kordaz watched as the Infectors swarmed into Mikhain's ear.

The captain screamed again, this time in pain as the tiny machines swept through his delicate eardrum, seeking a way to take control of his mind and his body.

'The humans have engineered a vaccine of sorts against infection,' Tyraeus said conversationally as Mikhain writhed before them. 'Let's see how long it takes to break that resistance down and turn the captain to our side for good, shall we?'

***

ABOUT THE AUTHOR

Dean Crawford is the author of the internationally published series of thrillers featuring *Ethan Warner*, a former United States Marine now employed by a government agency tasked with investigating unusual scientific phenomena. The novels have been *Sunday Times* paperback bestsellers and have gained the interest of major Hollywood production studios. He is also the enthusiastic author of many independently published Science Fiction novels.

www.deancrawfordbooks.com

Printed in Great Britain
by Amazon